Winterset

Also by Candace Camp
in Large Print:

Beyond Compare
Mesmerized
Secrets of the Heart

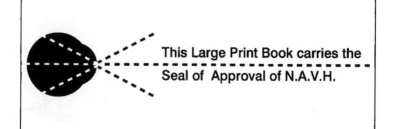

This Large Print Book carries the
Seal of Approval of N.A.V.H.

Winterset

Candace Camp

Thorndike Press • Waterville, Maine

Published in 2005 by arrangement with Harlequin Books S.A.

Thorndike Press® Large Print Basic.

The tree indicium is a trademark of Thorndike Press.

The text of this Large Print edition is unabridged.
Other aspects of the book may vary from the original edition.

Set in 16 pt. Plantin by Christina S. Huff.

Printed in the United States on permanent paper.

Library of Congress Cataloging-in-Publication Data

Camp, Candace.
    Winterset / by Candace Camp.
      p. cm.
    ISBN 0-7862-7269-4 (lg. print : hc : alk. paper)
    1. Mansions — Fiction. 2. Large type books. I. Title.
  PS3553.A4374W56 2005
  813′.54—dc22   2004024685

Winterset

As the Founder/CEO of NAVH, the only national health agency solely devoted to those who, although not totally blind, have an eye disease which could lead to serious visual impairment, I am pleased to recognize Thorndike Press* as one of the leading publishers in the large print field.

Founded in 1954 in San Francisco to prepare large print textbooks for partially seeing children, NAVH became the pioneer and standard setting agency in the preparation of large type.

Today, those publishers who meet our standards carry the prestigious "Seal of Approval" indicating high quality large print. We are delighted that Thorndike Press is one of the publishers whose titles meet these standards. We are also pleased to recognize the significant contribution Thorndike Press is making in this important and growing field.

Lorraine H. Marchi, L.H.D.
Founder/CEO
NAVH

* Thorndike Press encompasses the following imprints: Thorndike, Wheeler, Walker and Large Print Press.

Prologue

She ran toward him, her arms outstretched, her beautiful face contorted with fear, mouth opened in a scream. The terror was plain in her eyes, and though he did not know what caused it, the force of it hit him like a blow. He stood rooted to the floor, unable to move or even to reach for her, and though she ran as if pursued by demons, she never reached him.

She screamed his name. "Reed!" It echoed through the dark, wide hallways.

Still struggling to reach him, effort and strain in every line of her body, she was now receding from him, pulled back by some unseen force. He knew he would never reach her, never see her again, and his whole body shook in a paroxysm of grief and pain and fear.

"Anna!" Reed jerked upright, his eyes flying open, staring sightlessly into the darkness of his room. "Anna!"

This time her name was said more softly, a desperate, desolate moan of despair. He let out a great sigh, sagging back against the mattress. It had been a dream, that was all.

Reed lay for a moment, gazing up at the tester high above his bed, trying to pull the befogged shreds of his thoughts back together. It was not the first dream he had had of her, nor, he suspected, would it be the last. Indeed, in his sleep she had come to him times without number.

There had been hot, lustful dreams that left him wide awake, sweating and panting, and dark, angry dreams, full of pain. But his dreams of Anna had come less and less as the years had passed; it had been months since he had had one. And never had any of them filled him with a heart-pounding terror such as this one had.

She was in danger. Reed was not sure how he was so certain of that fact, but he was. Something was frightening her, threatening her, and the thought left him with a sick, powerless feeling.

He sat up, pushing aside his tangled bedsheets, and walked over to the window. The curtains were open and the window ajar, letting in a soft summer breeze that cooled his skin. He stood for a moment, looking out at the expansive gardens of

Broughton House. From the rose garden below drifted up the heady scents of hundreds of flowers.

Looking out at the moonlit gardens, he saw not their neat and well-tended order but the tangled, overgrown yard at Winterset. It had been three years since he had been there, but it was almost as clear in his mind as Anna's face.

He closed his eyes, the old bitter sorrow creeping over him. He thought of her dark blue eyes, the delicately heart-shaped face framed by a glorious tumble of light brown curls, accented by sunny streaks of gold. She had a firm mouth, with ends that seemed to turn up, giving her always a look of faint, suppressed amusement at the world. The first time he had seen her, standing in the garden at Winterset, one hand up to shade her eyes as she watched him approach, he had felt as if he had been struck a blow to the chest, and he had known that he had found the woman he would love for the rest of his life.

It was to his lasting regret that he had been right that day. The woman, unfortunately, had not felt the same way.

With a sigh, Reed turned and sank down into a chair. Leaning forward, he put his elbows on his knees and rested his head on his hands, thrusting his fingers back into his thick dark hair. He clenched his fingers, the tiny pain of his hair tangling in his fingers a kind of relief from the pain within him.

After three years, he thought, it should cease to hurt. Yet it had not. There was no longer the constant dull ache that had accompanied him the first few months when he had returned to London after Anna declined his proposal, but neither had his world ever completely righted itself. No woman since had caught his eye enough to warrant more than a dance or a polite conversation. He still thought of her now and then, and every time he did, there was a slice of pain. Reed supposed he should be glad that it was no more than an echo of the hurt that had once enveloped him.

He tried to pull his mind from the old wound and think about the dream instead. He remembered the fear in Anna's eyes, the scream that seemed to be issuing from her lips as she ran. *What was she running from? What did it mean? And, most of all, why was he so certain that the dream meant that Anna was in danger?*

Reed Moreland was not the sort of man who believed in visions and portents. He had had a grandmother who had claimed to converse with her dead relations — his mother had said that it was typical of her mother-in-law that she had pursued her hapless relatives even beyond the grave — but Grandmother was generally agreed to be a trifle dotty. Rational adults did not see things that were not there, nor receive information in dreams, nor hear heavenly voices. Reasonable, well-educated men such as himself lived their lives according to logic, not superstition.

Yet neither could he dismiss the things that had happened to his sisters two years ago. They were not hysterical females given to frights and vapors, yet both Olivia and Kyria had encountered strange mystical forces that could not be explained away rationally. Indeed, all of them had given up trying to explain things. If there were unseen forces at work in the world, a possibility that he could no longer dismiss out of hand, then it seemed that the Moreland clan had some sort of special connection to them.

More than that, irrational as it might be, he could not dismiss the force of the feeling that had shot through him during the dream. It had been too strong to ignore. *Anna was in trouble.* The only real question was: *What was he going to do about it?*

Chapter One

Anna Holcomb made her way downstairs to the kitchen area. It was still quite early; she had not even had her breakfast yet, but she wanted to make sure that Cook had remembered to bake something for her visits today. They were duty calls — one to one of the tenants whose wife had had a baby and the other her weekly call to the vicarage. She and her brother, Kit, were all that was left of the two major families that had lived in this area for centuries, so it was up to her to make sure that such niceties were taken care of. Anna had never been one to shrug off her duties. Indeed, there had been moments in her life when she had thought rather resentfully that her "duty" had consumed her entire life. However, those moments were few and far between; for the most part Anna accepted her life as it was without complaints. She had had, she knew, a most fortunate life, and it was both foolish and petty to bemoan the parts of it that had been hard.

As she strode along the main hallway toward the door into the kitchen, she saw the door at the end of the hallway open. It was a very short door and unevenly set, a quaint leftover from the medieval cloisters from which this part of the manor house had been built, and it was not frequently used. So it startled Anna a little to see it pushed open and a slender girl slip through it rather furtively.

The girl cast a quick glance down the hall and jumped when her eyes fell upon Anna. A guilty look crossed her face, and she glanced from Anna to the back stairs, only a few feet from her. Anna knew the girl; her name was Estelle, and she was one of the upstairs maids. For a moment Anna could not understand the girl's furtive entry, but then she realized that Estelle must be just returning to the house, which would indicate that she had spent the night somewhere other than upstairs in her bed.

Anna started to speak to her, but just at that moment, the housekeeper's voice came from the side hall. "Estelle!"

Both Anna and the maid jumped. The maid shot Anna a pleading look and sidled toward the back staircase.

"Drat it! Where is that girl?" the housekeeper said, treading heavily toward the intersection of the two corridors where Anna stood. From where Mrs. Michaels was, she could not see the maid at the back stairs. "Oh, Miss Anna, I did not realize you were here. I was just looking for that silly girl Estelle."

Anna smiled at her and lied blandly, "I believe I saw her upstairs earlier, cleaning the bedrooms."

Mrs. Michaels had been the Holcomb family's housekeeper for as long as Anna could remember. She was a faithful and efficient employee, but also a woman of stern character. Anna would have hated to have the woman supervising her.

Estelle cast Anna a grateful look and scurried up the stairs. Anna continued talking to the housekeeper, saying, "I came to check on the pies that I am going to take to the vicarage and to Mrs. Simmons."

"Oh, yes, miss," Mrs. Michaels assured her. "I have already made sure of that. Baked first thing this morning, they were, and Cook just set them out to cool."

"Thank you. Then if you would be so good as to send a message to the stables to have the trap brought around at ten, I will take the pies to the village."

"Of course, miss."

Anna went back down the hall to the

smaller dining room where she and her brother, Kit, normally took all their meals. Kit, always an early riser, was already seated at the table, sipping a cup of coffee, a habit he had picked up on his tour of the Continent a few years ago.

"Hallo, Annie," Kit said, rising to his feet and pulling out the chair on his left hand for her. "I trust you are well this morning."

"Very. And you?" She poured herself a cup of tea.

Theirs was a rather informal household. Their mother had died when Anna was fourteen, and she had taken over the reins of the household for her father and younger brother. It had seemed foolish to her to run their cozy manor house, with only the three of them in it, with the formality that their mother, a de Winter by birth and used to a grander lifestyle, had kept at Holcomb Manor. It had taken some sharp exchanges with the housekeeper, who regarded tradition as sacrosanct, and even a few appeals to her father for support, but Anna, strong-willed despite her seemingly placid nature, had won out in the end. As a result, their footmen did not wear livery, their meals were served by no more than two servants, and breakfast was unattended, with the food set out in chafing dishes along the sideboard, and Anna and her brother serving themselves.

As they ate, Kit and Anna chatted with the ease of people who had spent almost their entire lives in each other's company. The only two children of their parents' marriage and just two years apart in age, they had, since they were young, been each other's chief companions and confidants. They had perforce seen less of each other after Kit grew old enough to go off to school and, later, when he took the tour of the Continent that was customary among young men of their class. At their father's death two years ago, he had returned and taken up his position as the heir to Sir Edmund's title and estate, and he and Anna had fallen easily back into their old habits.

They were much alike in temperament, both of them possessed of calm, easygoing personalities, quick to laugh and slow to flare into anger. Both loved their old home, parts of which dated from the Middle Ages, as well as the land surrounding it, and as young as they were, they had taken on uncomplainingly the responsibilities of maintaining the largest estate in this part of Gloucestershire.

In looks they were somewhat less alike. Anna had a tall, willowy build like her father, and the dark blue eyes and light brown hair, streaked with gold, of their mother, whereas Kit was built along sturdier lines, and his blond, green-eyed coloring was that of their father. Anna's delicately heart-shaped face was unlike Kit's square-jawed countenance, but there was no mistaking the similarity of their mouths, which tilted up slightly at either end, giving them a look as if they were secretly amused.

They talked about the day that lay ahead of them. While Anna made her calls in the village, Kit would be spending much of the day closeted with the manager of the estate. The Holcomb family, long overshadowed by the grander and showier lords and ladies de Winter, was nevertheless a family of some distinction and wealth, their family having lived here since the early Middle Ages, and since their mother and her brother had been the last of the de Winter line, Kit was necessarily involved in that much larger estate, as well.

"I don't envy you the task," Anna told him, smiling. "I think duty calls are infinitely preferable."

Kit shrugged. "I don't know. Not if they involve going to see the squire's wife. Having to listen to her extol the virtues of her children is more than I can bear. Miles is all right, I suppose. A little moody —"

"Sensitive," Anna stuck in, her eyes dancing with amusement. "His mother assures me that he is sensitive, even poetic."

Kit gave a little snort of derision. "Well, at least he is usually quiet. His sister, on the other hand, is a blasted chatterbox. And she giggles. But to hear Mrs. Bennett tell it, you'd think she was the epitome of charm and grace."

"That is because her mother cherishes fond hopes of your marrying Miss Bennett."

Kit's jaw dropped. "You can't be serious."

"Oh, but I am. Why else would she be forever hinting at what a fine wife Felicity will make?"

"But — I mean, put aside the fact that Felicity is spotty and graceless and never ceases her prattle, the girl is only seventeen years old! She isn't even out yet."

"Those are the veriest trifles in Mrs. Bennett's mind, I can assure you. Fortunately, I am not visiting her today, or I would have to endure her trotting Felicity out. I think she hopes that we will become fast friends and that I will recommend her to you."

Kit let out a short bark of laughter. "Thirty minutes spent in her company would, I should think, ensure that you would never be friends."

Anna smiled in agreement, and they finished their breakfast in a pleasant silence. Afterward, Anna spent some time on the household books, then donned her hat and gloves and went out front, where the pony and trap were waiting for her.

Two of the pot boys carefully carried out the pies and settled them in a nest of towels on the floor of the trap, and Anna climbed up into the vehicle, taking the reins from the groom. She glanced across the yard and saw their gamekeeper standing several yards down the driveway. She gave the reins a little slap, and the horse started forward. As she approached him, the gamekeeper doffed his hat in respectful greeting, and Anna reined in beside him.

"Rankin," she said, nodding her head.

"Good day, Miss Anna." He looked up at her. "I delivered that package."

"Very good," Anna responded. "And how was everything?"

The man shrugged. "As usual, miss, as usual."

Anna nodded. "Do they need anything?"

"No'm, not so as Bradbury asked. I took 'em a pheasant, as well. He usually likes that."

"Good. Thank you, Rankin."

"Miss." He gave her a final nod, then turned and walked away.

Anna gave the reins a brisk slap, and the horse started off smartly. She drove along the familiar curving driveway, finally emerging onto the road that led to the village. She always enjoyed the outdoors, and today, with the June sun spilling its gentle heat over her and the blooming rhododendrons, it was a pleasure simply to drive along, looking out over the countryside. She belonged here. The land was as familiar and beloved as her own house, and sometimes, when she was inclined to feel a little self-pity, thinking of things that might have been, she reminded herself how much she had here, of the beauty that lay just outside her doorstep and the people who were part of her life.

She drove first to the tenant's house, where she handed over one of Cook's pies and dutifully admired the squalling newborn. Then she drove on to the vicarage, which lay beside the brown stone church.

She saw as she drew up that the squire's carriage was already there, which meant that Mrs. Bennett must be calling on the vicar's wife, too, and for an instant Anna was tempted to turn around and leave. However, she knew that she could not. She might have been spotted by one of the women through the front windows of the house, and such a departure would, of course, be quite rude. So she got down from her trap, tying the horse to the low fence in front of the vicarage, and picked up the remaining pie, telling herself that she would simply plead some excuse to make the visit as short as was polite.

The maid took the pie from Anna with a curtsey and ushered her into the parlor, where she found not only Mrs. Bennett and Mrs. Burroughs, the vicar's wife, but also the village doctor, as well. Dr. Felton rose to his feet with such a bright smile on his face when Anna entered that she could only assume that he had the same reaction to Mrs. Bennett's conversation as Anna did.

"Miss Holcomb, what a fortunate surprise," he said, crossing the room to bow over her hand. Unmarried and in his late thirties, Martin Felton was part of the small social circle in which Anna and her brother moved. She saw him frequently at parties and assemblies, and while he was not exactly someone she would classify as her friend, he was a good acquaintance.

"Oh, yes, Miss Holcomb, it's so delightful to see you." Mrs. Burroughs, a small, fluttery woman, jumped up and rushed forward to take Anna's hands. "How kind of you to come. And bringing one of your cook's delicious pies, as well. So considerate of you." She admired the pie in the maid's hands and fussed over Anna, taking her arm and leading her to the sofa, sitting down beside her.

Mrs. Bennett, who was as plump as her friend was thin, joined her in an effusive greeting. "Anna, so nice to see you. How is your brother, my dear? Such a fine young man, I always say. Wasn't I just saying to you the other day, Rachel, that Sir Christopher was the very model of a gentleman?"

"Oh, yes, of course, I'm sure. Such a gentleman," Mrs. Burroughs agreed.

"You must scold him for not coming with you today. We do so enjoy seeing him."

"I fear he is rather busy today with the estate manager."

"Oh, yes, such a responsible young man he is. I could only wish my Miles showed the same sort of interest in our estate, but, of course, he is not inclined toward matters of business. He is more of a scholar, I fear, forever locking himself in his room with his books."

Anna, having conversed with the young man on a few occasions, would scarcely have termed him scholarly, but she made no comment. Indeed, when Mrs. Bennett was talking, there was rarely any room to make a comment, even if one should be so inclined.

"Of course, I fear that Miles is feeling a trifle under the weather," Mrs. Bennett sailed on. "I hope he hasn't caught a chill. He got caught in the rain the other day. I told him to take an umbrella before he went out for his walk, but you know the young. . . ." She let out a titter and covered her mouth. "Oh, he would be furious if he heard me say that. He said to me only yesterday, 'Mother, I am scarcely young. I am all of twenty and one!' And, of course, he is, but still, it seems so young to me. Probably not to you, of course, as you are barely more than a child yourself."

"Hardly that, I am afraid, ma'am," Anna demurred.

Somewhat to Anna's surprise, the woman did not pursue the subject of her son's ill health any further than that. Nor did she even remark upon her daughter. Such a departure from Mrs. Bennett's normal behavior would have made Anna wonder what was the matter with the woman, but there was an air of suppressed excitement in her manner, a bright gleam in her eye, that to Anna, judging from past experiences, meant that the squire's wife was bursting with some prime bit of gossip.

Anna glanced over at her hostess and saw that Mrs. Burroughs' cheeks were also faintly flushed, her eyes bright. *What on earth was going on?*

As if she could hold it in no longer, Mrs. Bennett said in a rush, "Have you heard the news, Miss Holcomb? So very exciting . . ."

"No, I am afraid that I have heard nothing exciting." Anna looked at the doctor, and he shrugged imperceptibly, as though he had no idea what was going on, either.

"Well, the squire told me — and I am certain that he heard it directly from Mr. Norton, who is, of course, his solicitor — Reed Moreland is returning to Winterset!"

Mrs. Bennett paused, looking at Anna expectantly. Anna could do nothing but stare blankly at the woman. *Reed Moreland!* She felt as if her insides had suddenly fallen down to her knees.

"Isn't it wonderful?" the vicar's wife gushed.

"Yes," Anna managed to say through bloodless lips. "Yes, of course."

"Such a gentleman of refinement," Mrs. Burroughs went on happily. "So knowledgeable, so well bred. Everything one would expect from the son of a duke."

"But not at all proud," Mrs. Bennett stuck in.

"Oh, no, indeed, you are absolutely

right," her friend agreed. "Not proud at all, but not overly friendly, either."

"Indeed, just perfect."

"A paragon, it would seem," Dr. Felton put in, a faint note of amusement in his voice.

"You are absolutely right." Mrs. Bennett, incapable of irony, nodded her head. "Did you meet him when he was here before, Dr. Felton?"

"I was introduced to him at a party, I believe. He seemed a pleasant-enough gentleman."

Anna felt as if she might be sick, right there in front of everyone. *Why was Reed coming back here after all this time? And how was she to bear it?* She thought of seeing him again, of going to a party and finding him there. *It would be impossible.*

"I am sure you must be quite excited to hear of it," Mrs. Bennett said, with a playful smirk. "As I remember, the man danced attendance upon you quite a bit."

"I wouldn't say that," Anna protested faintly. "He was a very pleasant man, but I am sure he had no partiality for me."

The other two women exchanged knowing glances.

"Very prettily said, my dear," Mrs. Burroughs said approvingly. "Your maidenly reserve becomes you. But there is nothing wrong with attracting a worthy man's attention."

"And since you did not have a Season —" Mrs. Bennett rattled on.

"Of course it was very proper, very good of you to remain here and run the household for your father and brother —" the vicar's wife inserted piously.

"— no one is more deserving than you of catching such a man's eye," Mrs. Bennett finished triumphantly.

"You are very kind to say so," Anna said, putting all the firmness into her voice that she was capable of. "However, I assure you that there was nothing between Lord Moreland and myself but a very brief acquaintance. I imagine he scarcely remembers me."

That statement, Anna knew, was extremely doubtful. Reed Moreland might not recall her with any kindness, but the son of a duke was unlikely to forget the affront of a woman turning down his offer of marriage.

"One wonders why Lord Moreland is returning after so long," Dr. Felton commented, and Anna shot him a grateful glance for turning the conversation away from her relationship with Reed.

"He wrote to Mr. Norton that he intended to sell Winterset," Mrs. Bennett explained. "And he wanted to see what needed to be done to the place to put it in good condition. He instructed Mr. Norton to hire servants and have the house cleaned and made ready for his arrival."

"Do you . . . know when he is arriving?" Anna asked.

"Very soon, I would think, my dear," Mrs. Bennett replied. "The squire said Mr. Norton seemed to think that Lord Moreland was most eager to come here." She shot a meaningful little glance at Anna.

"It would doubtless be a good thing if he can sell it," the doctor mused. "It would be much better to have someone living there. Winterset is far too fine a house to stand empty so long."

"Oh, yes, it is beautiful," Mrs. Burroughs hastened to agree, adding somewhat hesitantly, "Although it is a trifle odd, don't you think?" She looked toward Anna apologetically. "I do not mean any offense, my dear. I know it is your ancestors' house. . . ."

Anna gave her a reassuring smile. "Please. Do not fear it will offend me. Everyone knows that the Lord de Winter who built it was, well, a trifle whimsical."

"Exactly." The vicar's wife nodded, pleased at Anna's understanding.

"It would be wonderful if someone would

27

live in it," Mrs. Bennett agreed, her eyes shining at the prospect. "Think of the parties . . . the balls. . . . Do you remember that ball Lord Moreland gave when he lived here before? Such a grand turnout."

"Oh, yes, indeed," Mrs. Burroughs agreed.

Anna said nothing, letting the conversational tide move on without her. She remembered the ball very well. Too well. The memories of it had haunted her for years.

She had looked her best. She had been aware of that. Her hair had been piled on top of her head in one of the intricate styles that her maid Penny was always trying to persuade her to wear, and she had worn a vivid deep blue gown that turned her eyes midnight blue. Her eyes had sparkled; her cheeks had been flushed with excitement. And she had glowed as if lit from within, her emotions turning her attractiveness into beauty.

The Winterset ballroom had positively glittered with lights, and the scent of gardenias had perfumed the air. Anna, knowing that she had told Reed once that gardenias were her favorite flowers, was aware, with a happiness so great she felt as if she were about to burst, that Reed had ordered them as a gift to her. His eyes as he smiled down at her had confirmed that knowledge.

It had been the most wonderful night of her life. She had danced only twice with Reed, the limit that propriety would allow, but those moments in his arms had been heavenly. She would never forget his face as he smiled down at her, his gray eyes warm and tender, the slash of dark eyebrows above them, the planes and hollows of his face as familiar and dear to her as if she had known him always, rather than only one month. The music, the other people, even the words they spoke, had been immaterial; the only important thing had been the way it felt to have his arm around her, her hand in his.

Later, after the midnight supper, he had taken her hand and slipped out onto the terrace with her, evading the countless prying eyes inside. They had strolled down the steps to the garden. The evening had been cool, but the chill had felt pleasant after the heat of the ballroom. As they walked, his hand had clasped hers, and Anna's pulse had begun to hammer in her throat. He had stopped and turned to face her, and she had looked up at him, knowing what was coming next, wanting it with every fiber of her being.

Then he had bent and kissed her, and she had felt as if something exploded within her.

Longing, hunger, a dancing, gibbering joy such as she had never experienced, all surged inside her, tangling and tumbling and racing through every inch of her. She had clung to him, lost to everything but Reed and the pleasure of his lips. And she had known at that moment that she had found the only man in the world for her, the love that would last her lifetime.

Even now, just thinking about it sent a shaft of pain through her chest so swift and hard that she almost gasped. Anna closed her eyes briefly, willing down the anguish that welled up in her all over again. Giving up Reed Moreland had been the hardest thing that she had ever done in her life. It had taken her three long years to reach the point of — well, not happiness, exactly, but at least contentment with her life.

It seemed the cruelest of jokes that Reed should decide to reappear in her life now. She dreaded the thought of what would happen if she saw him again. *Would the mere sight of him send all her hard-won peace of mind crashing to the ground?*

Anna could feel herself starting to shake inside, and she clenched her fists tightly to control it. She had to get away from here, had to be by herself, where she could reflect without having to worry about what everyone around her would think. Hoping she had stayed long enough to be polite, she inserted herself into the first conversational pause, saying that she must return home to give Kit the latest news.

She set the horse on the road back to Holcomb Manor, but before she reached it, she took the lane to the left that led to Winterset. She drove the trap along the driveway, edged on both sides with limes. Her hands grew looser on the reins, and the horse slowed its pace more and more. There were breaks in the trees where one or more had died and been cut down over the years, and there were shrubs that had grown up closer to the road. But it was still familiar enough to make Anna's heart ache within her chest. Winterset was their nearest neighbor, but she had not ridden along this drive for three years.

The rows of trees ended, opening onto a broad expanse of lawn leading up to the great house itself. Winterset lay on a slight rise in the land, like a jewel in its setting. The drive curved in a circle in front of it, ending just before the low stone wall, topped by an iron railing, that stood some yards in front of the house.

The wall was centered by two stone pillars standing higher than the iron railings, and atop each pillar lay a staghound *au couchant,* its ears pricked alertly. The fierce dogs were, it was said, modeled after the hunting hounds of Lord Jasper de Winter, who had built the house in the seventeenth century.

Between the iron fencing and the house lay a small inner courtyard, with a wide stone pathway leading from the drive to the front door of the house. The house itself was elegant and symmetrical, with a long central section flanked on either end by two shorter gabled wings. It had been constructed of yellowish stone, almost honey-colored when it was built, but now darkened in patches by age, and much of it spotted by lichen. As a result, when the sun shone on it, as it did this summer day, the stone was a mellow golden; on dreary days, it had a dark and gloomy cast.

Much of its graceful elegance came from its large windows and the stone balustrade that ran across the top of the house. Stone chimneys dotted the roof. The chimneys at the front gables were carved so that they appeared to twist upward in spirals. At various corners of the roof, statues of fierce griffins and eagles jutted up into the air.

Anna looked up at the building. She had always loved Winterset, even when she was a child, seeing the statues of the fantastical griffins and the twisting chimneys as delightful whimsy. But now, looking at the house, she understood the superstitious unease with which many people regarded it. The statues and twisted chimneys did give the place an odd air, even — especially on a gloomy day — an atmosphere of foreboding. The uncannily accurate renditions of the staghounds on the gate piers only added to the faint menace. Despite the ravages of time, the faces of the large dogs were eerily realistic, so that one felt almost as if the animals were watching one carefully. It was the sculptor's skill at creating the hounds, Anna thought, that had contributed to the local legend that on the nights of the full moon, the staghounds rose from their positions and, at the piercing whistle of their long-dead master, Lord Jasper de Winter, ran with him on a ghostly hunt through the night, eyes gleaming like red-hot coals.

There was a rustling in the bushes beside Anna's trap, and she whipped her head around. A man stood just beyond, scarcely visible, watching her.

Chapter Two

Anna's hands tightened on the reins, her heart suddenly in her throat. Then the figure moved, shoving through the shrubbery to the driveway, and she relaxed.

"Grimsley. I did not see you there."

The slight man, a trifle stooped from years of bending over plants and weeds, reached up and swept the dark cap from his head, revealing a shock of curly hair, the dark streaked through with gray.

"Good day to ye, miss," Grimsley replied, with a deferential bob of his head. He had once been head gardener here at Winterset and had stayed on as caretaker during all the years it had sat empty.

"How are you?" Anna asked politely, and the man moved over to the side of her trap.

"Very good, miss. Kind of you to ask." He grinned up at her, displaying a row of crooked teeth. "The old place is still a beauty, ain't she, miss?"

"Yes. I have always found Winterset quite

lovely." Anna paused, then added, "I hear that the owner plans to return."

He nodded his head eagerly. "Yes, miss, that's the truth. Mr. Norton came by and told me today. Says the grand folk are coming back. Mayhap ye will be coming over here again, then."

Anna quickly shook her head. "I wouldn't think so."

"Don't seem right, the house without a de Winter in it."

"I am sure Lord Moreland is a good employer."

"Not a de Winter," the man said unanswerably. He turned to look again at the building. "House is lonely without them. Don't seem right, Lord de Winter leaving Winterset like that. Going to some heathen place."

"Barbados," Anna said automatically. This was a familiar conversation; she had had it nearly every time she had run into Mr. Grimsley in the past few years.

"Selling the house." The middle-aged man's jaw set stubbornly.

"It was far too big a place for my uncle," Anna said. "And he did not wish to live there any longer."

Her mother's brother, Charles, was the Lord de Winter about whom the caretaker spoke. An unmarried, childless man, he — and Anna's mother, Barbara — had been the last of the de Winter line. When he left Winterset, he had put the house and all his other assets into the guardianship of Anna's father, as someday, when he died, all his belongings would be inherited by Anna and Kit. Kit still managed the de Winter lands and money, but their father had sold the house, as all of them preferred to live in their own home, Holcomb Manor.

Anna could see that her words had not mollified Grimsley; she knew that they never had before and doubtless never would. The man was peculiarly obsessed with Winterset and the de Winters. He had been born on the estate and had lived his entire life there. He had continued to occupy the small gardener's house on the grounds for the last three years, while the house had stood empty. Of course, he was also rumored to take a few nips of gin throughout the day, which Anna suspected had something to do with some of the odd notions he took.

She turned the conversation back to the subject that still nagged at her brain. "Do you know when Lord Moreland will be arriving at Winterset?"

Grimsley shook his head gloomily. "Soon, Mr. Norton said. 'Best be getting it in shape,

Grimsley.' That's what he said. How's one man to do that, I'd like to know."

"I am sure he will not expect you to do any more than what you can," Anna assured him. "Ree— Lord Moreland is a very fair man."

He nodded, but Anna could see the skepticism in his eyes.

"Well," she went on bracingly, though she knew that the assurance was more for herself than from the caretaker, "I imagine that he will not stay here all that long, anyway. I understand that he is merely looking it over to see about selling it."

"Aye." Grimsley shifted and looked away, and suddenly Anna understood what bothered him.

"Even if he does sell the house," she told him with the sympathetic understanding that had made her a favorite among all the people who worked for the Holcombs, "I would think that a new owner would keep you on as head gardener — and would probably even hire men to help you. Then you would be able to keep the grounds in the manner that you would like to."

He looked up at her, and a kind of odd, shy smile touched his lips. "Aye, miss, that he would — if he be the kind ye and yer brother be."

"If he is not, rest assured that there will always be a place for you on the Winterset lands," Anna replied.

"Thankee, miss. Good day, miss." Again he gave her the little head bob and began to move away, melting back into the shrubbery.

Anna glanced back at the house. She would have to tell Kit about Reed's return. It would seem highly odd if she did not. Kit did not know what had transpired between her and Reed. He had been abroad when their father had sold Reed the house, and she had never told him what happened. He might have heard rumors from others, she supposed, but he had never brought up the subject. He would have to call on Reed when he arrived. It would be impolite to do anything else, and it would cause talk. But surely Reed would not return the call, given what had passed between them, so if she avoided any parties that he might attend . . .

But she knew that idea was ridiculous. She could not pretend to be ill for however many days or weeks Reed decided to stay here. She was filled with a cowardly impulse to flee. If only there were some relative to whom she could make a sudden visit, but she was sorely lacking in relations on both sides of her family. Her uncle was childless, and the great-aunt who had raised her mother after her parents' tragic deaths had died a few years ago. The only other possibility was a cousin of her father's, but she was a busy woman with five adolescent girls whom she was continually in the process of trying to marry off, and she had made it quite clear to Anna years ago, when Anna should have made her debut, that she had little desire to have another girl in the house, especially one who would outshine her own plain daughters.

There was her good friend Miranda, of course, who had married a minister near Exeter. Anna had visited her many times, and Miranda would welcome her, but she was the mother of two children and was even now in her lying-in for her third baby. Her husband's mother had come to visit, in order to help with the new baby, and what with the nursemaid, the children and the mother-in-law, the small parsonage would be bursting at the seams.

Besides, such a sudden flight just when Reed returned would cause much talk and speculation, and that was the last thing Anna wanted. She knew that she would simply have to stay here and do everything she could to avoid seeing Reed. And if they met by chance, then she would simply have to get through it. She would smile politely and say some little formality, and that would be it.

After all, it had been three years. She no longer even thought about him — well, scarcely at all — and doubtless he had similarly gotten over her. He had been in London these three years, and there had been numerous girls there doing their best to lift his spirits, Anna was sure. *Why, for all she knew, he had gotten married.*

Anna's heart twisted in her chest at this thought, but she told herself sternly that that was both foolish and selfish. A man as eligible, as handsome, as charming as Reed would have had no difficulty finding someone else to love, and surely that was what she wanted for him. *Of course it was.* And she was over him; she had put away her girlish dreams. Whatever pain and embarrassment she might feel about meeting him again, it certainly was not because she still *loved* him.

With an irritated shake of her head, Anna clicked her tongue, turning her horse around and heading back down the driveway. Whatever lay before her, she told herself sternly, she was not going to act like a lovesick girl. She had done what she had to do three years ago, and she did not regret it. She *would not* regret it. That aspect of her

life was over. She refused to let Reed Moreland's return send her into a turmoil.

She slapped the reins, urging the horse
on, and firmly quelled the notion, deep inside her, that it felt as though she was running away.

Anna kept herself busy for the next few
days, doing her best not to think about Reed
or his impending arrival. She did all the
mending that had piled up in her sewing
basket and finished the little embroidered
baby gown she had made for her friend
Miranda's newest baby, as well as embroi-
dering a white linen fichu she had bought a
few months ago for the neckline of one of
her dresses. She caught up on all her correspondence and visited one of their aging
tenants. She also took a long walk every day,
something she had found helped to ease her
mind, whatever the situation.

Three days after she had called at the vicarage, she left her house for another long
tramp. She took the path that ran from their
garden to the east. The path forked, one
choice leading back into the woods that nestled at the base of Craydon Tor, one of her
favorite places to walk, but today she continued on the walk that curved around the
outer base of the tor. It then straightened

41

out and ran in a more-or-less straight line until one reached the edge of Winterset lands. Anna had walked this path hundreds of times in her life, but in the last three years she had never walked as far as Winterset. She did not plan to today, either, intending to turn off at the meadow halfway along and climb over the stile and cut across the meadow to the tree-lined stream that lay beyond. She often went there to think, for it was a calming place, shaded by leafy green trees and dappled with the sunlight that stole through their gently moving leaves, with the burble of the brook as a soothing background.

Rounding the tor, her head down and deep in thought, she did not look at the long stretch of path before her until gradually she became aware of the soft plip-plop of horses' hooves. She sighed inwardly. She did not wish to have to speak to anyone right now, and she cast about in her mind for some way to avoid it, but, of course, there was none, for the rider was sure to have seen her, and a retreat now would be rude. Bracing herself to smile and say a few polite words, she lifted her head.

The horse, a big, sleek black stallion, was trotting toward her, his rider moving with an effortless grace on his back. The man riding was tall and broad-shouldered, and his dark hair glinted with highlights of red in the sun. He was still too far away for her to make out the exact shape of his features or the color of his eyes, but Anna knew them well enough to supply the strong jaw and wide mouth, the straight slash of dark eyebrows above dark-lashed gray eyes.

It was Reed Moreland riding toward her.

Anna stood rooted to the spot, her mind a chaotic jumble. He had been in her thoughts often the last few days, but still, it was a shock to actually see him. Fate, she thought, had a firm sense of irony, to send him riding toward her as he had been the first time they met.

Reed stopped a few feet away from her and dismounted. For a long moment they simply looked at each other. Anna's heart was pounding in her chest until she felt as though it might explode. No matter how hard she had tried, she realized, nothing could have prepared her for seeing him again.

"Miss Holcomb." He came a step or two closer, holding the reins of his horse.

"My lord." Anna was a little surprised at how calmly her voice came out. It should, she thought, have shaken as she was shaking inside.

Her eyes searched his face, looking for each tiny difference. Was his skin more tanned? Were there a few more little lines radiating out from the corner of his eyes? It was a little something of a shock, seeing his eyes again; memory could not render exactly the silver-gray color of them, shadowed by lashes so thick and long they seemed almost ridiculous on a man.

She was aware of a strong desire to reach out and brush back his hair with her fingertips. Warmth started deep in her abdomen. She remembered the touch of his lips on hers, the way heat had flared along his skin, the hard iron of his arms around her. Anna swallowed and looked away from him, praying that her face showed none of what she was feeling.

Silence stretched between them awkwardly, until finally Anna rushed in with the first thing she could think of. "I was . . . surprised to learn that you had decided to return to Winterset."

"It seemed foolish to keep the house," he replied. "I thought I should look at it . . . put it up for sale."

"That will be good," Anna said, irritated by how stiffly her voice came out. She felt embarrassed and foolish, and she could not help but think about the fact that she was wearing her everyday bonnet and her sturdy walking boots and a quite ordinary dress. She must look like the veritable country mouse. Reed would probably wonder what he had ever seen in her. *Why had she had the misfortune to run into him this way? And why the devil had he returned so early?* She had thought she would have several more days to ready herself.

"Yes, I am sure you must feel so," he retorted in a clipped voice.

He still hated her, she thought. It was what she had expected. A person did not forget slights — the son of a duke probably even less so than others. But she had not been able to explain it to him. She could not have borne the way he would have looked at her after that, the way he would have thought about her. Better that he think her callous and careless, an inveterate flirt.

She cast about in her mind for something to say to alleviate the awkward silence. "I hope that they were able to get the house ready for you in time."

A trace of a smile so faint she wasn't even sure it was there tugged at his lips for an instant. "I fear the butler was not best pleased to see me. Especially since I did not come alone."

Her eyes flew to his face at his words. *Was*

he going to say that he was married? Had he brought his wife? His family? Anna's heart squeezed within her chest. "Indeed? You brought a party with you?"

"My sister and her husband. They thought they might be interested in purchasing Winterset. And my twin brothers — they were, once again, without a tutor." His mouth curved into an actual smile now, albeit a rather rueful one, and his eyes lit with humor and affection.

Anna remembered the look very well, and seeing it now was like a knife slicing through her. "Ah . . . Constantine and Alexander."

His eyebrows rose. "You remember their names? I am surprised."

She did not tell him that she remembered everything he had told her — nor that she had written them down in her journal like a lovesick schoolgirl. "They are difficult names to forget," she told him quickly. "Two Greats in one family."

"They are difficult boys to forget, as well," he went on in the same easy tone, without the earlier awkwardness that had been in his voice. Then he seemed to remember how things stood with them, for he looked away and his body shifted, returning to its former awkward stiffness.

"I — how are you doing?" he continued abruptly, frowning down at her.

"I am well, thank you," Anna said, noting that there had been no real concern in his voice. He had sounded, in fact, more annoyed than anything else.

"Then there has been . . . nothing unusual happening around here?"

Anna looked at him oddly. *What did he mean?* Was he pointing out to her the dull contrast of her life to the exciting London life that he could have given her? She stiffened, her face turning defiant. "No. I fear that only the most ordinary things occur around Lower Fenley. It is not the sophisticated sort of place that you are accustomed to, I'm sure."

He raised a brow, obviously nettled by her words. "You have no idea what I am accustomed to," he retorted sharply.

He stopped, pressing his lips together as if to hold back whatever words had sprung to his lips. "I should never have come back here," he went on, his voice bitter.

"No, perhaps you should not," Anna agreed, and turned quickly away to hide the sudden, unwelcome glint of tears that had sprung into her eyes.

"Anna . . ." He started toward her, then stopped, a soft oath falling from his lips.

47

Her throat was suddenly tight and full. She knew that she could not speak without bursting into tears. Hurriedly, Anna began to walk away. She could not bear it if he followed her, she thought. Yet when she heard the rustle of movement behind her, then his quiet command to his horse and the sound of the animal's hooves as he pounded away from her, she felt perversely insulted. *He was so eager to get away from her!*

She turned, looking back toward Reed. He was galloping away, a magnificent figure on his horse. Tears blurred her vision. Then she turned, blinking the water from her eyes, and strode toward home.

As he rode home, Reed called himself ten times a fool. He had rushed to Winterset, unable to rid himself of the uneasy certainty left by his dream that Anna was in trouble — and equally unable to convince himself that there was no reason why he should be the person to help her out of whatever it was.

But nothing had gone right since he made the decision to come here. He had come up with a most reasonable excuse for returning to Lower Fenley: He intended to sell Winterset. It made sense; he knew that a logical man — a man who was able to let go of a nonsensical romantic fantasy — would have sold it years ago. He could go back to Winterset to look it over and decide what repairs needed to be done in order to sell it, even stay to make sure that the renovations were done to his liking. It was a logical-enough idea that Anna would not assume that he had come there just to see her — especially not after three years had passed. It would also, he thought, be something that his family would accept without questioning him.

He had bought the house three years ago when he had been seized with the idea that he should purchase a country house, a home of his own, separate and apart from his beloved and eccentric family. He envisioned it as the place where he would someday bring a bride and raise a family. Inquiries had brought up word of Winterset, a large manor house in Gloucestershire that had lain vacant for almost ten years. It had been the seat of the de Winter family, a noble family whose numbers had dwindled away over the years until there was only the last Lord de Winter left. Unmarried and childless, Lord Charles had left England ten years earlier for Barbados. Apparently he had decided not to return, and the house had been put up for sale by Sir Edmund Holcomb, de Winter's brother-in-law and the guardian of his estate while Lord de Winter was abroad.

A description and drawing of the house had intrigued Reed, and he had ridden to Gloucestershire to see the place for himself. What he had not expected was that on the first day he saw the house, he would meet the woman whom he wanted to be his bride.

The house and surrounding grounds had been everything he had wanted — spacious and elegant, built of honey-colored stone, with just the sort of odd, piquant touches to make it intriguing — and he had bought it, then settled into the most-habitable wing while he began the process of rebuilding it. And as he did so, he courted Anna Holcomb. For a few weeks, he had spun happy dreams, but they had all ended the day he had asked her to marry him. She had rejected his suit in terms that allowed for no possibility of her changing her mind. The next morning Reed had left Winterset, and the house had once again sat empty.

He had told no one in his family about what had happened at Winterset three years ago, except for his older brother, Theo, his closest sibling and one whom he could count on never to reveal a secret. The sympathy of his sisters had been more than he had thought he could bear at the time, and he had an innate reluctance to reveal something so deeply painful even to those who loved him. Being a family rather given to odd fits and starts, no one had really questioned his abandoning the home he had bought, but he suspected that returning there out of the blue would set up just the sort of questions that he wanted to avoid. Selling the house would, he hoped, be the sort of logical, boring business matter that no one in his family would want to hear more about.

That much was true. His mistake, he knew, had been bringing the matter up at the breakfast table. He had hoped that only his father and mother, or perhaps his sister Thisbe and her husband, Desmond, might be there, all of whom had little curiosity about matters outside their chosen fields and who would accept his explanation for his sudden departure with few questions.

Unfortunately, when he had arrived in the breakfast room somewhat later than was his custom, he had found it a scene of great activity. His brother, Theo, Thisbe's twin and the heir to the family title and estate, had been home for almost six months now and was apparently growing restless again, and he had arisen early that morning for a ride in the park and was just then sitting down to breakfast. His sister Kyria and her husband, Rafe, had recently returned from their honeymoon in Europe, which had extended itself into two years and a tour of Rafe's native United States, as well, bringing with them their six-month-old baby, a strawberry-blond beauty named Emily. His other sister Olivia and her husband, Stephen, had come to London with their own toddler, John, when Kyria and Rafe returned, and they had come over early this morning to visit.

And shortly after Reed walked in, the twelve-year-old twins, Alexander and Constantine, had come charging into the room, their hair sticking out all over their heads and smelling faintly singed, to chatter excitedly about the experiment with electricity that they had conducted under Thisbe's supervision.

At that point, Reed knew, he should have kept his mouth shut and told his father later, in the duke's workshop, where he puttered about with his beloved objects of antiquity. But, foolishly, he had opened his mouth and stated his intention to return to Winterset to sell the house. Theo, who knew about Anna, had narrowed his eyes as he looked at Reed, and asked him one or two piercing questions.

Then Kyria had declared that perhaps she

and Rafe would be interested in buying the place themselves, as they were considering establishing a country home in England. Before he knew what had happened, Theo had suggested that Rafe and Kyria should accompany Reed on his trip to Gloucestershire and look at the house, and after that, the twins had begged to be allowed to come along, too. As Con and Alex were once again without a tutor, the last one having left in a huff when the twins' boa constrictor had mysteriously wound up in his bed one evening, the duchess had seized upon this suggestion with a great deal of warmth, saying that it would give her time to find a more suitable tutor. Then Kyria had decided that she would bring her friend Rosemary Farrington with her, as she had a remarkably good eye for interiors.

Reed had groaned inwardly, sure that Miss Farrington had been thrown into the mix in another one of Kyria's valiant attempts to find him a wife, as he had never before noticed that Kyria had trouble deciding on anything on her own. Kyria had always been an inveterate matchmaker, and marriage seemed only to have made her worse.

He had argued valiantly that he intended to leave as soon as possible, but Kyria had countered that after two years of traveling, she was an expert at packing quickly, and the twins, of course, were ready to go at a moment's notice, needing only to extract a promise from Thisbe and Desmond that they would make sure that the parrot and boa and the rest of the twins' menagerie were well taken care of. As for Rosemary, Kyria could vouch for her speed and efficiency, as well as her willingness to take off on a lark.

Finally Reed had given in, knowing that to continue to argue further against their joining him would only result in exactly the sort of curious questions that he was trying to avoid. He would have far preferred to have gone alone, but he had to admit that taking several members of his family with him would make the trip appear more normal and conveniently mask his real purpose.

Kyria had kept her promise of packing and moving with speed, and within a day they had set out, travelling not by train, as Reed had originally intended, but in Kyria's new victoria, an elegant low-slung open carriage that Rafe had recently bought for his wife, with Reed and Rafe riding alongside, followed by a slower wagon of personal servants and luggage, as well as a groom with several more horses for the twins, Kyria and their guest.

When they arrived at Winterset, Reed had immediately talked to the butler, then to the local solicitor, Mr. Norton, and even to the caretaker of the place, subtly inquiring about what had been happening in the area. Frustratingly, he had come up with no indication that there was anything amiss locally. He had tried to keep any inquiries about Miss Holcomb casual, but he thought there had been a definite spark of interest in Norton's eye when he answered that Miss Holcomb and her brother were in the best of health.

It occurred to Reed that he had been both precipitate and foolish in placing so much importance on a dream. No matter how vivid it had been, no matter how it had shaken him, it was, after all, only a dream. A rational man, he reminded himself, would not forget that.

Still, he could not dislodge the feeling deep inside that it had indeed been important, and he knew that he had to find out more. He needed, he knew, to talk to Anna, to see her and judge for himself whether or not anything was bothering her. For that reason, he had ridden out this afternoon, heading along the path to her house. It was one he had taken many times in the month he had spent courting her, and just riding along, looking at the beautiful landscape around him, had filled him with a poignant sense of loss and regret.

He wasn't sure what he intended to do. He had learned from the butler that Sir Edmund, Anna's father, had died two years ago, and her brother, Christopher, was now in charge at Holcomb Manor. He did not know Sir Christopher, and according to the polite code of society, it would be correct to wait until Christopher came to call on him, as Reed was the visitor to the area. On the other hand, Reed had called at Holcomb Manor many times before when he had lived at Winterset, so it would not be breaking any rule of conduct, really, to call upon Anna.

It would, of course, be awkward in the extreme.

However, he could think of no other way to talk directly to her. He certainly had no intention of sitting around, kicking his heels, waiting for Sir Christopher to call on him so that he could return the call, or for Anna to call upon his sister, which seemed unlikely, given the circumstances.

It had seemed heaven sent, then, when he had spied her walking in the distance, and he had kicked his horse into a trot, eagerness rising up in him.

He had seen the stricken expression on her face when she had looked up at him, and it was only then that he had realized his eagerness was out of proportion to what he should feel. His second thought had been that her beauty had not diminished in the three years since he had seen her. She had, if anything, grown even more beautiful — or perhaps his memory had simply been unable to recall the full extent of her beauty.

He had dismounted and then stood, feeling like a fool, knowing that she did not want to speak to him, or even see him; that was obvious from the way she stood, poised as if she might run away at any moment. Their conversation had been awkward and stilted, and he had found out nothing from her that he did not already know.

It had been impossible to ask her outright if she was in any sort of trouble. She would have thought him mad — and if he had told her about the dream that had sent him to Winterset posthaste, she would have thought him even more insane. He had no right to protect her; he had not even seen her in three years, and when last he *had* seen her, she had rejected him.

Worst of all, as he had stood there struggling through their awkward conversation, he had been aware of the fact that what he truly wanted to do was to pull her into his arms and kiss her. After all this time, despite her flat and unequivocal rejection of his proposal, he still wanted her.

What a fool he had been to come back here! Reed could not help but wonder if what had sent him running to Winterset had been less certainty in the portent of his dream than the long-dormant, but obviously not-quenched, fire he had felt for Anna.

There was no hope for him with her; there never had been. Coming back here had just stirred passions that were better left alone. He had spent three long years getting over the pain of loving her. The last thing he should do was place himself in danger of falling in love all over again.

He should leave, he knew. Forget his bizarre dream and just go back to London, where he had a perfectly enjoyable and trouble-free life. He should simply do what he had told everyone he was doing here: spend a day or two looking over the house, then order repairs and put it up for sale. Then he should return to London and forget all about Anna Holcomb.

And yet he knew, even as he thought it,

that he would not. However foolish it was to stay, he would not — could not — leave.

The girl walked as quickly as she could through the trees. She did not like to be alone here, where the trees grew thickly all around and the night was silent except for the occasional scrabbling of some nocturnal creature. There was an eerie quality to the woods that frightened her even during the daytime, but at night they seemed twice as ominous — secret and dark and full of things that she could sense but could not see.

Her lover scoffed at her fears. He said the woods were like a cloak, hiding and protecting them. They could meet no other way. It was only in the woods at night that the two of them could be alone together, could express how they really felt.

And it was for that reason that she plunged eagerly in among the trees. She would meet him here tonight as they so often did, and he would kiss away her fears, tease her for her foolishness even as his hands caressed her. She did not mind that he teased her, did not care that he talked of things she could not understand. He loved her, and that was all that mattered. Never in her wildest dreams had she imagined that one such as he could love her. She hugged that knowledge to herself like a kind of talisman against the darkness.

Something rustled in the bushes behind her, and the noise sent an icy prickle down her spine. She glanced uneasily behind her, but she could see nothing. She picked up her pace a little, her hands fisting nervously in her skirts. It would not be long before she was at their meeting place, and then everything would be all right.

There was a snap behind her, and she jumped and whirled, peering into the darkness behind her. "Hello?" Her voice came out quavering and thin. There was no answer.

It was nothing, she told herself, or perhaps it was her lover, playing a little joke on her. She did not always understand his jests. She waited, but the longer she stood waiting, listening, the more stretched her nerves grew. Again there came a rustling, but this time to the side of her. And as she whipped her head around, she glimpsed something — a flash of movement.

Fear tore through her, and she began

to run. She called his name, her voice swallowed up by the enormous silence of the woods. She ran, her pulse pounding in her ears, her breath rasping in her throat.

It was following her. She could hear the snap of twigs, the whisper of branches pushed aside, the soft thud of someone — something! — running. She ran with all the speed of terror, but it gained easily on her. She could hear its breath behind her, and then it slammed into her.

She went sprawling on the ground, the breath knocked out of her. Its weight was heavy on her back. She struggled to breathe, struggled to crawl. It growled, low and menacing. Tears of fear sprang into her eyes. She tried to turn, to face her attacker, but it held her head down.

Out of the corner of her eye, she glimpsed a face — fearsome, snarling, like nothing she had ever seen. Then, before she could even think, something sank into her throat, ripping, tearing. Her screams echoed and died in the stillness of the trees.

Chapter Three

Anna heard all about the arrival of Lord Moreland and his party at Winterset, first from her excited maid the next morning and later from the squire's wife and daughter. Anna carefully refrained from telling either one of her newsbearers that she already knew of Reed's arrival. She listened patiently as Mrs. Bennett repeated the chemist's description of Moreland's entourage as it had moved through the town of Lower Fenley, keeping a pleasant smile fixed on her face.

After the Bennetts left, Kit turned to his sister and said thoughtfully, "I suppose I ought to call on him — to be polite. Or do you think that's forward?"

Despite her inner turmoil, Anna had to smile at her brother's somewhat anxious expression. He had brought the same subject up days ago, when they had first learned that Reed Moreland was returning to Winterset, and obviously he had been considering the matter ever since. Kit was, after all, still rather young, only twenty-four years of age, and the prospect of new neighbors was a little exciting to him. There were few people his age or station anywhere around them, and his social life in London had been cut short by having to return to take over his father's responsibilities. He had accepted his lot with good grace, never complaining, and for the most part he seemed content to live quietly in the country.

But it was only natural that he should want to meet some new people. The social highlight of his life was a weekly game of cards in the village with Dr. Felton and a few of the local men. Indeed, Anna knew that had circumstances been different, she, too, would have looked forward with pleasure to meeting the occupants of Winterset. The last thing she wanted was for Kit to meet Reed, but she could not bring herself to tell him about the disastrous relationship that had formed between her and Moreland. Nor could she ask him not to call on the man.

"No, I don't think it's forward at all," she assured him, fixing a pleasant smile on her face. "I think it is just what is proper." She hoped that Reed would not be abrupt or unkind to Kit just because he was her brother. "And you will get a better idea of whether or not they intend to stay and if they are friendly or too snobbish to mingle with us country folk."

"Is that the way Lord Moreland is?" Kit asked. "You knew him. Mrs. Bennett seemed to think —"

Anna forced a chuckle. "Come, Kit, surely you are not relying on Mrs. Bennett's version of events. Why, to hear her talk, one would think that you are quite taken with her daughter."

Kit made a wry face. "Point taken. But you did at least talk to the man."

"Yes. At parties and such. He was . . . a nice man. He did not seem puffed up with pride, as I had expected of the son of a duke. But it has been three years. He may have changed."

Kit smiled at her. "Don't worry. I will not be disillusioned if he offers me a set down."

As it turned out, Kit was far from offered a set down. In his eagerness, he rode over to Winterset not long after their conversation, and when he returned, he was smiling and bubbling over with liking for their new neighbors.

"He's a jolly good sort," Kit told her, a boyish grin on his face. "Just as you said — not at all proud or puffed up. I quite liked him."

"Good. I'm glad," Anna responded with genuine pleasure.

"There were several other people there, as Mrs. Bennett said," he went on. "His sister, Lady Kyria, and her husband, who is an American."

"And what are they like?" Anna remembered hearing Reed speak of Kyria more than once, as well as his other sisters, and she could not help but be interested in her.

"Very nice. Lady Kyria is stunning. Actually, I had seen her when I was in London. A friend took me to a party once, and she was there. Unforgettable."

"What does she look like?" Anna pressed.

"Red hair, very tall. Just . . . just beautiful," he finished lamely, shrugging. "And quite charming. Not a bit of snobbery about her, either. Strangely enough, the family seems a bit egalitarian."

"I understand that the duchess is very forward-thinking," Anna told him.

"Lady Kyria's husband is a chap named Rafe McIntyre. He's an American — shook my hand, acted as if he'd known me all my life." He paused, and his expression shifted subtly. "There is another woman in their party . . . Miss Rosemary Farrington."

Something cold touched Anna's heart. "Another woman? A relative, do you think?"

"Oh, no, I didn't get that impression. I think she is perhaps a friend of theirs."

"What — what is she like?" It was common to bring friends along to stay at one's county estate, but it betokened a certain interest in a woman if a man asked her to come with his family to his estate, especially if she was there by herself, not just a member of a family invited to stay. "Is she — are her parents there?"

Kit looked at her oddly. "No, I don't think so. No one said anything about them. Why?"

Anna blushed, realizing how peculiar her question had sounded. "I don't know. I was just wondering . . . if there were any other people there. You know, if it was a large party or small. One cannot rely on Mrs. Bennett for accuracy, you know."

"No, I think they are the only people who came to Winterset."

"Tell me about Miss Farrington." Anna strove to keep her voice light. It was absurd, she knew, for her to feel this quiver of jealousy at the thought that Reed might have an interest in Miss Farrington. After all, she expected him to go on with his life. Indeed, she *wanted* him to. She wanted him to be happy.

"She is a beautiful woman. Not, perhaps, as beautiful as Lady Kyria is, but, to my way of thinking, much better — more normal, you know, more approachable. Her hair is blond and her eyes are blue. She is quite small and just a little bit shy, I think."

It was only then that Anna noticed the moonstruck look on her brother's face, and a different sort of anxiety crept into her. "Kit . . . you are not — you sound quite taken with Miss Farrington."

Her brother's expression hardened, the rapt look in his eyes replaced by something a little bitter. "Don't worry. I'm not a fool. I know that there is no possibility —"

Anna's face filled with sympathy, and she went to her brother, slipping her hand into his. "Kit, I am so sorry. . . ."

"I know. It is not your fault." He smiled faintly down at her, squeezing her hand a little. "You, after all, suffer just as much as I. One cannot choose one's lot, can one? And, for the most part, I am well content."

"For the most part."

He shrugged. "I cannot help but see, can I? Cannot help but feel?"

"No," Anna replied, her voice threaded with sorrow. "One cannot help but feel."

After her talk with Kit, Anna felt the need to get outside. She had always loved the outdoors, and she refused to let Reed's proximity deter her from her almost-daily walk or ride about the estate. Whatever the problem, it always helped clear her head to go on a long ramble.

She would be careful this time, though, not to head in the direction of Winterset. She would go into the woods toward Craydon Tor. So, putting on her walking boots and grabbing her hat, she left the house. She took the same path out of the garden that she had used the other day, but this time she headed into the leafy green trees leading toward the tor, an upthrust of land that on this side was a gradual elevation and on the other was a more-or-less sheer drop to the valley below. It loomed over the village of Lower Fenley and was the most distinctive landmark for miles around.

As she walked through the trees, the vegetation grew thicker around her, and the path became less and less clear. Anna knew the area, however, and she had no fear of getting lost. There were some, she knew, who disliked the woods, finding them dark and gloomy, even frightening. But she had always thought them peaceful and serene, and she liked the glimpses of wildlife that she found in them, from the red flash of a bird flitting from branch to branch to the jittering antics of a squirrel on a limb.

The woods worked their usual magic today, calming her. At one point she came upon a fawn with its mother, both of which turned and shot off as she approached. She sat on a large stone for a few minutes, just listening to the sounds of the woods — the twitter of birds, the soft stirring of the branches, the rustle of some small creature in the leaves.

Holding her skirts up with one hand and grabbing at branches and saplings with the other, she made her way down into a small depression where a little pool had formed. She chuckled as a startled frog jumped off a stone at her approach and landed with a splash in the large puddle. Past this indention in the land, she climbed upward at a slant, taking a narrow path. It led, she knew, to a small, enchanting glen not much farther on, where a fallen, mossy tree trunk provided a natural seat. Perhaps she might go even farther than that; she might go to the hut and see how things were there. She too often avoided her duty there, she thought. Her father would not have been pleased; he would have said that the distress she felt when she went there was no excuse.

Anna came to an abrupt stop. A terrible cold assailed her. Her hand flew to her chest as if to hold in the pain that flowered there, sharp and icy. Instinctively she closed her eyes, seeing in her mind the nighttime darkness of the woods, deep and pervasive. Her breath caught in her throat as fear and panic flashed through her.

She bit back a moan and stumbled away. She leaned against a tree, struggling to calm her breathing. The panic and the pain receded, leaving her shaken.

Anna turned, looking back at the innocuous copse of trees from which she had just fled. She pressed her hand against her forehead, where a headache had formed. She waited for the shaking and the weakness to subside. They always did, though the headaches tended to linger longer.

It was not the first time she had felt this sort of strange sensation, where she seemed abruptly to be outside of her body somehow, assaulted by emotions she did not understand. Sometimes she simply felt these emotions; other times she might smell something, like the sharp scent of burning wood, and often she "saw" something.

Once, when she had gone to visit one of their tenant farmers whose child was ill, as she had approached the door, she had been struck by a wave of sorrow so severe that tears had sprung unconsciously into her eyes. It had been no surprise to her when the farmer had opened the door, his face a mask of grief, and told her that his child had died only minutes earlier.

Usually they were quite commonplace things that she saw or felt — a spring day and an upswelling of joy even though it was winter at the time, or a sentence or two in another's voice suddenly running through her head, completely out of context with anything that was happening around her. When Kit was away in Europe, she had awakened one night thinking she had heard him speak her name, but, of course, he had not been in the house.

She did not know what caused these "visions," and she had kept them hidden from those around her, ashamed and embarrassed by her oddity. It was only rarely that they seemed connected to anything real, as they had been with the tenant farmer. She did her best to suppress and ignore them when they came upon her. But never had one hit her with the intensity or pain she had just felt.

Anna took a deep breath and smoothed back her hair with her hands. She looked at the quiet scene again. It was ridiculous to think that there was anything about it that could cause such fear. She took another steadying breath, turned and began to walk away. Her desire to go farther up the hill had vanished, and she decided to walk home.

She had not gone very far when she heard the faint sound of a voice. She paused, listening. She was on Holcomb land, and it was unusual for there to be anyone else here.

Again there was a voice — no, two, she thought. Curious, she turned in the direction of the sound, walking quietly and carefully. There was always the possibility of poachers, though Rankin kept a sharp eye out for them. She had little desire to meet anyone who was roaming deep in these woods.

She saw them now, some twenty feet or so away, though they were still somewhat hidden by the trees. They were lads, and they were bent over something on the ground. As she drew closer, she saw that what interested the boys was an animal, lying on its side.

Anna hurried forward, worried now. Obviously there was something wrong with the animal, which she could see now was a dog. She wasn't sure whether she was more worried that the boys had hurt the dog or that the wounded animal might bite them in its fear.

"Boys!" Her voice came out more sharply than she had intended.

The two adolescents whirled around. The first thing she noticed was the evident relief on their faces, which reassured her that they were concerned for the animal, not hurting it, and the next thing was that they were as alike as peas in a pod. They were slender as whips, and both had thick dark hair, disheveled. Their eyes were wide and light-colored, and intelligence shone in them. They looked, she realized with a little clutch in her chest, very much like Reed.

The twins! Reed had spoken of them often, with a wry affection — and had he not mentioned the other day that they had come here with him?

"Ma'am!" one of them exclaimed, and they started toward her.

"Can you help? We found this dog."

"And he's badly hurt."

They stopped before her, looking earnestly at her. There were leaves and twigs caught in their hair and on their clothing, and dirt smudged their faces and clothes. Anna could not help but smile at them.

"What happened to him?" she asked, moving around them to the dog.

"I don't know."

"Some other animal hurt him, we think."

"His side's slashed open."

"And one of his legs is hurt."

Belatedly, one of the boys added tentatively, "Well, actually, you might not want to look."

"It's all right," Anna assured them. "I have seen wounded animals before."

The boys, who had come up on either side of her, grinned.

"Wizard!" said one, and the other told her, "Sometimes girls get squeamish."

"So I've heard." Anna looked down at the dog, which did not move, only rolled his eye up warily at her. "Well there, fellow, you *have* gotten yourself into a mess, haven't you?"

He was a medium-size dog, with short yellowish fur. His front leg was torn open and bent at a strange angle, and there were several slashes along his side, blood matting the fur.

She crooned to the animal, reaching her hand slowly toward his head while at the same time she pulled a handkerchief out of her pocket. The dog regarded her, and his tail gave a feeble thump. "That's right. You know we're only trying to help you, don't you? But just in case . . ."

She stroked his head gently as she slipped the handkerchief beneath his snout, then brought the ends together and tied them. She looked more closely at his wounds, then stood up.

"I think he's going to need more help than I can give him," she said. "If anyone can save him, it'll be Nick Perkins."

"Who's he?"

"Someone who lives not too far away and is an expert with animals. I've gone to him with every animal I've ever had who was sick or wounded. Everything I've learned about helping them, I learned from him."

"Good." One boy nodded.

"Let's go," the other one said.

"The only problem is, we will have to carry him."

"We can do that," the boys told her confidently.

"But we want to jar him as little as possible," Anna went on. "So if you two young men will turn your backs, I'll see if I can provide a litter of sorts."

They looked a little confused, but obediently turned their backs to her. Anna quickly stepped back and reached up under her skirts to untie one of her petticoats, then slipped it down, off her feet.

"All right," she said, carrying it over to the dog and spreading it out beside him.

"Jolly good idea!" one of the boys approved.

"Let's tie knots at the ends to make it easier to carry," the other suggested.

Anna smiled and agreed. They were engaging lads and obviously quick-minded, as well as kindhearted. They were, she supposed, what one would expect from Reed's brothers.

With as much gentleness as they could, they slid the dog over onto the petticoat, and while he let out a whimper, he seemed to know that they were trying to help him and did not even growl. The two boys picked up either end of the makeshift sling, and, with Anna in the lead, they started off.

Their progress was slow, and Anna was sure that the boys' burden must have gotten very heavy, but they did not breathe a word of complaint, and when she offered to take over carrying one end of the sling, they refused, pointing out that as they were perfectly matched in height, it made the ride much more comfortable for their patient.

They introduced themselves politely as Con and Alex Moreland, but the only way that Anna could tell them apart was that Alex had a streak of dirt across his forehead, whereas Con had a thin red streak on his left cheek where a twig had snapped him.

"I am Anna Holcomb," she told them in turn, and when they politely called her Miss Holcomb, she protested, "Call me Anna. I think that formalities can be dismissed after an experience such as we are sharing, don't you?"

Alex grinned. "You're true blue, ma'am. That's what Rafe would say."

"Bang up to the nines," Con agreed emphatically.

"Lots of girls would have fainted," Alex went on. "Not our sisters, of course, 'cause they're bang up, too. But one of Kyria's friends fainted one time when I showed her a mouse, and it wasn't even hurt."

"Mmm. Well, perhaps she hadn't the advantage of being reared in the country, as I was."

"She was just hen-hearted," Con said flatly, his disgust for the puny friend of his sister plain in his eyes.

Their eyes were green, Anna noticed, different from Reed's silvery-gray ones, but apart from that, she suspected that she was looking at something very much like Reed's image when he was twelve. It made her heart swell with a strange bittersweetness.

"It's a good thing you came along when you did," Alex continued.

"Yeah. We were thinking we'd have to go back and get Reed or Rafe, and by the time we got back, we were afraid he might have died," Con added.

Alex nodded. "But we thought if we tried

to pick him up and carry him back home between the two of us, it would hurt him too bad."

"Are you sure this Nick Perkins can save him?" Con asked.

"No," Anna replied honestly, for she felt sure that these two weren't the sort of boys who would rather hear a sweet falsehood. "But if he *can* be saved, Nick's the man to do it."

She had first met Nick Perkins when she was eight. She had ridden over to his cottage with her father when he had gone to consult Perkins about his favorite dog, which had been wounded in a fight and was barely clinging to life. Formerly a farmer on Winterset lands, Perkins knew more about animals than anyone else around, and he had learned about remedies and herbs from his mother, who had learned from her mother before her — back generations and generations of lay healers, Nick said. Nick had given her father an ointment that time, and steady application of it had saved the dog's life.

Anna, who had loved animals from an early age, thereafter regarded the man as a miracle worker, and she had brought every sick stray she found to Perkins for his healing touch. Over the years he had imparted not only much of his knowledge and skills regarding animals to Anna, but his knowledge of remedies, as well. She had turned a small room off the kitchens into a stillroom, and there she made her own ointments and syrups. She had even had the gardener enlarge the cook's herb garden to include several that she needed in her concoctions.

There were other plants, of course, that she had to search for in the woods and meadows, and Perkins had taught her to look for those, as well. She regularly went on such expeditions with Nick, for he, despite the fact that he was now in his late seventies, was still a strong and healthy man, and had an eagle eye for spotting their growing quarry.

She was also, quite frankly, as likely to rely on Nick's remedies as the village doctor's for combatting the illnesses of her household — though she would never have admitted as much to Dr. Felton.

They cut through the meadow and across the stream, then followed a wider, more well-defined path until finally they arrived at Nick Perkins' cottage. It was a cozy little house, only two rooms and a kitchen, tucked in beneath some trees. Ivy grew up one side of it and crept around to the front, spreading its tendrils toward the steep thatched roof. Before the house lay a small garden, redolent with the scents of herbs and roses mingling. The last few years, since he had stopped farming, he had turned his still-considerable energies to his garden, bringing forth a riot of flowers every year, as well as the herbs he needed for his remedies.

He was kneeling in his garden now, digging in the earth before one of his rose bushes, and he turned at the sound of their approach. When he saw Anna, a smile spread across his leathery face, and he pushed up from the ground, rising a little creakily to his feet. Although he was old, there was nothing feeble about Nick Perkins. He was still a large man, his broad shoulders only slightly hunched, and though he was slower in his movements, there was strength in his grip and the bright flare of intelligence in his blue eyes.

"Miss Anna!" he exclaimed, coming toward them, and then his eyes went to the boys and the bundle they carried, and the grin vanished.

He moved forward more quickly. "What have you brought me this time, eh?"

He bent over their burden, taking in the injuries at a glance, and said, "Carry him

into the kitchen, lads, and let's get him up
on the table."

He led them into his house and through
the front room to the kitchen. It was cool inside the thick-walled cottage, lit only by the
sunshine pouring in through the open door
and windows. The cottage was, as always,
tidy and swept, and the kitchen was thick
with the scent of herbs and flowers and
other plants that hung drying from the
ceiling, which mingled with a delicious odor
wafting from the iron pot that hung over the
fire.

Perkins caught the glances that the boys
unconsciously sent toward the fire, and he
said, "Mayhap you lads'd like a bowl of that
stew. Looks like ye've prob'ly worked up a
bit of hunger, with what ye've been carrying."

"Oh, no, we'd rather watch you, sir, if
you'll let us," Alex told the old man politely.

Con nodded, adding, "But we could
probably eat a bowl later, if that's all right
with you."

"Of course." Perkins smiled at them and
bent down to help them lift the dog onto the
table. "But this won't be pretty."

"No, sir. But still, we would like to
watch."

He nodded, saying, "Just don't get in my

way. Miss Anna, fetch me the cleaner and some cloths."

Anna went to do as he bid, taking a stack of clean, though stained and worn, cloths from one of the drawers and picking up a bottle of thin green-tinted liquid from the counter.

Perkins spoke soothingly to the dog as he bent over it, gently turning back its fur as he searched the wounds. Then he began to clean the wounds, all the while talking to the animal. The boys stood on one side of the table, and Anna took up her familiar position on the other side, by the animal's head. She held the dog's head firmly in her hands even as she kept up a litany of soft, soothing words and sounds.

The twins watched with interest, though they did at times pale a bit or scrunch up their faces with empathy. After Alex had asked a question about what he was doing, the old man explained every step he took as he cleaned out the wounds with care, then stitched up the longer gashes and decorated them all with an ointment. When the leg wound was clean, he carefully set the fractured bone, splinting it with small sticks that Anna brought him from another drawer, and wrapping it around tightly with a bandage.

When he was through, Nick finished the

job by rolling up some herbs into a small ball and popping it into the dog's mouth, stroking his throat until he swallowed it.

"That is to ease his pain," he explained to the twins, whom he then set to creating a soft place with an old blanket near the hearth for the wounded animal to lie.

They helped him lay the dog carefully on the blankets, and the boys bent over the dog to admire Perkins' work. After Anna had cleaned up and had made sure the boys did the same, Perkins dished up some of his stew for the lads, and they ate it hungrily, all the while peppering Nick with questions ranging from the operation they had just witnessed to the care and feeding of boa constrictors, a matter on which Nick Perkins allowed he had no knowledge.

They would doubtless have remained longer, except that Anna, glancing out the window, noticed how low in the sky the sun had sunk.

"Oh, my goodness, we have been here much longer than I realized!" she exclaimed, standing up. "It won't be long before the sun is setting." She turned and looked at the boys, guilt clear on her face. "And your brother has no idea where you are. I am afraid that your relatives will be terribly worried."

The twins considered this, and Alex said fairly, "Yes, they will probably worry — but not as much as you would think. They are accustomed to our staying out."

"When did you leave the house?" Anna asked.

"Sometime this morning. Around ten, I think."

"Oh, my. They will have every right to be angry. I must get you home right away."

Her heart quailed a little inside at the thought that she might have to face Reed again, but she had to escort them to their house. They were unfamiliar with the country and had come to Nick's house from the woods behind Holcomb Manor, not from Winterset, so they would have no chance of finding their way back alone. Well, she told herself, she would just have to steel herself to face him — and hope that she could manage to hand them over to their sister and avoid Reed altogether.

The boys got up without demur, bidding goodbye to their new friend Nick and politely requesting permission to come back to check on their patient's progress. Anna hustled them out the door and headed toward Winterset.

She should have taken them back earlier, she knew. Of course, she had not known at the time that the boys had been gone from their house since before noon, but, still, she should have thought. . . . Reed would be so worried — and their sister, too, of course. And he would have every right to be angry with her.

They had just crossed the footbridge over the stream and emerged from the trees on the other side when, in the distance, Anna saw a man on horseback. Her heart sank. It was Reed.

Beside her, the boys waved. Reed waved back, then reached inside his coat and brought out a pistol, which he fired up into the air. Then he urged his horse forward.

"There's Rafe!" Con exclaimed, turning to look off to the west, where another man on horseback was now traveling toward them. The boys waved at him, too.

"I must say, you don't seem particularly worried about what your brother will say," Anna commented.

"He'll only scold a little," Alex assured her. "They get worried, you see, but they know we can take care of ourselves, mostly."

"We often go off on our own," Con added.

Anna was not as assured as the boys seemed to be that their relatives would not be furious, but when Reed pulled his horse to a stop in front of them and dismounted, his expression was more one of resignation than fear or anger.

"Well," he said lightly, crossing his arms and looking down at the twins. "I see that this time you have managed to embroil Miss Holcomb in your peccadilloes."

"She was great guns, Reed!" Con told him. "You should have seen her. She helped Perkins sew up a dog — and Perkins said we could have him, if we wanted, when he's better, as he seems to be a stray — and she didn't faint or anything at all the blood."

"Indeed?" Reed's eyes turned to Anna, cool and appraising.

She blushed under his gaze, realizing that once again she must look like a ragamuffin, her hair every which way and wearing her old boots and bonnet and a dress that was not only everyday, but was now dirty from kneeling beside the dog and, moreover, splotched with unappetizing stains.

"I am sorry, my lord," she began stiffly. "I am sure you and your family must have been quite worried about where your brothers were. I am afraid I did not realize how late it had become. I should have brought them home earlier."

A smile tugged at one corner of his mouth as Reed said, "Oh, no, pray, do not apologize. I am well aware that all fault lies with these two." He cast a severe glance back at his brothers.

The two seemed supremely unconcerned by his stern demeanor. "You weren't really worried, were you, Reed?" Alex asked. "It isn't even dark yet."

"Mmm." Reed cast an expressive glance around at the fast-encroaching dusk. "Not pitch-black, no." He turned back to Anna, explaining, "Con and Alex are well known for their explorations, I'm afraid. Actually, we were not overly worried, except that the terrain is unfamiliar to them. I feared that once it grew dark, they would have some difficulty finding their way back."

At that moment the other horseman reached them, and he, too, dismounted, grinning at the boys. He was a large man, as tall as Reed, and very handsome, with tousled brown hair threaded through with golden strands, and vivid blue eyes. There was a deep dimple in his cheek when he smiled, as he was doing now.

Winking toward the twins, he said, "Well, now, got yourselves into brand-new trouble, haven't you?"

He was the American, Anna realized, his voice soft and slightly slurred, and he sounded as if he found the entire world amusing. He looked over at Anna and swept off his hat, giving her an elegant bow. "Rafe McIntyre, ma'am, at your service. My sympathies on having gotten tangled up with these two rapscallions."

"I found them very pleasant and admirable young men," Anna said stoutly.

McIntyre laughed and winked again at the twins. "Won her over, did you? You are a treasure beyond price, then, Miss —"

"I'm sorry," Reed interrupted. "Miss Holcomb, allow me to introduce my brother-in-law, Rafe McIntyre. You will have to forgive his informality. He is an American." He countered his words with a glance of true liking toward the other man. "Rafe, this is Miss Anna Holcomb, our neighbor to the west. Her brother is the young gentleman you met earlier."

"My pleasure, ma'am." Rafe bowed to her again, and Anna smiled back, unable to resist his infectious personality.

"We didn't mean to stay out so long," Alex began, "but we found this poor dog. He was in terrible shape, and Con and I didn't know what to do. But then Miss Holcomb came along, and she helped us. She knows a man who knows all about healing animals. You should see his house! He has all kinds of plants hanging from the rafters, drying, and he makes potions and ointments."

"And he sewed the dog up," Con continued excitedly, "and he let us watch. And Miss Holcomb held the dog's head for him and didn't sick up or anything!" He beamed at his new friend.

Anna chuckled and ruffled his hair affectionately. "I've helped Nick all my life, just about. Believe me, it took me a while to get used to it."

There had been another rider approaching them as they conversed, also apparently in response to Reed's gunshot. He was a small, wiry man, and he led two saddled, riderless ponies. Now, pulling up beside the others, he slid easily from his horse and marched over to the twins.

"There ye are, ye two!" He scowled at them. "Young scapegraces, worritin' yer sister like that. Ye ought to be ashamed of yerselves, and that's a fact."

"We're sorry, Jenkins." For the first time, the boys looked abashed.

Reed turned toward Anna and said, "We needn't worry about reprimanding the boys. Jenkins usually does the job well enough for us."

"Aye, an' if I didn't, who would, I'd like to know?" The man in question turned his fierce gaze on Reed. "There's not a one o' ye who takes 'em in hand like ye should."

"I know. That is why we are so fortunate to have you."

"Aye, well, I've kept ye all in line, and that's a fact," the man agreed, with a sharp nod of his head. "An' I can tell ye that ye and Theo were just as bad as these two, in yer day."

The groom turned back to the boys, continuing his scolding as he tossed them up onto their ponies and handed them the reins. Reed turned to Anna.

"Thank you for helping the boys. It relieves my mind that they were with you."

"I should have brought them home earlier."

"It sounds as though you had plenty to occupy you. It's no wonder the hour slipped your mind." He paused, then said a trifle awkwardly, "If you will allow me to put you up on my horse in front of me, we can ride back to Winterset, and then I will send you home properly in our carriage. I — I am sure that the boys' sister would like to thank you in person."

Heat rose up in Anna at the thought of riding on Reed's horse with him all the way back to Winterset, and she was sure that she must be blushing. "Oh! Oh, no, you needn't worry. Now that the boys are with you, I can just go on to my house from here, while you take the boys back."

"And leave you to walk alone in the dark all the way back to Holcomb Manor!" Reed stiffened. "Is that what you think of me? That I would repay your kindness toward my brothers with such shabby treatment?"

"No, no, of course not," Anna demurred quickly. "But it is no problem — it isn't that far, and I am quite familiar with —"

"Nonsense, I could not allow it," Reed retorted flatly, adding, not without a certain calculation, "Of course, if you feel you cannot ride double, then Jem will give you his mount, and he can walk back to Winterset."

Anna narrowed her eyes at Reed. He knew, of course, that she would not force a servant to trudge all the way back to Winterset in the dark, especially one who was as unfamiliar with the territory as the boys.

Reed gazed back at her blandly, his eyebrows slightly raised.

"All right," Anna agreed, knowing that she sounded ungracious, but she could not help it. She dreaded the thought of being in such close physical proximity to Reed Moreland.

Without comment, Reed helped her up onto the horse, then mounted behind her. He took up the reins, and his arms closed around Anna. She was suddenly surrounded by his heat, his scent, breathtakingly familiar and yet so long absent. Anna could not control the shiver that ran through her as he dug his heels into his steed and they set off through the night.

Chapter Four

Anna sat stiffly, afraid to relax against Reed, incredibly aware of his body only inches from hers, his arms around her. It was impossible, with the movements of the horse, to keep from brushing against him, and every time she did so, her skin flamed at the touch. She gritted her teeth, telling herself she was being ridiculous. His closeness should not affect her so much. Yet no matter how much she told herself that, her words could make little headway against the sensations rampaging through her.

They said nothing, the silence between them almost as awkward as their proximity. The twins chattered away about their adventure, and Rafe threw in a comment or a question now and then, leaving Anna and Reed alone on their island of silence. Anna closed her eyes, trying desperately to think of something to say, anything to distract her from the only thing that was in her mind, which was the feel of his iron-hard arm against her back or the occasional brush of his thigh against hers as the horse moved.

It was a distinct relief when at last they reached Winterset and Reed swung down from the horse, reaching up to lift her from the saddle. Their faces were only inches apart for a moment as he swung her down, and their eyes locked. His were a dark, mysterious gray in the dim light of dusk, and Anna felt, for a strange, weak moment, as if she could simply sink into their depths and be lost forever.

Then she was on her feet again, and she took a quick step backward, trying to suppress her inward trembling. Tongue-tied, she turned away, and at that moment the front door was flung open and a tall, redhaired woman swept out into the small courtyard.

"There you are!" Her strong voice held a mixture of relief, exasperation and amusement, and she shook her head as she strode toward them. "You two will be the death of me!"

She wrapped an arm around each of the twins and hugged them to her, then stood and scowled down at them. "Where have you been? You don't even know the countryside!"

The woman looked up, her gaze sweeping across the others, and for the first time she noticed Anna, standing beside Reed.

"Oh! I am sorry. I did not know anyone else was here." She started toward Anna.

"This is my sister, Lady Kyria," Reed told Anna. "Kyria, allow me to introduce Miss Anna Holcomb, who, I am happy to say, was looking out for Con and Alex."

"My lady," Anna greeted her.

Lady Kyria reached out and took her hand, smiling. "You have, no doubt, rescued Con and Alex from some frightful thing — for that is always the way with them," she went on, tucking her arm through Anna's and steering her toward the front door. "Do come in and have supper with us and let me thank you properly."

"Oh, no, I couldn't —" Anna began. "I am sure that my brother is expecting me, and —"

"Your brother is that charming young man who was here earlier?" Kyria asked. "Such a nice gentleman. We'll send one of the footmen over with a note explaining that you are going to dine with us. I am sure he will understand."

"But I — I am not dressed for dinner," Anna pointed out, blushing a little, as she gestured down at her plain dress, which she now noticed was not only dirty and stained, but had also somehow acquired a tear near the hem, so that a piece of it trailed behind her, filthy and ragged.

"We do not care about formality here," Kyria assured her, ignoring her own elegant black off-the-shoulder gown and the glitter of a diamond necklace and earrings. "Our family is shockingly careless about such things, as anyone will be happy to tell you."

"You might as well give in, Miss Holcomb," Rafe McIntyre told her, coming up beside them. His eyes rested lovingly on his wife's face. "I can assure you that for every objection you bring up, Kyria will have a dozen reasons to override them. Once she sets her mind to something, I've learned, you might as well give in."

Kyria favored her husband with a dazzling smile, then turned it back to Anna. "There, you see? It's all settled. Do come in and meet our houseguest, Miss Farrington."

She led Anna down the hall into the drawing room, managing at the same time to signal to one of the footmen to inform the kitchen that they were ready and also to send another one for paper for Anna to write a note to her brother, as well as pay attention to her younger brothers, who had launched into an account of their afternoon.

A dainty blond woman was sitting in the

drawing room, and she rose at their entrance, smiling.

"Rosemary!" Kyria said, pulling Anna forward. "I want you to meet our neighbor, Miss Anna Holcomb. Her brother is that handsome young man who called on us, Sir Christopher."

Introductions were quickly made, and before she knew it, Anna found herself ensconced in a chair, pen and paper in hand, jotting a note to her brother, while Con and Alex described to their sister the torn and mangled dog they had discovered. Kyria responded with appropriate horror, though she did notice that her guest, Miss Farrington, was turning a pale shade of green, and she suggested that the boys not inform them of the wounds in quite such detail.

Before supper was served, Kyria whisked Anna upstairs, where she could clean up a little, and even insisted on lending her one of her own dresses, which, while too long for Anna, was such an improvement over Anna's own bedraggled frock that she was quite grateful to wear it.

At the meal, Anna found herself seated at Reed's left hand, with Lady Kyria across the table from her and Rafe on her other side. It was fortunate, she thought, that Kyria and her husband seemed well able to carry the conversation by themselves, as neither Anna nor Reed contributed much. The boys, after their afternoon's adventure, had been shuttled off to their rooms for baths and a quick meal before going to bed, and Miss Farrington was apparently a rather quiet woman.

Anna knew that she should contribute more to the conversation, and she was normally able to make polite chitchat, but she found Reed's presence beside her too unnerving for her to think of much to say. She wished that she had more poise. She wished that she did not want to know so badly what Reed thought of her in this much-more-attractive blue dress, with her hair brushed and pinned into subjugation.

She realized suddenly that everyone was looking at her expectantly and that she had let her mind wander, losing the thread of the conversation. "What? I am sorry. I'm afraid I was woolgathering," she said, coloring in embarrassment.

Kyria smiled. "I was just saying that I am planning to have a small gathering Friday evening — nothing grand, just a small party to thank everyone for welcoming us so graciously to Lower Fenley. I am hoping that you and your brother will be able to attend."

"This Friday?" Anna cast about frantically for some excuse not to attend, but none came to her. It would be absurd to say that they had other plans, for if Lady Kyria was throwing a party, it was certain that everyone around here would be attending it. And, besides, she was certain that Kit would like to go, and she could scarcely refuse her brother the chance to attend. "Yes, of course. That sounds lovely. We would very much like to come."

She would simply have to come down with a headache or something, so that she would not have to go. Anna cast a quick, covert glance at Reed and found him watching her, his eyes unreadable. She wondered if he wished she had refused to attend — or if her presence there made no difference to him either way. Perhaps he was only interested in Miss Farrington's attendance. What few remarks Reed had made this evening had been primarily addressed to that young lady. Anna wondered, as she had when Kit told her about Miss Farrington, whether she had been included in this party because Reed had a particular interest in her. Anna had not seen anything loverlike in his face when he addressed Miss Farrington, but, then, he was not the sort of man who would expose a young woman to gossip by singling her out for his attention.

Anna realized that her eyes had been fixed on Reed's face for several moments now, and she hastily turned away. Her gaze fell instead on Kyria, who was watching her with a certain amount of speculation in her eyes. Anna could feel a blush beginning to rise up her throat, and she was relieved when Kyria turned casually away and addressed a remark to her husband.

When the meal was over, the company did not split up into male and female groups, as was the custom, with the men going off to smoke and have a glass of brandy. The Morelands were, as Anna had always heard, "different," so Anna was unable to quietly take leave of just her hostess, as she had hoped. When she told Kyria that she must be getting back home now, Reed jumped in and told her that he would escort her back to Holcomb Manor in the carriage.

"Oh, no, there is no need —" Anna assured him hastily, her stomach jumping nervously at the thought of being enclosed in the small confines of a carriage with Reed.

"I insist," Reed said with quiet firmness. "After the way you helped my brothers, it is the least I can do."

"But there is no need for you to put yourself out so," Anna protested faintly. "I will be perfectly fine by myself in the carriage. I have traveled the road hundreds of times."

"Please, Miss Holcomb, allow me the opportunity to play the gentleman. My sisters rarely do, so I must inflict myself on our guests."

Kyria rolled her eyes affectionately at her brother and said, "You might as well give in. Reed is like a dog with a bone — especially when it comes to one's safety. He is terribly overprotective, but, then, I suppose that is much better than the alternative, is it not? Besides, he really is quite a pleasant companion."

"I am sure — I did not mean —" Anna stopped, embarrassed. *Had her reluctance been so obvious?* The last thing she wanted was to stir up any suspicion in Reed's sister, and she had already seen curiosity in the woman's gaze earlier at the table. As Rafe had pointed out earlier, Reed was not the only member of the family who was like a dog with a bone when his or her interest was aroused.

So she wound up a few minutes later back in her old walking dress — though Kyria's efficient maid had sewn up the torn ruffle at the hem and also made a stab at removing the dirt and stains from it — and sitting in the carriage across from Reed. It was a sporty open-air victoria — brand-new, from the shiny looks of it — and the expandable top was pushed to the back, opening it up to the mild summer night.

The moon was full, casting a soft romantic glow over the evening scene. The trees arched over them as they went down the driveway, so that the moon and stars flickered through the branches, and a gentle breeze stirred the leaves, caressing Anna's cheeks.

She looked across the small carriage at Reed. Though they were quite close, his face was only partially visible in the dim light, his eyes dark and unknown, the ridges of his cheekbones highlighted. She could not help but think what a sweet, romantic ride it would have been if he had been sitting beside her . . . if she had not refused him . . . if life had turned out differently. . . .

Anna gave herself a mental shake and said brightly, "This is a beautiful carriage."

"It's Kyria's. Rafe gave it to her when they returned to England a few weeks ago. Beautiful and a little impractical — very much like Kyria." A smile took the sting from his words.

"I can see that you are very fond of your sister."

Reed nodded. "I am fond of all my

family." He paused. "I want to thank you for what you did for the twins today."

"How could I not?"

His mouth quirked. "There are a number of women, I think, who would not have helped them carry a wounded dog to a healer. Of course, they really had no business being on your property."

Anna shrugged. "That is no problem. Kit and I are happy for them to explore." She frowned, then added quickly, "Of course, they probably should not go farther into the woods — up Craydon Tor, you know. I fear they could easily get lost."

"They generally take their compass. I imagine they could have found their way back today if you had not come along. But I will speak to them about Craydon Tor — though I fear that, with those two, any word of warning seems to make them only more eager to do something."

"Typical boys, I think." Anna smiled. "Kit was always most eager to do whatever had been forbidden. But I do hope you will impress on them not to go alone into those woods. They could fall or — well, there must be some sort of animal, perhaps a wild dog, that inflicted that damage on the dog they found. I have no idea what it was, but the dog's wounds were severe. I do not like to think of Con and Alex coming upon that fierce a creature." She brightened. "If they will but come to the Manor, I will send our gamekeeper, Rankin, out with them to explore the woods. He is a very good sort. They will enjoy their outing with him, I assure you."

"That is very kind. Was the dog as badly injured as the boys said?"

Anna nodded. "Yes. Nick Perkins is a wonderful healer, but I hope Con and Alex will not count too much on his curing the animal."

Reed studied her for a moment. "You truly liked them, didn't you? Alex and Con."

"Why, of course." Anna cast a startled look at him. "How could I not? They are delightful boys."

"There are many who do not find them so," Reed commented wryly.

Anna wrinkled her nose. "Then they must be very stodgy sorts."

Reed chuckled. "They are, many of them. However, it does seem as though wherever the twins go, things just seem to . . . happen."

"Things?"

"Oh, frogs in a tutor's bed, for instance, or an escaped parrot . . . or boa constrictor . . . or rabbit. Then there was the fire in the nursery — that was when they were pretending to be frontiersmen in America, I believe, and using a tinderbox. Or the time they went down an abandoned well after a kitten. Or —"

Anna chuckled, raising a hand in a stopping gesture. "All right, I believe you."

They smiled at each other across the short space separating them, and suddenly Anna was struck with a shaft of longing — not physical desire, but a yearning for the closeness they had once shared, however briefly, a mental and emotional intimacy, the spark of fun and humor and excitement that had underlain the more urgent physical desire. They had *liked* each other, had simply enjoyed each other's company, and Anna realized with a pang how much she had missed that closeness. She wanted to ask him if they could continue like this, if there was any chance that they could be friends after what had happened, but even as the thought was born in her head, she dismissed it.

It was foolish to even think of it, she knew. After what had happened between them, they surely could not be friends. If she had handled things differently from the beginning, perhaps. Or if she had known . . . But, she had not, and it had happened as it had happened, and she could really hope for nothing except to keep a certain polite distance between them.

Anna dropped her eyes to her lap, and a sudden, awkward silence fell upon them.

"Anna," he said urgently, leaning forward, closing the short space between them.

Anna looked up at him warily. He was much too close, and it was suddenly difficult for her to breathe.

"What happened to us three years ago?" he asked, his voice a harsh whisper. "Was I so wrong in what I thought? Did you never feel for me what I believed you did?"

"Please . . ." Anna whispered back, her voice choked. "No, do not ask. . . ."

"I loved you, and I thought you loved me. Was I so blind? So wrapped in conceit that I could not see what was right before my eyes?"

"I beg of you, do not press me." Anna's eyes glittered with tears, and she looked away from him, certain that if she continued to look into his face, she would start to cry. "Why did you come back? Why did you insist on riding with me tonight? Can you not leave well enough alone?"

"Because it isn't well enough," he grated back. "It was never so for me." He reached out, wrapping his hand around her wrist, and Anna looked at him, her eyes wide and frightened, her heart pounding. "When you sent me away before, I was too hurt to question it. Too heartsore to do anything but crawl back to London and lick my wounds. But now . . . I return and find that you are still here, unmarried. A beautiful young woman, in the prime of your life, and no other man has captured your heart. Why is that?"

"I choose not to marry," Anna said, drawing herself up with dignity and pulling her arm out of his grasp. For an instant he retained his grip; then he let her go and sat back. "A woman does not have to marry, does she? I enjoy my life as it is."

"Your brother will marry someday. It is the way of things. And you will no longer be the mistress of Holcomb Manor. It is not a position many women would like. Most women would choose to have their own home, a husband and children. . . ."

"Clearly I am not most women," Anna said lightly. "I hardly think I need to explain myself to you."

"No, I suppose you do not. Yet I cannot help but wonder, if you did not love me, that you have found no one else."

"Must one love a man?" Anna retorted. "There must be women who do not. And, may I remind you, if it is so strange that I have not married, then it is equally strange that you have not."

"Ah, but I was the one whose heart was broken. It takes time to be able to once again place one's heart in the hands of a woman. You, on the other hand, were heart-whole."

There was a flash of pain in Anna's eyes, quickly covered by her glance away, out into the dark night. "Perhaps I am heart-whole because I do not have it within me to love. Surely you must have thought of that."

"Yes, I have thought of it," he agreed. "There was many a night when I was convinced of that very idea. But looking at you today with Con and Alex, I found it harder to believe. The warmth and compassion that was so evident in you . . . the kindness and gentleness. I cannot believe that you do not want children."

"Of course I want children!" Anna flashed back, her eyes snapping. She stopped, drawing a deep breath and pushing down the tumult of emotions that bubbled up in her at his words, thinking quickly of how to cover her slip. She went on in a calmer voice. "That does not mean that I will marry just to have them, any more than I would marry to have money or position."

"And that, I take it, is a slap in the face to me," Reed said, settling back into the cushioned seat behind him. "Money and position being the only reasons you would have had for marrying me."

"I do not know why you insist on pursuing this," Anna went on in a stifled voice. She hated the coldness that had come over his face and voice. "I never wanted to cause you pain. I still do not. Please, can you not just let it be?"

"I guess I am as stubborn and contrary-minded as my brothers," Reed replied dryly. "I am told it is a Moreland trait."

Anna knotted her hands in her lap, looking down at them. "I could not marry you," she said flatly. "I did not have the feeling for you that a wife should have for her husband." She lifted her head to look straight into his eyes, keeping her own eyes steady and cool. "I have never regretted my decision, nor would I change it if I could."

She swallowed, feeling faintly sick to her stomach.

"I see. Well, I suppose I could hardly ask for anything clearer than that."

Anna looked away. To her relief, she saw the lights of Holcomb Manor in front of them. This unbearable trip would be over in just a few minutes.

Silence reigned in the carriage until it pulled to a stop in front of Holcomb Manor.

Anna stood up and scrambled out before Reed could put out a hand to help her down.

"Thank you," she said breathlessly, and hurried toward the front door without waiting to hear Reed's response. She was grateful when the front door was opened wide, casting a rectangle of golden light into the night, and one of the footmen stepped out, bowing, to greet her.

Anna hurried up the steps into the house, and the footman closed the door behind her with a solid thud. She stood for a moment, waiting for the trembling in her limbs to stop.

"Miss Anna? Are you all right?"

She turned toward the footman. "Oh, yes, John. I am perfectly all right." She forced a smile, then turned and hurried down the hall and up the stairs to the sanctuary of her bedroom.

Her maid Penny was waiting for her, and Anna was glad that she was there to help her out of her clothes and into her nightgown, for frankly, at the moment, she wanted nothing more than to crawl into her bed, pull the covers up and give way to a bout of tears. In her own state of distress, it took her a moment to realize that Penny's face was splotchy and red, and her eyes were so puffy they were nearly swollen shut.

"Penny!" Anna took a second look at her. "What's the matter?"

"Oh, miss!" Penny's face crumpled, and she began to cry. "I'm so sorry! Please don't let Mrs. Michaels turn me out!"

"Turn you out?" Anna repeated, dumbfounded. "What on earth are you talking about?"

"She said I should be turned out. She called me an ungrateful wretch, and said I had be-betrayed the family's trust. And I never meant to, miss, I swear I didn't. You know I love you. I would never do anything to hurt you or bring dishonor to the Holcombs."

"Of course not," Anna assured her, bewildered, and took the maid by the hand, leading her over to her easy chair. She sat down in the chair, pulling Penny down onto the hassock in front of it. Taking the girl's hands in her own, she looked into her face. "Now. Calm down and tell me, step by step, what it is you are talking about."

"I didn't mean to do anything wrong," Penny said, drawing a long, quavering breath. "I was only trying to not get Stell into trouble. That's all. That's why I didn't say anything earlier."

"Stell?"

"Estelle, miss. The upstairs maid. She

111

sleeps in the same room with me, you see. She asked me not to tell, 'cause Mrs. Michaels'd turn her out without a reference, and that she would have, too, miss. And Estelle's me friend. We have our little fusses now and then — who doesn't, I ask you? But we help each other out, you see."

"Of course. But why is Mrs. Michaels angry at you? What happened?"

"It's Estelle, miss. She's gone."

"Gone? I don't understand — she's gone where?"

"I don't know, miss." Penny looked at her with rounded eyes. "That's the thing — Estelle has disappeared."

Chapter Five

For a long moment, Anna could only stare at Penny. "What? What do you mean, she's disappeared?"

"Nobody knows where she is," Penny said, and tears started in her eyes again. "She left the house last night, and she never came back."

A shiver ran down Anna's back, and she thought — she wasn't sure why — of her feeling in the woods today, the cold, eerie stab of panic and pain. She shook the feeling off and forced herself to concentrate on Penny's words.

"She told me she was goin' out last night to see her fella, and I didn't think anything about it. Sometimes she doesn't come in until awful late when she does that."

Anna remembered the morning only a week or so ago when she had seen Estelle sneaking in the back door and suspected that the girl had been out all night. "She has been doing that a lot recently?"

Penny nodded, looking remorseful. "She

begged me not to tell anybody. She said Mrs. Michaels'd be that mad at her, and she was right. She was so happy, and it didn't seem right that she should have to stop seein' him just 'cause Mrs. Michaels wouldn't like it. She was just — she was so happy! I felt glad for her, and so I promised not to tell anybody when she sneaked out and came in in the middle of the night. Then, this morning, she didn't come back by the time we had to get up and go to work. It has happened before, so I figured she'd be in soon. She shouldn't 'ave stayed out all night like that, but I couldn't just turn her over to Mrs. Michaels."

Anna nodded. She could understand the girl's feelings. Mrs. Michaels was a formidable woman, especially when someone had broken one of her rules. "What did you do, then?"

"I didn't do nothin'. Well, not till Mrs. Michaels asked me where Estelle was, and then I said she wasn't feelin' well and had stayed in bed. 'Cause I figured it was like the other morning, and she'd come sneaking in late, you see. But she didn't. And later, Mrs. Michaels sent Rose up to see about her, and, 'course, when she wasn't there, Rose told Mrs. Michaels she couldn't find her. So Mrs. Michaels came back to me, breathin' fire, she was, and I had to tell her."

"Of course you did."

Penny shot her a grateful look. "Thank you. I knew Estelle'd be furious with me, but what else could I do? She shouldn't have stayed out all night like that, leavin' me to explain it! So I told Mrs. Michaels that I lied about it, and that Estelle had gone out last night and never come back, and then she wanted to know how long she'd been doing it, and I had to tell her for a couple of weeks or more. And she was that mad. She said I was a traitor and an ingrate, and I don't even know what that is! But I know I'm not a traitor. I'd never do anything to hurt you or Master Kit, and that's the truth."

"I'm sure you wouldn't."

"I didn't think I was doing anything to hurt you by doing it, but Mrs. Michaels says it re-reflects badly on the Holcombs, having a maid that's a slut. But she's not a slut, miss! Or, I mean, she never was before. She's always been a good girl." She looked at Anna pleadingly. "You won't let Mrs. Michaels turn me off, will you? My mum would slap me silly if I lost a position like this. And I never meant to do anything wrong. I wouldn't damage your name for anything."

"No, I am sure you would not," Anna told the girl soothingly. "And doubtless the

Holcomb name can stand up to more than a maid sneaking out to meet a man at night." She hesitated, frowning, then said, "But why did Estelle not come back? Where did she go?"

"I don't know, miss, and that's the truth. Mrs. Michaels and Mr. Childers kept askin' and askin' me, but I truly don't know any more. Mrs. Michaels says she's run off, and I guess maybe she has." Penny's mouth drooped a little. "I never thought she'd just go off like that and not even tell me."

Anna rose to her feet. "I'll just go down and talk to Mrs. Michaels. She won't turn you out. I am sure that after she has had a chance to think about it, she will see that that is too harsh a punishment for what you did."

"Oh, thank you, miss." Penny grabbed Anna's hand and squeezed it fervently, dropping a quick curtsey, as well.

Anna left her room and hurried down the narrow back stairway, the quickest way to the kitchen area. After walking past the already-dark kitchen, she knocked quietly on the door to Mrs. Michaels' bedroom. The housekeeper opened it a moment later. She was obviously ready for bed, with her hair up in a ruffled sleeping cap and a cotton wrapper over her high-necked sleeping gown.

"Miss Holcomb!" The housekeeper looked startled, then frowned. "Did that silly girl bother you with her story?"

"Penny was rather upset. She is quite afraid that you will turn her out without a reference."

"And so I should," the housekeeper said sternly, the very bows on her nightcap quivering with remembered indignation. "Covering up for that doxy Estelle! In my day, we would never have dreamed of hiding such a thing from the housekeeper, I can tell you."

"Yes, I am sure she was foolish," Anna said quickly before Mrs. Michaels could warm to her story. "However, she is a very skilled personal maid, and I should not want to lose her."

"Oh, no, miss, I would never presume to turn out your personal maid," Mrs. Michaels told her, looking shocked.

"But I wanted to ask you about Estelle."

"That pert baggage!" Mrs. Michaels made a face of disdain. "Looking back on it, I can see that we should never have hired her! Always giving herself airs . . ."

"I am rather worried about what might have happened to her," Anna said, cutting into the other woman's tirade.

"Happened to her! Why, nothing's happened to her. I'm sure she just ran off with that man she's been meeting. She was a sly one."

"Well, but — doesn't it seem rather sudden? Why didn't she tell Penny if she was not planning to return?"

"Probably didn't want Penny fussing at her. For all her silliness, Penny's a more sensible girl than that. She'd have told her it was wrong to just take off with some man."

"Yes, but, you see, we don't know that that is what she has done," Anna pointed out. "Did she take any of her things with her? I would think Penny would have noticed if she had."

"No, miss, Penny looked through her things, and she didn't think she took anything other than what she was wearing."

"Wouldn't she have taken her things if she was planning to run away?"

Mrs. Michaels looked thoughtful. "Mayhap she didn't run away with the man. Maybe she was just so late that she realized she couldn't come back without getting into trouble. So she took off."

"Without any of her possessions?" Anna asked skeptically.

"It wasn't much, miss, just a few bits of clothes and a brush and such. She was wearing her earrings, Penny said."

"Yes, but if you haven't much, I would think what you do have is precious to you," Anna said.

Mrs. Michaels frowned. "I don't understand, miss. Why do you think she didn't run away? I mean, what else could it have been?"

"I don't know." Anna thought again of her shivery feeling in the woods. She wasn't sure why she connected it with Estelle's disappearance. It probably had nothing to do with it. And yet . . . she could not shake the feeling that there was something wrong. However, she could scarcely tell her very practical housekeeper that she was worried because of a strange sensation that had come over her in the woods that day.

"But it seems to me," she went on, "that we ought to make a push to see if we can find her. Ask her family, tell the constable that she's gone missing, send some men out to search around a bit. I mean, what if she fell down as she was returning to the house and is out there somewhere, hurt?"

"Well, yes, miss, of course, if that is what you want," Mrs. Michaels agreed, her expression plainly stating that she found Anna far too softhearted in her dealings with the servants.

"Yes, that is what I want," Anna told her

firmly. Mrs. Michaels had been the house-keeper at Holcomb Manor since before Anna was born, and she would never have dreamed of replacing her. The Holcombs were known for their loyalty. But she had learned early on that unless she was firm and spoke with authority, the older woman would run everything exactly as she pleased, rather than as Anna wanted.

Anna went to bed feeling easier in her mind, knowing that whatever Mrs. Michaels might think, now that Anna had given her an order, she would do whatever she could to find the girl.

As the week wore on, however, there was no news of Estelle. Her family had not seen her in several weeks, nor had anyone else in the village. The gamekeeper had taken the grooms and some of the gardeners and had fanned out around the garden and grounds the next day, searching all the way back into the woods almost to Craydon Tor. There was no sign of Estelle, and Anna was forced to agree that the maid must have run away, probably with the man she had been sneaking out to meet at night. No one, including Penny, seemed to know who that man had been, so there was no way of checking whether he was still around or had left town, too.

The twins took her up on her invitation to visit Holcomb Manor, and the three of them hiked over to Nick Perkins' cottage to check on the dog. They found the patient alive and apparently healing, though he was able to do no more than lift his head and thump his tail somewhat feebly when they drew near him. The boys wound up spending most of the afternoon there, helping Nick with his garden and learning about all his herbs and their healing properties.

Anna enjoyed the afternoon thoroughly. Having grown up with a younger brother, she was well used to boys, and she found the twins bright and entertaining, if at times almost too full of energy. Looking at them, she could see Reed at that age or the children they might have had if she had agreed to his proposal. But that, of course, was not worth thinking of, as she quickly reminded herself.

She had planned not to attend Kyria's party on Friday evening, intending to come up with a headache at the last minute, but as the days went by, she found herself thinking about what she would wear and discussing hairstyles with Penny, just as if she was really going to go. Finally, on Friday, she had to admit to herself that she wanted to go to the party. Social occasions were not that common here in their rural backwater, and she hated to miss out on the one that would probably be the highlight of the season. Kyria had seemed quite nice, and it would be rude, she told herself, not to attend, especially with no better excuse than a mere headache. Besides, even though she would insist that Kit go on without her, it would put something of a damper on his enjoyment of the evening. And the prospect of spending the evening in her bed, with a lavender-soaked cloth on her head, pretending to be sick and thinking about the gaiety that was going on without her, struck her as a thoroughly unpleasant way to spend an evening.

It wasn't as if she would have to spend the evening with Reed, she reasoned. There would be an ample number of other people there with whom she could mingle. And after their talk in the carriage the other night, she suspected that he would have as much interest in avoiding her as she had in avoiding him. Besides, she could not resist the ignoble urge to let Reed see her looking her best instead of the ragtag way she had looked the other times he had run into her recently.

And so Friday evening found her dressed in her newest ball gown, a sky-blue dress that did wonderful things for her skin and eyes, and which, with its wide scoop neck and small puffed sleeves, showed off her creamy white shoulders to perfection. It was adorned in back with the smallest of bustles, over which the skirt was pulled back and gathered to fall in a cascade of blue satin. A simple pearl necklace and eardrops completed the outfit, and Penny had arranged her golden brown hair in a fall of ringlets from a knot at the crown of her head, with soft curls escaping around her face. She did look her best, she was pleased to think, and she hoped it was not terrible of her to hope that when he looked at her, Reed would think that she was as pretty as she had been three years ago.

Not, of course, she reminded herself, that she wanted anything to come of it. She did not. That part of her life was over, and it was best that way. But surely there was not so much wrong with just a little vanity on her part.

She smiled at her brother as he helped her up into their carriage, her stomach tightening with anticipation. Kit looked equally eager, she thought, and she wondered if his anticipation centered around the lovely Miss Farrington. The thought worried her a trifle. Kit, of course, was both realistic and dutiful; he would not do anything he should not. But that did not mean that his heart might not get bruised. However, she said nothing, not wanting to cast a pall over their first evening out in weeks. In general, she loved the country and her life there, but at times the quiet life could be almost stifling.

Winterset was ablaze with lights as their carriage approached, following a few yards behind the doctor's one-horse rig. A footman opened the door and ushered them into the large drawing room, where Lady Kyria and her brother and husband stood in line to receive them. Lady Kyria was a vision in emerald green, but it was to Reed that Anna's eyes went first. He wore formal black and white, with the only spot of color a tasteful blood-red ruby tie pin nestled in his snowy cravat, but he was easily the handsomest man there, Anna thought.

Her pulse speeded up, and it occurred to her suddenly that it had been a definite mistake on her part to come. She was playing with fire, she realized, wanting to come here tonight to see Reed again, wanting him to see her. The flash of silver in his eyes as they fell on her confirmed that. It was not Kit whose heart she should be worried about endangering, it was her own.

She looked quickly away from Reed, smiling at Kyria and murmuring a polite greeting. But then there was no avoiding him, for he stood next in line and took her hand smoothly from his sister, bowing over it.

"Miss Holcomb, a pleasure to see you again. I hope I am not forward in saying that you are a vision tonight."

Anna could feel a blush starting in her cheeks, and she was suddenly hopelessly tongue-tied. "Thank you, my lord," she replied faintly, not looking into his eyes. "It is so kind of you to have us in your home. I believe you know my brother Kit?" she hurried on, turning to include her brother.

"Yes. Sir Christopher, of course." Reed released her hand, turning toward her brother, but Anna could still feel the warm imprint of his fingers against hers.

For once in her life, she was glad for the distraction of the squire's wife, who bustled up to her, her gray curls fairly quivering with excitement. "Anna, there you are. Poor Miles was afraid you would not come. He's been wanting so to dance with you — and while it is not a ball, per se, I don't doubt but what Lady Kyria will let you young folks have a few dances. She's hired a string quartet, you see. So elegant."

Anna smiled and nodded, letting the woman lead her toward the rest of her family. She had her doubts that Mrs. Bennett's son Miles had expressed any longing to dance with her; that was simply the sort of foolish thing Mrs. Bennett liked to say. While Mrs. Bennett did not cherish any hopes regarding her son and Anna — or, at least, Anna sincerely hoped she did not, since the boy was barely twenty-one to her own twenty-six years — as she did with Kit and her daughter, she liked to link the members of their family in any way possible, feeling, Anna thought, that it gave her the same social status.

The squire was standing with their daughter Felicity, and Miles lounged against the mantel a few feet away from them, doing his best to look interesting. His brown hair was worn a trifle long and shaggy, and his cravat was carelessly tied. The effect he was looking for, Anna thought, was that of an artist or poet — moody and enigmatic, even a little bit dangerous. In truth, he simply looked a trifle unkempt and unsure of himself. He should, in Anna's opinion, take a look at Reed, for the elegant set of his shoulders and the flash of silver in his eyes was inherently more dangerous to any woman's heart than all of Miles Bennett's posturing.

Anna greeted the squire and Felicity.

Squire Bennett was a stolid, quiet man, the opposite of his chatterbox of a wife, and he greeted Anna and her brother, whom Mrs. Bennett had managed to seize and drag along with them, with a brief bow and a few words. Then he fell silent, nodding along as he let his wife and daughter rush forward with the conversation. Mrs. Bennett talked, and Felicity giggled and bridled and flirted with her eyes over her fan at Kit, who remained politely oblivious to her efforts.

Miles apparently realized after a time that his pose by the mantel, while artistic, kept him apart from the conversation, for after a few minutes he lounged over to join their circle.

"Miles, there you are!" his mother exclaimed with delight, as if he had appeared from some distance. "I was just telling Sir Christopher and Miss Anna how you have been spending your days writing." Mrs. Bennett turned toward Anna, saying with a smile, "You should see him. He just scribbles and scribbles away in there, for hours on end. Of course, he won't let me read a bit of it — young men are so secretive, are they not?"

She beamed at her son, who was looking acutely embarrassed. Her daughter picked up the conversation, tittering and saying,

"That is all he ever does, read and write, write and read. I cannot think what he finds in it."

"You wouldn't," Miles retorted rudely, shooting his sister a dark look.

"I love to read, as well," Anna put in, with a smile toward Miles. He had been rude, of course, but it must be a severe trial to have the mother and sister that he did.

Miles smiled back at her, and his face was instantly more attractive. He would be better served, Anna thought, to put aside his brooding-writer pose and smile more.

"I am certain that you understand," he told Anna warmly, and it occurred to her that perhaps his mother's words hadn't sprung entirely from her imagination. It was just possible that Miles was suffering from a mild case of puppy love. She sighed inwardly, knowing that she would have to watch her words and gestures carefully from now on, so that he would not receive any unintended encouragement.

She was glad when Dr. Felton joined them and asked her if she cared for a stroll around the room. Large and rectangular, it was really more an assembly room than a drawing room, with several straight-backed chairs placed about the walls and a massive teak table in the center. It was perfect for a social affair such as this: large enough to accommodate several areas of conversation, while having plenty of space to stroll about in. Later, if Lady Kyria did indeed allow dancing, the large table could simply be pushed back to create a small ballroom. It was also one of the rooms for which Winterset was justly famous — the barrel-vaulted plasterwork ceiling was covered in representations of animals, both real and fantastical, running the gamut from jumping trout and oddly formed elephants to hippogriffs, chimeras and dragons.

"Interesting ceiling," Felton remarked, looking up at it. "I've heard about it — my father used to sing the praises of Winterset — but I haven't ever actually seen it."

"Yes, my uncle rarely entertained," Anna agreed, keeping an eye out for Reed's whereabouts so that she could avoid running into him.

"How is your uncle?"

"Doing well, thank you."

They had drawn close to the vicar and his wife, and Mrs. Burroughs turned toward them, smiling. "You are speaking of your uncle, I collect?"

"Yes. Dr. Felton kindly inquired after his health."

"Dear Lord de Winter," Mrs. Burroughs

said, beaming. "We do miss him, don't we, dear?"

As her uncle had rarely darkened the door of the church, Anna rather doubted that sentiment, but she merely smiled and nodded.

"How long has he been away now? Ten years, is it?"

"Yes."

"Likes the tropics, does he?" the vicar said with his kind smile. "Can't say I blame him. Sometimes, when my elbow aches in the winter, I could wish I were in Barbados myself."

"Yes. It is very pleasant there, I understand. Of course, we do not hear from Uncle Charles very often. He was never much of a correspondent, I fear."

Out of the corner of her eye, Anna could see Reed walking toward them, so, with a smile, she eased out of the group and made her way over to where Kyria stood, chatting with Kit and Rosemary Farrington. In the same manner she managed to avoid him for much of the next hour.

As the party wore on, Kyria did indeed open up the floor for dancing. Anna took to the floor first with her brother, and after that she stood up with Dr. Felton, then Miles Bennett. She had danced often enough with both of them, for generally the same people attended every social gathering. Dr. Felton was an adequate, if methodical, dancer, but Miles Bennett was a poor partner, concentrating on his footwork to the exclusion of all else, including the music, so that while he did not tromp all over her feet, he did tend to push and pull her about the floor without much regard to the beat of the music.

It was a relief when the dance ended and she was able to curtsey to Miles and leave the floor. However, as she turned to walk away, she found Reed standing in her path, a cup of lemonade in his hand.

"You look as if you could use this," he told her, a smile quirking the corner of his mouth as he held out the cup to her.

Anna could not help but chuckle and take the drink from him. "It is a rather energetic exercise, dancing with Miles," she agreed, then sipped thirstily.

"Perhaps you will allow me to lead you out for the next dance, then. I promise I am not so quick-footed."

Anna remembered all too well how Reed danced, and just the thought of it set up nervous trembles in her stomach. She looked up at him. There was nothing in his face of the anger or bitterness that had been there the last time they had talked, nothing but polite interest. She should not waltz with him, she knew, but, on the other hand, it would seem odd and impolite not to dance with her host.

"I — thank you. Of course." The truth was, she knew, that she wanted to dance with him again. It was foolish, just as it had been foolish to come here, but she could not seem to keep from doing it. She took another nervous sip of the lemonade.

Then the first notes of the music sounded, and Reed took the cup from her, setting it aside on a nearby table, and gave her his arm to lead her out onto the floor. She took it, hoping he could not feel the faint trembling of her fingers through his suit jacket. He turned to face her, one hand going to her waist, the other curving around her hand, and they swept out onto the floor.

Anna's heart lifted with the music. Dancing with Reed was like heaven after Miles' clumsy efforts. She floated across the floor, very aware of the warmth of his hand at her waist. She remembered the first time she had danced with him, in the ballroom at Holcomb Manor. She had been giddy, already tumbling head over heels into love with him, and she had never known anything so wonderful in her life. She had been twenty-three, but she had felt like a girl of eighteen at her first ball.

She tried to thrust the memory out of her mind. It was dangerous to think about it. She knew better now; she could not let herself stumble into that same quagmire. Anna looked up at Reed, and her breath caught in her throat. He was gazing down at her, his eyes gleaming in the candlelight. His gaze flickered to her mouth, and his eyes darkened. Anna's insides quivered in response.

It did not surprise her when he danced her closer to the bank of French doors, open to catch the cooler evening air, or that before the notes of the music ended, he whisked her out the doors onto the terrace.

Taking her hand, he walked over to the balustrade. They stood silently for a moment, looking out over the moon-washed garden, still largely untamed despite the recent efforts of Reed's gardeners, who had come to help old Grimsley. The heady scent of roses hung on the night air, heavy and seductive.

Reed took her by the shoulders, turning her to face him, and Anna looked up reluctantly into his face. His full lips were drawn tight, and he was scowling down at her, but the heat in his eyes was at odds with his irritated expression. "I must have been mad to come back here," he said. "You are more beautiful than ever . . . or perhaps I'd just forgotten."

Anna let out a shaky breath. Her mind was a blank. She knew she should say something, end the moment, but she could not make herself turn away. Her heart was thudding in her chest, and she knew that all she wanted at this moment was for him to kiss her.

As if he had heard her thoughts, Reed leaned down, his face looming closer, and then his lips were on hers and all other thoughts fled from Anna's head. She trembled, her hands going up to his chest as if to ward him off, then sliding instead around his neck. His lips were soft and seeking, the pressure gradually increasing as passion flared up inside him. Reed's arms went around her tightly, pulling her up and into him, as his mouth pressed harder against hers.

Anna let out a soft sound of pleasure, clinging to him, her head whirling. It had been so long since she had tasted his lips; she thought she had forgotten how it felt, but the memories flooded back to her now, hot and fierce. Desire thrummed in her, as though the years between had only made it stronger. She wanted the world to go away, wanted the kiss never to stop.

His hands roamed up and down her back,

caressing her shoulders and back and hips, and he lifted his mouth briefly from hers only to change the angle of their kiss. Reed's skin was searing where he touched her bare back and shoulders; his heat enveloped her. One arm curled around her back, supporting her, and his other hand moved slowly up her side from her hips, curving around to the front and coming to rest on the underside of her breast.

Anna shuddered, heat lancing straight down through her abdomen and exploding in her loins. No one had ever touched her like this, not even Reed three years ago, and the sensation was both shocking and intensely exciting. She had never before experienced the hot flowering of yearning between her legs or the sudden fullness of her breasts, the tightening of her nipples. Hungrily, she pressed herself even more tightly against him, her arms locking around his neck.

He kissed his way across her cheek to her ear, and his teeth and tongue worried at the sensitive lobe, sending wild darts of sensation shooting through her. His hand tightened on her breast, his thumb stroking across her nipple, and even through the material of her dress, her nipple responded, hardening and pointing.

"Anna, Anna . . ." He breathed her name

as his lips trailed down her neck, nibbling and kissing until at last they reached the pillowy softness of her breast.

She gasped, rocked by pleasure, and somehow the very intensity of the pleasure brought her out of the haze in which she had been floating. Anna straightened, pulling sharply away from Reed, her hand going to her mouth. For a long moment they simply stared at each other, too stunned to speak or even move. Then, with a low cry, Anna turned and hurried away.

"Anna!" Reed called her name in a hoarse whisper, but she did not turn around.

She paused at the open doors, looking into the lighted room. She straightened her dress and patted her hair, then took a deep breath and slipped inside. No one seemed to notice her entrance.

Anna glanced around the room, looking for her brother. At last she spotted him at the other end of the room, talking to Kyria and Rosemary, and she began to make her way around the edge of the dancers toward him. She hated to tear Kit away from the party, which he was so obviously enjoying, but she did not think she could bear to remain here any longer. She would plead a headache and tell him that she had to leave, but would send the carriage back for him.

She cast a look back toward the outer doors as she moved up the room. Reed had reentered, as well, but was making his way toward the opposite end.

The music came to a stop, the dancers left the floor, and Anna started directly across the room toward her brother. Then there was a stir at the door leading out into the hall, and Anna turned her head to see the constable, Carl Wright, standing in the doorway, looking ill at ease and twisting his cap in his hand. As she watched, Reed strode through the other partygoers to the constable and bent to say something to the man.

By now, almost all the heads in the room were turned toward the door, watching curiously. Reed raised his head and glanced around the room, and his gaze fell upon Dr. Felton. He gestured to the doctor, and Felton slipped through the other guests to join the knot at the door. A murmur rose from the those nearest the three men, moving back through the room.

"A body . . ."

"They've found a body. . . ."

Anna stiffened, her hands clenching at her sides. *Estelle!*

Chapter Six

Anna was not sure why she was so certain that the body they were speaking of was the maid Estelle, but she was. She felt suddenly weak in the knees, and her concerns of a few moments earlier fled her mind. Turning, she hurried over to where her brother stood with Lady Kyria and Miss Farrington, and slipped her hand through his arm. He glanced down at her, his hand going protectively over hers.

"Do you know what's happening?" Anna asked Kyria, who shook her head.

"I just heard someone say they'd found a body."

At that moment Rafe McIntyre came up beside his wife, sliding a supporting hand around her waist. She leaned into him a little, casting him a grateful glance. "Who is that man?" Kyria asked, nodding toward Reed and the others.

"The constable," Anna replied. "I think he must have come to fetch Dr. Felton."

"Oh, dear, how awful," Rosemary Farrington gasped, looking pale.

"What if it's Estelle?" Anna asked her brother.

"Who?" Kyria asked. "Who is Estelle?"

"We don't know that it is she," Kit protested. "It could be anybody."

"She is one of our maids," Anna explained to the others. "She has been missing the past few days. Everyone thought she had run away with a man, but . . ."

Anna cast another look toward the door. Dr. Felton and the constable were no longer there, and Reed was walking toward his sister, the rest of the party falling around him, clamoring with questions. When he reached his sister, he said quietly, "I am sorry to spoil your party, my dear."

"Never mind that," Kyria said, shaking her head impatiently. "What is going on?"

"Apparently a body has been found."

"Where was it?" Anna asked, her mind going again to the woods and the strange feeling she had had there the other day — though surely the body could not have been found there, for she had seen nothing.

Reed shook his head. "I'm not sure. I believe the constable said something like Hutchins' farm. I think a farmer found her."

"Sam Hutchins?" Kit supplied. "He is one of our tenants. I mean, one of my uncle's tenants."

"Yes, I got the impression it was on de Winter land."

"Do they know who it is?" Kit asked, and Reed shook his head.

"He did not say. Only that they needed the doctor to examine the body."

"Miss Holcomb is afraid that it might be one of their servant girls," Kyria explained.

"Estelle Akins. She left the house several days ago. We thought she had gone off with someone." Distress filled Anna's voice. "We should have looked harder. Done something more."

"Now, Anna, you don't know that the body is Estelle's," Kit pointed out. "Nor do we have any idea what happened. And how could we have known? She obviously left the house on her own."

"I know. It's just —" Anna thought again of her feeling in the woods that day. She *had* known something was wrong; she had felt it strongly. No one would have believed her, she supposed; she scarcely believed it herself. But she could have pushed the issue, she thought; she could have sent the men out searching farther afield than she had.

Yet even as those thoughts went through her head, she knew that she would not have thought to send the men as far away as Hutchins' farm, where the body had been

140

found. The "vision" she had seen — or felt, or whatever one called it — had been in the woods.

Anna looked at Reed and asked, "What happened?"

Again Reed shook his head. "I'm not sure."

"There were claw marks," said the squire from behind them. "I heard Wright say there were claw marks on the body."

Anna's eyes widened, and her mind went immediately to the dog that the twins had found, its side slashed. Her eyes went to her brother. There were gasps from several of the guests, and the vicar's wife said in a horrified whisper, "The Beast!"

"Now, my dear . . ." the vicar began in a soothing tone.

"The beast?" Kyria repeated, glancing around. "What beast? What are you talking about?"

"The Beast of Craydon Tor," Mrs. Bennett said in tones of awe.

"It's nothing," Anna said flatly. "Just a local legend."

"My dear, how can you say that?" the vicar's wife admonished her.

"The area is full of legends," Kit said. "All of them apocryphal, I'm sure."

"I told you one of them," Reed said to his sister. "How the staghounds on the columns at the gate come to life at the full moon and follow their dead master as he races on his phantom horse through the countryside."

"Yes, you did," Kyria said with a dramatic shudder, "and it gave me the shivers, I can tell you. But is that what they call the beast?"

"The Beast is something altogether different," the squire's wife said.

"Long, long ago," piped up Felicity Bennett, in the tone of one telling a fairy tale, "there was an important nobleman — one of the de Winters, perhaps, but it was so long ago, no one knows who. He had a beautiful young daughter, and he betrothed her to another lord. But the daughter had already fallen in love with a local lad, and when her father told her that she was to marry the lord, she refused. He locked her in her room, but the local lad helped her escape and they fled into the forest. Lord de Winter and his men hunted them down and killed the girl's lover right in front of her. He took her back to the castle, and that very night, the girl, crazed with grief, flung herself to her death in the castle courtyard."

"A rather typical legend," Mr. Norton, the solicitor said, somewhat pompously.

"I don't understand," Rosemary Farrington said. "It's very sad, but what does it have to do with a beast?"

"That's the next part." Felicity picked up the story. "The boy the nobleman killed was the son of a witch, and she was furious. She went to the nobleman and put a curse on him for having killed her son, and for causing his own daughter's death, as well. She changed him into a beast, part man, part animal, and doomed him to roam the earth forever, reviled by everyone." She stopped with a pleased look on her face.

"A lot you know about it," her brother put in scornfully.

"Oh, and I suppose you know better?" Felicity pouted, putting her hands on her hips.

"There are other variations of the story," the solicitor said. "That every seven years the present Lord de Winter turns into the Beast, or that every generation a de Winter is born a beast. But Miss Bennett's version is the most popular."

"They call him the Beast of Craydon Tor," Reed went on. "I was told all about it when I bought Winterset. The Beast supposedly lives in the woods around Craydon Tor."

"It's all nonsense," Anna said. "Just a bogeyman to frighten children."

"But he's been seen!" Mrs. Burroughs

protested. "Many, many times. I read about it in a book Dr. Felton lent me."

"There have been stories that he has been sighted," Anna replied. "But none of them have ever described him in the same way, have they?"

"No," her brother agreed. "Some have said it was a dark animal, like a panther. Others have said it walked upright and had a head like a lion. And then there are those who said it looked like a man, but with claws and hair all around his face and long, sharp teeth."

"Besides," Mr. Norton, clearly a skeptic, put in, "it's nothing but hearsay — some priest recounting legends of beasts, or a newspaper story full of things like 'a local farmer said.' "

"But what about those killings?" the squire asked. "Those were the work of the Beast. I was just a baby when they happened, but I remember everyone talking about them when I was young."

"Killings?" Kyria asked, her eyes wide. Beside her Reed looked almost as surprised.

"Oh, yes," the squire nodded, looking important. "It was nigh on fifty years ago when it happened. Four years or so before Lord and Lady de Winter died in that fire — " He turned toward Anna and Kit, adding, "Your grandparents, your uncle's parents. Terrible tragedy, that." He gave a sigh and a lugubrious shake of his head, then went on. "But a few years before that, the Beast killed two people."

"Really?" Kyria looked amazed.

"I never heard about this," Reed commented.

"There were killings at that time," Mr. Norton said, in the carefully precise way he spoke.

"The victims were clawed," Mrs. Burroughs said, much more firmly than was her wont. "That is what everyone says. One of them had his throat ripped out."

Her words seemed to hang in the silence, harsh and terrible.

"Did they find who did it?" Rafe McIntyre asked.

Several people shook their heads. The solicitor was the first to speak. "A number of people didn't think it was a person. They thought it was this 'Beast.'"

"One can hardly believe that a person would do such things," the vicar added.

"People were scared about it for years afterward," put in the squire. "I remember my nurse used to tell me about how people would bar their doors and windows, even in the heat of the summer, afraid of the Beast."

Even disbelieving as she was, Anna could not help but feel a little shiver run down her back at his words.

The party broke up shortly after that. There seemed little more to say, and the natural inclination for most was to seek the shelter of their own homes.

When their guests had gone, Rafe slid his arm around his wife, pulling her against his side, and Kyria laid her head gratefully on his shoulder.

"Sorry about your party, darlin'," Rafe said, kissing her gently on the temple.

Kyria shrugged. "I don't mind that. . . . It's that poor girl."

"Do you think it's the Holcombs' maid?" Rosemary asked, frowning in concern.

"It seems likely, given the fact that she is missing," Reed commented. "I did hear the constable say that the body was that of a woman."

Miss Farrington shuddered and said in a subdued voice that she was going up to bed. Reed cast a look at his sister and Rafe, saying, "Join me for a drink in the study?"

"I think a bit of brandy is exactly what we need," Rafe agreed, and the three of them strolled down the hall into Reed's study. A large, comfortable room, it was still furnished with the large leather chairs that had been there when Reed bought the place, all well worn into a buttery softness.

Reed walked over to a cabinet against the wall and took out a decanter of brandy, pouring a healthy dollop of cognac into three small balloon glasses.

Kyria sighed as she sat down on the sofa. "It's so awful. Poor Anna. She looked white as a sheet. Did you notice?"

Rafe nodded as he sat down beside her. He linked his hand through hers and brought it up to his lips, kissing it tenderly. Kyria smiled at him and snuggled up against him.

Reed, pouring the drinks, turned at his sister's words, his eyes narrowing. "I wasn't with you when she heard. Was she much distressed?"

"I would say so," Kyria said. "She was quite pale. Of course, she assumed it was their servant. That is much worse than just hearing that a stranger has died."

"I wonder . . ." Reed murmured, staring down at the glasses without really seeing them, the decanter still in his hand.

Rafe and Kyria exchanged a glance. "Wonder what?" Rafe asked bluntly. "Did you know this servant girl, or whoever it was that was found?"

Reed shook his head. "No. But . . ." He set down the decanter, then picked up two of the drinks and brought them over to Rafe and Kyria. "You will probably think me mad. I told Theo about it, and I'm fairly certain that he did."

Kyria raised her eyebrow. "Told Theo what? How is Theo involved in this? He's in London."

"He's not involved. But I told him why I was coming here."

Kyria stared at him. "I thought you were coming to put the house in order so that you could sell it. That is why Rafe and I came along, to look at the house in case we wanted to buy it. Is that not why you came here?"

"Not entirely, no."

Rafe and Kyria exchanged a glance, then looked back at Reed. "Reed . . . what are you saying? Are you not planning to sell Winterset?"

"I don't know. I — I had thought I might." He sighed. "I don't use the place. And it seemed like a reasonable excuse to come."

"Excuse?" Rafe picked up on the word. "Why would you need an excuse to visit your own house?"

"Because it has been three years. Because . . . I thought it would stifle any awkward questions."

"From the family?" Kyria asked.

Reed nodded. "Yes. And from everyone here. I thought it would seem a trifle odd to go off for three years and then come running back."

"The odd thing was buying it and then leaving it in a few months and never going back," Kyria said shrewdly. "That is what I have always wondered about." She paused, then said, "Why did you really come to Winterset? Is it because of Anna Holcomb?"

Reed looked at her sharply. "How did you know?"

Kyria grimaced. "I'm not blind, you know. I saw you this evening — you scarcely took your eyes off her all night. And the other day, when she came back here with the twins, it was the same. Then you insisted on escorting her back to her home, when it would have been enough simply to have sent her home in the carriage. And when you came back, you were in such a terrible temper, I didn't dare talk to you."

Reed shot her an expressive look. "As if you've *ever* hesitated to say anything to me."

"Well, that is true," Kyria admitted, giving a little grin. "But no doubt others would not have dared to approach you, you looked so grim. And I have seen how Miss Holcomb looks at you, too."

"She looks at me?" Reed leaned forward, his eyes intent on his sister's face. "How does she look?"

"The way a woman does when she is interested in a man," Kyria replied. "Her eyes kept straying about the room this evening, and whenever they lit on you, she would stop. Then, a few minutes later, she would do the same thing."

Reed grimaced. "Most likely she was looking for me so she could avoid me."

Kyria smiled a little smugly. "I don't think so. There is a certain warmth in her eyes when she looks at you." She cocked her head to the side, studying her brother. "There is also the little matter that she is far too attractive and likable a woman to be still unmarried. What happened when you were here three years ago, Reed? Did you break her heart?"

"I? Why would you assume that it was *I* who broke *her* heart?" Reed asked.

"Are you telling me that it was the other way around?" Kyria asked.

"I offered for her. She refused me."

Kyria stared. "She turned you down?"

A faint smile touched Reed's lips. "I suppose it is gratifying that you find that so startling."

"But of course it is! There are always women dangling after you, you know that. Why, the only bachelor who is more sought after than you is Theo, I warrant, and that is only because he will be a duke one day." She paused, frowning, then said slowly, "Unless, of course, she was already in love with another . . ."

Reed shrugged. "I have no idea what happened. I will doubtless appear insufferably arrogant, but I was certain that she would accept my proposal. She seemed . . . well, we had not known each other long, but from the moment we met, there was a . . . a certain feeling between us. I cannot explain it."

Kyria smiled and glanced at Rafe. "I know what you mean."

Reed smiled. "Yes, I suppose you do. But apparently the feeling was entirely on my side. I thought it must be clear to her what my feelings were, and she — well, I thought she encouraged them. I called on her frequently, we went for rides together — I even held parties, just so that I could have an opportunity to dance with her."

"My goodness, you must have been bewitched," Kyria teased.

"I was. I knew almost as soon as I met her — the way Papa says he felt when he met Mother."

"What happened?"

"I'm not sure." Reed shook his head, his face tinged with the old sorrow. "She had been ill. I had not seen her for a few days. Looking back on it, I suppose she wasn't really sick at all those days, simply avoiding seeing me. But at the time, I had no suspicion. Certainly, when she did see me, she looked pale enough to have been ill. I thought I should wait until she felt better to ask her, but I could not. As soon as I started proposing to her, she looked as though I had struck her. She would not even let me finish. She was quite agitated. She popped up, then sat back down, then got up again and paced about the room. Then she said all the things that women are taught to say in such circumstance — what an honor I had done her, how surprised she was, how she had not realized how I felt, how she had not meant to mislead me, but there was no possibility. We would not suit."

He stopped, his mouth grim.

Kyria looked at him, frowning. "I scarcely know what to say. It sounds so . . . so odd. I would never have guessed, from seeing her with you, that she had turned you down. I would have said that she had . . . well, feelings for you."

"I thought so, but obviously I was wrong. And tonight, I —" Reed stopped, looking uncomfortable. "It seemed to me again that she felt something for me, that she would not be averse to my suit, but then she turned and all but ran from me. I don't know what to think."

They were silent for a moment, then Rafe said, "What made you decide to come back now, after all this time?"

"Oh." Reed grimaced. "You will think I'm mad if I tell you. That's why I said I was coming to see about selling the house. The real reason is absurd."

"I am sure we will not think you are mad," Kyria assured him. "We have had some rather bizarre things happen to us, as well, you know."

"I came back because of a dream," Reed said with the air of a man owning up to a dreadful flaw.

"A dream?"

He nodded. "Yes. I dreamed that I was with Anna, and that she was in trouble. Something was pulling her away from me in the dream, and I could not move, could not reach her. It sounds foolish when I say it, I know, but you cannot imagine how real the

153

dream was. Even after I woke up, I was seized with something close to terror because I could not help her. I tried to tell myself that it was only a dream — and that whatever happened to Anna was not my concern, anyway. I felt sure that she would not welcome my help. But I knew I could not stay away. I had to see if she was all right. I had to help her if I could." Reed cast his sister an abashed glance. "You have every right to think I am insane."

"Why? Because you've had one of the famous Moreland dreams?" Kyria asked lightly. "I am the last person who would say you were foolish to do something on the basis of a dream — or a feeling. You know what happened with that reliquary."

She paused, thinking back to two years ago, when a man had died at the Morelands' house, bringing with him a reliquary and setting into motion a strange chain of events that had brought her love and almost cost her her life. Kyria could remember quite clearly the sense of connection she had felt with the reliquary and the huge black diamond on its side, and the peculiar dreams she had experienced after she held it.

"Or what happened with Olivia and Stephen," Rafe added, alluding to Reed's and

Kyria's sister and the man she had married, Lord St. Leger. Rafe had been Stephen's best friend and had shared part of their eerie adventure. "The dreams they shared . . . the couple seemingly speaking to them from the past . . ."

"Maybe Grandmother was right," Kyria told Reed. "Perhaps there is a special . . . sensitivity in our family."

Reed rolled his eyes. "I have a little trouble believing that Grandmother was sensitive in any way. I think her 'visions' were more a way of keeping everyone's attention focused on her than anything else."

Kyria chuckled. "That may be. But I know what happened with me, and I don't doubt that there were forces at work there that were far beyond my understanding. When that happens, I think it's best not to fight it. You felt that she was in trouble and you should come here. And I think that is what you should have done."

"I felt a fool when I got here and spoke with her. Everything was obviously all right with her, and she wished me gone. I could see that. But now, after tonight, I wonder. . . ."

"You think your dream was prophetic? That she is going to be in trouble before long?" Kyria asked.

"And that this maid's death is part of the

trouble that she is in — or will be in?" Rafe added.

"I don't know. Obviously, it is a terrible thing, although I cannot see how it connects to Anna — I mean, more than superficially. But clearly I am dealing with something that I don't understand. If I heard someone else say the sort of things I've just been saying, I would be certain he was an idiot."

"Well, murder is very real," Kyria said.

"*If* the maid was murdered. It could have been an accident," Reed pointed out.

"You think she was really killed by an animal?" Kyria asked skeptically.

Reed cast her a sardonic look. "I doubt it was some mythical beast, if that is what you mean. That is simply the sort of sensational story people seem to prefer to the truth."

"People always love a good story about a supernatural beast," Rafe put in, taking a sip of the fiery cognac. "I remember a story that used to go around home about the swamp cat. There was some swampland not too far from where I lived, closer to the coast, and people swore there was a black panther that lived in there. But not just any old panther — no, sir, this one was bigger and stronger than any ordinary cat, and he had eyes that glowed like red coals in his head. People said he couldn't be killed, no matter how many times you shot him. The devil's cat, they said, and if you got lost in the swamp, when nighttime came, you were likely to meet him. Thing was, he didn't just kill you — he took your soul, as well."

"I think it's most likely that the maid was attacked by an actual animal," Kyria put in.

"Like what?" Rafe responded. "That's the problem I see. I haven't noticed too many wildcats or bears or such running loose in England."

"No. But it could have been a mad dog, I suppose."

"What I find the most intriguing about it," Kyria said, "is the fact that it's like those killings that took place almost fifty years ago."

"If it *is* like them," Reed pointed out. "We have very little information about either the original killings or the body that was found."

"Well, it seems clear to me that we need to find out more about both this death and the murders that took place fifty years ago," Kyria decided.

" 'We?' " Reed asked. "I was just about to suggest that you and Rafe take the twins, Emily and Miss Farrington, and go back to London."

"You are kicking us out?" Kyria asked with mock indignation.

Reed grimaced. "Hardly. But if there was a murder here, it scarcely seems like the place for children or a gently reared young lady like Miss Farrington. And someone has to take them back."

Kyria started to speak, then stopped and sighed. "Yes, I can see your point. It's all so different when one has a child, isn't it? But I cannot really see how this woman's death, even if it is murder, could affect one of us. I mean, obviously it has to do with the local people and something that was going on before we arrived."

"Mmm. Probably this fellow that Miss Holcomb was saying they thought the girl ran away with," Rafe agreed.

"That may be. But I think you will agree that investigations of evildoing have a way of getting out of hand," Reed said.

"I won't go out investigating," Kyria protested. "I am a mother now. I'm not going to endanger my child or her future. Or the twins or Miss Farrington, for that matter. And with both you and Rafe here, I can't think there will be any danger to us in this house."

"I should hope not." Reed glanced over at Rafe, who smiled wryly, and Reed knew that he was thinking the same thing Reed was: the more one tried to push Kyria into doing something, the more determined she became not to be moved.

"It would be quite bad of you to toss us out," Kyria went on teasingly. "It seems the least you could do is to let us stay here awhile longer, since you don't mean to let us buy Winterset, do you?"

Reed looked faintly surprised, then thoughtful. "No, I think you are right. I don't want to sell this house. I'm sorry. I thought I would, but now that I'm here — I really can't give it up. I suppose I had better send a note to Mr. Norton tomorrow telling him I've changed my mind." He paused, then looked at his sister seriously. "But you will promise me, won't you, Kyria, you'll leave and take the children if there appears to be any real danger?"

"Of course I will," Kyria agreed. "If there is real danger." After a moment she added, "But right now, I think we had better concentrate on finding out what we can about what's going on."

"Whose body it was, whether or not she was murdered, and how, if at all, it's linked to Anna," Reed said.

"We might do well to find out about those old murders, too," Rafe pointed out. "I have a little trouble believing that somebody now, as well as two people back then, were all killed by wild animals. I have even more trouble believing that there's some ancient man-beast popping up every fifty years or so to kill somebody."

"So where will you start?" Kyria asked, looking at Reed, the expression on her face challenging.

He sighed. "With Anna, of course. I'll ride over there tomorrow and see what I can find out about this servant."

They finished off their brandies, and Kyria and Rafe left the study, starting up the stairs toward their bedroom. Rafe's arm was looped around his wife's shoulders, and he held her close against his side.

He leaned down and nuzzled her hair, saying in a low voice, "Why do I get the feeling that you were trying to maneuver Reed into going to see Miss Holcomb tomorrow?"

Kyria smiled and turned to kiss his cheek. "Perhaps because I was."

"And your reason for throwing the poor man together with the woman who broke his heart three years ago is . . . ?"

"My brother is a wonderful man, but he has a maddening habit of listening only to his head and not to his heart. She told him she wouldn't marry him, and he accepted it because that was the logical thing to do. But his heart obviously has a different opinion. I don't know whether Miss Holcomb is in trouble or not, but I do know that he dreamed of her, and that when he thought she was in trouble, his first instinct was to fly to her rescue. That is his heart speaking, and he should follow it."

"And what if she turns him away again? What if she still does not want him?"

Kyria cast him a sideways glance. "I looked around the room this evening and saw that neither my brother nor Miss Holcomb were there. A few minutes later, she came sliding back into the room from the terrace, her cheeks flushed, her eyes sparkling, a certain expression on her face, as if she'd just barely saved herself from falling off a cliff. I don't know why Miss Holcomb turned him down three years ago. But I think I can definitely say that it is not the case that she does not want him."

She smiled her cat-in-the-cream smile at Rafe. "Maybe they just need to be thrown together until finally they figure out that they belong together." Her smile curved up even more as she said, "After all, that's what happened with us."

Then, with a giggle, she pulled away from him and ran lightly up the rest of the stairs. Rafe, grinning, went after her, taking the stairs two at a time.

Chapter Seven

Anna met Dr. Felton with a subdued smile,
extending her hand to him. "It was very kind
of you to come here today, Dr. Felton."

She gestured him toward the couch, and
she and her brother sat down on the pair of
blue velvet chairs that faced the sofa. It was
the afternoon following the party, and she
had been waiting anxiously all day for news
about what had happened the night before.
When the butler had announced Dr. Felton,
she had been filled with a combination of relief that she would at last find out and dread
that the body must indeed have been
Estelle's, for why else would the doctor have
come straightaway to tell them?

"I wanted to tell you myself," Felton
said.

"It was Estelle?" Kit asked. "You identified the body?"

"Yes," the doctor answered. "I was fairly
certain as soon as I saw the body, but her father identified her, too."

"I feel terrible," Anna murmured. "We

should have done something more. Looked farther afield for her."

"I am sure you did all you could," Felton said comfortingly.

"We thought she had run off with a man," Anna explained. "And all that time, she was dead!"

"We had no reason to think otherwise," Kit told her. "You mustn't blame yourself. By the time we became aware that she was missing, she was probably already dead. Why else would she not have come home? Even if we had searched in the right place and found her, we could not have helped her."

Anna turned toward Dr. Felton. "Is that true? I keep thinking, what if she had fallen or something, and she was lying there all this time. . . ."

"No, you must not worry yourself about it. Sir Christopher is right. There was nothing you could have done for her. She had been dead for several days — doubtless she was already dead when you were searching for her. It was no accident. She was murdered."

"Oh!" Anna had known in her heart that such was probably the case, but still the words hit her like a blow.

Murder was something that happened in

London and other far-off places, not right here at home. And not to people one actually knew. Anna had seen Estelle every day for years now; she had come to work for them when Anna was only twenty-two. She had spoken to her often, had given her remedies for her toothaches and catarrh. She remembered again that day in the servants' hall when she had seen Estelle return, and the grin that had touched Estelle's pert face when Anna had protected her from the housekeeper.

"I knew," she said, her voice sinking almost to a whisper. "I saw her come in one morning from the outside, and I realized that she must have been out all night. But I didn't tell Mrs. Michaels, because I hated to get her into trouble. If only I had, she probably wouldn't have been able to sneak out again. And she would still be alive today."

"Or Mrs. Michaels might have let her go right there and then for moral turpitude," Kit reminded her. "In which case, she would probably have been in exactly the same place."

"I suppose you're right," Anna agreed. "Still, I cannot help but feel . . . responsible somehow."

"You take too much upon yourself, Miss

Holcomb," Dr. Felton assured her. "I doubt very much that there was anything you could have done to prevent this."

At that moment the butler appeared silently in the doorway, and when they looked toward him, he said, "Lord Moreland is here, Sir Christopher. Shall I show him in?"

"Yes, of course," Kit answered.

Anna's stomach tightened. She did not want to deal with Reed today; she was in too much turmoil already. But there was nothing she could do about it now. She could scarcely stand up and flee the room just as he walked in.

The butler returned with Reed, announcing him with a certain pride. It was not often that they had titled guests. Reed took in the room at a glance, nodding to Kit and the doctor, and bowing over Anna's hand. Her heart sped up at his nearness. She could not help but think of those moments in his embrace last night, the feel of his lips on hers, of his hand sliding up her body.

"How do you do, my lord?" Anna said tightly, steeling herself to conceal her reaction to him.

"I am well, thank you. I came to see how you were faring after what happened last night." Reed's eyes looked on hers for a long moment, then went to the doctor. "I take it that the girl turned out to be Miss Holcomb's maid?"

Dr. Felton nodded. "Yes, I was just informing them. It appears that she was murdered."

"Do they have any idea who did it?" Reed asked as he took a seat beside Dr. Felton on the sofa.

The doctor shrugged and glanced toward Kit and Anna. "I understand that she had been sneaking out to meet a man. . . ."

Anna nodded. "That is what she told Penny — the maid who shared her room."

"Obviously this man must be the most likely suspect," Kit said. "A lover's quarrel, perhaps, gone terribly wrong."

"But what about the marks?" Anna asked, turning toward the doctor. "They said there were claw marks. Could it not have been that she was attacked by some animal?"

Dr. Felton frowned. "Yes, there were claw marks —" He glanced at Anna, hesitating. "This is a most gruesome subject. I hesitate to tell a lady . . ."

"No. I want to know," Anna said firmly. "I have to know what happened to her."

"There were claw marks in several places — her arms and chest, her face, her throat. Her throat, particularly, was torn. She died from exsanguination — a loss of blood. Most of it had soaked into the ground."

Anna felt a little queasy at his words, but she did not ask him to stop. She nodded. "Then it *was* an animal? Could she not have been going to meet her lover and been attacked by —"

"It did not resemble anything I have seen done by an animal," Dr. Felton said grimly. "It would have had to be a very large animal. The scratches —" He hesitated again, looking at Anna uncomfortably. "They were fairly deep and spaced rather far apart — not nearly close enough together to be a dog or even a wolf — if there still are any wolves in this area. I have not heard of any. And dogs are much more likely to bite and tear as they fight, not use their claws."

"What could it have been, then?" Reed asked.

"I would have said something much larger, some sort of animal that one would find only in the London Zoological Park — a lion, say, or a bear."

The others simply looked at him. Finally Kit said, "It doesn't seem very likely, does it?"

"No. That is why I'm more inclined to think that it was murder," Dr. Felton said. "I suspect it was the work of a man."

Anna paled even more and said, "With claws?" She glanced toward Kit, and he shook his head slightly. She turned back to the doctor, saying "But a man would not have —"

"No. Not claws. I think it merely resembled that. I would be inclined to say some sort of instrument — a gardening tool, perhaps. There is one, I'm not sure what you call it as I'm not much of a hand in the garden, but it looks something like a small rake, less than a foot long, with tines that curve down."

"Oh, yes," Anna said. "I know what you mean. It is a cultivator. One breaks up the earth with it before one plants. Of course. I can see how it would look that way."

"I cannot take credit for the idea, I'm afraid. It was my father's," Felton said.

Kit and Anna looked confused for a moment, then Kit said, "Oh, from the killings before . . ."

"The ones fifty years ago?" Reed asked. "I had wondered about those. Were they that similar?"

Kit nodded toward the doctor. "You had best ask Dr. Felton. He is the expert on the Beast of Craydon Tor murders."

Reed turned surprised eyes toward the doctor, who looked no more than five or ten

169

years older than himself. "But surely you were not alive then."

Dr. Felton smiled. "No. My father was the physician here at that time. He was young, had only been a doctor a few years when they happened. I was born a good many years later in his life. However, he kept all his notebooks from his practice, including the ones that he made regarding the two victims in those killings. He left them to me when he died a few years ago." He shrugged, looking faintly embarrassed. "I have always been somewhat fascinated with the Beast of Craydon Tor from the time I was a boy. Of course, back then, I believed wholeheartedly in a magical beast, part man, part animal, doomed to live that way eternally by a vengeful witch. Of course, those murders were part of that lore. I collected what writings I could find on the Beast, and several years ago, one of my older patients gave me a box of clippings she had collected on the subject — newspaper articles and such about the murders."

"I see. So you have the definitive library on the subject?"

"Yes, I do."

Reed looked at him speculatively. "I must say, I would be rather interested in looking at some of those articles."

Felton looked surprised, but said politely, "You are welcome to come look at them if you wish."

"Thank you. I will take you up on that offer. My sister and brother-in-law and I were speculating on the murders last night after everyone left."

"Yes, I imagine it caused quite a stir at the party," Felton commented.

"Oh, yes, no one talked of anything else after you left," Anna told him. "The party ended soon after, needless to say."

"What happened in the original murders, if you don't mind my asking?" Reed asked the doctor. "Everything everyone said last night was rather, um, speculative."

"You mean, there was a lot of wild talk about the Beast," Anna said tartly. "People are willfully superstitious."

"I was rather surprised to find that the vicar's wife believed in the legend so enthusiastically," Kit commented.

"I find it not that unusual for someone who has faith in God to also have faith in a good number of other things," Reed said dryly. "And," he added, "in all fairness, even I have to admit that I have seen some events that have shaken my disbelief in things magical or legendary."

"Well, there was nothing magical or legendary about the murders forty-eight years ago," Martin Felton put in. "When one reads the articles and books and such, they are written in a lurid way that sounds as if they were eerie and otherworldly, but once you have seen the drawings of the bodies in my father's notebooks and read his notes, it is hard to view them as anything other than cold-blooded murders."

"Who was killed that time?"

"The first was a servant girl, and the other was an old man, a farmer. Both had similar disfiguring marks upon them, as if a giant cat had scratched them. But the man actually died from a deep puncture wound in his back, and amid the cuts on the girl's throat, there was the distinct slice of a knife." Felton glanced over at Anna. "I am sorry, Miss Holcomb, I forget myself. This is not fit conversation in front of a lady."

"No, please, Dr. Felton, go on. I am fine," Anna assured him. "I am made of sterner stuff than that, I think. I, too, would like to learn what happened. I have heard about the murders since I was a child, of course, but no one ever really explained them properly."

"The culprit was never found, was he?" Kit asked.

"No. When the servant girl was killed, it

was assumed that her fiancé had probably done it. He was arrested, but he was a tapster in the tavern, and there were a good number of witnesses who had seen him there, at least until closing. Then the second person was killed in the same way while the fiancé was still in jail, so they released him. No one could ever find any connection between the two victims, and there were no witnesses, no proof of anything. They never found who did it, and there were no more murders . . . at least, until now."

"But it could not possibly be the same person," Kit said.

"No, I wouldn't think so. I mean, the murderer could still be alive, if he was fairly young at the time, but he would be quite old — at least in his seventies, I would think. It seems unlikely that he would have the strength to subdue a healthy young woman," Felton responded.

"It would seem to me that whoever did it must be imitating the original murders," Reed said. "Wouldn't you think? That it is someone trying to make everyone believe that this Beast is the culprit."

"That would seem reasonable," the doctor agreed.

"But it tells us nothing useful about the killer," Kit pointed out. "I mean, all we know is that he had heard about the original killings, which could be almost anyone in the area."

"It would seem most likely that the killer was the man she was sneaking out to see," Anna said. "Kit was saying so earlier."

"It makes sense," Reed agreed. "They quarrel about something. He kills her, then tries to cover it up by making the claw marks."

"Yet it seems unlikely that he would have been carrying a gardening tool or whatever he used to make the marks when he was going to a rendezvous," Anna pointed out.

"True," Reed agreed. "That would make it seem premeditated."

"It would not be the first time someone chose murder to get rid of a lover whom they no longer wanted," Dr. Felton mused.

For a moment they were all silent, considering the doctor's words. Then Dr. Felton said, "I should go back to the village. I have stayed too long, I fear. There will doubtless be patients waiting for me at the surgery."

He rose, and the others stood up with him. Anna thanked him again for bringing them the news about Estelle, and Kit offered to walk the doctor out. Reed and Anna were left alone in the drawing room, and they looked at each other awkwardly.

"I am glad to see that you are all right," Reed said at last.

"It was something of a shock," Anna admitted. "Still, it was not a complete surprise, I suppose, since Estelle has been missing for several days. I had hoped that everyone was right in saying that she had simply run away, but . . ."

"But you thought it was something more. Why?"

Anna looked at him. "I — I'm not sure." She had told no one about what had happened to her in the woods. She certainly was not about to admit her odd feeling to Reed. She cast about in her mind for another explanation for her uneasiness. "Perhaps it was because we found that dog in the woods the same day."

Reed's eyebrows lifted. "You think they are connected?"

"No. Well, I don't know. I did not really connect the two things. It is just that the way the dog was so badly wounded made me feel a little uneasy. And then, when I came home, I learned that Estelle was missing. I didn't really think at the time that they had anything in common, but I think that the feeling of uneasiness carried over when I heard about Estelle."

"At the time?" he repeated. "Do you

mean that now you think that they do have something in common?"

"I'm not sure. It was just that when the doctor described the marks on — on Estelle's body, it occurred to me that the wounds on the dog's side looked something like that. I assumed he had gotten into a fight with a larger dog, but the marks were rather far apart to be a dog's claws. I didn't really think about it then, but when Dr. Felton was talking about how they were wide-spaced, I realized that what he said could apply to the twins' dog, as well." She shook her head deprecatingly. "It's probably nothing."

"But it could be that whoever killed your maid might have injured the dog, as well." Reed studied her for a moment, then said, "I noticed that when the doctor was talking about the claw marks, you exchanged a look with your brother."

Anna glanced at him, startled. Her heart began to beat a little faster in her chest. "I don't know what you mean. I — I don't re-member looking at Kit particularly."

"You did. I wondered if the claw marks meant something to you."

Anna stiffened, her expression turning chilly. "Just what are you saying? That I know something about the murders?"

"No, of course not," Reed said quickly. "Damn my tongue. I always seem to say the wrong thing to you. All I meant was that you seemed to pay particular attention to that detail. As if something about it was familiar or —"

"That's ridiculous," Anna snapped. "I looked at Kit, I suppose, because he hates those tales of the Beast. He thinks them ignorant and foolish, and he dislikes the fact that people continue to repeat the legend. This will only further confirm people's belief in it."

"I see." Reed looked at her for a moment. Her gaze was direct and challenging. After a moment, he glanced away. "Anna, I hope you will take care where you go, what you do. I know you have always loved to tramp about, but . . . well, that doesn't seem very safe at the moment. I hope you will take someone with you when you go out."

Anna gaped at him. "But this has nothing to do with me. No doubt it was the man Estelle had been meeting, as everyone says. There isn't some wild animal roaming the countryside looking for victims. And even if there were, it did not happen in the woods or anywhere around our house. They found her clear over at Hutchins' farm."

"I know. But there is no reason to take any

chances. The consequences are too horren-
dous. It is little enough trouble to take a
groom with you when you ride or your maid
when you walk —"

"That is easy enough to say when you are
not the one who has someone following
your every step," Anna retorted. "The
whole point of my long walks is to be alone,
to — to think and look at the world around
me."

Anna did not know if it was because her
mother had died and she had taken over the
reins of the household at an early age or
merely because her father was a most understanding man, but she had, since she was
an adolescent, been allowed to go around
the countryside on her own. She cherished
that freedom — valuing it even more so
when she had seen her friends like Miranda
had been plagued with the propriety of
never venturing out without a companion.
The idea that anyone would try to take away
that freedom was enough to arouse her
anger; the fact that it was Reed seemed to
make it even worse.

"I cannot believe that you, after all the
things you told me about your mother and
how you were raised, would be advocat-
ing —"

"Blast it, this isn't about propriety!" Reed

retorted, stung by her words. "It is about your safety."

"But that's absurd. There is no reason why I am not safe," Anna said flatly. "Do you plan to go about armed, or take a servant with you?"

"No, of course not. But I am able to take care of myself."

"Against a man with a gun?" Anna asked, looking at him coolly. "I don't think the fact that you are a man or even your size would help you there."

"I'm not likely to meet up with a man with a gun."

"I am not likely to meet up with a murderer, either," Anna shot back.

"I just want you to be safe!" His voice rose in anger.

"It is no concern of yours!" Anna cried. "There is nothing between us!"

His chin came up a little, as if she had hit him, and there was a flash of hurt in his eyes before they turned blank and cold. "You do not need to remind me that I have no connection to you," he told her, his words clipped. "No right to protect you. You have made that amply clear. I can only wonder at my own stupidity that I even care about your safety."

Anna had seen the wounded look that had

touched his eyes, quickly repressed, and regret pierced her. "Reed . . ." She took a step toward him, instinctively reached toward him. "I am sorry."

He stepped back, out of her reach. "No. Do not apologize. No doubt I overreached myself."

"I never wanted to hurt you," Anna continued in a low voice.

"Fortunately, I no longer love you, so you cannot hurt me," Reed told her, and the lack of emotion in his face confirmed his words. "I did not ask you to be careful because I was trying to assume some right over you. I was concerned, as I would be concerned about any young woman who might come into a killer's path. I apologize if my concern offended you."

"No, Reed, it —" Anna stopped. She looked down at her hands. It was ridiculous, she told herself, to feel so rebuffed. After all, there was nothing between them. She had just told him so a moment before. It was foolish of her to feel hurt by his abrupt words. Of course he did not love her. It had been three years. She did not *want* him to love her still. It was best to just leave the matter alone.

"I will take my leave now," Reed went on. "Kindly give my regards to your brother."

"Of course."

Anna stood, watching him walk across the room, her heart heavy within her chest.

At the door, he stopped and turned and delivered his parting blow, "It did not seem that you believed there was 'nothing between us' last night when you were in my arms."

He turned and walked out the door. Anna sank down into her chair, her legs suddenly trembling too much to hold her up. She clasped her hands together in her lap and stared down at them. It shamed her to think how readily she had given in to passion last night. Reed could certainly be forgiven for thinking that she was a woman of easy virtue — to claim that she did not care for him, yet to practically swoon at his kisses.

She was still sitting in the same position a few moments later when Kit came strolling back into the room. "I saw Lord Moreland on his way out," he said cheerfully, his voice dying as he took in Anna's posture. "Oh, Anna . . ."

He strode across the room and squatted down beside her chair. "Don't worry. I know what you were thinking when Felton said that about the claws, but I am sure that you are wrong."

"Am I?" Anna looked at her brother. She glanced out the window of the drawing room toward the massive upthrust of Craydon Tor. "He could not have done such a thing. Surely not."

"Of course not."

"But if anyone knew . . ."

"No one does. No one will." He slipped his hand around hers and squeezed it reassuringly.

"No doubt you are right," she said.

"Of course I am. Now, promise me you will stop thinking about this murder."

Anna summoned up a smile for him. "All right. I will."

Despite her words, Anna could not keep from glancing out the window again. *What if they were wrong?*

Chapter Eight

Anna discovered that her promise to her brother turned out to be one more easily made than kept. She could not banish thoughts of what had happened to Estelle from her mind any more than she could stop thinking about Reed and the words they had exchanged that afternoon.

It seemed to her that she should do something, find out something, about what had happened to Estelle. She knew, as Kit had pointed out, that she could not have kept the girl from coming to harm, but still, she could not help but feel responsible for Estelle. She could not simply sit back and wash her hands of the matter. It was her duty to do what she could to help bring the girl's murderer to justice. And besides . . . there was the suspicion, the horrible thought that had sprung up in her mind at the doctor's words. She could not rest until her mind was easy on that score.

She had little idea how to go about tracking down the killer, but there was one area that she knew she could explore — the identity of the man whom Estelle had been sneaking out to meet at night.

Therefore, that evening, when she was seated in front of her vanity, as Penny took Anna's hair down from its pins and was brushing it out, Anna looked into the mirror, catching her maid's eyes in the glass.

"Penny . . . ?"

"Yes, miss?"

"Did Estelle ever talk to you about this man whom she was meeting?"

The girl's eyes welled with tears, and she quickly looked down at her task. "I should have asked her more. I feel so terrible. It's all my fault, isn't it? I should have told Mrs. Michaels what she was doin'."

"You couldn't have known," Anna assured her, reaching up and curling her hand comfortingly around Penny's. "You thought you were helping her. I will tell you something — I didn't tell on Estelle, either." She told her maid about seeing Estelle sneaking into the house one morning, and when she was through, Penny visibly relaxed, breathing out a sigh.

"Oh, miss, I'm that glad to hear you say that. Mrs. Michaels says I'm a terrible person not to have told her. She says I'm a sinner and —"

"Never mind that. I am sure that what you did was not a sin. You were trying to be a good friend to Estelle. It isn't your fault she was killed. It is the person who killed her who is to blame."

"You think it was the man she was seeing?" Penny asked. "John the footman thinks it was the Beast. He says he got her because she was out alone in the woods at night, going to meet that man."

"I don't believe in the Beast. I have never seen it. Have you?"

"No . . ."

"And if it is the sort of thing that kills people like this, don't you think it would do it more often? Or that it would kill animals the same way? But I've never heard of a farmer losing a cow or a sheep or even a dog to this creature." Anna pushed from her mind the thought of the wounded dog she had taken to Nick Perkins.

"No. I haven't, either," Penny agreed, although she did not look entirely convinced.

"Kit thinks that there was a lovers' quarrel, and he killed her, maybe even accidentally, but then he tried to make it look as if the Beast had done it, just to avert suspicion from himself."

Penny nodded. "Master Kit has always been a brainy one."

"So I thought, if we just knew more about this man she was meeting, perhaps they would be able to find him," Anna went on persuasively.

"Yes'm, but the thing is — I don't know much about him. She never told me his name. Fact is, she was dead quiet about him —" Penny sucked in a breath, looking shocked "— ooh, I didn't mean that. That's an awful expression, isn't it, miss?"

"Yes. I guess we frequently say things without thinking about them. But, Penny, if Estelle never said his name, surely she must have said something else about him — how he looked, for instance, or where he lived."

Penny frowned, concentrating, and her hands stilled on Anna's hair, the brush poised above her head. "She kept him a secret, miss, and that's the truth. I asked her about him. I was curious, like. But she wouldn't tell me anything 'cept that he was a gentleman."

"A gentleman?" Anna asked, surprised.

Penny nodded. "I was that surprised. I told her she was fibbing, but she swore it was true." She hesitated. "I think it was the way he talked and dressed. She told me he looked as fine as Master Kit, and he treated her real polite, like she was a lady."

Anna nodded. It made sense that Estelle's judgment of a man as a "gentleman" would have had more to do with his manner of speech or his way of dressing, rather than his status in life. Estelle might have labeled anyone from a lawyer's clerk to a dancing tutor as a "gentleman."

Moreover, while she had been assuming that the man lived nearby, the fact was that he could even live in a neighboring village rather than right here at Lower Fenley. He could easily have ridden a few miles from Eddlesburrow or Sedgewick to meet with Estelle. Of course, she could not imagine how Estelle would have met someone from one of those villages, given the fact that she spent all but one day every other week working here at the Manor. But, then, Anna would not have thought that the girl could have kept up secretive meetings at night for weeks on end, either. Obviously Estelle had been more resourceful than anyone had realized.

Penny had nothing else to tell her, Anna felt sure. Therefore, she would have to ask someone else. The other people who seemed most likely to know anything about Estelle's secret lover were her family. It would be expected of her to call on the family, anyway, Anna thought, to offer her condolences. She could easily ask them a few questions, as well.

The next afternoon, Anna embarked on her plan. She had just come downstairs, gloves and bonnet in hand, to have her trap brought around when there was a knock on the door and the footman opened it to reveal Lady Kyria on her doorstep.

"My lady!" Anna paused in the midst of pulling on her gloves. "What a pleasant surprise."

"I am sorry," Kyria said, glancing down at Anna's hands. "You are obviously about to go somewhere."

"Yes, I was going to drive into the village to call on Estelle's family. But I can postpone it for a bit. Won't you come in?"

"Oh, no, I wouldn't wish to make you change your plans." Kyria paused for a moment, then went on. "If you wouldn't mind, I could go with you. My carriage is already at the door, and I would like to make my condolences to the family. I did not know her, I realize, but since we are living at Winterset, it seems as though I should."

Anna understood doing one's social duty. She had spent much of her life occupied with such things. "I am sure they would be honored, my lady."

"Please, call me Kyria. I have spent the

last year in America, and I have come to like the lack of 'lady this' and 'lady that.' "

"All right. Kyria. And you must call me Anna." Anna smiled at the other woman. She liked Kyria, and she suspected that if things had happened differently between her and Reed, she and Kyria would have become good friends.

They took Kyria's open-air victoria into town, enjoying the summer day. They made a stop at the chemist first, for Kyria to pick up headache powder for Miss Farrington.

"Poor thing. I fear this killing has completely overset her," Kyria said. "But your brother has been so kind — he quite took her mind off it for a while yesterday when he came to call. I believe they are going riding this afternoon."

"Really? I did not know." Anna felt another tug of worry.

As they left the chemist's and started toward their carriage, they saw Mr. Norton standing beside the vehicle. The solicitor turned at their approach and bowed, smiling broadly. "Ah, my lady, Miss Holcomb. I thought this was your equipage, my lady. A very well-sprung vehicle, if I may say so."

"Mr. Norton." Kyria nodded toward the man.

Lawrence Norton was a thin, bony man, and though he was rather tall, hours spent hunched over books had given him a stooped appearance. Anna had never liked his obsequious manner, though she could not fault his competence, and she discovered as they talked that he was even more fawning with Kyria. After he complimented her carriage and horses, he went on to wax enthusiastic about the party she had given the other evening.

"Mrs. Norton and I were so honored to attend," he gushed. "It was most generous of you. Such a beautiful affair — the musicians were excellent, the food divine."

"Thank you, Mr. Norton," Kyria said, continuing to move toward the carriage as they talked. "I am sorry that it had such a sad ending."

"Oh, yes, terrible thing, terrible. It is awful that such a thing should spoil your visit here. I hope it will not leave you with a bad impression of Lower Fenley. Now that your brother is planning to remain here, I hope that you will return often."

Anna felt the shock of the lawyer's words all through her. *Reed was planning on living here?*

It was all she could do to maintain her composure as Kyria skillfully extricated them from the conversational tentacles of Mr. Norton. She sat down in the carriage, feeling a little breathless, and they pulled away from the curb, Norton waving after them as if they were embarking on a long journey.

"Ree— your brother is intending to live at Winterset?" Anna asked, struggling to keep her voice light. "I had thought he was planning to sell it."

Kyria looked at her. "I believe he has decided not to sell the house after all. It is such a pleasant place, don't you agree?"

"Oh, yes. Yes, it's beautiful." Anna's mouth felt dry as cotton. *What would she do if he stayed here?* She was so wrapped up in her own thoughts that she did not even notice Kyria studying her thoughtfully.

Somewhat numbly, Anna directed the coachman to the house in the village where Estelle's family lived. Fortunately Kyria did not talk much as they drove or Anna would have had trouble following the conversation, for her mind was racing, considering the prospect of Reed living at Winterset.

When they reached the Akins' house, Anna forced herself to put Reed out of her mind for the moment and went inside to talk to the grieving parents. She and Kyria visited with the family at some length, expressing their regret and sympathy, and listening to Mrs. Akins explain what a good girl her Estelle had been.

When Anna asked if they had known the man whom Estelle had been seeing, Mrs. Akins fired up, saying, "She wasn't like what that Mrs. Michaels is saying. She wasn't seein' no man — I don't care what that woman says. Estelle wouldn't 'a' been sneaking out like that."

Anna nodded and murmured something consoling. Clearly she would not be getting any information about the man from Estelle's family. However, as they were leaving the cottage, Estelle's next-oldest sister caught up with them. "Miss?"

Anna turned, and the girl slipped out of the door, closing it behind her. "I wanted to ask you — when you asked about that man?"

Anna nodded. "Yes?"

"It could be him what killed her, couldn't it?"

"It might be, yes."

The girl nodded. "She was seeing someone, no matter what me mum thinks. Stell told me she was."

"Did she say anything about him? His name? What he looked like?"

The girl shook her head. "Not much. She

just said he was goin' to change her life, like. She said she wouldn't be cleanin' houses forever. But she wouldn't say who he was, even when I teased her."

Anna asked the girl a few more questions, but she could learn nothing more from her. The girl went back inside the house, and Anna and Kyria strolled out to the carriage.

"She was certainly secretive about this man, wasn't she?" Kyria commented.

"Yes. She told my maid that he was a 'gentleman,' though what that meant in Estelle's estimation, I'm not sure. However, she refused to tell Penny — who was, I think, her best friend — what his name was or, really, anything about him. I am not even positive that he was from Lower Fenley. He could have ridden over a few nights a week from a nearby village."

"Still, it makes one think that he must be from around here. Else why would she be so determined to keep him a secret? I would think it must be because he was someone her family or her friends would know."

Anna looked at Kyria. "It gives one the shivers, doesn't it? What if he *is* the one who killed her? What if it is someone we know?"

As they stepped up into the carriage, Anna turned and looked down the street. A horseman was riding toward them. Her throat tightened.

"Reed!" Kyria exclaimed.

He pulled up for a moment, then urged his horse forward, coming to a stop beside their carriage. "Ladies." He swept off his hat. His eyes went over to Anna. She could not read his expression.

"Have you come to pay a sympathy call, too?" Kyria asked. "I did not know you were riding here."

"I did not know you were, either," he responded.

"Yes, I happened to catch Anna as she was leaving, so I came along."

"Stay here," he told them. "I will be back. I want to talk to you." Again his eyes slid toward Anna.

He dismounted, handing the reins of his horse to the coachman, who had jumped down to take them. Kyria heaved a sigh.

"Well, if that isn't just like him," Kyria said. "He's always been inordinately bossy. Much worse than Theo, and he's the oldest. I've half a mind to tell Henry to tie Reed's horse to that tree and drive on." She shrugged. "Of course, he'd just catch up with us later, so it's hardly worth the trouble."

Anna nodded. The way he had looked at

her, she couldn't help but think it was she to whom he wanted to talk. She would have liked very much to leave, but she could scarcely tell Kyria that she wanted to flee her brother.

"How are Con and Alex?" Anna asked, to make conversation.

"As rambunctious as ever. Of course, they are morbidly interested in this killing. They want to investigate, but Reed put his foot down about that. Told them they are not to leave the house and gardens without a groom along. So they have been having to create what deviltry they can within the confines of the house and yard. Of course, they are up to the task. They've tied a rope to the railing on the second-floor landing and have been climbing up and down it. It frightened a maid so badly she dropped a load of dishes, the first time Alex came swinging over the side."

Anna chuckled. "I shall have to come and take them to Nick's again to see the dog they found. They seemed to enjoy that last time."

"Oh, my, yes, they revere your Mr. Perkins. They would love to go again, I'm sure. But only if you don't mind — I wouldn't want them to be a bother to you."

"They are no bother," Anna assured her. "I had an excessively good time with them both times we were out. They are lively, intelligent boys."

Kyria smiled at her, pleased at her assessment. "I quite agree. Not everyone is so understanding, I'm afraid." She looked past Anna at the Akins' house. "Ah, there is Reed. I wonder what it is he's wanting to say. He has been grim all day."

His grimness was unabated, Anna thought, as she watched him approach the carriage. His face was set in stern lines; his gray eyes were unreadable.

"Miss Holcomb," he said without preamble, "will you walk with me? I — I wish to speak to you."

Dread gathered in Anna's stomach. She had no desire to talk to him, but she could see no way out of it, not when she was sitting in his sister's carriage. She glanced at Kyria. The other woman's face was alight with curiosity, but she could see no sign that Kyria knew what Reed's intent was.

"Of course," Anna said, climbing down from the carriage. She took his hand to help her down the step, but withdrew it as soon as her feet were on the ground. She looked up at him, her chin lifted a little defiantly. He gestured toward the street in front of him, saying, "I would offer you my arm, but I have the feeling you would not take it."

Anna swept past him, holding her skirt up a trifle to save it from the dirt of the road. When they were far enough away that their words could not be heard, she began crisply, feeling it was better to attack than to wait for whatever he intended, "Lord Moreland, if you intend to lecture me again, let me —"

"No, no, I assure you. I have no intention of lecturing. I — I did not mean to yesterday. I wanted to talk to you because I wanted to apologize for what I said to you. I was . . . unkind."

Anna glanced at him, surprised.

"Please, do not look so amazed," he said, half smiling. "You will make me think I must seem the veriest ogre."

"No. I just — it is an awkward situation."

"I was concerned for your safety. You are correct in saying that I have no right to be. Whatever I thought we once had, it is, of course, long over. I did not really mean to assume any rights. It is just that I —" He sighed and looked off into the distance. "I don't know how to put this without you thinking that I have run mad. But I did not want you to think that I am arbitrarily meddling in your affairs."

Anna looked at him, curious now. "What are you saying?"

"Not long ago, I — I dreamed about you."

Anna felt a blush rising in her cheeks, and she looked down at the ground. She, too, had had dreams about Reed, ones that left her crying and bereft, and others that she awoke from in a hot daze of passion.

"It was not the first time — I will not pretend that," Reed went on. "But it was the first time in a long time, and it was . . . different. It left me afraid."

Anna glanced at him, startled. "Afraid? What do you mean?"

"I dreamed that you were in trouble, that you were calling out to me for help." He looked at her ruefully. "I realize how absurd it sounds — to place so much importance on a dream. But it was a different sort of dream from any I have ever had. It was so vivid, so . . . intense. I could not help but feel that it meant something."

"That I am in trouble?" Anna asked, still staring at him.

"Yes." He turned to face her, his face set as if he were facing a firing squad.

"You dreamed this before you came to Winterset?"

He grimaced, his gaze flickering away from her. "Yes. It is why I even thought to come here. I did not know what was wrong. I could not write such gibberish to you. All I could think was to come here and see what was the matter."

Anna's heart warmed inside her chest. Despite the way she had hurt him, despite what he had said yesterday, when he had thought she was in danger, he had ridden to help her. Tears threatened to flood her eyes, and she glanced away to hide them.

"I am sure you are now convinced that I am mad," Reed added, his voice rough. "No one but a fool would believe in dream portents. But I cannot help but believe it is true. I felt it so strongly. I cannot tell you why I was so sure, I can only say that I knew — without a doubt. There are things that cannot be explained away rationally. I have seen things, learned things, in the past few years that defy logic."

"I do not think you are mad," Anna said, looking up at him seriously.

"What?" He looked surprised, his brows rising slightly. "Then you believe that I was right?"

"I believe that you felt it. That you believe it. As to whether or not it is true — I do not know. I don't know if I believe that dreams and . . . and visions are the truth. I do not know of any trouble that I am in. But the other day . . ." She hesitated. She had never told anyone about the "visions" that she had experienced all her life. Even after what Reed had told her, she felt a flutter of fear in her chest at the thought of exposing her oddity to him.

Finally she said, "The day when I met your brothers, when I was walking through the woods, I was suddenly struck by a — a feeling I can hardly describe. A feeling of pain and fear so sharp it made me nearly sick. And I was cold, so cold. . . . In my mind I saw the place where I was, but at night, and I felt this pain."

"My God, Anna." Instinctively Reed reached out and took her hand. "What was it?"

She shook her head, her fingers curling around his. "I do not know. There was nothing there, and in a moment it passed. I did not know what it meant. But that evening, when I heard that Estelle was missing, I thought of that moment in the woods, of what I had felt, and somehow I — I connected it with her." Anna paused, collecting her thoughts, and looked down, realizing suddenly that Reed was holding her hand.

Hastily she let go of his hand, a blush starting on her cheeks. Reed glanced at her but said nothing about her gesture.

"I have no reason for thinking so," she went on a little stiffly. "Her body was found somewhere far from there. The time when I felt it was not when she was found, and I doubt that it was when she was killed, either. I would think that happened the night before, when she went missing. I suppose, if the feeling actually meant anything, it was perhaps connected to that dog the twins found and what happened to him. But it was because of my 'feeling' in the woods that I had the servants look for her, that I could not quite believe she had simply left with a man."

"And you were right."

"I suppose. I did not know that that was what my . . . vision meant. I still do not. But I — I could not ignore it, either. As you said, I felt it meant something."

Reed frowned. "I have no idea what either of our 'omens' means, but it worries me."

Anna attempted a little laugh. "Yes, it rather concerns me, as well. I can tell you I would prefer not to feel that sensation again."

"I, too, would rather you did not suffer it," Reed agreed. He caught himself, then said, "I would not want anyone to feel it. But more than that, I am concerned about what will happen if this thing you felt, what I dreamed, are actually presaging something worse to come — something that will involve you."

"Stop. You will frighten me."

"I would like to," Reed told her. "I want you to take a care for yourself."

"I will. You need not worry about me."

Reed looked as if he would like to say something else, but he merely sighed and glanced back to where his sister sat waiting for them in her carriage. "And, please, I beg you, do not let Kyria lead you into doing anything rash."

Anna chuckled. "What an unkind thing to say about your own flesh and blood."

"I say it because I know her," he retorted, but he smiled. He turned back toward the vehicle, offering Anna his arm. She hesitated for a moment, then slipped her hand into the crook of his elbow. It felt very comfortable, very natural, to walk with him this way. Indeed, she thought, it felt almost too good. She reminded herself that she must keep her guard up with Reed.

As they walked back to the carriage, Reed said, "I know that we have exchanged some harsh words. And the past makes it difficult. But I would like, if I could, to be a friend to you. I do not mean to try to rekindle what we — what I *thought* we once had. But I have been thinking about not selling the house and instead living here at least part of the year. I would like for the situation not to be . . . awkward."

"I — I see." So he *was* going to stay! Anna felt a little breathless at the thought.

"Can we put the past aside and agree to be — well, not friends, perhaps, but at least good acquaintances? People who are able to meet on occasion and to speak without drawing swords?"

"I do not wish to fight with you," Anna replied carefully. She did not think it was possible for her to forget her past with Reed. Nor was she sure that she could be around him with any degree of equanimity. But she could scarcely explain to him that his presence made everything inside her start to tingle. "I would hope that we can be civil."

"Good. I am glad to hear you say that." They had by this time reached the carriage, and Reed extended his hand to help Anna up into it. He smiled up at his sister and Anna. "Now, if you ladies would allow me, I should be happy to escort you home."

Reed was, Anna admitted, the perfect picture of the casual acquaintance as he rode beside them to her house. He talked to her and Kyria equally, his manner friendly but somewhat distant when he spoke to her. And she found it frankly irritating. She could not help but wonder how he found it so easy to act as if they had only recently met, as if nothing had ever passed between them, when she found herself tongue-tied and awkward. It was enough to make her wonder if only she had felt the surge of passion when they kissed the other night. Perhaps it was nothing but her own lack of experience that had made the moment seem so important, while Reed — more experienced — had merely found it a bit of passing pleasure.

The idea left her feeling perversely disgruntled when she arrived home. It was for that reason, perhaps, that her voice was sharper than she intended when she ran into her brother on the way up the stairs and he told her that he had just come back from riding.

"You went riding with Miss Farrington?" she asked.

Kit glanced at her, his eyebrow lifting. "Yes. Why?"

Anna sighed. "Kit . . . you paid a call on her yesterday, then there was the party, and now you go riding?"

His jaw tightened. "Yes. What of it? Are you keeping an account of my coming and goings?"

"No, of course not. But it scarcely seems wise —"

"Wise? No, perhaps it is not wise. I am not sure that I can be eternally wise. Mayhap you can always put your head above your heart, but I cannot!"

"Kit! Are you saying — are your feelings engaged?" Anna's hand went unconsciously to her stomach, where a feeling of dread was coiling. "Are you coming to care her?"

He glanced around. "This is scarcely the time or place to discuss this."

He started down the stairs, and Anna turned and followed him. In the hall below, she took his arm and steered him into the drawing room, closing the door behind them.

"All right," she said, facing him. "Let us discuss it now. Are you . . . falling in love with Miss Farrington?"

"No. Perhaps. I do not know," Kit said, flinging up his arms. "I like her. I like being around her. Is it so much to ask to spend some time with an attractive woman?"

"No, of course it is not too much." Anna's heart went out to her brother, and she took a step toward him, her face filled with sympathy. "It is exactly what you should have."

"Yet it is exactly what I *cannot* have," Kit snapped, and whirled away. "Don't you think I know that it is impossible?"

"Oh, Kit . . ." Anna felt tears start in her eyes. "I am sorry. I should not have questioned you. I don't mean to be overbearing.

I am not your watchdog. It is just — I hate to see you get your heart broken," she finished, her voice dropping almost to a whisper.

"Like yours was?" Kit asked, turning back to her.

Anna froze. "I don't know what you mean."

"Come now, Anna. I am not a fool. It is pointless to try to pretend with me. I have known you for twenty-four years, you know. I may not have been here when it happened, but that doesn't mean I haven't figured it out. I saw the two of you dancing together the other night, and I also saw how you avoided him the rest of the evening."

Anna could think of nothing to say. She sat down on a chair, suddenly weary.

"Don't you ever just want to forget it all?" Kit asked, his voice filled with emotion. "Don't you want to say, 'The devil with my duty' and just grab for your own happiness? God knows, I do."

"We cannot," Anna said. "You know we cannot."

"No, I don't know!" Kit flashed back. "I don't want to live this way forever. Do you? Are you satisfied with half a life?"

"Of course not!" Anna retorted. "Of course I want more. That doesn't mean that I can have it."

"But you can!"

"Yes, if I ignore what is right! If I think only of myself!" Anna jumped to her feet, facing her brother. "I know that is not your way any more than it is mine."

"But what is life worth if one can never know love and happiness?" Kit shot back. "What is the point?"

"There are also honor and duty!" Anna exclaimed. "There is the satisfaction of doing what one knows is right."

"And is that really enough?"

"Sometimes it has to be," Anna told him, her voice tinged with sorrow.

"I don't know if it is for me," Kit said, then turned on his heel and stalked out the door.

The young man walked across the footbridge, his hands in his pockets. He was whistling. He was eighteen years old, and it had been a good evening. He had spent it in the tavern, laughing and talking with his cronies, and the girl who brought him his drinks had smiled at him with what he definitely thought was an invitation in her eyes. Maybe next time he would stay until closing, and he would talk to her afterward, offer to walk her home. . . .

But tonight he had to get home. It was

summer, and tomorrow would be a full day in the fields. Pops would have his hide if he stayed out to the wee hours and came home with a snootful. He didn't care about the drinking, of course; it was his shirking at work the next day because his head ached and his eyes felt as swollen and red as tomatoes.

He staggered a little as he stepped off the footbridge, and he had to grab for the rail. He snickered at his tipsy state, thinking that perhaps he hadn't left early enough.

Picking up his tune again, he walked into the stand of trees beyond the footbridge. As he entered the trees, he heard a sound and turned, looking behind him. He could see nothing in the darkness, made deeper by the trees now spreading above him. The moon was no longer full, as it had been the other night, when Estelle Akins had met her death.

A little shiver ran through him as he thought about her. He didn't know her, but it seemed a shame that anyone had to die like that. He'd heard it had been the Beast, back again after all these years, thirsty for blood.

Of course, he told himself, he wasn't in any danger, not a healthy, strapping farm lad. He could take care of himself. Still . . . he would be glad when he got through the trees and reached the edge of his father's farm on the other side. It wouldn't be long. It wasn't as if these were the deep woods.

There was a snap behind, and he started to whirl around just as something slammed into him from behind, knocking him to the ground. His fall knocked the breath out of him, and it was a struggle even to draw air. Something hard rapped against his skull, and pain exploded in his head.

Chapter Nine

Anna walked briskly along the path, Con and Alex Moreland on either side of her. She had driven over to Winterset this morning in the trap, but it was far easier and less roundabout to walk to Nick Perkins' cottage than it was to drive a vehicle, so she and the boys had set out on foot from their house.

They were full of questions, as they always were, asking about this plant or that, and regaling her with stories of the plants and animals that their brother Theo had seen in his travels.

"Do you think that Perkins will let us bring the dog home with us today?" Alex asked as they drew near the footbridge over the stream.

"We'd take very good care of it," Con added. "We could change his bandages and put on ointment and everything."

"I don't know." Anna smiled at them. "I suppose it will depend on how well the dog is doing. He may not be well enough to be moved, you know."

They reached the footbridge, and the

boys stopped to look over the sides at the stream below it. Anna dawdled a little bit, too, gazing down at the clear water tumbling over the stones. As she reached the end of the footbridge and stepped off, she felt faintly uneasy. She glanced around, not sure why she felt that way. The feeling grew as she took a few more steps, and she paused, her hand going to her stomach.

"Miss Holcomb?"

"Are you all right?"

The twins' voices came to her as if from a distance, and there was an odd buzzing in her head. She was afraid she was about to faint, and she started toward a large rock just off the path ahead, under one of the trees. But before she could reach it, a wave of pain and fear slammed into her, and she stopped, almost doubling over.

"Miss!" The boys were beside her in an instant, taking her arms and guiding her over to the rock.

In her head it was night, and she could see the rock, paler than the dark around it. She could see the trees and hear the rustle of their leaves. Her mind was muddled except for the fierce welling of panic in her chest. And suddenly the ground was coming up at her, and she was falling, and then there was a burst of terror inside her.

"The Beast," she murmured.

"What?" Con bent closer to her. "What did you say?"

Anna raised her head. The "vision" was gone, and the pain was receding, leaving her sick and shaken.

"Are you all right? Are you ill?" Alex, too, leaned down to look in her face. "One of us can go back to the house and get Reed or Rafe to take you back to Winterset."

"I — just give me a moment. I'll be all right, I think."

"Are you sure?" Alex straightened and looked around him. Suddenly he stiffened, and he made a strangled noise.

Con and Anna turned toward him and saw him staring ahead. They followed his eyes and saw a man lying just to the side of the path. Anna drew in her breath sharply, her hand flying to her mouth. Con and Alex started forward, and Anna let out a sharp cry.

"Wait! No, I don't think you should —" she began, but the boys were already gone.

She jumped up and hurried after them. They stopped abruptly beside the body, and Anna almost stumbled into them. For a long moment all three of them stared at the body of the man lying before them. He lay on his back, his arms and legs splayed. He was young, barely a man, and his bright blond hair spread like a fan around his head. His eyes were open and staring lifelessly up at the leaves above him. His shirt was torn across the front and arms, revealing long scratches.

There was blood everywhere — his hair, the raw, gaping wound of his throat, spilling all over his chest and arms and onto the ground around him. It was dark and sticky, pooled in some places, and the stench of it was everywhere, filling the air.

Anna stumbled back, pressing her hand tightly to her mouth. Con and Alex turned toward her, their eyes huge in their white faces. They stared at her for a moment; then suddenly Alex turned and ran a few steps away, falling to his knees and retching. Con came over to where Anna stood and sat down abruptly on the path, pulling his knees up and bracing his elbows on them, and dropping his head to his hands.

Anna swallowed hard, willing herself not to give in to the nausea that washed over her. She had to be strong, she told herself. She had to take care of the twins. But her legs were trembling so much, she thought it was a wonder she was even able to stand up.

She leaned over Con. "Let's go back to that rock. All right?"

He nodded, and she gave him a hand to help pull him up. They went over first to Alex, who had stood back up and wiped his mouth. He looked at Anna shamefacedly.

"I'm sorry, miss."

"Nonsense. I feel the same way myself," Anna assured him, putting a hand on each boy's shoulder. "Let's sit down for a moment and collect ourselves."

They walked back to the rock and sat down, the boys dropping onto the ground at Anna's feet. They were silent, their eyes turning back now and again to the body that lay a few yards from them.

"What happened to him?" Alex asked at last.

"I don't know," Anna said.

"The Beast. That's what all the servants are saying killed that girl," Con said.

"That's just a story," Alex said scornfully, but his mouth trembled a little as he looked back at the body.

"It certainly looked as if an animal attacked him," Anna admitted. "But my suspicion is that it was a person."

"The same man who killed the girl?" Con asked.

"It seems likely."

"We had better tell Reed," Alex said, looking up at her.

"Yes, we had," Anna agreed. "Can you boys run back to the house and get him? I — I think I should stay here with . . ." Her voice trailed off, and she turned to look again at the body.

Con and Alex looked at each other.

"We shouldn't leave you alone," Alex said doubtfully.

"I'll be all right," she assured him. "That poor man cannot hurt me, and I am sure that whoever or whatever killed him is no longer around."

"It doesn't seem right." Con and Alex looked at each other again, and then Con said, "Alex can go, and I will stay with you."

"No, I don't want one of you alone," Anna said immediately.

"But you said that he was long gone."

"Yes, I imagine, but . . ."

The boys, however, had made up their minds, and they were, apparently, as stubborn as their brother. In the end, Anna agreed, and Con dropped down beside her, while Alex started off at a trot across the footbridge.

Anna leaned down and put her hand on Con's shoulder. "Thank you for staying with me. It was very kind of you."

"We could not leave you here by yourself," Con told her gravely. "It is not the sort of thing a gentleman would do."

Anna smiled. "I think that you and Alex are very fine gentlemen."

Con gave her a smile that held a glimpse of his normal cheeky grin. "Not according to most of our tutors."

"Then they are not very discerning men."

"That is what Kyria says."

They were silent for a moment, and Anna saw Con's eyes drift over toward the body. To keep his mind off it, Anna asked, "How did you two decide that it was Alex who should go? I did not see you discuss it."

Con shrugged. "We didn't have to discuss it. We just . . . knew. I always know what Alex thinks."

"And he knows what you think? It must be nice to have that sort of communication with another person."

"I don't know. Makes it hard to play a trick on him," Con pointed out practically.

"Yes, I can see how that would be."

Anna kept the conversation going in order to keep both their minds from returning to what lay only a few yards away from them. They talked about tutors and governesses, and Anna soon had a good idea of the educational views of the boys' mother, the duchess of Broughton.

She did not know how long it had been when she heard a noise. She whipped around, her heart pounding, and saw Reed running toward them.

"Reed!" She jumped to her feet, and Con leaped up and ran toward his brother, meeting him just this side of the footbridge.

Reed lifted Con up, giving him a hug, then set him down and hurried on toward Anna. His arms opened as he neared her, and, without giving it a thought, Anna rushed into them, throwing her arms around his chest and holding on for dear life. Suddenly, after all the time that had passed since they reached the body, she found herself crying.

Reed held her close, stroking her back and murmuring soft words of sympathy. The meaning of them scarcely registered with Anna, only the feeling of comfort. She had no idea how long they stood that way. She was aware only of the strength and warmth of his body against hers, enfolding her, protecting, comforting. . . . She felt his lips press against her hair and heard the murmur of her name.

There was the sound of a horse's hooves, then splashing as it crossed the stream. Reluctantly, Anna and Reed pulled away and turned to face the arrival.

It was Rafe McIntyre. He pulled to a stop and dismounted, and Anna saw that he wore a belt with a holster into which a pistol had been thrust. After tying his horse to a low branch, he strode over to them.

"Kyria sent a groom with a message to the doctor and the constable. I reckon they'll be here pretty soon." He tipped his hat to Anna. "Ma'am. Con." He ruffled the boy's hair and pulled him against his side for a brief, hard hug. "You all right, son?"

Con nodded. Rafe gave his back a pat and nodded toward the body. "I'll go take a look."

Anna made a sound of dismay, reaching out her hand toward him and shaking her head. Rafe paused and gave her a faint smile. But she could see in his eyes something she had not noticed before, something hard and world-weary.

"Don't worry, ma'am," he told her. "I've seen a good many of them before now."

He turned and walked over to the body, leaning over it, then carefully dropping down on one knee beside it.

Reed turned to Anna. She wished that his arms were still around her, but she pushed down the treacherous thought.

"Did you recognize him?" Reed asked.

"I don't know his name. I think — I think it is one of the Johnsons. There are several cousins. Their fathers are farmers." She looked away, feeling again the queasiness she had experienced when she looked at the body. "The way he looked — I am not sure I would have recognized him even if I had known him well."

"Don't think about it," Reed advised, taking her arm gently. "Just let it go."

"I'm not sure I can." Anna passed a shaky hand across her forehead. "I fear that I shall be seeing . . . that whenever I close my eyes. Oh, Reed, I so hate it that the boys saw him." She looked over at Con, who had wandered back to the footbridge and was sitting, gazing down at the water.

"There was nothing you could do," Reed told her. "I will talk to both the boys. And Rafe will, as well." He glanced toward the other man, who had finished looking over the body and was walking back toward them. "Rafe was in the war in America. He has seen worse things than I can even imagine. He will help them."

Reed turned toward Rafe inquiringly as he reached them. "What did you find?"

"There'll be a hell of a lot more talk about your 'Beast,' " the other man said dryly.

"It looks like an animal attack?"

Rafe shrugged. "That's what it's set up to look like. But the only animal involved here is a man."

"Are you sure?" Anna asked.

"Those aren't the marks of any animal I know. Only thing that big is a bear paw, and I don't think you have many bears lurking around here. Besides, he was laid out there. It looks . . . staged, like he was arranged this way for someone to find. To see."

"But why?" Anna asked.

"Now, that, ma'am, I don't know. People do things that surpass all comprehension, I've found." He turned to Reed. "I'll stay here while you take Miss Holcomb and Con back to the house."

Reed nodded. "Yes. Thank you. I will return as soon as possible."

He took Anna's arm, and they started toward the footbridge. "I should have ridden over, as Rafe did, I suppose. That way I could have brought you a mount. After what you experienced, I am sure you are very tired."

"My knees are a trifle shaky," Anna admitted, summoning up a faint smile. "Oh, Reed! That poor boy! His poor parents. It doesn't bear thinking of."

"No."

They joined Con at the footbridge and crossed it, heading back to Winterset. It seemed a much longer way returning than it had been walking over that morning. Anna was glad for the support of Reed's arm.

When they reached Winterset, Reed led them inside and up the stairs to Kyria's sitting room, where she and Miss Farrington were sitting with Alex, anxiously awaiting their arrival.

"Anna!" Kyria cried when Anna and Reed walked into the room, and she jumped up to rush over and enfold Anna in her arms. "You poor dear. Come sit down with us. I'll ring for some tea, shall I? And then perhaps you would like to lie down."

"Take good care of her, Kyria," Reed said. "I am going back to wait with Rafe. Send the constable and the doctor on as soon as they come."

"I will," Kyria promised, looping an arm around Anna and guiding her over to the sofa.

Reed followed, and when Anna was seated, he bent down to take her hand. Anna's fingers curled around his tightly as she realized how much she did not want him to leave.

He smiled into her eyes, giving her hand a squeeze. "Let Kyria cosset you for a while. I will return as soon as I can. Try to put it out of your mind."

Reed left, and Anna did as he suggested, letting Kyria and Miss Farrington fuss over her, arranging pillows around her on the couch so that she was comfortable and plying her with tea. Alex and Con retreated to their room. The boys would, Kyria explained to Anna and Rosemary, handle what had happened to them as they did everything — together.

Kyria thought Anna should lie down, but Anna did not think she could sleep, and, frankly, she was reluctant to close her eyes, for she knew that the image of the dead boy would come flooding back. Miss Farrington read aloud from *The Moonstone*, but Anna found it difficult to concentrate on the story. She kept waiting for the sound of Reed's return.

The constable and Dr. Felton arrived, and Anna, more familiar with the area than Kyria, directed them to where Reed and Rafe waited for them. After they left, Rosemary once more gamely took up reading. She was, Anna thought, really a sweet girl. She could see why Kit was drawn to her. *If only things were different . . .*

Time crawled on, and tea had long been served before the men came back to the house. They had little new to say. The doctor had confirmed that the wounds were very similar to those on Estelle Akins' body, and the constable had recognized the victim as Frank Johnson, whose father's farm lay not far from the footbridge where they had found the boy's body. The constable had seen him, in fact, in the tavern only the evening before. He had apparently been walking home from the tavern when the killer had struck.

When tea was over, Reed drove Anna back to Holcomb Manor in the trap she had driven over in, his own horse tied to the back. They sat side by side, the trap small enough that his arm pressed against hers, and Anna found it comforting to have him next to her, large and solid. They said little, for which Anna felt grateful. She was still too shocked by the events of the day to talk much. It was soothing to feel the fading glow of the summer sun on her skin, to have her cheek brushed by a stray breeze, to soak in the familiar beauty of the land and the slowly setting sun.

When they reached the Manor, Reed walked her to the door, and she found herself slipping her hand into the crook of his arm as if it were the most natural thing to do. He covered her hand with his own for a moment.

"Will you be all right? Is your brother here?" He looked down into her face, his own brow knotted in concern.

Anna nodded, smiling at him reassuringly. "Yes, I shall be fine. I imagine Kit is here, and, if not, there is a whole houseful of servants. I will be perfectly all right."

They stood for a moment, looking at each other, and Anna thought that he was going to lean down and kiss her, and she was not sure what she would do. She was so tired and heartsore, and it seemed too great an effort to erect her customary barrier between them. But just then the door was opened by one of the Holcomb footmen, and the moment was gone.

Reed bowed over her hand and went back down the steps to his horse, and Anna went inside. She found Kit in his study, going over some papers, and he looked up at her entrance with a smile.

"Ah, thank heavens. I hope you have come to save me from an accounting of the farm rents."

"No. I —" Tears sprang into Anna's eyes, surprising her almost as much as her brother.

"Anna! What is it?" Kit rose and moved around the side of his desk to her.

"Someone else has been killed," she told him tersely.

"What!" Kit took hold of her arms. "Are you sure?"

"Yes. I — I found him."

He stared at her, stunned, as she described to him how she and the twins had stumbled upon the body just beyond the footbridge, leaving out the feeling of cold pain and terror that had swept her just before they saw the body. She had never told even Kit about her visions.

"My God," he said weakly when she had finished, his hands dropping from her arms. "What is happening here?"

"He was marked as Estelle was," Anna went on. "Dr. Felton said so, and I saw it. It was horrible — as if some large animal had torn at him. His throat —" She stopped and swallowed, unable to describe what she had seen.

Kit turned and looked at her, his eyes narrowing. "What are you saying?"

"I cannot help but wonder . . ."

"No!" Kit told her sternly. "I know what you are thinking, but it isn't true. It's impossible. How can you even wonder? He would never —"

"Are you so sure?" Anna asked, her eyes searching her brother's face. "I am not."

"It cannot be," Kit reiterated, but his eyes fell from her face. He stood for a moment, staring down at the carpet as if it held some secret. "All right," he said finally. "We will go up there tomorrow. Will that help you?"

"Yes," Anna replied. "I think we have to."

They set out the next morning not long after breakfast, walking through their garden and along the path that wound back into the woods. Anna avoided the path that led to the spot where she had experienced the chilling pain the other day as they walked deeper into the trees. The land began to rise as they approached Craydon Tor. On the far side of the tor, the land dropped in a sheer cliff face down to the ground below, offering a clear view of the countryside for miles. On that side it was a towering edifice, looming over everything else.

On this side, it was a gradual rise, thick with trees and bushes, climbing, then leveling out a little, then climbing again. Because of the thick woods, it was not a particularly popular place to walk, and even those who did climb the tor stuck to the marked path.

Kit and Anna, however, veered off the path, going deeper into the forest, winding around trees and stones. After a time, they reached a line of stones that seemed to curve in a large circle, disappearing at either end into the underbrush. Stepping over the stones, they continued, grasping at branches of trees and saplings to help them up the steeper parts. They went around an outcropping of rock and came upon a narrow path. It led them up toward the side of the tor, and though the ground there was still a slope that was easily enough traversed, ahead of them the hill became a sheer rock face.

There, against the rock, was nestled a small, dark hut, barely distinguishable from the trees and bushes around it. A man sat on a stool in front of the small house, whittling away at a piece of wood in his hand. There was a small fire built in front of him, and over the fire hung an iron pot. A semicircle of rocks, much like the ones they had already passed, ran in front of the hut and around to the cliff face on either side of the house.

Almost unnoticed at first, another man lay rolled up in a blanket beneath one of the trees, a wooden marker stuck into the ground at his feet, another at his head. A twig cracked under Kit's feet as they approached, and the sleeping man sat straight up, staring at them wildly.

"It's all right, sir." The other man, too, had looked up and seen them, and he stood up and walked toward Anna and Kit. "Master Kit, Miss Anna. It's good to see you."

"Hello, Arthur," Kit replied to the man

walking toward them. He and Anna stepped over the line of stones and walked closer, their steps slow, their demeanor calm.

The man who had been sleeping rose to his feet, glancing back at Arthur Bradbury, then again at Kit and Anna. He was a man of medium height, dressed in a simple cotton shirt and serge jacket and trousers, and his feet were bare. His hair, a brown color mixed with gray, was bushy and long, hanging below his shoulders. The lower half of his face was covered with an equally long beard, much more streaked with white than the hair on his head. His face was smudged, a dark streak across his brow and one more on each of his cheeks above his beard. His eyes were light-colored, and they did not stay on Kit and Anna, but kept flickering from them to the ground beside him, then back to them.

He raised one hand toward them, palm out, as if to stop them, and they came to a halt. On his upraised hand, the fingernails were bizarrely long, curving down at the ends, so that they resembled claws. The fingernails on his other hand were the same, though one had been broken off shorter than the others. His feet, if one looked down, had nails that grew out from his toes at a much greater length than normal.

"I know you," he said finally.

"Yes, you do," Kit said.

He nodded slowly. "Hello."

"Hello, Uncle Charles," Anna and Kit replied.

Chapter Ten

Their uncle nodded again, a short, decisive nod, then did it twice more. "How are you? Are you well?" he asked, his polished voice at odds with his rough clothes and bizarre appearance.

"We are," Kit replied. He and Anna carefully did not move any closer to their uncle. Uncle Charles disliked anyone standing too close to him. "How are you?"

"I'm fine," Charles de Winter replied. "I am looking out for her. I am careful. You know that."

"Yes, we do," Anna agreed. "You are always very careful."

His gaze skittered to her, then away again. Anna was accustomed to it. Her uncle did not like to look anyone in the eye, either. "One has to be," he said firmly. "She has spies everywhere. They are always trying to find me." He gave them a quick, crafty smile. "I have outfoxed her, though."

He gestured toward the stones encircling the hut, then patted one of the slats of wood that stood where he had lain. Things that looked like letters in some foreign tongue — Arabic, perhaps, or something like it — decorated the marker, running in a row downward. Anna knew that the other wooden slat was decorated on the far side with similar figures. What they said, she had no idea. All she knew was that her uncle insisted on sleeping between the two markers, feeling that they kept him safe.

She and Kit, like nearly everyone else who lived in the area, had thought that her mother's brother had sailed to Barbados ten years earlier. It had not been until three years ago that her father had finally taken her aside and told her the truth. Her uncle was mad.

Anna could remember clearly the day her father had told her. It had been the day all her dreams had died.

Arthur had reached them by now, and he swept off his cap, bobbing his head first toward Kit, then to Anna. "We're that pleased to see you, aren't we, my lord?"

"Yes, General. But I —" Charles cast a worried glance at the ground where he had been sleeping. "It is time for my rest." He looked back at his niece and nephew, then over at a point a little to the right of them. "It is important. You know I have to stand guard at night. That is when they are most likely to come."

Kit nodded. "We know, Uncle Charles. Don't worry. Go ahead and sleep. We'll just talk to Arthur for a while."

Their uncle looked a little doubtful as he glanced at his servant, but Arthur nodded reassuringly, saying, "I'll keep watch, my lord. Master Kit and Miss Anna will help me look."

"Yes. All right. But I'm not sure they'll know what to look for."

"I'll tell 'em. Don't you worry yourself, sir. We'll keep a good lookout, and it's daytime, after all."

"Yes. You're right, of course. And I have my protection." Charles de Winter showed them the backs of his hands, where more of the unreadable figures were drawn in charcoal. "I changed them, you see. Much better than the old ones. Gabriel told me."

"Good. I'm glad." Anna nodded and smiled. It was the easiest course to take with her uncle.

They walked with Arthur back up to the front of the hut, and Arthur dragged out two straight-backed chairs from inside for Anna and Kit to sit in.

"How is he doing?" Kit asked Arthur, nodding toward his uncle, who was now wrapping himself carefully in his blanket and lying down between the markers.

"He has his good days and his bad days," Arthur said noncommittally. He had looked after Lord de Winter from the time Charles was a child, separated from him only when Charles had gone off to school. Many another young man would not have taken Arthur on as his valet when he returned from Oxford, for he was rougher in manner and speech than most valets, but Charles had wanted no other manservant. Arthur, for his part, was intensely loyal to Charles. Anna knew that only a deep affection could have made anyone willing to take on the sort of life he had in order to care for her uncle.

"How has he been the last two or three days?" Anna asked.

Arthur looked at her, faintly surprised. "Same as ever, miss." He nodded toward where Charles lay. "He's been fairly quiet, just drawing them designs on his hands. He's happy, thinks they'll keep him safer."

"At night — does he stay here?" Kit asked.

Arthur drew back, studying them, a frown starting. "Why are you asking all these questions? What's the matter?"

"We just want to make sure that Uncle

Charles hasn't gone anywhere the last few nights. That he has been here."

" 'Course he's been here. Where else would he go? He spends most nights right here outside the hut or up in one of the trees, keeping watch to make sure the 'Queen's assassins' don't somehow make it past the rocks."

"Doesn't he patrol sometimes?" Anna pursued. "Roam the whole area?"

"Sometimes," Arthur agreed somewhat reluctantly. "But I haven't heard him say anything about it lately."

"But you are asleep during the night. So you wouldn't know for sure whether or not he left this area?" Anna asked.

Arthur slowly shook his head. "No, miss. I'm not absolutely sure. Why does it matter?"

"There's been some trouble."

"Someone's found out about Lord de Winter?" Arthur asked, worried.

"No. Nothing like that. Some people have been killed."

"Killed!" Arthur stared at her. "What are you saying, miss?"

"The manner in which they were killed was very odd. There were marks on them that looked as if an animal had clawed them," Anna explained.

For a moment Arthur's face was blank; then understanding dawned on him. "Oh! His nails. But, miss, he would never hurt anyone. He couldn't. Why, no matter how upset he gets about things, he's never made the least effort to hurt me. He's gentle. You know that. He's just . . . confused, like, and scared."

"But, Arthur, what if — what if he thought those people were the Queen's spies or her assassins? What if he thought they were going to hurt him? Can you swear that he would not kill them to keep them from harming him — and you?"

Arthur looked troubled. "Well . . . no, miss, I might not could swear to it. But he's been peaceful the last few days. I told you. He thinks this angel told him to draw these other marks on his hands, and he feels safer."

Anna bit her lip. She wished Arthur's answer had been more reassuring. Of course he would not think Charles had done anything so terrible; he was devoted to the man. Nor did she really think that her uncle was capable of murder. Still, there was a niggling little worry in the back of her brain. She wasn't sure exactly what Uncle Charles might do when he was in the grip of one of his delusions.

"Keep a careful eye on him, won't you?" Kit said to the servant.

"I always do that, sir," Arthur told him somewhat reproachfully.

"I know you do. You are excellent with him. But we need to make especially sure that he doesn't go out anywhere, that no one sees him."

"Nobody comes this way, sir. Most people don't like the woods, and you can't get to the top of the tor this way, anyway. The time or two anybody's shown up, trying to climb the tor, they haven't seen him, and I've sent them on their way. He always hides if he hears voices. You know how he is." He nodded at them gravely. "Don't you worry. I'll take care of him. Nobody's going to find out about him — and nobody's going to be hurt, not by him."

"Do you feel better about it now?" Kit asked a few minutes later as he and Anna made their way back down from their uncle's hideaway.

"Yes, I suppose." Anna agreed. "I mean, he says Uncle Charles has been calmer. Surely he would not be calm if he had killed someone, even if he thought they were spies or assassins."

"Arthur would have noticed if he had

been acting strangely. He is devoted to him, but I don't think he would cover up something like that for him."

They made their way carefully down a slope, not speaking until they reached more level ground. When they did, Anna said with a sigh, "It makes me so sad to see him like that. Do you remember him when we were young? How he always had that bowl of sweets in his study, and he would give us one?"

Kit smiled faintly. "Yes, I remember. It is sad." After a moment, he added, "What frightens me is — what if it strikes me later, as it did him?"

"I know. It's a terrifying thought. I think about it, too."

Their uncle's madness had not come upon him until after he was grown, and at first, his "spells" had come upon him only now and then. During his "good days," he had seemed normal. Gradually the spells had become more frequent and his behavior had grown more bizarre, until it was difficult to hide from the servants. His insistence on living outdoors had been the final oddity, impossible to explain, and it was then that Anna's father had hit upon the plan to hide Lord de Winter's madness from the rest of the world.

It was impossible not to look for signs of

incipient madness in herself and in Kit, to examine every little oddity for an indication of something worse. Beneath everything that she did, running like a thread through the everyday fabric of her life, was the knowledge that one day her uncle's fate might be hers or Kit's, as well.

When they reached Holcomb Manor, they were surprised to see Kyria McIntyre's carriage sitting in front of their house. Kyria and her friend Rosemary were in the front drawing room, sipping at the cups of tea that their butler had hastened to provide.

"Kyria!" Anna exclaimed as she and Kit strode into the room. "What a delightful surprise."

"You will think me utterly rude, I'm afraid, to insist upon waiting for you, but your butler said you had already been gone some time on your walk, and I did so hope to catch you."

"Of course I don't think you are rude," Anna assured her. "I am glad that you waited. May I offer you anything more than tea?"

"Oh, no," Kyria said with a chuckle. "Your butler has already offered us most of the contents of your pantry, I think, but we had a late breakfast."

As Kyria and Anna talked, Kit had taken

the opportunity to speak to Rosemary Farrington, and now he extended to her an offer to show her the Holcomb gardens. Blushing a little, Miss Farrington did not hesitate to agree, and the two of them slipped out the door. Kyria looked after them for a moment.

"I think," she said, turning to Anna with a smile, "that there is a certain fondness between your brother and Miss Farrington."

"Miss Farrington is a very pleasant young woman," Anna replied noncommittally.

"Unfortunately, I am afraid that I am going to throw a spanner in the works."

Anna looked at Kyria questioningly.

"We came over here today to tell you that we are leaving for London as soon as we can get ourselves packed and ready — probably by tomorrow afternoon."

Anna's heart sank as she thought of Reed no longer being there. She knew it was the best thing, of course, for both of them, but that did not make the future seem any less empty. However, she kept her expression schooled to a mild disappointment as she said, "I — I am sorry to hear that."

"Normally I would not be such a coward," Kyria went on. "But I have to think of baby Emily and the twins, not to mention my guest. It — well, it just seems too dangerous for us to remain here with them, now that there is this person killing at random. . . ."

"Yes, of course. You cannot expose the children or Miss Farrington to danger," Anna agreed. "I perfectly understand. Still, I will be sorry to see you go."

"Thank you. I will miss you, too. The twins, of course, are most loath to leave. They have been trying to convince us that they should stay and help find the murderer. But I can see that their pleas are lacking their usual spirit. I think that finding that body yesterday has affected them more than they would like to admit."

"I am sure it has. I am so sorry they were with me."

"You could have had no idea," Kyria reassured her. "I am very glad you were with them and they did not stumble upon it by themselves." She leaned forward, impulsively reaching over to take Anna's hand. "I do hope that this will not be the end of our friendship. I would like it very much if you and your brother would come visit us in London. We could do all sorts of things. It is the height of the Season, and I would love to show you around. Please say you will come and stay with us. I shall have my mother write you an invitation. She would love to meet you. And Broughton House is huge, far too large for our family. You would not have to worry about being squeezed in with all of us."

Anna flushed a little with pleasure. She liked Kyria, and she could not help but wish that things had been different, that she and Kyria could have become fast friends. But, of course, they could not. She could not go for a visit to the ducal mansion, living in the same house as Reed. It would be an impossible situation. No, no matter how empty the upcoming days would seem, it would be far better for Reed and Kyria and all the rest of them to leave. In the long run, it would be far easier on her heart.

"I am sorry," she said, real regret in her voice. "But I am afraid that Kit and I do not often visit the City. We are simple country folk."

"What nonsense. That is the sort of thing Rafe says — usually when he is trying to put something over on someone."

Anna laughed. "No, I promise you, I am not trying to 'put anything over' on you. But the summer is a very busy time here. Kit has to keep track of everything for both estates, and I could not leave him to do it all by himself."

"Well, I shall write you, and you must promise that you will write back to me."

"I will, yes."

"And I will convince you to visit. You'll see."

Rosemary and Kit strolled back into the room soon after that. Their faces were flushed, and Anna thought that Miss Farrington looked a little teary-eyed. Kyria rose, and they took their leave. Kit and Anna walked with them out to their carriage.

"Please say our goodbyes to Lord Moreland, as well," Anna said, carefully keeping her voice neutral.

Kyria looked at her in surprise. "Reed? Oh, but Reed is not going with us to London. I am sorry, I did not realize you thought that he was leaving, as well. No, it is just Rafe and I and our baby and Miss Farrington and the twins."

"Oh." Anna's heart was suddenly much lighter. She told herself that the news should not make her happy; she should not be looking forward to seeing Reed again. "He — he really should leave. You must persuade him to go with you for his own safety."

Kyria let out a lilting laugh. "Oh, no! If I were to tell Reed that, it would only make him even more determined to stay."

Kit handed the women up into the carriage, bowing toward them, his eyes going to Rosemary. She lifted her hand to him, and the carriage pulled away. Anna glanced over at her brother. He was watching the carriage as it receded down the drive.

"I am sorry, Kit," Anna said, slipping her hand into his.

He did not look at her as he said, "It is better that she leave now. It will make it easier in the end."

"Yes, but I know that it is hard right now."

He squeezed her hand. "We have not fallen in love. But I did like her . . . very much. She wanted me to come to London to visit. She said that Kyria was inviting us to stay with them at Broughton House."

"She did."

"I told her it was impossible. It hurt her. I could see it in her eyes, though she tried to hide it. And that makes me feel worse than ever."

"Oh, Kit . . ."

He mustered up a smile for her. "What a sorry pair we are, eh? Ah, well, I do not suppose I could ask for a better sister to grow old with here. Can you not see us when we are Nick Perkins' age? Playing cribbage in front of the fire every evening?" He turned back into the house, standing aside for her to walk through the door before him and saying lightly, "It's the very devil behaving responsibly, isn't it?"

Anna was surprised the following morning when the butler interrupted her in a conference with the housekeeper to tell her that Lord Moreland and his two younger brothers were there to see her.

She hurried out of the servants' area, stopping at a mirror in the hall to examine her face and hair, and to repin a lock that was threatening to slip out. Reed and the twins were waiting for her in the formal drawing room. Alex and Con, who had been tussling with each other, straightened, letting go of each other, and turned to grin at her.

"Anna!"

"Hello, Con. Alex." She went over to them and took their hands. "How glad I am to see you. I was afraid that you were going to leave without saying goodbye to me."

"Never!" Con declared stoutly. "Reed told us he would bring us."

Anna looked over at Reed. He smiled and made a slight bow to her. Warmth stirred in her. "Thank you," she told him.

"I was glad to do it," he replied.

"Reed took us to see Perkins yesterday," Alex told her.

"Really?" Anna glanced toward Reed,

surprised that he would have taken them along the same route where they had found the body.

"We drove by way of the road," Reed explained, obviously aware of what she had been thinking.

"I see. And how was your patient?" Anna asked.

"Ever so much better. He can get up and walk around, though he still wears a bandage," Alex went on.

"And Perkins said he was well enough that he thought we could take him back to London with us if we wanted," Con finished.

"That's wonderful news."

"We'll be very careful to keep him away from the boa," Alex assured her.

"I am sure that would be a good idea."

"And the parrot," he added after a moment's thought.

Anna smiled. "Well, I have no doubt that he will enjoy his new home. And I think it's good that you are going home."

Con nodded. "Rafe explained it to us — how Kyria would feel she would have to stay if we stayed, and if she stayed, the baby and Miss Farrington would, too, so the only way he can get them back to London is if we go, too."

"That's a very clever plan," Anna said, her eyes twinkling.

"Yes," Alex agreed, and his eyes twinkled back at her. "Rafe is very good at persuading everyone to do what he wants."

"No doubt he told the same thing to Kyria," Con added. "I told him so, and he laughed. But, still, it's true. And, actually, I wouldn't mind seeing Mama and Papa again."

"I think you are both very wise," Anna assured them. "You *should* go back to London. But I have to tell you that I will miss you both very much."

"Will you?" Alex's smile was radiant. "You're the best, Anna."

Con nodded. "I think you are the first woman who likes us who's not one of our sisters."

"Come, now. Surely not all the women you have met are that foolish."

"I think they are," Alex told her confidentially. "And quite a few men, as well. Kyria had to get rid of more than one suitor because he didn't like us."

"Well, obviously Kyria is not foolish. Now, will you let me give you a hug before you go, or are you too big?"

In answer she was seized in a double hug. Tears started in her eyes, and she realized, a little shocked, how very much she would miss the twins.

"All right, boys, we'd best be getting on," Reed told them. "Why don't you go on out to your ponies while I say goodbye to Miss Holcomb?"

The boys did as he suggested. They were, as Kyria had pointed out the day before, more subdued than usual, though "subdued" was a relative term in regard to them.

"I hope they will be all right," Anna commented after they had gone. "I would hate for this to have hurt them."

"I think they will get over it," Reed replied. "Children are very resilient. Rafe and Kyria will be a great help to them. But it was a terrible thing to see. I — I wanted to make sure that you were recovering from the shock, as well."

"Thank you. I think I am. I have had nightmares the last two nights. I suppose it is inevitable. But last night was better than the night before." She looked at him, remembering how comforting it had been to lean on him, how strong and safe his arms had felt around her. She knew that if only she could go into his embrace now, she would feel better.

Anna glanced away, hoping that her

thoughts did not show in her face. "Have you heard anything further about the murders?"

He shook his head. "No. Anna . . . I intend to find out who killed those people." The tone of his voice made it a promise.

Startled, Anna looked up at him. Reed's face was set, his gray eyes determined. "But why?" she blurted out. "Is that not the constable's job?"

"Yes, no doubt. But the last time this was happening, the constable did not solve the matter. We cannot presume that he will this time. He is not accustomed to dealing with problems like this. A constable in a small village . . ." Reed frowned. "I just think he probably needs all the help that he can get."

Anna nodded. She knew the constable better than Reed, and she knew that he was a simple man, accustomed to dealing with simple problems. She had to admit that the murders of the past week would be overwhelming to him.

"I have to make sure that no one else gets hurt," Reed went on, and Anna realized suddenly that he was looking into the murders for her sake. He was afraid that his dream meant that she would be a target for the killer. He had said that he did not love her, but he must still care for her in some way. She told herself that it was terrible and selfish of her that this knowledge warmed her heart.

"You think that these deaths are somehow connected to me," she told him. "Don't you? Because of your dream."

"I cannot help but wonder."

"Perhaps your dream — if it meant anything — was nothing more than an indication that I would stumble upon the body. I do not see how the murders threaten me more than anyone else who lives here."

"I don't, either, at the moment. But we have no idea why he has killed those he did — or who else he might decide to kill. The only safe way to deal with the problem is to find out who has done these things."

After a long moment, Anna said, "Did you notice that the first murder was of a servant girl and the second victim was a farmer — just as in the murders fifty years ago?"

"It occurred to me. One can only wonder why someone has decided to imitate what happened before. It seems that it must have some significance for the killer."

"Yes, but what? The style of killings would be enough to raise the fear of the Beast in everyone. Why make them so exactly alike?"

"God only knows. I cannot think that we are dealing with a rational person. It may mean something to him that would never occur to a normal human being."

"There were only two deaths the other time. Perhaps he will stop now."

"We can hope, but I would not rely on it."

"What are you going to do?" Anna asked.

"First, I want to look into the legend about the Beast, and also the earlier murders. There must be some reason why the killer wants us to think that the Beast is running amok again . . . why he has copied those other two deaths so closely. I plan to look through the Winterset library. I haven't really had a chance to — it's extensive. I thought there might be something there about the local legends. And I would like to look at those records the doctor spoke about. His father's notes and the newspaper articles of the time. Perhaps something in the old murders will give me a clue as to what is happening now."

"I want to help you," Anna told him.

Reed looked at her, his eyebrows lifting. "But —"

"Don't tell me that it is unsafe," Anna warned. "You are already afraid that I am somehow involved. I don't see how poking about would endanger me any more."

"It is just that it is an unsavory subject,"

he responded. "Are you sure you want to look at the doctor's drawings and such?"

"I'm not sure that 'want' is the correct word. But I have seen one of the victims, and I do not think that the drawings of two murders in the past could be any worse than that. I feel an obligation to Estelle and that poor young man. I want to do something."

"Of course. I will be glad for the help. You can escort me to the doctor's. You know him far better than I." He paused, then continued. "Tomorrow, perhaps. And we can look through the library at Winterset."

"All right." Anna felt suddenly a little breathless. It occurred to her that she might be playing with fire, being alone with Reed in his library, but she pushed the thought aside.

He arranged to come by the next day to take her to the doctor's, and then he bowed over her hand and left. Anna stood for a moment, her hand pressed to her stomach, which was suddenly dancing with nerves.

Several times that evening, she started to write a note to send to Winterset, telling Reed that she had changed her mind, that she was not going with him to look at the doctor's notes. She even got so far as actually writing part of the note, but then she tore it up. However much she told herself that it could be dangerous, she could not bring herself to refrain from going.

The next morning, she took extra care with her appearance, then grew angry at herself for doing so, and instead put on one of her plainest dresses and had Penny redo her hair in a bun at the nape of her neck. However, she did not realize that nothing could detract from the glow of her skin or the sparkle in her eyes, so that no matter how much she tried to look ordinary, her very anticipation at being with Reed enhanced her beauty.

Dr. Felton was somewhat surprised at their arrival on his doorstep, but when Anna told him that they wished to look at his father's notes on the fifty-year-old murders, he agreed amiably and led them into the office behind his surgery. Unlocking a cabinet, he pulled out a metal box and opened it. Inside were a series of bound journals, which looked identical. Dr. Felton searched through them and, after a time, took out one.

"This is for the year of the murders," he told them, handing the volume to them, and closing and replacing the box. "Would you like the newspaper accounts, too? Mrs. Ross, his old housekeeper, gave them to me several years ago. I don't know, really, how helpful they are."

He closed the cabinet and relocked it, then moved to another, unlocked, cabinet and dug through it until he came up with a plain box. He turned toward them, holding out the box. "These are all the articles she clipped. I haven't read all of them. One can only describe the tone of most of them as hysterical. I am not sure how accurate they are." He gave a faint smile. "I discovered that our newspapers' ancestors were almost as given to hyperbole as the present-day issues."

"This is perfect," Anna assured him.

"You can look at them in here, if you'd like," Dr. Felton told them, gesturing vaguely around his small office, which was almost entirely filled by his large desk and several cabinets. "Or you may take them home if you would rather. . . ."

They agreed that it would be easier to look at them at Winterset, and Anna promised solemnly that they would return the materials as soon as possible. They went back to Winterset and sat down in the library with a pot of tea, then opened the journal between them on the table. They sat side by side at the table, leaning in to look at the book. Their arms touched — it was impossible not to — and even though Anna could feel only the material of his suit coat against her own skin, bared by her summer dress, the contact made her flesh tingle with awareness.

In her mind, she imagined covering his hand with hers, feeling his warm skin beneath hers. *He might open his fingers slightly, allowing hers to slip between his.* . . . Her skin warmed, and she shifted a little in her chair, so that their arms were separated by a fraction of an inch. But she could not escape the other ways his nearness affected her. There was still the faint scent of his skin in her nostrils; she could still feel the warmth of his body; she could still glance at his profile and see the curve of his jaw, the straight line of his nose, the curl of his impossibly long eyelashes, the dark shadow of beard that was already beginning to lurk beneath his skin, even though he had doubtless shaved only hours earlier.

Reed turned to glance at her, and their eyes caught and held. Anna's breath was shallow in her throat; she could not turn from his silver gaze. Yearning for what she would never have pierced her. If she had married him, they would have sat often like this, but then she would have had the right to slide her hand through his, to lean her head against his shoulder. She would know every line and curve of his face, would have touched them many times, tracing a loving finger over his brows and nose and lips.

Reed's gaze darkened as he looked at her, and for an instant Anna thought that he was about to kiss her. She waited, her heart pounding ferociously, not knowing what she would do if he did lean toward her. But then he broke the contact of their gazes and turned back to the journal in front of them, flipping through the pages until he reached the first of the murders.

"Here it is."

Anna leaned in, looking at the doctor's notes. There was a detailed drawing of the servant girl's body, with lines leading to the places where she had been stabbed. The stabbed areas were then drawn in insets, enlarged, with the marks detailed. It was a gruesome drawing, even with the doctor's dry, clinical remarks attached. On the next page, the doctor had jotted down such information as where she was found and when.

"Look. She was found on a farm, also," Anna said. "Weller's Point. That is on one of the Winterset tenant farms. Not the same one as where Estelle was found, but still . . ."

"A definite similarity," Reed agreed. "It seems clear our killer is imitating the first."

"Let's look at the second drawing," Anna suggested, reaching out to flip through a few more pages. She stopped, running her finger down the center of the book. "This — it feels as if a page has been torn out here."

Reed nodded. "I noticed that earlier on." He flipped back toward the front of the journal. "Pages are missing here, as well. And here."

"Hmm. Why do you suppose that is?"

Reed shrugged. "I suppose there could have been mistakes, a drawing done wrong and ripped out."

"Or something that he did not want anyone even to read," Anna put in.

"Yes." He glanced at her. "Are you suspecting the doctor of the earlier murders?"

"I don't know. I don't suppose he should be ruled out, though. What if the cuts were made with a scalpel, just spaced apart to look like claws?"

"Then why write in here that he thought they were too even to be an animal's claws? If you go to the trouble to do that, trying to fool everyone, you aren't likely to write down the truth in your journal."

"I suppose that is true," Anna conceded as she turned the page and found the drawing of the old farmer who had been killed next. She peered at the drawing. "I don't think these marks look exactly like the ones on the Johnson boy. I mean, they aren't in the same places."

Reed nodded. "You're right. And this old man's throat was not as damaged as Frank Johnson's. So the killer imitated the killings, but not in every point. Perhaps he had only heard that they looked like an animal attacking but had never seen these drawings showing exactly where they were."

"Which would be almost anyone in the area," Anna commented with a sigh.

"Yes, I am afraid it's not a terribly useful supposition."

"There must be some reason for the imitation, though. I mean, the killings are the same in so many particulars that he has to be copying the earlier murders."

"I think you're right," Reed agreed. "I mean, unless you subscribe to the eternal man-beast theory. Then it would be the same, er, person."

Anna grimaced at him. "I think we can safely discount that theory. Nor does it seem likely that it was the same person, even if he is not a supernatural being. He would be far too old now to be doing such things, wouldn't you think?"

That also, Anna thought with inward relief, tended to exonerate her uncle. He had been only a boy at the time of the killings, no more than seven or eight. Of course, she reminded herself reasonably, perhaps talk of the killings had been so significant to him that he had incorporated them into his madness.

She flipped back and forth a few times between the drawings, studying them, then went back to the notes the doctor had written about the first victim. Suddenly, something toward the bottom of the page caught her eye.

"Look. He says here that she was a servant at Winterset."

"What?" Reed leaned closer, his eyes going to the spot where her finger pointed. " 'Susan Emmett, a parlormaid at Winterset, was found beneath the large tree at Weller's Point.' "

He looked at Anna. "Well, I suppose it makes sense. If she was a servant girl, she would in all likelihood have served either here or at Holcomb Manor. You say Weller's Point was a de Winter tenant farm. How far away was it?"

"Not too far."

"It says here it happened on a Sunday evening. She might have been off that Sunday and had gone to see her family, then was walking back to Winterset when he attacked her." Anna couldn't suppress a little shudder at the thought.

"Do you suppose there would be anyone here who might remember her?"

"I should think it was all too long ago for any of them to still be working here, but if we could find out their names, some of them might still be alive."

Reed nodded, and they bent their heads to the pages once again. Finally he sat back, letting out a groan. "I think I have absorbed all I can for the moment." He looked at Anna. "Care for a walk?"

"That sounds very nice."

They went out the back, wandering through the garden, which had obviously been cleaned up quite a bit, weeds pulled, and overgrown bushes and trees cut back. There was some semblance of order now, although the roses still grew in wild profusion, casting their heady scent in the air.

Anna's hand was tucked into Reed's arm. The sun was warm on her back, shielded from her eyes by the brim of her bonnet. It was a delightful day, she thought, seemingly far removed from the tales of murder they had been studying inside. And yet, murder had taken place not far from here only a few days earlier. It seemed impossible.

She breathed in the roses with a sigh of

enjoyment, and Reed, a smile touching his full lips, broke off a bloom, carefully stripping it of thorns, and handed it to her. Anna brought it to her nose and sniffed deeply, her eyes shining with thanks above it. Her heart welled with feeling. This, too, could have been hers, she thought — long summer days with Reed, walking in the garden, side by side. Perhaps they would have been holding hands, laughing as they talked about their lives. There might even have been children running about. She pictured them laughing and intelligent, full of questions, something like the twins — perhaps even with their black hair, but with Reed's silver eyes.

It was a picture so compelling that she almost let out a soft moan of longing. She had done the right thing, she knew. The honorable thing. It had been her only choice. But she knew with an ache just how much she had cut out from her life.

They strolled through the arch, covered thickly with a flowering vine, and a figure popped up in front of them, startling them.

"What the devil — oh, Grimsley. You gave us a turn."

It was the caretaker, Grimsley, small and dark, wearing a cap pulled low on his head to shield his eyes from the sun. He swept the cap off now to Reed, revealing his stringy mop of graying hair, and bobbed a bow.

"My lord. Miss." He nodded at them, grinning and twisting his cap in his hand. "Out for a stroll, eh? The old place is lookin' better, innit? Now that I got some help. We'll have it lookin' tip-top in no time."

"Yes, it is much improved," Reed agreed.

"Sorry her ladyship and the young'uns left," Grimsley went on. "They was interested in all the plants, them boys."

"Yes. They are generally interested in everything."

"Too bad about them folks being killed." Grimsley shook his head. "Strange it happened again."

Reed shot Anna a look. They had not even thought about the gardener when they had been talking about the Winterset servants earlier.

"You were here then?"

"Oh, yes, I were just a lad then, twelve or so, I guess. But I helped me dad out sometimes. He was head gardener here before me."

"And did you know the girl who was murdered?"

"Oh, no, sir, she worked at the Manor, now, didn't she?"

"No, I meant the murder that happened a long time ago."

"Oh. Aye, I think she did work here, now I think about it. But I didn't know her, like. I only worked out here, you see."

"Yes. Of course." Reed paused, then asked perfunctorily, "And the murders — do you think they were committed by the 'Beast'?"

"The Beast," the old man repeated scornfully. "Nay, my lord, I don't believe in any Beast. That's just a tale, now, innit?"

Reed looked at him in surprise. "Yes, that is what I think. But most of the servants I've talked to believe that it is indeed the Beast of Craydon Tor who has been doing the killings."

"Oh, them . . ." Grimsley made a dismissive gesture toward the house. "They're new here, ain't they? They don't know nothin'."

"And do you have a theory as to who it is, then?" Reed asked, his interest piqued.

"Sure," Grimsley replied easily. "It's clear as day. It's the ghosts."

Chapter Eleven

There was a long silence as Reed and Anna stared at the gardener.

"Ghosts?" Reed repeated.

"Aye, sir. It's ghosts right enough."

Anna cast a glance toward Reed, then said, "Why do you think that?"

"Well, miss, it's like this," Grimsley began confidentially, coming a step closer to them. "I been workin' out here fifty years or so. I spend all me time outdoors, workin' here, walkin' places, goin' to visit me sister what lives in the Fell. And in all that time, I never seen any beast other than a fox or dog or such. But, now, ghosts — ghosts I've seen."

Anna caught the scent of gin coming from the man, now that he was nearer to her, but she asked gamely, "You have? Where?"

"Why, right up there, miss," Grimsley replied, looking surprised, and gestured toward the house. "I seen 'em at night. Lots of times. It's the late lord and lady. Not your uncle, miss, but his father and mother, what died right here in the summerhouse." He gestured off toward the left to where the summerhouse had once stood, Anna presumed.

"Why do you think it is they?" Reed asked.

"Well, they'd be the ones walkin', now, wouldn't they?" Grimsley answered unarguably. "Happens, dying sudden like that. 'Orrible death, burnin'. 'Sides, the lights always come along the gallery, you know, where he liked to walk." Grimsley pointed toward the long row of windows on the right side of the house, where the gallery lay, then lifted his finger higher and over to the left, pointing to a set of four smaller windows, all covered with wrought-iron bars. "And they're in the master's old bedroom, too. It's the old lord walkin', like he used to late at night. I seen him oftentimes."

"You saw lights?" Reed pressed, frowning. "When was this?"

"Oh, before you come back, my lord. Not all the time, of course. They don't always walk. Stopped once you come back. I guess the old lord's shy, like."

"And how long has this been going on?" Reed continued.

Grimsley contemplated this question, his head to one side, and finally said, " 'Bout a year now. More or less." He smiled a little apologetically. "I'm not so good with the time anymore, you understand."

"Yes. Of course. Well, thank you, Grimsley."

The man nodded, seeming satisfied, and turned, going back to the bush he had been tending and picking up his shears. Reed offered Anna his arm again, and they strolled away.

When they were securely out of earshot of the old caretaker, Anna looked at Reed, saying in a wry voice, "Now ghosts?"

Reed half groaned, half laughed. "That is all I need. As if it isn't bad enough to have homicidal man-beasts roaming about . . ."

Anna turned to look back at the house. "Do you think he really has seen lights in there?"

Reed shrugged. "I suppose it is possible. The house has been empty. Someone could have broken in — though the place certainly did not look as if it had been ransacked. And why else would someone break in except to steal things?"

"Well, I understand that ghosts don't really steal things," Anna told him, her eyes dancing.

He grinned at her. "Laugh if you like. I have a sister — not Kyria — who came to believe quite seriously in ghosts."

"Really?" Anna looked at him with interest.

"Yes. I will tell you the story sometime. It's the sort that sends shivers down your spine."

"Thank you, I have no need of any more of those," Anna replied.

"However, I find Grimsley's story somewhat less reliable than Olivia's," Reed went on. "For one thing, when he pointed to the old lord's bedroom, he was pointing not at the master's bedroom but at the nursery, I think. Did you see the bars?"

Anna nodded. It was a common practice to bar the windows in nursery rooms so that children could not fall out of the high windows. "Yes, I thought that must be where those windows were."

"Nor does it seem likely that the old lord — or lord and lady, if you will — should come back to haunt the place a year or two ago, after resting quietly in their graves for the past however-many years."

"Forty-four or forty-five, I think," Anna said. "They died a few years after the first Beast killings."

"How did they die?" Reed asked.

"They were caught in a fire in the summerhouse," Anna said. "I'm really not sure of the details. They died when my mother was quite young, only three or so, and she didn't remember her parents. She was raised by her aunt — my grandmother's sister — who lived in London."

"She did not grow up here?" Reed asked, surprised.

"No. My uncle was away at school when their parents died. He was ten or twelve years older than my mother, and he had already gone off to Eton. Except for occasional visits, I presume the house must have stood empty for several years then, too. I believe he returned here when he finished at Eton, but my mother, of course, remained with her aunt until after her debut."

"Did she meet your father in London, then?"

"No. After her first Season, she came here to stay with her brother for a few months. It was then that she met my father. An unequal match, some said. She was a beauty, and the de Winters were of higher birth. But she didn't care for that. She and my father loved each other very much."

Anna was unaware of how her face softened and her eyes warmed as she talked about her parents, but Reed could clearly see her grow even lovelier as she talked. He looked down at her, a more carnal heat stirring in him.

"My parents, too, were a love match," he

told her, and he could not keep his fingers from trailing lightly down her arm.

Anna's breath quickened in her throat. She looked up at him, her eyes meeting his, and the heat she saw in them set up an answering warmth in her own loins. She remembered the moment earlier in the library when she had thought that he was going to kiss her. She wondered if he was going to now.

She wanted him to kiss her. However foolish or wrong it was, she wanted to feel his lips on hers, wanted to have his hands on her arms, sliding up over her bare skin, his fingers pressing into her flesh. Anna trembled, her lips parting slightly.

His eyes went to her mouth, and they burned suddenly with a silver fire. "Anna . . . you are so beautiful."

Would it be so wrong? she wondered. Would it be so terrible to kiss him, to taste for a moment the joy, the pleasure, that she would never have?

But she knew the answer, even as she thought the question. Kissing Reed would only make everything harder. A taste of what she had given up would only leave her wanting more. And Reed . . . it would be unconscionable to do that to him. To stir his desire again. To let him know that desire still burned in her.

Anna stepped back, her gaze shifting away from him, even as everything inside her screamed not to.

"We ought to get back to the doctor's journals," she said stiffly.

"Of course."

Anna glanced back at Reed. His face was set, his eyes unreadable. He extended his arm to her in a stiff, formal way. Anna took it; his muscles felt like iron beneath the sleeve of his jacket. They walked back to the house, the distance between them palpable.

They spent the rest of the afternoon in the library. Reed took a seat across the table from Anna, and he started on the doctor's notes again, while Anne read some of the articles from the clippings that the doctor had given them.

The newspaper articles were by and large lurid accounts, full of overblown language and possessing few facts. They wrote of the innocent girl "ripped from life" and made references to the bloody legend of a "ravening beast" who roamed the area. They made, in fact, a great deal out of nothing, and Anna soon realized that they had learned far more from the few pages of the doctor's notes than they would from the stacks of articles.

"These are useless," she said at last,

tossing down the clipping she had been reading.

Reed glanced across at her with a rueful smile on his face. He had finished with the doctor's journals and had read a few of the articles, too. "I fear you are right."

He stood, rolling his shoulders to get out the kinks put there by hours of reading. He strolled across to the window and glanced out. "It's gotten dark." He paused for a moment, then said neutrally, "Will you stay for supper? If I know the cook, it is nigh ready. We adhere to country hours here, apparently."

Anna glanced down at the papers as if they could tell her what to do. "I — Kit will be expecting me."

"I can send a groom over with a note, explaining."

She wavered. The thought of dining alone with Reed, chatting and laughing, was appealing. That was the problem, of course. It was too appealing.

"No," she said firmly, standing up and giving him a false smile. "I must go. I have spent all day on this, and there are things I need to attend to at home."

He acquiesced gracefully, with no further urgings for her to stay, and a few minutes later the carriage was brought around. Anna found, perversely, that she was a little disappointed by his seeming lack of interest in whether or not she left.

He rode home with her in the carriage, making plans for the morrow, and bade her a polite goodbye at her door. Anna went inside, only to find that Kit had sent a note home saying that he had been delayed at one of the farms and would be taking his evening meal there. So she dined in lonely state in the small dining room and spent the evening reading in her room, reminding herself now and then why she had chosen to live her life without Reed Moreland.

It was something she had to remind herself of on several occasions during the next few days. She spent most of her time with Reed, searching for answers about the murders, both past and present, and, despite the gruesome subject, those days were some of the happiest she had spent in years.

She had forgotten how much she enjoyed Reed's conversation, how witty he could be, the way his gray eyes danced with amusement. In quiet moments, she found herself turning to look at him, her eyes drawn to the full curve of his lower lip, the firm line of his jaw. Once, feeling her eyes on him as he read, Reed glanced up, and a slow smile spread across his face. Anna could not keep from smiling back, and she ducked her head quickly, returning her eyes to the pages she had been reading.

In every moment that they spent together, there was always the subtle running under-current of attraction between them. When he smiled, heat curled within her abdomen, and when he laughed, the corners of his eyes crinkling up, she felt a visceral tug. Anna could not look at his hands without thinking of the way his fingers had felt on her skin. When they looked together at a piece of paper, they leaned closer in, and his scent, his warmth, stirred her, making it hard for her to concentrate.

She wanted him, wanted him perhaps more than she had three years ago. He had never kissed her three years ago in that raw, desperate way in which he had kissed her at Kyria's party, and that kiss had awakened something within her that was strong and primal, a hunger she had not felt before, even when she had been most in love with him. He was older and harder, and the changes in him drew her. He no longer treated her, she noticed, as if she were made of glass, and she enjoyed it.

After examining the doctor's notes, Reed and Anna decided the best course would be to try to locate someone who might have had more immediate knowledge of the case. Since Susan Emmett had been a servant at Winterset, they set out to find another servant who had worked there. Reed started with his butler, who informed him a little haughtily that he was not a local, having been hired from an agency, and his last posting had been in Brighton. It turned out that the housekeeper, too, had been hired in the same way and was, in fact, from Devonshire.

"I remember Uncle Charles' butler," Anna told him. "His name was Merriman — although he was one of the sourest men I have ever seen. I believe he retired when Uncle Charles left, but I cannot remember where he went. I suppose he could have been the butler during that time, as well. He looked as if he might have been here since the house was built, frankly. But I don't remember anyone else. I'm sorry."

In the end, they turned to Anna's housekeeper, Mrs. Michaels. Anna was surprised to see that formidable woman all but gush at being asked to sit down in the presence of the son of a duke and talk to him.

"Oh, yes, I remember Merriman," she said, nodding. "Always had his nose up in the air because he'd once worked for an earl

— as if the de Winters hadn't come over with William the Conqueror himself. But I'm sorry, miss, he wasn't the one who was the butler back when they had those other awful killings." She gave an expressive shudder. "That was Cunningham. But he died several years ago. That was why his lordship took on Merriman."

"Oh," Anna said, disappointed. "What about the housekeeper back then?"

"Well, that was before my time, you understand," Mrs. Michaels told her. "But when I came here to the Manor, I remember that it was a woman named — oh, what was it?" She frowned. "It will come to me in a moment, I'm sure. A regular tyrant, she was. That's what all the girls who worked for her said."

Anna wondered what the woman must have been like for Mrs. Michaels, who now made a bed check of all the servant girls every night at ten, to find her too dictatorial.

"Hart?" Mrs. Michaels said tentatively. "No . . . Hartwell! That was it. Mrs. Hartwell. I believe that she was there until your uncle left for that heathen island. And where did she go after that?"

"It's all right, Mrs. Michaels," Anna assured her. "We can find her whereabouts, I think. It just occurred to me that my uncle would have given her a stipend." Though he might not remember, it was a certainty that her father would have. "Mr. Norton would be the one sending it, I imagine."

Reed nodded. "Yes, of course. We'll ask Norton."

It took no more than a note to the solicitor, delivered by one of Reed's grooms, and within an hour they had a missive in return, stating that Mrs. Hartwell resided with her son in the nearby village of Sedgewick. This seemed to them a hopeful development, and they set out the next morning in good spirits to visit the housekeeper.

They rode, rather than taking a carriage, and Anna could not help but enjoy the morning. When Reed had courted her three years ago, they had often gone riding, and simply being out with him this way again was enough to make her feel the way she had then — at least a little.

The cottage to which Mr. Norton had directed them was a pleasant half-timbered house of Tudor construction, well kept up, with a small, fragrant garden in front. When Reed knocked on the door, it was opened by an apple-cheeked young girl, who stared at them a little shyly and bobbed them a curtsey, then called for her mother.

A middle-aged woman appeared next,

and when Reed explained that they were there to see the Mrs. Hartwell who had once been the housekeeper at Winterset, she gave them a puzzled look but invited them inside.

"It's John's mum you're wanting to see, then?" she asked, leading them into a small but pleasant parlor.

"Yes. I am Lord Moreland. I live at Winterset now. And this is Miss Holcomb. We were — I had some questions regarding Winterset that I wished to ask Mrs. Hartwell."

"Well, I — of course you can see her, if you wish, but I doubt there'll be much you can get from her. Please, sit down, and I'll get you some tea. Lizzie!" She bustled out of the room, and Reed and Anna exchanged a look.

The apple-cheeked girl returned not long afterward with a tea service on a tray, and a few moments after that, Mrs. Hartwell came in, her steps slowed to accommodate the old woman who leaned heavily on her arm.

The girl, who had been uneasily waiting, shifting from foot to foot, sprang forward to help her mother lower the old woman into a chair.

"Mother Hartwell," the middle-aged woman said loudly, bending down and looking directly into the old woman's face. "You have visitors."

The elder Mrs. Hartwell turned to look blankly at her daughter-in-law, then swiveled her head to cast the same blank look at Reed and Anna, sitting on the couch across from her.

"Mrs. Hartwell, I am Lord Moreland. I own Winterset now, where I understand you used to be the housekeeper."

The old woman blinked and turned back to the other woman, opening her mouth and making a few garbled noises. The middle-aged woman shot Reed and Anna an apologetic look.

"I'm sorry. It's hard to understand what she says. She hasn't been the same for the past few years, ever since she had the apoplexy. The doctor said it was a miracle she lived, but she hasn't been able to walk or talk right since then."

"No, it is we who should apologize for intruding upon you like this," Reed replied. "We did not realize . . ."

"If you want to go ahead and ask her, I can tell you what she says," the woman offered.

"We were going to ask her about some of the other servants who worked at Winterset while Mrs. Hartwell was housekeeper there," Anna began.

They all looked at the old woman, who

was nodding pleasantly. Encouraged, Anna went on, "We were especially interested in Susan Emmett. She worked there almost fifty years ago."

The old woman continued to nod, smiling a little. The younger Mrs. Hartwell bent and asked her, "Do you remember Susan Emmett, Mother? At Winterset."

The old woman made a few more garbled sounds, and her daughter-in-law turned to them apologetically. "I'm sorry. Sometimes she doesn't make much sense. She said . . . I think she said something about an animal."

"The Beast?" Reed asked.

The other woman looked surprised. "Yes, that is what it sounded like. Does it mean something to you?"

"A little." Again Reed and Anna exchanged a look. It would be almost impossible to get any useful information about the murders from Mrs. Hartwell. "We were hoping she could tell us about Susan's death."

"Beast gor 'er," the old woman managed to get out, the clearest thing she had said yet.

She added something, and her daughter-in-law cast them an embarrassed look. "I think she said that the girl was a silly chit."

"Could you tell us, Mrs. Hartwell, the

names of some of the other servants who worked at Winterset then?"

There was another long struggle to speak from Mrs. Hartwell, translated by her daughter-in-law. "I think she said, Cutting or Cunning."

"Cunningham," Anna supplied.

"Oh. Yes, I see. And then she said Arabel or Anabel, but she gave no last name. And then Josie — I'm pretty sure of that one — but I think she was saying that all of them are dead."

Reed and Anna soon took their leave, thanking the women for their help. He threw her up in the saddle, then mounted his own horse, and they started down the street.

"I'm afraid that didn't get us much of anywhere," Reed commented.

Anna cast him a sympathetic look. "I'm sorry."

He looked at her and smiled. "No one's fault, really." He sighed. "I wish we could get the names of the other servants. In his note, Norton said that only the butler and housekeeper had received stipends. He did not know the names of any of the other servants who had been in your uncle's employ, and, of course, those may not even have been at Winterset almost thirty years before Lord de Winter left."

Anna sighed. "No, I would imagine that most of them were too young to have been there that long ago."

After a moment, Reed said, "There must have been record books."

Anna glanced at him. "Why, yes, I am sure you're right. I wonder we didn't think of it earlier. They would have had household accounts books, and it would have listed the wages they paid the servants."

"Now, if we just had any idea where those are."

"Father probably took the most recent ones over to the Manor when he took over my uncle's business dealings. But I would think he would have left all the old books at Winterset."

"If the old books were still there, of course," Reed inserted.

"It is a long time to keep them, I suppose, but our estate manager's office has books dating back a hundred years or more. Of course, my Holcomb ancestors were a good bit more methodical than my de Winter ones, I'm afraid."

"The de Winters were erratic?"

"The de Winters were colorful," Anna said with a grin. "They tended to live their lives on a grander scale. Like old Lord Jasper — the one with the staghounds."

"Mmm. 'Colorful' can be rather trying sometimes. And I can tell you that I speak from experience."

"I cannot believe that your family is as odd as you say," Anna told him.

"No? That is because you have never met them."

"I've met Kyria. And Con and Alex. And they were all charming."

"But just look at their names. Who would name twins Constantine and Alexander?"

"Someone who envisioned great things ahead of them?" Anna ventured.

"No. I'll tell you who — the same person who named the other set of twins, my older brother and sister, Theodosius and Thisbe."

"Oh, my."

He flashed a smile at her, and she felt her insides melt. "You see? My father thinks little of importance happened after the fall of Rome."

"And did not your mother object?"

"My mother, I believe, proposed my name and my sister Olivia's. Kyria was something of a compromise, being Greek for Father and pleasant-sounding for Mother. But she is inclined to give in to my father on such issues as names, because her mind is concerned with more important things — social reforms, the vote for women, child labor laws."

"I think your mother sounds like a very good person."

"Oh, she is. So good, in fact, that one can sometimes find it difficult to live up to her expectations."

"Surely *you* have not failed her expectations."

"Of course I have. We all live in fear of her."

Anna laughed. "What a piece of flummery! I don't believe you for an instant. I have never met people who are less afraid of anything than you and your brothers and sister."

"Ah, but you have never met my mother," he retorted with a smile.

They continued with such banter as they rode back to Winterset, but once there, they set about looking diligently for the old household records.

First they searched the small locked room where the household silver had always been kept, but there was no sign of records there. They moved on to the study, then the library, but found no household accounts, new or old.

"The estate manager's office!" Anna exclaimed after a moment. "I don't know why I didn't think of it earlier. He had a small house on the grounds — it's beyond the stables, and when my father took over the estate, he transferred everything to our own estate manager. The cottage has been closed up ever since, but I wonder if maybe they left all the old records there in his office."

"It's worth a try," Reed agreed.

It took some time to find the appropriate key, and in the end, they came up with four that might open the office. Taking them all in hand, Reed and Anna strode across the yard and past the stables, walking the path that led past a copse of trees to a small house. There was a door on the side of the house that opened directly into the estate office.

One of the keys worked, although the lock turned with the creak of age and disuse, and Reed pushed the door open, revealing a small room containing a desk and some cabinets, as well as a few open bookcases. There were also two large trunks lying behind and beside the desk, and smaller boxes stacked up in every available space. A layer of dust coated every surface in the room.

Leaving the door open for the light and air, they stepped into the room. Anna looped up the trailing train of her riding habit and tucked it through her belt so that it would not drag across the dusty floor. She made her way through the maze of boxes to the single window and pushed the curtains aside, letting in more of the summer sunlight.

Reed sighed, looking around him. "This could take us hours. I should have brought a lamp."

"Let's start, anyway. If it grows dark before we find it, we can go back for light."

"You're right. Where do you suggest we begin?"

"Are there labels on any of the boxes?"

"I think so." Reed brushed off the top of one. " 'Farm Accounts' and a date. That's not it."

They ruled out several other boxes, but the trunks did not have labels attached to them, so they simply opened one and began to dig through it. It was impossible to avoid the dust, and their clothes were soon liberally smeared with it. Once they had reached the bottom of the first trunk, they opened the second. A cloud of dust rose from the surface as they lifted the lid. Anna let out a low cry of dismay.

"Oh! Look at this!" She gazed down at the dust that coated the front of her skirt. "Penny will never get this clean. She will think I have been out rolling in the dirt." She wiped ineffectually at the dust, succeeding only in furthering the damage. "Oh, dear." She sighed and raised a hand to brush back a strand of hair from her forehead.

Reed chuckled, his eyes dancing with amusement. "Wait. You are only making things worse. Now you have a streak of dirt across your forehead. No, don't touch it. Here."

He dug in his pocket and pulled out a large white handkerchief. Taking her hand in his, he turned it palm up and wiped the handkerchief over it.

Anna watched his hands at work on hers. His fingers were long and nimble, dusted with a sprinkling of black hair. She had always loved the look of his hands, she thought, strong and masculine, but not blunt or square. They were very capable hands, yet they could move with great gentleness and tenderness. A quiver of sensation ran through her, startling her, and she drew in a sharp breath.

Reed's hands froze on hers, and he looked up at her. They stood that way for a moment, their gazes locked, his hands still around hers. Then he looked back down and continued to wipe away the dirt, his fingers moving slowly, gently on hers. Anna felt each stroke of his hand, his skin separated from hers by the silken cloth of his handkerchief.

"You should not," she said a little breath-lessly. "You are ruining your handkerchief."

"It's all right," he replied, his voice faintly roughened.

He let go of her hand and took the other one, applying the same treatment to it. The silk cloth caressed her skin, stirring up a slow, curling heat in her abdomen. She felt suddenly, tinglingly alive, her nerves aware of every sensation — the slide of the cloth over her skin, the touch of air against her throat with each breath she took, the heavy thrum of her pulse.

Reed straightened, letting go of her hand. He took her chin between his fingers, holding her head steady as he wiped at the smudge of dust on her forehead. He was very close to her now, only inches away, his gaze locked on hers. Anna felt as if his eyes could see right down into her soul, as if they could discover the secrets of her heart. She gazed back at him, unable to look away.

His hand stilled on her face. The hand-kerchief fell from his grasp, fluttering to the floor between them, unnoticed. His hands slid around to cup her face between them. His skin was searing, and Anna could feel an answering heat flaring in her. A trembling began deep inside her, and she thought that her legs might give way beneath her.

Unconsciously, she leaned closer. She saw a light flare in Reed's eyes. Then his lips were on hers, his hands sliding into her hair, sinking into the soft mass of her curls. All Anna's firm resolutions went flying out of her head, driven away by the fierce heat of her desire. A tremor shook her, and she curled her fingers into the front of his jacket, holding on to him.

The passion she had kept hidden since the night he had kissed her flamed up again, fiery and demanding. He kissed her again and again, his hands tangling in her hair, popping loose the hairpins that Penny had carefully placed there. Her hair fell in a silken tumble over his hands and down to her shoulders.

Whatever small amount of control Reed retained fell away in that moment. His arms went around her tightly, grinding her into his body, and he kissed her as if he could never get enough of the taste of her mouth. They twisted and turned in a slow, heated dance of passion, locked together.

Anna clutched his shoulders, her fingers digging in, as he rained kisses over her face and down her neck. When the high collar of her riding habit impeded him, he cursed and fumbled at the large buttons that marched down the front of the military-style jacket. The two sides of the bodice came apart at last, and Reed shoved the sides of it back onto her shoulders.

His eyes went down to the front of her chest, exposed by her opened habit. She was clad in a white cotton chemise, her breasts swelling above the simple oval neckline. A pink ribbon was laced through the material below her breasts and tied in the front, and another ribbon ran along the neckline, tightening it halfway up her breasts.

Slowly his hand came up, and he took the top ribbon between his thumb and finger, then tugged. The bow came undone, and the chemise sagged open, revealing even more of her breasts. Reed ran his forefinger down between the soft orbs, then up across the top of one breast as it swelled above the chemise.

Anna's breath caught in her throat. She knew that she should be embarrassed to have a man see her like this, but all she could feel was heat snaking through her body. It aroused her to see him look at her . . . aroused her even more to see the glitter that came into his eyes as he watched her, the way his face slackened with desire. She was aware of a shameless urge to be naked before him.

Reed slipped his hand beneath her chemise, cupping her breast, and Anna let out a little gasp of pleasure. He looked up at the noise and smiled at what he saw stamped on her face — not outrage or dismay, but pleasure and a sensual hunger that matched his own. Watching the play of emotions across her face, Reed squeezed her breast gently, his thumb playing across the nipple and making it harden.

Anna closed her eyes at the sensations that flooded her. Desire flowered between her legs, hot and wet, turning her restless and yearning. With every flicker of his thumb against her nipple, the pulsing ache increased.

Reed lifted her breast free of the fabric and bent to kiss the hard button of her nipple. His tongue circled it provocatively, and then he pulled it into his mouth, his tongue and lips working on her sensitive flesh. Anna jerked a little at the jolt of desire that shot down through her, and a soft moan escaped her lips. She sagged against him, and his arm went tightly around her waist, holding her up.

His mouth continued to roam her breasts, and with each new delight, the past slipped away from Anna, all reason and duty lost amid the onslaught of physical pleasure. She could feel nothing but want, understand only the pounding urgency of her own desire.

She murmured his name, her voice low and throaty with passion. He groaned deep in his throat at the sound of his name on her lips, and his mouth returned to hers, taking her lips in a long, deep kiss. Anna melted into him, her arms going tightly around his neck, and she stretched upward, pressing her body into his. The buttons of his jacket bit into her tender bare flesh, but she didn't notice the discomfort. She wanted only to be closer, still closer, to him.

Reed's hand smoothed down her back and curved over her buttocks. His fingers dug into the firm flesh, lifting her into him. Desire pounded in him, filling him and driving out everything else. He ached to sink deep inside her, to feel her around him, hot and tight. All the emotions he had ever felt for her tangled inside him, melding into a hunger so fierce he could feel nothing else. Driving into her, feeling her convulse around him, seemed, at that moment, more necessary than breath itself.

He bunched up her skirts in his fists, pulling them up until his hand touched her leg, separated from him only by the thin cloth of her pantalets. His hand trembled as he caressed her thigh and buttocks, sliding around to the front, seeking the hot center of her desire. His hand slid between her legs, and Anna shuddered, heat slamming through her.

And it was, oddly enough, this sudden, unexpected surge of pleasure that shocked her into awareness of what she was doing. She froze, then jerked back from him. For an instant she stared at him, her eyes wide, her heart pounding insanely in her chest, as the full realization of her actions swept over her.

"No!" she gasped, her hands flying up to the sides of her bodice and yanking them together. "No! I cannot!"

With a choked cry, she turned and ran out of the room.

Reed stood, stunned, then ripped out an oath and ran after her.

Chapter Twelve

Anna ran from the cottage, fumbling at the buttons of her bodice.

What an idiot she had been! Tears sprang into her eyes, whether from anger or regret, she was not sure. She wanted to cry, to throw herself on the ground and dissolve into tears.

"Anna! Stop!"

She whirled around. Reed was running after her. His face was frightening, dark with anger, his brows steep slashes above his eyes. She held out both hands as if to stop him.

"No! Please, don't!"

"Don't what?" he barked, coming to a stop before her. "Are you going to pretend that I attacked you? That anything that happened back there was not entered into by you willingly, even eagerly?"

"No. No, of course not. I was as fully at fault. I don't deny it." Anna blinked back tears. Her breath was coming in gasps, and she knew that she was close to breaking down. She clenched her fists, struggling to regain control of herself.

Reed looked at her. Anna's face was pale, with bright splashes of color in her cheeks, and her hair was tumbling wildly down over her shoulders. He did not think he had ever seen her look so desirable, and even now, while anger and frustration filled him, he could not keep from wanting her.

"There is no *fault*," he told her roughly. "I am not trying to excuse myself or blame you."

"Then let me go," Anna told him.

"Not until you tell me why you ran from me!" he exploded. "I don't understand it. Any of it."

"I was wrong to come here," she said, her voice catching as if on the edge of tears. "There can be nothing between us."

"Why?" he shot back. "Because you feel nothing for me? Isn't that what you told me three years ago? You would not marry me because we wouldn't 'suit'?"

"I don't know!" Anna cried. "I don't know what I said!"

"You cannot remember why you did not want to marry me?" he asked incredulously. "Was it such a small matter that it somehow slipped your mind?"

"No, of course not. Reed, I beg of you . . ."

"What? What do you beg of me? I have no idea what you want from me. You told me you did not love me. That there was no possibility of love growing in you for me. But back there —" He pointed toward the cottage that they had just left. "Those kisses, the way you melted in my hands — those were not the actions of someone who does not care. You are not indifferent to me. I felt you tremble. I felt the heat of your skin, the eagerness of your mouth. Do not tell me that you did not desire me!"

"That isn't love!" Anna shot back. "I don't love you."

"When you refused me," he said, his eyes boring into hers, "I was so shocked, so stunned, that I could not think straight. I told myself that I had somehow mistaken the hours we had spent together, that when you had laughed with me, talked to me, you had not felt what I felt. That I had just been too blind to see how bored you were, that I mistook a polite smile for the warm glow of true liking. I told myself that you were false, that you had been playing a game with me, leading me on only to crush my heart beneath your heel. I lived on my anger and my hurt, cutting myself off from you, from this place, removing myself so that I would not have to see your face and feel the pain. . . ."

Anna raised her hand to her mouth, struggling not to give way to tears. Her heart ached. "I'm sorry," she breathed. "I am so sorry. I did not want to hurt you. I was too bold, too unthinking."

"Nay. I think you were too honest. Because of my pain, I did not examine what had happened. But now, since I've been back, seeing you again . . . I don't believe you."

"What?" Anna raised her brows. "You are saying that I lied?"

"Yes," he said bluntly. "I am."

"Are you so puffed up with pride?" Anna made her voice scornful. "So sure of your charms? Do you think that no woman can resist you? That any woman should be glad to fall into your arms?"

"No. It is just that I am done with stupidity. I have spent the past few days with you. We have talked and laughed just as we did before. I have seen you smile at me. I have felt your lips on mine. You want me, just as I want you."

"It was a mistake!" Anna cried, desperation rising in her. "It was just a mistake! I shouldn't have —"

"You shouldn't have what?" he exclaimed, closing the gap between them and grabbing her arms. "You shouldn't have slipped? Shouldn't have let me see what really lies within you? Bloody hell, woman, what is wrong with you? Why won't you tell me the truth? Why do you run from me?" His fingers bit into her arms. "Why did you refuse to marry me?"

"Stop! Please. Let go of me!" Anna could no longer hold back the tears.

"Tell me why you sent me away, dammit," he growled.

"I can't!" Anna cried, sobbing.

"Can't?" he repeated, and suddenly the anger seemed to drain out of him. He dropped her arms. "You won't, is more like it. Sweet Jesus, Anna, I loved you with all my heart. I would have given you anything, done anything for you. And you won't even give me an honest answer." He turned and started to walk away.

Anna's heart squeezed within her chest. She hated herself for what she had done to him, hated him for putting her through this, for forcing her to look at the depths of her own cowardice.

Reed stopped and looked back at her. His face was drawn, his eyes dark with emotion. "Did you never love me, Anna? Am I a fool to even suspect you did?"

"I loved you." Her voice was hoarse, as if the words had been ripped from her, and tears streamed down her face. "I loved you to the very depths of my being. I couldn't marry you. I *couldn't*."

"Why?" He came quickly back to her. "What on earth kept you from it?"

"Please . . ."

"Tell me." His voice was harsh. "You lied to me. You ripped my heart from me. Surely I at least deserve the truth. Why could you not marry me?"

Anna looked away from him, unable to meet his eyes. "Because my blood is tainted. I — my family is mad."

There was a long silence. Reed stared at her, astonished.

"What?" he asked finally.

Anna drew herself up, forcing herself to meet his gaze. "There is insanity in my family."

"Insanity," Reed repeated blankly. He shook his head. "Anna . . . every family has a few eccentrics. Why, my own family is known far and wide as the 'mad Morelands.' Surely —"

"No." Anna stepped back, crossing her arms across her chest. "I am not talking about a harmless eccentric or two. There is madness in the de Winters. It has been passed down to Kit and me." She drew a long breath. "A few days before you asked me to marry you, my father took me into his study and told me the truth. He had wanted to spare me, but when he saw how — how things were between the two of us, he grew frightened. He knew he had to tell me. That is why I pretended to be sick those days when you came to call. I could not bear to face you. Finally I realized that I had to send you away. I hadn't expected you to propose that day, but, clearly, when you did, I could not accept."

Stunned, Reed passed his hand across his face. "Are you sure about this?"

"Of course I am sure," Anna retorted. "Do you think I would cut myself off from love, from ever marrying, if I were not sure?"

"No. I just —"

"What my father told me that day was that there had always been rumors of . . . *oddities* . . . within the de Winters. Obviously the de Winter who built Winterset was, at the least, peculiar. But my mother, raised as she was from an early age by her maternal aunt, was unaware of the possibility. And it — the madness comes upon them late. She did not know about it, not for sure, until after she had married my father. It was only then that her brother, my uncle, began to exhibit symptoms of his madness."

"Your uncle? The one who left Winterset?"

Anna nodded her head. "Kit and I had thought, like everyone else, that my uncle had moved to Barbados. But what my father told me that day was that my uncle's madness, which began with episodes of bizarre behavior in his late twenties, had become increasingly worse in character, and more and more frequent. In one of his few rational periods, he realized that he had to do something, and so he and my father concocted this scheme to — to allow my uncle to live as his . . . illness dictated and also to spare the family embarrassment. Uncle Charles did not want Kit and me to know. He didn't want us to be shamed by his behavior."

Her voice wavered, close to tears, and Reed took a step toward her, saying, "Oh, Anna . . ."

She shook her head sharply, moving back. "No. Please. I don't want your pity. I don't want you to feel *anything* for me. Just let me finish."

Reed stiffened, color flaring on his cheeks, but he only gave her a formal nod of the head. "Go on."

She sent him a searching look. "If I tell you this, you must promise me that you will never breathe a word of it."

"Of course."

"My uncle did not leave. He moved into a

small house deep in the woods, by Craydon Tor. He lives there with his valet. No one else knows of this besides Kit and me and our gamekeeper, who takes them food. Even Norton, who drew up the power of attorney, believes that Uncle Charles moved far away. Uncle Charles has elaborate delusions. He believes that —" She sighed, then continued. "He thinks that he is somehow the legitimate descendant of the Stuart kings. I don't understand it, though he is able to draw a long chart showing one how the line comes down to him. He is quite certain that the Queen wants to get rid of him, because he is really the one who should be sitting on the throne."

"Good Lord."

She gave him a long look. "That is perhaps the sanest of his beliefs. He thinks that the Queen sends spies and assassins after him. He also believes that the angel Gabriel comes to him and tells him how to protect himself from the Queen's assassins. He has laid out circles of rocks around his house in a certain pattern that is intended to somehow thwart the Queen's men. He paints strange symbols on his skin and sleeps between two wooden slats painted with the same symbols, because he thinks this makes him invisible to the assassins — or something like that. I have trouble following his logic sometimes. He cannot bear to live indoors. He spends very little time in the hut where he lives, and he will accept it only because it is so hidden against the rock, with trees and shrubs all around it.

"The Queen's men come mostly at night, he says, and so he does not sleep at night, but roams about the area outside the house, looking for enemies. Sometimes he watches from up in the trees. Other times he slips around, hiding behind rocks and bushes and trees. He sleeps outdoors, but only during the daytime, when his valet can keep watch for him. He is certain that cutting his hair or nails will sap his strength, or that letting his hair and beard grow conceals his true identity — I'm not sure which. He looks . . . In recent years, when people have sworn that they have seen the Beast of Craydon Tor, I have wondered if they actually saw my uncle. He looks like a wild creature." She stopped and looked at Reed.

He gazed back at her, his face still stunned. "Anna . . . I — this is so difficult to take in." He frowned. "Maybe your uncle's condition is an aberration, something peculiar to him, and would not affect you."

She shook her head. "No. There have been others. My father said that after my mother found out about Charles, she talked to her aunt, Margaret. Margaret was the sister of my mother's mother, Lady Phillippa, who married Lord de Winter. After Lord and Lady de Winter died in a fire in the summerhouse, Great-Aunt Margaret took my mother and raised her in London. My mother forced her aunt to tell her what she knew, and Great-Aunt Margaret said that their parents had some suspicions about the de Winters. There were rumors. But they were so eager for their daughter to marry well that they ignored the rumors. My aunt said that my grandmother Philippa told her that her husband had described a great-uncle of his who heard voices and saw visions. He was kept out of everyone's sight."

Reed ran his hands back through his hair. "But that's not you. You aren't mad."

"No. Not yet. But I could become so. What if my visions are a precursor of madness? Besides, do you really think that I would risk passing it on to our children? That I would contaminate your family's blood? I would have had to be without honor to do something like that! Is that what you think of me?"

"No. No, of course not." He paused, then said, "Why did you not tell me this three years ago? Why did you just turn me away?"

"I could not tell you! I didn't want you to know. I couldn't bear to have you think of me with pity and shame. To know that about my family."

"But I loved you. And you let me think that I meant nothing to you. Less than nothing. You didn't trust me enough, didn't love me enough —"

"How can you say that?" Anna flared. "If I had loved you less, I would have married you and said to hell with all the consequences. What would I have cared about your family and its reputation? What would I have cared about burdening you with a wife who might turn mad in a few years?"

"Oh, yes, it was noble of you, all right," Reed snapped. "But you gave me no say-so in the matter. You shut me out, gave me no opportunity to say or do anything. You arranged my life for me, without even the courtesy of asking what I wanted."

"It didn't matter what you wanted. Or what *I* wanted!" Anna cried. "There was only one course of action. We could not marry."

"It didn't have to work out the way you envisioned. We could have talked about it, decided what to do. Perhaps we could have done something."

"What?" Anna flung her arms wide. "It

doesn't matter how rich or powerful you are, or how clever. There was nothing to be done. Nothing could take away the madness in my family. Nothing could have changed the terrifying possibility that lies within my body. How could anything have been any different? There was no way that we could be together. You had to build a life without me. I had to build a life without you."

"An empty life," Reed retorted. "A life without love."

Anna drew herself up. "Whatever you call it, it is my life. I worked very hard at driving you out of my heart. I cannot allow myself to love. Never again."

"I marvel at your ability to turn your feelings on and off at will," Reed told her. "I, unfortunately, was never able to."

Anna looked at him for a long moment, then said tightly, "I did what I had to do."

She turned and strode away. Reed stood, looking after her. This time, he did not follow her.

The following days passed in a haze of misery for Anna. She did not see or hear from Reed. She presumed that before long she would hear that he was moving back to London. She had driven him off, just as she had done three years ago. It would have seemed, she thought, that once would have provided all the pain she should have to endure.

She went about her daily tasks, searching out every little thing that she could do to busy herself, and though she did them somewhat numbly, at least they kept her mind from returning again and again to the thought of Reed. The nights were much worse, for when she went to bed and extinguished her candle, there was nothing to stave off her thoughts, and soon she would turn her face into her pillow and cry.

Anna wanted to continue to look into the killings, but she was unsure how to go about it. Obviously, she could not go back to Winterset and help Reed look through the records there for former servants. Beyond that, she was not sure what to do. Frankly, she could not tell that their investigation into the killings almost fifty years ago had any relevance to the two killings that had taken place recently.

However, she had no idea how else to proceed. She had talked to Estelle's roommate and to her family, and she had come no closer to discovering the identity of the mysterious man Estelle had been meeting. Nor could she think of any way to discover who had killed the young farmer a few days later.

Had the killer specifically meant to kill Frank Johnson? Had he seen him at the tavern and followed him home? Or had he lain in wait at the footbridge and simply killed the first person who happened by?

It seemed to her that he must have intended to kill a farmer in order to make the murders like the ones that had occurred in the past. Therefore, he must have known that Johnson worked the fields with his father and brothers.

Anna experienced a shiver down her back at the thought. For the killer to have known that Frank Johnson was a farmer would indicate that he must be someone local, not, as she had hoped, someone from another village who had ridden over to see Estelle. The second killing, she thought, also made it more unlikely that it was Estelle's lover who had killed her — unless, of course, he had set out to kill a maidservant and had taken up with Estelle with the intention of killing her.

That idea brought another shiver. It all seemed too horrible to contemplate. Whether the killer was cold and meticulous, choosing his victims — taking up with Estelle, following the Johnson boy home — or someone who prowled the area at night, killing whoever happened to cross his path,

Anna could not imagine how anyone could do what he had done. He must be mad, she thought.

That idea brought her back to her uncle. Anna could not bear to think that he had done it. He was her flesh and blood; she loved him even though he no longer was the man she had known and loved as a child.

There was no wickedness in him, of that she was certain. But she was less certain that he was incapable of killing someone if he was in the grip of one of his delusions. He heard and saw things that other people did not, but they were as real to him as the events in Anna's life were to her. If the "Angel Gabriel" told him he must kill Estelle, wouldn't he do it? If he thought the Johnson lad was one of the Queen's assassins, might he not fight him?

On the other hand, the fact that the killings so closely mirrored the original killings seemed to Anna to indicate that Uncle Charles could not be responsible. How could his fogged brain have been up to the task of planning murders to resemble the old ones?

Anna prayed that she was right, that the killer could not be her uncle. If he was, then she and her family were ultimately responsible for those poor people dying, for they had hidden and sheltered her uncle, and allowed him to live freely instead of locked up in an asylum.

As she was pondering these matters one morning, it occurred to her suddenly that she knew a person of very sound mind who had been alive at the time of the original killings — Nick Perkins. So that afternoon, taking a meat pie from the cook, she drove the long way around to his house — she still could not face walking over the footbridge on the way there.

He was working in his garden, as he usually was, and he stood up with a smile when he saw her. "Miss Anna. What a pleasure to see you."

"Thank you." She smiled, climbing down from the trap, and handed him the pie. "A little something for your table from Cook."

"Your presence is gift enough," he told her with a twinkle in his blue eyes. "But I'll take the pie, anyway."

"I cannot imagine how you never came to marry," Anna said teasingly. "A charmer such as yourself."

"Ah, now, Miss Anna, mayhap I was just too crafty for the matchmakers."

In fact, Anna had wondered more than once why the old man had not married and grown old with children and grandchildren around him. Even in old age, his was a handsome face, and Anna could well imagine that when he was young, he had had the local lasses swooning over him. When she was younger, she had dreamed up several romantic tragedies to account for his single state. In more recent years, it had seemed to her less romantic and more sad that the man had grown old alone.

Leading her inside, Perkins put the pie away and brewed a pot of tea for them. "How are those two young rascals? Bright as tacks, they were, and good with their hands, too. I didn't worry about letting them have the dog."

"I haven't heard from them. They have gone back to London, you know. Their sister did not feel it was safe to have the children around here with all that has happened."

Nick shook his head somberly as he brought the teapot to the table and poured the golden-brown liquid into their cups. "Bad business, that."

"Yes, it was. Very bad." Anna took a sip of tea, then said, "Nick . . ."

"Yes, miss?"

"You were here, were you not, forty-eight years ago? When the first murders happened?"

He glanced over at her. "Aye, I was."

"What do you remember about them?" Anna asked.

"What do you want to know about those for? They're long past. It's better to leave the dead buried."

"But someone won't let them," Anna countered. "Have you heard the details of the current murders? The first was one of our maids, and the last was the son of a farmer. They were slashed with what looked like claws. Just like the murders forty-eight years ago."

"It couldn't be the same person," Nick said flatly.

"No. I think it's clear that someone is imitating him. But perhaps the answer to these murders lies in those old ones."

"I don't see how," he said with a shrug.

"Did you know the people who were killed back then?" Anna asked.

"I knew Will Dawson. He was an old man. He didn't deserve for his life to end that way." Perkins' usually cheerful face was grim.

"No one does. So you didn't know the servant at Winterset?"

He shook his head. "No. Oh, I'd seen her once or twice, I suppose, but I didn't know her."

"Who do you think killed them?" Anna asked.

"Everyone said it was the Beast," he replied.

Anna cocked an eyebrow at him. "Surely you don't believe that."

"It would take a beast to do those things." His eyes slid away from her.

"Was there no one they suspected?" Anna persisted. It seemed to her that Nick, usually such an open, even talkative person, was being peculiarly vague with his answers.

"The girl's fiancé," he replied. "But when Dawson was killed, they let him out of jail. He couldn't have done that one."

"But no one else?"

"I never heard that there was."

Anna looked at him with narrowed eyes. She could not shake the feeling that her old friend was holding something back from her. "Did you never suspect who it was?"

"I had no way of knowing," he replied. "I didn't spend much time worrying about it. It was harvest, and I had a lot of work to do. And then the murders stopped, so . . ."

"Isn't it peculiar, though? How the killer just stopped after two? Why did someone kill those two and no one else?"

"Mayhap he left the area," Perkins suggested. "More tea?" He lifted the pot.

Anna nodded, with a little sigh. When she

had thought of Perkins, she had been so sure that he would be able to tell her something useful. He must have seen her disappointment, for he reached over and patted her hand, a more familiar gesture than he would normally have made.

"Don't worry about it now, Miss Anna." He smiled at her. "It was all a long time ago. Just let it lie."

"I can't. What if there's some connection to the present murders?"

"Someone is imitating them, that's all. Finding out what happened back then, even if you could do it, wouldn't tell you who's doing it now." He stood up. "By the way, seeing that you're going back to Holcomb Manor, would you take this liniment to the head groom? I promised to make him up a new bottle."

"Of course." Anna accepted the change of conversation, even though she could not understand why Perkins seemed so reluctant to talk about the matter. Perhaps, since he'd known the farmer who had died, the incidents held too many bad memories for him.

She left a few minutes later and drove home, mulling over her conversation with Perkins. When she stopped the horse in front of her house, she wished that she had left Nick's cottage several minutes later. The squire's carriage was in front of their house.

There was no way she could sneak in without being seen, so Anna put on the best smile she could and walked into the drawing room. Kit, looking rather beleaguered, glanced up at Anna's entrance and smiled with relief.

"Anna, dear." He stood up, giving her his seat in a straight-back chair positioned between Mrs. Bennett and her daughter, Felicity.

Mrs. Bennett beamed at Anna, and Felicity giggled for no apparent reason. Anna saw that they had brought Miles with them this time. He was slouching on the sofa beside his sister, looking bored, but he rose at Anna's entrance and bowed deeply over her hand.

"Oh, pray don't leave us, Sir Christopher, just because your sister has returned," Mrs. Bennett said with a little laugh. "We should love to chat with both of you. Isn't that right, Felicity?"

"Oh, my, yes," Felicity replied inanely, letting out another giggle.

"I am sorry. I offer you my deepest apologies, but I have a great deal of work waiting for me at my desk," Kit told her. "I am afraid

I must leave Anna to entertain you." He left the room as quickly as politeness would allow.

"Such a responsible gentleman," Mrs. Bennett said warmly, with an approving smile at Kit's back. "You see, Miles, how he attends to his estate. One day your father will no longer be with us, and you will have to assume his duties. You could have no better model than Sir Christopher."

Miles cast a dark look at his mother. Anna suspected that this was an argument he had heard more than once from her.

Mrs. Bennett turned to Anna, leaning forward confidingly to say, "I cannot get Miles even to accompany his father round the estate. That boy." She cast an affectionately exasperated glance at him. "He would rather work on his poetry. Isn't that right, dear?"

"Mother, I am sure that Miss Holcomb doesn't want to hear about our family matters," he said, with an agonized look at Anna.

"He's right," Felicity agreed unexpectedly. "It's horribly boring, poetry."

A flush stained Miles' cheeks, and he shot his sister a furious glance. Anna hastily put in, "I am rather fond of poetry myself."

"Of course you are," Mrs. Bennett said,

smiling at her. "Such a smart girl you are. La, Felicity and I are such featherheads." She said this happily, as if such a character trait would endear them to Anna.

Anna murmured some response, not sure exactly what was appropriate to this remark. Mrs. Bennett, however, did not notice her hesitation. She was already plowing ahead with her typically one-sided conversation.

"I am sure you are sorry to see Lady Kyria go," she said. "Such a lovely woman — and not at all high in the instep, as one would think she would be. Wouldn't you say so?"

Anna had barely parted her lips to answer before Mrs. Bennett went on, "And her husband — such a charming gentleman, even if he is an American. I was so surprised. He seemed quite genteel."

"I hear that civilization has reached their shores," Anna replied dryly.

Mrs. Bennett gave her a puzzled look, then chuckled. "Oh, yes, I see. You are joking. You are such a clever girl, I always say. But you know, dear . . ." She leaned forward, lowering her voice confidentially, "Gentlemen don't always wish a woman to be quite so clever."

"Mama . . ." Miles' word was a groan.

"Now, hush, Miles. Miss Holcomb understands what I'm saying, don't you, dear?"

"Of course, ma'am," Anna replied politely.

Mrs. Bennett proceeded to rattle on in her usual way for some minutes, discussing everything from Lady Kyria's party to the horror of the deaths — and the deplorable way they were cutting into the area's social life — to the continued presence of Reed Moreland at Winterset, which she attributed, with an arch smile in Anna's direction, to Anna's own charms.

It was a vast relief to Anna when the Bennetts finally left almost an hour later. She strolled down the hall to the door of her brother's study and knocked, then stuck her head inside.

"You are safe now. The Bennetts have gone."

Kit grinned somewhat sheepishly. "Are you very mad at me for abandoning you with them? They had been here almost half an hour already, with Mrs. Bennett urging that silly Felicity to talk, though she is able to do nothing but giggle, as far as I can tell."

"Yes, I think you are right." Anna smiled back at him. "I know your limits were tested. That's why I didn't send for you to bid them farewell, even though Mrs. Bennett kept hinting broadly at it."

"You're a dear."

Anna stayed for a few more minutes, discussing their respective days; then she went upstairs to dress for dinner. The evening meal was their usual quiet affair, with Kit and Anna talking companionably about this and that through the courses. It occurred to her that this would be the pattern of the rest of her life: visits with the neighbors, quiet meals with her brother, evenings spent in front of the fire with a book.

She glanced at Kit. They had agreed three years ago that they could not marry, that it would be unfair to bring their strain of madness into an unsuspecting family. They would not have children who might someday succumb to the illness. It was not a bad life; there were others, Anna knew, who had made much greater sacrifices than they had. But there were times, like tonight, when the ache of it brought her close to tears.

After the meal, Kit rode into the village for his weekly card game at the doctor's house. Anna spent the evening catching up on her correspondence. However, she had difficulty keeping her mind from turning to Reed. She wondered what he was doing this evening, if he found his mind going to her no matter what he tried to concentrate on.

He had been stunned by her news, that was clear — and angry because she had not told him the truth when she rejected his proposal. He had every reason to be angry, she told herself. It would doubtless have been easier for him to accept her rejection if he had known the real reason. Though he might have been sad, he would have realized that they could not marry. Finally, with a sigh, she put aside her paper and pen, and went upstairs to her bedroom.

She felt bored and lonely and too restless to sleep. So she picked up the book she had been reading lately, but a few minutes of reading the same page convinced her to put it down. Finally she went to her secretary and lowered the front, then sat down to write.

On the left side of the page, she listed all the things she knew about the old murders. On the right side, she listed all that she knew about the recent ones. It was not, she thought, a very impressive list. She drew lines connecting the items in each column that matched up. She looked at it for a few minutes. Still, no idea sparked in her head.

She rose and crossed to the window, then stood for a few minutes looking out. The moon was only a sliver, and the landscape below lay largely in darkness. She looked up at the bright stars in the dark sky, and her mind drifted.

Suddenly, sharp as a knife, fear lanced

through her. Anna gasped and swung around, almost expecting to see something horrific behind her. There was nothing there, but the fear in her did not abate. Her chest was tight, as if steel bands had wrapped around it, and her breath was loud and harsh in her ears.

Her vision began to blur, and she dropped down into a chair, her knees suddenly weak. She could feel the night air against her cheek; she was aware of a faint feeling of goodwill and a certain fuzzy-headedness. She saw a dark road stretching out in front of her, the moon and stars blocked out by the overarching trees. She saw the tangled branches of the trees moving gently in the evening breeze. Then, blindingly, pain burst in the back of her head and radiated through her skull, pitching her forward onto her knees on the floor.

Kit!

Anna pushed herself up onto her feet and ran to the door. "Kit!"

Chapter Thirteen

Anna tore down the hall to her brother's room, even though she knew he was not there. She threw open the door, not bothering to knock. The bedchamber was empty. She turned and pelted down the stairs, calling his name, and went to his study. It, too, was empty.

Anna pressed her hands against her head. Her heart was pounding so hard she could hardly think. *Oh, Reed!* She wished desperately that Reed were here, that she could turn to him for help.

"Miss? Is something the matter?" One of the footmen hurried toward her, drawn by her screaming of her brother's name.

Anna shoved aside her momentary weakness. "Have you seen Kit? Has he come home yet?"

"Why, no, miss, he hasn't. Is something wrong?"

"Yes. I — I'm not sure." Anna could not explain why she was so convinced that something had happened to her brother —

or was about to happen. But she was certain of it, and she could not stand by and do nothing. "Go out to the stables and tell them to saddle my horse."

The man goggled. "At this time of night, miss?"

"Yes! Don't just stand there! I have to go to Kit!"

"Yes, miss." He nodded quickly and scurried off.

Anna ran back to her room. She didn't have time to change into her riding habit, but she could not ride in these evening slippers. She kicked them off and pulled on her boots as fast as she could, then grabbed her riding crop and dashed back downstairs.

She raced across the yard to the stables, her heart pounding. There she found not only her mare, saddled, but a groom saddling another horse.

The head groom was holding her mare's reins, and he turned as Anna approached. "I'm going with you, miss," he told her, his chin thrust forward stubbornly, as if he expected a fight.

"Good," Anna replied, taking the reins and letting him toss her up into the saddle. If Kit was hurt, she would need help, and Cooper was a good rider; he would not slow her down.

"Shall I bring others?" Cooper asked.

Anna hesitated. If she was wrong, they would doubtless think she was mad, but she could not worry about that now. "Tell them to bring round the carriage and follow. We're riding into town. Kit may be . . . in trouble."

Cooper turned to the other groom, barking out a few quick orders, then mounted his horse. Anna was already turning her mare and heading down the driveway, going as fast as the dim light of the waning moon allowed.

At the end of the driveway, she turned right onto the lane. Her mind had been working as she ran, and she thought she knew what stretch of road she had seen in her vision. Not long before the lane ended at the larger road into town, there was a stretch where the trees formed a long canopy. She was sure that that was what she had seen right before the blinding pain had exploded in her head. She didn't understand how she had known that Kit was the object of her vision; she had not seen him. But she was certain that it was about him; she felt it in every fiber. She hoped it had not happened already. She hoped she was not too late.

Cooper did not waste any time trying to question her. He simply kept up with her, his eyes searching the road in front of them intently. Finally, up ahead of them, Anna saw the beginning of the rows of trees. It looked almost like a tunnel, the road disappearing into its black maw.

Her heart was in her throat as they drew closer. It was difficult to see, and she had to slow her horse as they rode into the deeper darkness created by the trees arching overhead.

There, halfway through the "tunnel," stood a horse, moving about restlessly, his saddle empty, reins dragging the ground. Only a few feet away from him, a dark shape was stretched out on the ground. A figure crouched over the body on the ground, head bent down, a cloak spread wide around him.

"Kit!" Anna screamed, and spurred her horse forward.

The figure threw one quick glance over its shoulder. Anna had a glimpse of something both light and dark, not really a face, and then the creature scurried away, melting into the darkness at the side of the road.

Anna pounded down the road, heedless of injury to herself or her horse, desperate to reach her brother. The groom sped after her. She reached the body on the ground and jumped down from her horse.

"Kit!" She ran the last few feet to the figure and dropped to her knees beside him.

It was Kit. The darkness beneath the

canopy of trees was so thick that Anna had to lay a hand upon his back to see if he was breathing. Her own breath came out in a long sigh when she felt his back move against her hand.

"He's alive!"

Cooper knelt on the other side of Kit. "Is he all right? What happened, miss?"

"I don't know." She looked across her brother at him. "Did you see —"

He gave a quick, emphatic nod. "I saw something. What was it?"

"I — I think it was a person in a cloak."

"Should I go after 'im, miss?"

Anna glanced into the darkness beyond the road, where trees and bushes clustered. "No. It's too dark."

She wished she had thought to bring a lantern. She also wished she had brought a gun. She shivered as she remembered the figure she had seen bent over Kit.

Anna leaned closer to her brother. "Kit?"

He let out a moan, which relieved her a little. His hair was darkened with dirt, but then she realized with a gasp that it was not dirt that matted the side of his hair; it was blood.

Quickly she reached under the hem of her skirt and grabbed a ruffle of her petticoat. "Do you have a knife?"

"What? Oh, yes, miss." Cooper dug in his pocket and produced a small clasp knife, which he opened and handed to her.

Anna cut through the ruffle and ripped off a long piece of it. Folding the piece of cotton, she pressed it as gently as she could against Kit's head.

He stirred, moaning again.

They heard the thud of horses' hooves and looked up to see the carriage rattling toward them, the coachman, looking most unlike his usual dignified self in his shirtsleeves and suspenders, handling the reins. The footman Anna had spoken to earlier sat beside him, clinging to the seat for dear life as the vehicle rocked along.

When the carriage rolled to a stop a few feet away from them, the groom they had left behind sprang down from the rear of the carriage, where he had been standing, hanging on to a strap. The coachman climbed down from his high seat, bringing a lantern, and the footman followed him at a much slower pace.

"Thank heavens you brought a lantern," Anna exclaimed. "Bring it here, Gorman. Kit has been injured."

The coachman approached and held the lantern up over the scene. In the light, Anna could see that the only blood on Kit came from the wound on his head. She lifted the makeshift pad she had pressed against it. It was still difficult to see the exact nature of his wound, but the blood seemed to have stopped flowing.

Quickly Anna and the groom felt along Kit's arms and legs. Nothing seemed to be broken. Carefully, they turned him over. Anna breathed a sigh of relief when she saw no sign of blood on his chest, either.

"Thank goodness. Let's put him into the carriage and take him home. Cooper, ride into the village and get Dr. Felton, and tell him that Kit has been injured."

"Yes, miss."

Cooper jumped back on his horse and took off as the other three men lifted Kit and carried him into the carriage. Getting him inside the vehicle was a difficult process, and Kit groaned, his eyes opening and staring blankly at them for a moment before closing again. Anna gave her horse to the groom to ride back to the Manor, and she got into the carriage with her brother. The ruffle she had torn off was now soaked in blood, so she tore off the remainder of it and held it against Kit's head during the ride home.

She took one of Kit's hands with her other hand. It lay limply in her clasp. She wished that he would wake up. It seemed to her a very bad sign that he had not awakened. She had heard of head injuries from which one never awoke, simply lay in a sort of limbo somewhere between death and life. Fear welled up in her, threatening to overwhelm her. Anna thought again of Reed. What she wanted more than anything at the moment was to lean against him, to feel his strong arms go around her and hear the reassuring sound of his voice.

Tears filled her eyes, and she blinked them away. She had to be strong for Kit, she reminded herself. She could not give way to weakness. Reed was not with her. He would never be with her. She had lived the great majority of her life without him; she could live the rest of it the same way.

Keeping a stern grip on her emotions, she sat through the rest of the ride home, holding the makeshift bandage against her brother's head and refusing to think of anything but the hope that Kit would soon wake up.

The house was brightly lit when they reached it, and as the carriage rolled to a stop in front of the door, it opened and the butler and several other servants hurried out. Anna climbed down out of the carriage and held up her hand, forestalling any questions.

"Kit is hurt. I don't know what happened, but he has a head injury, and he's unconscious. Take him up to his bed, and we'll clean the wound and wait for the doctor."

Shock stamped the faces of the servants, but they hurried to do as Anna had told them. As they carefully lifted Kit out of the carriage and carried him toward the house, there was the sound of hoofbeats. Anna swung around, a crazy hope swelling inside her.

A horse and rider thundered up to the house from the east, moving much faster than was safe in the dim light. He had obviously come the faster route through the fields instead of along the road. He pulled to a stop and jumped down from his horse, his long strides eating up the ground between him and Anna.

"Reed!" Something inside Anna snapped, and she flung herself against him, heedless of all the watching eyes of the servants. His arms went tightly around her, holding her to his chest.

"Anna! What's happened?"

She could not answer. The fear she had been holding in check swamped her now, and she burst into tears. She clung to him, crying, and Reed smoothed his hand down her back, murmuring to her comfortingly.

Over her head, he watched the servants carry the limp form of her brother into the house, and he tightened his hold on Anna.

Gradually Anna's arms loosened a little around his waist. She stood for a moment longer, listening to the reassuring thud of his heart beneath her ear, her tears drying. She thought of the servants watching and knew that there would soon be a wealth of gossip in the servants' quarters, but at the moment she could not bring herself to care.

Finally she stepped back, wiping her tears from her cheeks with her hands.

"Here." Reed pulled his handkerchief from his pocket and gently dabbed away the moisture.

Anna gave him a trembling smile. "Thank you." She glanced back at the front door. "I — I must go to Kit."

"Of course." Reed took her arm, and they started for the door.

"How did you — how did you know?" Anna asked, looking up at him. "I mean, what are you doing here? It must be near midnight."

"I had a dream," he replied. "I think. I was in my study, reading, and I — I suppose I had begun to drift off. And then I heard you call my name. It was so clear, so real. I don't know how, but I was certain that you needed me. So I had my horse saddled, and — well, here I am."

Anna thought of the way she had cried out to him in her mind, of how everything inside her had yearned for him to be with her. She had needed him. And, somehow, it did not even seem strange now that he had known.

They walked through the house and up the stairs to Kit's room. The servants had laid him down on the bed, and removed his jacket and boots. There was a bowl of water on a table beside the bed, and it was pink with diluted blood. Kit's valet was cleaning the wound on Kit's head with a washcloth, and he turned as they entered the room.

"Miss Anna."

"Thompkins. How does it look?"

"There was a lot of blood, but I've cleaned most of it off, and I don't think the wound itself is very big."

"What happened?" Reed asked.

"I don't know," Anna replied. She leaned over her brother, bending down to inspect the wound. Behind her, Reed picked up an oil lamp and held it closer so that she could see.

She let out a little side of relief. "It looks as though he's been hit on the head, doesn't it? I don't think it's a bullet wound, do you?"

"No," Reed agreed. He set the lamp down

and pulled a chair up to the side of the bed. "Here. Sit down. Is the doctor on his way?"

"Yes. Cooper went to get him."

Reed turned to the valet. "Why don't you go down and bring us a pot of tea? I'm sure Miss Holcomb could use a cup, and the doctor will doubtless appreciate one, too, when he arrives."

Anna thought that she should not let Reed give her servants orders, but at that moment she was too tired to care. Once she had seen Kit's wound, all her energy had seemed to leave in a rush. She leaned forward, taking Kit's hand in one of hers and propping her head against her other arm on the bed.

As soon as the valet left, Reed squatted down beside her, looking into her face. "Now. What happened?"

"I don't know. I had a . . . a feeling, the sort I told you about, like the one I had that day in the woods. Somehow I just knew that Kit was in trouble."

"So you went looking for him?"

She nodded. "I knew he had gone into town tonight to play cards. He does it once a week. Some of the local men meet at Dr. Felton's every Tuesday for cards — the squire, Mr. Norton, Miles. So, when I had that feeling, the only thing I could think to do was to ride into town. Of course, if I had ridden there only to find Kit peacefully playing cards with the other men, he would have been enormously embarrassed."

"But your intuition was correct."

"Yes. I saw trees, and, when I thought about it, I was fairly certain that what I had seen was a certain stretch of road, before you reach the larger highway. It is a little finger of the woods that stretches out, with the lane cut through them, and the branches arch overhead, forming a kind of roof."

Reed nodded. "I know where you're talking about." He frowned. "So you actually saw what was happening? You had a vision?"

"Yes. I . . . well, I was just looking out the window, and my mind was drifting, I guess. And suddenly I was filled with fear. It swept over me. And I knew, I just knew, that something was terribly wrong. I had to sit down. I felt weak. And then I saw these branches, and I could feel the night air on my cheek. Suddenly there was a tremendous pain in my head, and I was certain that there was something wrong with Kit."

"Pretty accurate, I'd say," Reed mused. He reached over and cupped his hand against Anna's cheek. "You may have saved his life."

Tears threatened again as she whispered, "I think I did." She blinked away the tears, muttering, "Damn." She drew a breath, then went on, looking into Reed's eyes. "When we rode up, I saw . . . someone bending over Kit."

"What! Who was it?"

Anna shook her head. "I don't know. It was very dark beneath the trees. I only saw this — this shape bending over him. I could tell nothing about him — height or size — except that he wore some sort of cape. He turned, and I glimpsed . . . something."

"What do you mean? You saw his face?"

"I'm not sure what I saw. It must have been his face, but there was something odd about it. It was only for a second, and then he turned and ran. It was terribly dark, and I couldn't send Cooper after him. It would have put him in too much danger."

"Of course." Reed rose and began to pace about the room. "Do you think it was the same man who murdered the other two?"

"It seems unlikely that there is another person running about attacking people."

"Yes. It rather stretches one's credulity." He turned to her. "When you say odd, what do you mean?"

"I can't tell you. It was only an impression. It just — it didn't exactly look like a person. You can question Cooper. He saw it, too, but he seemed as uncertain as I about what he saw. It's the sort of thing where you expect to see something, and then it isn't what you expect. It takes you a moment to adjust, but he was gone in a flash. I can't tell you what was wrong with his face, but the whole scene gave me the shivers. It was so eerie. . . ."

There was a knock on the door, and Anna jumped, then let out an apologetic little laugh. "Come in."

It was the doctor, followed by Thompkins with a tray containing a teapot and cups, as well as a few sandwiches and cakes that the cook had added. The doctor looked at Anna, then over at Reed, but if he found anything odd about Reed's presence there at this time of night, he said nothing. His eyes went to Kit's form on the bed.

"Good heavens!" he exclaimed. "I scarcely believed your man when he told me. I just saw Sir Christopher not an hour ago."

"Then he did play cards with you this evening?" Anna asked.

"Yes, of course. He was the last to leave, in fact. Not half an hour after I bade farewell to him, your man was knocking on my door."

The doctor strode across the room and

bent over Kit, examining the wound. "Hmm. Looks like he got a good crack on his head. Do you know what happened?"

"No," Anna admitted. "We found him like this. He was lying in the lane, and his horse was near him." She described the location.

The doctor frowned as he took out a bottle and cloth and began to clean the wound. Kit winced and let out another noise.

"I suppose he could have fallen from his horse," the doctor mused. "And struck his head. He had a few drinks, although I certainly would not have thought him drunk."

"Kit is a good horseman. Even when he's been drinking, he can stay on a horse. And I can't imagine that he was riding fast through there. It was rather dark."

"Perhaps he did not see a branch and it knocked him from his horse. The trees are very low-hanging there."

"There was someone with Kit," Anna said. "When we rode up, someone was bending over him."

The doctor looked at her, startled. "Who?"

"I don't know. He ran away."

Dr. Felton stared at Anna. "You mean, you think someone attacked Sir Christopher?"

"Why else would he have run away from us?"

"This is mad. Why would anyone have attacked your brother?" Dr. Felton asked.

"I have no idea. Why would anyone have attacked Estelle or Frank Johnson?"

Dr. Felton glanced from Anna to Reed, then shook his head. "It seems as if the world has run mad. Who could be doing such things?"

Anna shook her head. The doctor sighed and finished cleaning the wound, then bandaged it.

"Shouldn't Kit have awakened by now?" Anna asked worriedly.

The doctor shrugged. "It's hard to say. He got a hard knock. It tore the scalp, and there is a contusion. Normally, I would not have thought he would remain unconscious this long." He bent, lifting Kit's eyelids one by one and peering into his eyes. "He isn't in a coma. I — he almost seems to be deeply asleep."

He straightened, frowning, and looked at them. "Give him until tomorrow morning and see what happens. It may just be the effects of a hard knock after a few whiskies. Let me know if his condition is unchanged. Here is a powder for his headache. Simply empty the packet into a glass of water."

The doctor had a cup of tea with them afterward, and then Anna and Reed walked with him downstairs, leaving Kit's valet to sit with the patient.

As they reached the front door, Reed thanked the doctor for loaning them his father's journals, then went on. "One thing puzzled us, however."

"Oh, really?" Dr. Felton turned to him inquiringly.

"Yes. We noticed that there were some pages torn out of the journal."

"Ah." Dr. Felton nodded. "I should have mentioned those. Unfortunately, I'm not really sure what was on those pages. My father left the journals to me upon his death, so I could not ask him. I noticed the missing pages, as well. I asked my mother, but she had no idea. She had never read his journals."

"We thought it might have been pages where he made a mistake in a drawing or something, and so tore it out and started over."

"It is possible," Felton agreed. "However, there are other places where he has simply crossed something out. I have given the matter some thought, and what I decided was that there were perhaps records of a patient that he considered too private, too confidential, to be revealed even to his son after his death." He shrugged. "I am sorry I can be no more help than that."

"Oh, no, we are very grateful for your help," Anna assured him.

"Did you get any ideas from the journals?" the doctor asked. "I mean, about who could be copying the killings?"

"No, not really," Reed told him. "Except that it must be someone who knew enough about the killings to imitate them."

"I am afraid that might encompass all too many people," Dr. Felton said. With a slight bow, he bade them good-night and left.

Reed and Anna turned back down the hall. Reed reached out and took her arm, pulling her to a stop. "Anna . . . about the other day . . . could we talk privately?"

"Yes, of course." She led him into the music room, which was nearby, and closed the door, turning to him.

"I wanted you to know — I am sorry I was so harsh with you when you told me your reason for not marrying me. I had no right to blame you. You only did what you thought was right."

"Thank you." Anna could feel the anxiety and sorrow that had plagued her for the last few days loosening within her. "It is generous of you to say so. I have thought about it, too, and I see that you were right. It was my fear that kept me from telling you the true reason. I should not have hidden behind the falsehoods I told you. I thought only about myself and my fears, not about you. It was wrong of me."

"But understandable," Reed told her. "People have called my family mad for as long as I remember, and though I know that the epithet is untrue, still, it stings." He paused, then went on. "I would hope that we can be friends now, however, that we will not have to shun each other's company."

Anna smiled, her face lighting up. She would not be completely cut off from Reed, would not have to face the rest of her life without ever seeing him.

"I am so glad," she said. "It is what I want, as well." It occurred to Anna that she seemed too eager, and she hastily explained. "I — I had hoped that we could continue to try to find the killer. I want to do so even more now that he has attacked Kit."

"I would like it, too," he told her.

"I went to talk to Nick Perkins today," Anna said. "I can't imagine why I did not think of him before. He is still quite alert and was a young man at the time of the earlier killings."

"You went by yourself?" Reed frowned.

"It was broad daylight, and I took the pony trap. I did not walk," she protested. "I was perfectly safe."

"And did you learn anything from him?"

Anna frowned. "Not really. He said that he knew the farmer who was killed, but not much beyond that."

"I dug through those records," Reed said. "It took me a day, but I finally found the household expenses for forty-eight years ago."

Anna brightened. "Did you find the names of the servants?"

"Yes, though I must say, I had the devil of a time figuring out the handwriting. And several of the servants had only their first names written down. But I gave the rest of the names to Norton, and he had his clerk track them down. Out of all the names, he did find one of the maids still alive and living in Eddlesburrow."

"Really? That's not too far. An hour's ride, perhaps."

"Yes. It is also where the records of the coroner's inquests are held."

Anna's eyes widened. "I had not thought of those."

"I don't know how much more we will find in them than was in the doctor's journals, but there might be something."

"Of course. We should look at them. I couldn't go, of course, until Kit is better."

"No. We will wait. The maid and the records will still be there." Reed hesitated, then continued, "Anna . . . I wanted to ask you about your uncle."

Anna's eyes flew to his face, and one hand moved unconsciously to press against her stomach, where her nerves were already fluttering. "What?"

"I thought about what you said quite a bit over the last few days. And I realized . . . Are you worried that it might be your uncle who is doing these things?"

Anna's heart began to hammer. She stared at Reed, unable to speak.

"No, pray, do not look at me like that," Reed said quickly, moving closer to her. "I do not mean to suggest that he is. I only thought that you might fear it."

"I do," Anna said, and her voice came out barely above a whisper. "Oh, Reed, I do. . . ."

She pressed her lips together tightly, struggling for a moment to overcome her emotions. She had been carrying her fears silently for more than two weeks, and while it hurt to admit what she had been thinking about her uncle, it was a relief, as well. Once she started, the words seemed to come tumbling out of her.

"I cannot think that he would hurt anyone. He is not a violent man, not at all. He is a good man, truly he is. But I cannot help but wonder, because of the marks. I told you that he refuses to cut his nails, and they grow quite long, and Dr. Felton said the marks were spaced wide apart, like a bear's claw. A man's fingers would be similarly spaced."

"Anna!" Reed took her hand between both of his. "Please do not distress yourself so. Those marks do not prove that it was your uncle."

"I know." Anna drew a calming breath. "And yet . . . everyone keeps saying how mad it is that someone would kill people this way. There is no rhyme nor reason. Uncle Charles has reasons for what he does, but they are so bizarre that no normal person would understand them. He is a gentle man — a pitiful figure, really, because he lives in such fear, even though all of it is created in his own mind. But he roams the woods at night. His keeper cannot keep track of him all the time. He has to sleep. And if, for some reason, my uncle thought that those people were the Queen's assassins — well, it seems ludicrous to us, but to him it is very real, and I am afraid that if he was laboring under a delusion such as that, he could kill them."

"Have you seen him, talked to him?"

"I have seen him. He seems much the same as ever. He did not mention anything about having had to do away with any enemies, but I'm not sure he would. He is so very secretive, even with Kit and me, or Arthur, his valet."

"What did his keeper say?"

"He does not believe that Uncle could have done it. But he admits that he does not know where he was on those nights, as he was sleeping. And he is the most loyal of people — I mean, he has been willing to stay with Uncle for all these years, and it is a hard, thankless task. No one would do it just for the salary. He truly loves my uncle and has looked after him since he was a boy. For that reason, however, I don't know how much I can rely on his opinion. He is not at all objective."

"What about tonight? Would he have hurt your brother? Does he — would he not recognize Sir Christopher?"

"Surely he would not harm Kit! He is not mad in that way. He knows who we are. And he seems still to have some fondness for us, though it is largely overwhelmed by his fears and delusions. He has never accused one of us — Kit or me or Arthur — of trying to harm him. But he did — well, before he left

Winterset, there was a certain turnover of staff because he would decide one of them was watching him or wanted to harm him or had stolen something. I cannot be sure but what he might come to decide that one of us is somehow trying to harm him. Oh, Reed, if it is he who is doing these things, then I am responsible for leaving him free!"

Tears glittered in her eyes, and impulsively Reed put his arm around her, pulling her against him. He bent and pressed his lips to her hair. "Shh. Sweet girl, do not cry. I promise you, you are not at fault."

Anna leaned against him, letting herself depend on Reed for another brief moment. She could not continue to be weak, as she had been tonight, she knew. *But just for a little while, surely it would not cause any harm. . . .*

With a sigh, she stepped away from him, wiping the tears from her face. "I am sorry. I seem to be a veritable watering pot tonight."

"It has been a very disturbing evening," Reed told her. "You have every right to be upset. I want to help you, Anna."

"I need your help," she admitted. Her eyes were huge and luminous as she looked at him. "I am very grateful for it."

"I don't want your gratitude," he responded tightly. "I am not doing it for that. I want — I want you to be happy."

"Thank you." She would not tell him that what he wanted was impossible. She had known real happiness once, when she had loved him, and now she was sworn to live without it.

"We will work on this and find out who did it," Reed went on firmly. "Whoever it is, we will put a stop to it."

Anna nodded and drew a steadying breath. "I should go see about Kit."

"Yes, of course. I will take my leave of you."

"Reed . . ." Anna reached out a hand, touching his sleeve. "Thank you."

"Of course." He took her hand and pressed a brief kiss on the back of it. It would have passed for a polite gesture, if not for the heat of his skin and the thrill that ran up Anna's arm.

She drew a shaky breath, unable to say anything.

Reed turned and left, and Anna sank down onto a chair. It took her a moment to recover her composure. Then she rose and made her way up the stairs to Kit's room.

Thompkins was sitting there, and he jumped up at her entrance.

"How is he?" Anna asked.

"Unchanged, miss. I — he is breathing

regularly. He seems to be asleep. I will sit up with him tonight," the valet offered.

"That is very good of you, Thompkins. But I think that I will sit up with him, at least for the first while. Perhaps you should go and get some sleep, and I will call you later if I need you."

"Very good, miss."

Thompkins left the room, and Anna sat down in the chair beside her brother's bed. The oil lamp was turned down very low, so she could barely see Kit's face, but he did seem, as Thompkins had said, to be sleeping peacefully.

She sat for a few minutes, watching him, then rose and walked over to the window. Pushing aside the drape and leaning close to the window, she looked out at the night sky. The stars were shining, but she could not see the moon any longer, and she knew it must by now have climbed high in the sky.

Anna looked down at the garden. Directly below were flowers and small shrubs, with paths winding through them and back into the larger trees that lay beyond. As she looked, she thought she saw a flicker of movement, a shifting of something in the trees. Pulling the sides of the drapes close to her face to cut out the dim light inside the room, she peered into the darkness.

Yes, there, beneath the mulberry, a shadow moved, resolving itself into a dark shape. It was blocky and foreshortened from this angle, and it took a moment for Anna to realize that it was the figure of a man in a hat and cloak. As she watched, he turned his face toward the house.

She could see no features, only darkness beneath the wide brim of the hat. The head turned, looking first one way and then the other, moving with an eerie slowness. The head stopped when it reached her window.

A chill ran through her. He was waiting, watching them.

Chapter Fourteen

Anna drew in her breath sharply and stepped back from the window. For an instant her thoughts were scattered, and she could not move. Then she whirled and ran out of Kit's room and down the stairs, calling for the butler. She ran to the side door and checked to make sure it was locked. She ducked into the next room, which was the study and almost directly across from where she had seen the figure in the trees. She did not light a lamp, but hurried over to the window and peeked through the drapes.

But even though she was closer to the spot where the *creature* had stood, she could not see it clearly, for the shrubs in the garden blocked her view. She went to each window, making sure that it was securely locked. By the time she reached the hallway, the butler, Hargrove, had arrived, followed by one of the footmen. The butler had already retired, and his dignity was considerably diminished by the nightcap he wore on his head and the robe wrapped around his ample girth.

"Miss? Is something amiss?"

"I saw — I saw something outside," Anna told him. It sounded weak and foolish now that she said it. "A person in the trees beyond the garden."

The footman gaped at her, and though Hargrove was better at hiding his astonishment, his voice could not completely conceal a note of disbelief as he said, "A person, miss?"

"Yes," Anna said firmly, and looked him in the eye. "My brother was attacked tonight. I do not know who I saw just now or why he is here, but I think that, considering the things that have been occurring lately, we cannot take anything lightly."

"No, miss, of course not." The man hesitated. "Should I . . . send someone outside?"

"No. Just make sure that all the doors and windows are locked. Don't overlook any of them."

"Of course, miss. Right away."

Hargrove turned to the footman, snapping out orders, and then the two men bustled away. Anna hurried back up the stairs to her brother's room. She crossed to the window and parted the drapes, looking out into the night. There was no sign of anyone beneath the trees.

She could feel little relief. She turned away from the window and crossed over to her brother's bed. Kit was still sleeping. She sat down in the chair, scooting it a little closer to the bed, so that she could lay her arm down and put her hand on Kit's. Right then, she needed to have contact with him. She settled down to wait.

"Anna?" Kit's groggy voice woke her, and Anna lifted her head, confused for a moment.

"Oh." Her brain cleared as she realized that it was morning, the sun creeping around the cracks in the draperies, and she had fallen asleep. In the next instant it sank in on her that Kit's eyes were open and he was looking at her. "Kit, you're awake!"

She sprang to her feet, ignoring the painful twinge in her neck and shoulder from falling asleep with her head on her arm on Kit's bed.

" 'Course I am," Kit replied a little thickly. "What is happening? Why are you here?"

"Do you not remember?" Anna asked.

"Remember what?" Kit frowned and raised one hand to his head. "I have the very devil of a headache. Was I — in the bag?"

Anna had to smile a little. "No. At least, I don't think so. Dr. Felton said that you had only a few drinks."

"The doctor?" He looked even more puzzled. "Was he here? Was I — was last night our card game?"

"Yes. Do you not remember it?"

He closed his eyes for a moment, then opened them again, saying, "The last thing I remember is Mrs. Bennett and Felicity being here."

"Well, you received a bump on the head somehow," Anna said. "We found you lying in the road, unconscious."

Kit stared at her. "You're not serious."

"Unfortunately, I am."

"But how — I couldn't have fallen off my horse," he said in a mortified voice. "Not even if I was dead drunk."

"I don't think you did. I think someone attacked you. I only wish you could remember."

"Attacked me!" Kit clearly found the idea ludicrous. Anna related everything she knew about the matter, but he could not bring himself to believe that anyone had tried to harm him.

"I think the doctor's right. I knocked my head on a low-hanging branch, that's all."

"And what about the figure I saw bending

over you?" Anna asked, folding her arms and raising one brow.

"Well, you said it was quite dark. . . ."

"Not dark enough that I conjured up a person who was not there! And Cooper saw him, too."

Kit had no answer for that, but she could see in his face that neither could he really accept what she had said.

"But who could — why would anyone do that?" he asked.

"I don't know. I can't understand this person's mind. But, Kit, even if you cannot believe that someone harmed you, you must promise me that you will act as if you do," Anna told him urgently. "You must take care. Guard yourself against danger."

"What are you suggesting?" Kit asked, looking appalled. "That I hide here in the house? I have work to do. There is the estate — 'tis the busiest time of the year, apart from harvest."

"I know. And you have your pride, as well," Anna added dryly. "I am not suggesting that you hide in the house — although I do hope that you will be sensible enough to rest today and take the powder Dr. Felton left for you. It will ease your headache."

"I will be more than happy to do that," Kit told her fervently. "I feel as if someone has taken a hammer to my head."

Anna went to the table and unwrapped the paper the doctor had left, shaking a fourth of it into a glass and filling it with water. As she stirred, she turned back to her brother. "I trust that whoever it is will not try anything during the daylight hours. He seems to confine his activities to the nighttime. But, please, try to make sure that you are around other people as much as possible. And look out for danger. Take a groom with you."

"Take a groom with me?" Kit repeated, outraged. "Like a child?"

"Like someone with sense," Anna retorted, handing him the glass.

Kit took a drink and made a face. "This is bitter."

"It's medicine. It's supposed to be bitter. Drink up."

Kit obediently drank the rest of it, and Anna took the opportunity to press her point. "At least take a groom with you if you go out at night. Personally, I think you should stay in in the evening, but I know you well enough to assume that you will make it a point of going out at night, just to prove that you are not afraid." She directed a pointed look at him. "So if you do, take a groom with you. Do not go alone."

"And how long am I supposed to do this?" Kit asked, setting down the empty glass and adding sarcastically, "For the rest of my life?"

"That won't be very long if the killer gets hold of you again," Anna replied acerbically.

Kit groaned theatrically and flopped back against his pillows. "Anna . . ."

"Reed and I are trying to find the killer. With luck we will be able to do so, and then you won't have to keep looking over your shoulder."

"What?" Kit bounced back up from his pillows. "You are telling *me* to be careful, and all the while *you* are actually trying to track down the killer? Good Lord, Anna, are you mad?"

"No, I'm not mad. I am sure he doesn't know we are trying to find him. It isn't as if we advertised that we were looking into the murders."

"Is that what you have been doing lately?" Kit went on. "Obviously I should have been spending less time on the estate and staying here to keep an eye on you."

Anna cast him an exasperated look. "Don't try to turn this around on me. We are talking about your safety. I haven't been doing this on my own. I have been with Reed the whole time."

Kit frowned. "Anna . . . how much time are you spending with him? Do you really think it is wise? You took me to task for seeing Rosemary too much, yet it seems to me that you are putting your heart into worse danger."

"It is in no danger," Anna replied, somewhat untruthfully. "Reed knows that we can never be together. I told him why."

"You told him about Uncle Charles!" Kit exclaimed, then glanced toward the door to make sure it was closed and no one had overheard his hasty words.

"Yes. He will tell no one," Anna assured him. "I simply could not hide it any longer."

Her brother looked at her searchingly. "Are you sure? A man in love —"

"He does not love me," Anna interrupted. "Not any longer. How could he, after my refusal three years ago? He has spent the last three years disliking me, I assure you. He was upset that I had not told him the truth, but he told me that he understood."

"Lord Moreland seems to me to be a man who does not give up easily."

"Of course not. But he sees the impossibility of tying his line to mine." Anna's throat closed a little, the pain of her lost love welling up in her, but she swallowed hard and went on. "How could he not? His father is a duke, after all."

"I suppose you are right," Kit replied, but there was still skepticism on his face. "Still, it cannot be good, the two of you working closely together like this, seeing each other so often. . . ."

"Kit, don't," Anna said sharply. "Don't tell me I should not see him. Reed and I can be friends, at least."

There was pity in her brother's eyes as he looked at her. "Anna . . . I don't want to see you hurt. That is all."

"I know." She gave him a smile. "I won't be. I will be quite careful with my heart — as you must promise me you will be with your life."

He smiled faintly. "All right. I promise."

He held out his hand, and she took it, squeezing it tightly.

In truth, she was well aware that she was placing her heart in danger. But she could not bear to stay away from Reed. Even though she ached inside whenever she looked at him, wanting him, wanting a life with him, and knowing that could never happen, still she was willing to endure that pain. However much she hurt, however much she yearned, there was a greater pleasure in looking at him and talking to him, simply *being* with him. It was foolish, she suspected, but at the moment, she didn't really want to examine her actions.

Kit was feeling better by evening, and the next day he insisted on being up and about his work. Anna returned to her investigation. She and Reed rode to Eddlesburrow, where the records were kept for the local coroner's inquests. But first they planned to stop at the house of the former Winterset maid whom Reed had located.

Her name was Margaret Lackey, and she lived in a small stone cottage on the edge of the village. A series of stepping-stones led from the street to her front door, and on either side of the path grew a neatly cultivated garden.

As they approached the house, they saw a woman kneeling in front of a flower bed, busily tugging up every weed within reach. A wide-brimmed bonnet shielded her face from the sun and from their view, but she looked up as Reed and Anna dismounted and tied their horses. Black button eyes peered out of a wrinkled face, and she smiled as Anna and Reed started toward her.

"Good day to you, madam," Reed said, sweeping off his hat and bowing formally to her. "We are looking for a Miss Margaret Lackey."

"Then you have found her," the woman replied cheerfully. "Except that the name is Margaret Parmer, for the past forty years." She looked at Anna and Reed with curiosity.

"Mrs. Parmer," Reed amended, and introduced Anna and himself. "We would like to talk to you, if we may."

The woman whipped off her gloves and extended a hand to Reed. "If you'll help me up, here, then we can go inside, where we can talk a little better."

Reed reached down, took her hand and helped her to her feet. She brushed the dirt from her skirt and led them inside her house, leaving her gardening tools where they lay.

It was a pleasant house inside, small but well kept, and Margaret Parmer showed them into the parlor. She called to someone, and a moment later a middle-aged woman came into the room, wiping her hands on a towel.

"Tea, Gert," Mrs. Parmer said cheerfully. "For three, and some of those biscuits you made yesterday." As Gert left, Mrs. Parmer turned to Reed and Anna, smiling. "Gert helps me out. I can't keep a house up by myself any longer." She wiggled her fingers; the knuckles were knobby and swollen.

Mrs. Lackey took off her bonnet, revealing white hair, pulled back and knotted in a bun at the crown of her head. Stray hairs had come loose as she removed her hat, and she smoothed them back behind her ears as she sat down in a chair.

The former maid was the opposite of the housekeeper whom they had interviewed the other day. Though her fingers were knotted and her movements careful, she was still spry and alert. Her dark eyes gleamed with intelligence and curiosity as she looked at them, waiting for the purpose of their call.

"Mrs. Parmer, I live at Winterset," Reed began.

The woman's eyes widened a little, but she said nothing, waiting for Reed to continue.

"We found in our records that you were once a maid there."

"Yes, I was," the old woman agreed. "That was before I married Mr. Parmer."

"The time we are interested in is forty-eight years ago," Anna put in. "When Susan Emmett was killed."

The lively interest in Mrs. Parmer's face blinked out, as if a candle had been snuffed.

"Oh. Why are you asking about that?"

"Because some similar murders have happened recently," Reed told her. "Perhaps you have heard."

Mrs. Parmer shook her head. "No. I don't get out much. But I can't see what that has to do with Susan. That was years and years ago."

"Yes. But there are similarities. Miss Holcomb and I are trying to find out what we can about what happened to Susan Emmett."

"The woman who was killed recently was a maid in my house," Anna explained, and the old woman's dark eyes slid to her for a moment.

"I'm sorry, miss."

"The way she died was quite like the way Susan Emmett died," Anna added.

Mrs. Parmer studied her for a moment, then asked, "Are you Miss Babs' daughter?"

Anna looked at her, surprised, then said, "I am Barbara de Winter's daughter."

The old woman smiled. "Aye, that was Miss Babs. She was a cute baby, that one. I missed her when her aunt took her off to London. 'Course, it wasn't too long afterward that I met my Ned and left the house. I'd heard that Miss Babs married the Holcomb lad."

Anna nodded. "Yes. Sir Edmund was my father."

They had wandered rather far afield from the subject, Anna thought, and she wasn't sure how to bring it back. Fortunately, Reed stepped in.

"Mrs. Parmer," he began, "do you remember Susan Emmett?"

"Oh, yes. She worked at the house with me for two or three years, I guess."

"What can you tell us about her death?" Reed asked her.

She looked at him blankly. "I — I don't know what you mean. I didn't know much about her death. One day she wasn't there, and we didn't know what happened to her. Then they found her and said she'd been killed."

"Didn't you think about who might have done it?" Anna asked. "I mean, didn't you and the others talk about who the killer might be?"

Mrs. Parmer looked down at her hands, twisting the gold band on her ring finger around and around beneath the swollen knuckle. "It wasn't my place to talk about things like that. That was for the magistrate and such."

"Did you talk to the magistrate? The constable?"

Mrs. Parmer shrugged. "I remember the constable came and talked to all of us. I didn't know anything to tell him."

"You don't remember any speculation about who could have killed Susan — or the farmer?" Anna asked.

"Everyone said it was the Beast," Mrs. Parmer offered.

At that moment Gert trundled in, carrying the tea tray, and their conversation was interrupted. A few minutes were taken up with the niceties of serving the tea.

Finally, after Anna felt she had taken enough sips to be polite, she said, "Did *you* believe that Susan was killed by the Beast, Mrs. Parmer?"

"Who else would have done it?" the woman replied.

"Well, at first, did they not believe it was her fiancé?" Reed put in.

"Oh, him." Mrs. Parmer grimaced and made a dismissive move with her hand. "That one didn't have it in him to kill anyone, let alone Susan. It was daft to think he had done it."

"What about some other man?" Anna asked. "Was there anyone else with whom you saw Susan talking? Or someone who seemed interested in her? Jealous, perhaps, because she had chosen another?"

The old woman shook her head. "No. We weren't allowed to have callers at the house. The only time Susan saw her fiancé or anyone besides the rest of us servants was when she went home on a Sunday."

"Did she go home on the day she was killed?"

Mrs. Parmer looked at her. "It's been a long time, miss. I don't remember."

"Were you off that Sunday, Mrs. Parmer?" Reed inquired.

"Oh, no. I was working. We got every other Sunday off. Reduced staff, you see, so that there would be someone there to wait on the family."

Anna looked at Reed. She felt dissatisfied, but she could think of nothing else to ask the woman. Reed gave a ghost of a shrug, as if he felt the same way. He turned to Mrs. Parmer.

"Thank you very much for talking to us today. I hope we have not disturbed your day too much."

"Oh, no, indeed." The old woman smiled a little archly at Reed, not too old, apparently, to feel his charm.

They took their leave of Mrs. Parmer and mounted their horses, riding away from her neat little house. Anna cast a glance over at Reed.

"Did you think —" She cast about in her

mind for a way to express what she felt.

"That she was hiding something?" Reed suggested.

"You felt it, too!" Anna exclaimed. "Well, perhaps not that she was hiding something, but at least that she was not telling us everything she knew."

"She seemed cagey," Reed agreed. "The way she sidestepped gossiping about the event."

"Yes, and the pious statement that it wasn't her place to speculate about such things. As if that ever stopped anyone from doing so."

"The thing is," Reed went on, "I cannot imagine why she would do so. After all these years, what difference does it make? Almost everyone involved in the matter must be dead. Who would she hurt? Who would care?"

"I don't know. It was frustrating. I kept thinking, if only I could ask her the right question, she would start chattering. But I couldn't think what it could be."

They rode to the center of town, where they stabled their horses at the inn and took a private dining room for a bit of lunch before continuing to the records office. They were shown to the best room by an obsequious innkeeper who, while he did not know them, knew well enough the cut and quality of their clothing, as well as the high breeding of their horses, and had great expectations of a large bill.

The private room was well apportioned, but small, creating a sense of intimacy. They seemed much more alone, Anna thought, than they ever did in either of their homes, with all the servants about. Here, once the maids had bustled in with their meal and laid it on the table, they were left quite alone, the door closed between them and the rest of the world. The room lay at the back of the inn, and the windows were open to the summer breeze, letting in the peaceful sounds of birds and the occasional distant noise of a horse and wagon, or the laughter of one of the ostlers.

Anna glanced over at Reed, who was busy carving the roast. She enjoyed looking at him this way, without his knowing how long her eyes dwelled on him, or seeing the warmth that she was afraid crept into her face when she saw him. Her eyes went to his hands, strong and quick, then back up his arms, the muscles moving beneath his coat.

"Anna?"

"What? Oh." Startled, she looked up into Reed's face to find him watching her, holding a slice of meat ready for her. Color flamed in her cheeks, and she quickly held out her plate. "I'm sorry. I was thinking . . . about the murders."

"Yes?" he said questioningly.

"I was wondering whether we are actually accomplishing anything," Anna said. It was a thought that had occurred to her more than once in the past few days. "Even if we are able to find out something about the murders that took place forty-eight years ago — and I frankly wonder how we can accomplish that when no one was able to at the time — will it really help us to find out what happened to Estelle and Frank Johnson?"

"I've wondered, too," Reed admitted, slicing off another piece of meat and laying it on his own plate. "Anyone could have decided to copy the murders. He wouldn't have to have a connection to the earlier ones. Yet I can't help but think that it would be wrong of us not to pursue those killings. What if we do find something that will give us a clue about the recent murders?"

"I know. I don't mean that we should abandon what we are doing," Anna told him. "But I wish we could think of some way we could find out more about what happened to Estelle or that boy."

Reed glanced at her somewhat speculatively. Anna's eyebrows went up.

"What?" she said. "You are thinking something."

A half smile touched his lips. "You are right."

"And you're thinking I won't like it," she continued.

"Right again." The partial smile turned into a full one, and Anna felt her insides melting. If he only knew, that smile would probably have her agreeing to almost anything. "I have been thinking about your 'gift.' "

"My gift?" Anna looked puzzled.

"Your ability to — to sense what has happened. Or is about to happen. As you did with your brother, or what you felt when you found the Johnson lad."

"Oh." Anna put down her fork and leaned back in her chair, looking at him warily. She did not know what he was going to say, but she disliked the thought of talking about her visions. She feared that he wondered, as she often did, if these strange occurrences were evidence that she, too, might be slipping into madness. "What were you thinking about this 'gift'?"

"Only that I wish we could use it."

Whatever she had been expecting, it had not been this. "Use it? How?" she asked, leaning forward a little.

"To tell us more about the case. I don't understand it. But what you sensed about your brother was remarkably accurate, don't you think?"

Anna nodded. "Yes, I suppose it was."

"You saw the place where it occurred. You felt something of what happened to him. I wish there was some way you could direct that ability onto these killings. Maybe you could get some sense of who had done them, or how."

Anna shifted in her seat. "I — I don't know."

"I'm sorry. I don't mean to push you," Reed said quickly, reaching out to lay his hand over hers on the table. "I wouldn't want you to do it if you didn't want to. If it made you uneasy or . . ." His voice trailed off.

Anna was very aware of his hand resting on hers, of the warmth and texture of his skin. It sent a tingle up her arm and into her chest. She shifted in her chair, sliding her hand from his and folding it with her other hand in her lap.

"It's not that I don't want to, exactly," she said. "I just . . . don't know how to do it. It isn't something I have ever tried to do. The visions, the feelings, or whatever you want to call them, just come upon me. There is no warning, and I don't do anything that causes them. I just suddenly feel them. I'm sorry, but I wouldn't know how to go about encouraging them."

Reed removed his hand and started in on his food, nodding.

"Perhaps . . . I could try thinking about Estelle," Anna mused. It sent a little shiver through her to think about trying to open her mind up to thoughts about the murder.

Reed looked over at her and saw the way her face had paled. "No," he said quickly. "It isn't worth it. I didn't think — the effect on you would be too terrible. It was a foolish idea."

Anna was warmed by his concern, just as she had been by the way he talked about her visions as if they were something normal and natural, an asset, rather than something to be hidden and denied.

"No, it wasn't foolish at all. If it would help us find the killer, it would be worth a bit of discomfort for me."

"I think it would be more than a bit of discomfort," Reed guessed shrewdly. "I saw the look on your face just now when you were considering it. They must be very difficult for you."

"They are . . . rather frightening," Anna admitted. There was something freeing about being able to talk about her visions to someone. "I — I feel the pain and the terror that they are feeling — or at least a part of it. The way I felt the burst of pain in my head when I was thinking about Kit."

"Then you certainly shan't do it," Reed said in a voice that brooked no denial.

Anna smiled a little. "Don't you think that it is for me to decide?"

He grimaced. "You are as bad as my sisters. Well, promise me this — tell me you will not try to experiment with your ability unless I am with you, so that I can help you if you need it."

Anna looked at him. She realized that her visions would be easier to bear if Reed was there with her. His presence would give her strength, make her feel safer.

"All right. I will not try unless you are there."

Reed nodded with relief, and they returned to their meal. Putting aside the gloomy topic of their research, they talked about lighter and more general subjects as they finished their food.

When they were done, they walked to the records office. There, Reed, looking and behaving every inch the son of a duke, informed the clerk of the records they wished to search, and after a brief and futile protest, the man disappeared into the back and returned some time later, bearing a wide, stiff book fastened by brads.

There was no convenient place to sit, so they stood at the long oaken counter and opened the book, thumbing through the yellowed pages until they reached the inquest they wanted. There were several pages of testimony from witnesses regarding the discovery of Susan Emmett's body, beginning with the senior Dr. Felton, who expounded on the wounds he had found on the woman's body. There was nothing in his testimony that had not been included in his notes. Indeed, there was less, as there was none of his speculation about the manner in which the wounds might have been inflicted.

The next witness to testify was the man who had discovered the maid's body lying beneath a tree at Weller's Point. As Anna looked at the name of the witness, she stiffened, staring in stunned surprise. The man who had testified about finding the body was Nicholas Perkins.

Chapter Fifteen

"Did you know Nick found Susan's body?" Reed asked.

Anna shook her head. "No. I just talked to him the other day. I asked him about it, and he didn't say a word!"

Her voice had gone up as she spoke, and Reed glanced across the counter toward the clerk who had retrieved the records for them. The man was watching them with unabashed interest. Anna drew a breath.

"Let's finish this first."

Reed nodded, and they resumed reading. Nick Perkins had given his testimony, and the coroner had stopped him from time to time to ask a question. Details rolled out about the time and place and position of the body, the manner in which he had found her and what he had done. Anna dutifully read it all, but she could scarcely think about what she was reading. It was a good thing Reed was there, as well, and jotting down notes from time to time. All she could think about was Nick Perkins and the fact that he had told her none of this.

"He never said anything!" Anna exploded when at last they finished reading through the inquest records for both murders and left the building.

"You specifically questioned him about the murders?" Reed asked, frowning.

"Yes. It occurred to me the other day that he had been alive when they happened, and that he was still in full possession of his faculties, so I went over there to talk to him about it. He seemed unusually close-mouthed. I had a feeling that maybe he wasn't telling me everything. But I never dreamed that he was hiding something like this."

Anna could not understand it. She felt betrayed by someone whom she had regarded as a friend. "Why would he have lied to me — well, as good as lied?"

Reed cast her a sideways glance. "Do you think he knows more about the murders than he told the coroner?"

Anna looked at him blankly. "What do you mean?"

"I mean, do you think Perkins was involved in the killings?"

"No!" Anna gasped. Her hand went to her chest as if to cover her heart. "No, he couldn't have been. Nick is a kind person.

He — why, you've seen how he tended to that dog. He has been healing animals all his life."

"Some people like animals much better than humans."

"Well, he may feel that way. But he wouldn't — he *couldn't* — kill a person. Certainly not in such a terrible, cold-blooded way."

"He discovered the body. That could be because he was the one who murdered her."

"The twins and I discovered Frank Johnson's body," Anna reminded him.

"True. But you wouldn't have concealed that fact years later — not when someone you liked and trusted asked you. When what you could tell them might help solve another set of murders."

"Are you saying you think Nick could have killed Estelle? That's absurd!"

"Why? Look, he is the only person I've seen so far who could have killed the first two and been able to kill two more people now. Even if he is almost eighty, he's still quite sturdy. He could subdue a girl, don't you think? Or even a young man, if he took him by surprise."

Anna stared at him. "Surely you don't believe this."

Reed shrugged. "It's possible. And the

fact that he was not truthful with you when you asked him about the original murders makes me wonder."

"He could not have been the man that Estelle was seeing," Anna said flatly.

"No. I'm sure not. But we don't know that her lover is the one who killed her. It may have been that the killer simply came across her as she was going to or from a meeting with her lover."

"Then why hasn't the lover come forward? Said something?"

"Because he is afraid that everyone will think he is the one who did it," Reed replied.

"I don't know why Nick didn't tell me about finding the body. I — it hurts me that he didn't. But that doesn't mean that he killed anyone. Let's just go to him tomorrow and ask him about it. Confront him with our knowledge and find out why he wouldn't talk about it."

Reed nodded. "All right. But we're going to have to listen to what he says with an open mind." He paused, then added, "You know, Anna, whoever committed the recent murders is likely to be someone you know."

She cast him a glance, then sighed. "I know. Obviously it has to be someone who knows about the earlier murders. I have wondered . . ."

He glanced at her when she hesitated. "Wondered what?"

Anna cast him a shamefaced look. "I feel a traitor to even think it, let alone say it."

They had reached the inn. There was a bench outside it, and Anna sat down. Reed followed.

"What are you thinking?"

"I have wondered about . . . Dr. Felton." Anna looked at him to see his reaction to the news.

A little to her surprise, he nodded. "I have, too."

She let out a sigh of relief. "I keep thinking I'm being foolish. The man is a doctor, dedicated to saving lives. How could he kill anyone?"

"Yes, but he would not be the first doctor to take a life," Reed pointed out. "And he, above anyone else, knows all about the earlier murders."

Anna nodded. "They have long been an area of fascination for him. That and anything to do with the Beast. That is why his patient gave him all those clippings she had collected — she knew he was interested in the subject."

"Even before his father died and left him the journals?"

"I think so. His father died about ten

years ago. Of course, he could have talked about the murders with Dr. Felton."

"So he was interested in the killings. He found out everything he could about them."

"In all fairness, so have we," Anna pointed out.

"True. Many people are fascinated by unsolved murders. It's human nature, I suppose. But what if his interest went beyond curiosity? What if it turned into obsession? He could have studied those journals, thought about what instrument was used. What if he decided to try out an instrument to see if it would work? He knew all the details — where the victims were found, the type of wounds. . . ."

"Yes, I know," Anna agreed. "That is why my mind keeps coming back to him. But still, I cannot bring myself to believe it. I've known him all my life. I have never seen any violence in the man. And why would he attack Kit? That doesn't fit with the other murders. There were only two the first time."

"Maybe he liked it. Maybe he could not stop."

"But Kit had just been at his house. How could he have gotten to that spot to waylay Kit before Kit got there?"

"Perhaps he followed him. Didn't he say that Kit was the last to leave?"

Anna nodded. "But if he followed Kit, Kit would have heard him. He would have turned around and seen him. Why would he risk that?"

"He planned to kill Kit, so Kit would not have been alive to testify against him."

"Then it would certainly be his good luck — whoever *he* is — that Kit can't seem to remember what happened," Anna mused.

"Yes," Reed agreed. "And I would say that places Kit in danger still. The attacker cannot be sure that Kit will not remember."

"The other night, I thought — I thought I saw someone outside our house. In the trees."

"What!" Reed's head snapped around and he stared at her in consternation. "The killer was lurking outside your house?"

"I don't know that it was the killer. It was dark, and he was under the trees. I — I keep thinking perhaps it was only a shadow, and my imagination was overactive."

"Good God. We must do something. You aren't safe there. You and Kit should move into Winterset."

"How would we be any safer there?" Anna protested. "Holcomb Manor is smaller, with fewer doors and windows where an intruder could enter. I alerted the servants, and made sure all the doors and windows were locked. And Thompkins has been sleeping across Kit's door on a cot."

"It isn't Kit I am worried about. It is you!" Reed responded, scowling.

"But no one has tried to kill me," Anna said.

"That doesn't mean he won't. What is to keep him from seizing the opportunity to do away with both of you?"

"But why?"

"Why does he do anything? I don't know. Whoever we are dealing with has some twisted sort of logic of his own that you and I cannot hope to understand. He might think killing two people at once would be a special sort of thrill. An accomplishment. He might not have any intention of killing you at all, but what if you were to wake up and see him sneaking into or out of the house? He would kill you just to get rid of a witness."

"There is nothing to say any of that will happen," Anna pointed out.

"Perhaps not, but I don't want to take the risk." Reed took her hand, holding it between both his own. "My God, Anna, if he hurt you, I don't know what I'd do."

The honesty, the raw need, in his voice touched Anna on some deep, primitive level. She looked into his eyes, and she saw the heat of anger and fear changing, turning into a different sort of heat. Her own blood warmed in response. She curled her fingers around his. His head lowered, drew closer to hers. She looked into his eyes, turned smoky by the subtle lowering of his thick black lashes, and she felt the curl of desire deep within her abdomen. He wanted her, just as she wanted him, and Anna knew that she need only raise her lips to his to send their desire spiraling out of control. There was an inn behind them; it would be easy to get a room. No one would wonder if they returned to the Manor a little bit late.

It took all her willpower to turn her head aside, breaking the contact of their eyes. "I — it's getting late. We had better return."

She felt the stiffening of his body, could almost hear the gritting of his teeth. But he said only, "Yes, of course."

It was a long ride home, and they did not speak much. If Anna had hoped that during the course of it, Reed had forgotten about his worries over her safety, such hopes were dashed when he insisted on going into the house with her to see Kit.

They found her brother in his study. He was seated at his desk, a pile of papers in front of him, but he was not working, only staring off into space. He looked up, startled, when they came in, then gave a sheepish grin.

"Come in. You've caught me woolgathering."

"You are entitled to, after that crack on the head you received," Reed commented.

"I still don't remember getting hit," Kit commented. "But I have remembered the time before that, though."

"You have?" Anna and Reed drew closer, sitting down in the chairs across from her brother's desk.

"Yes. I remember playing cards at Dr. Felton's house," he said. "I had a couple of whiskies, and I lost a little money. Then I remember taking my leave of Martin and starting out for home. But I don't remember even reaching the lane where you found me. The strangest thing . . . I felt so sleepy."

"What?" Reed leaned closer, his eyes sharp. "What was strange about it? It was late."

"Yes, but I was terribly sleepy. Not like I am normally at bedtime. It was as if I could barely stay awake. I remember having to struggle to keep my eyes open. It was a good thing Nestor knew the way home, or God knows where I might have ended up."

Reed and Anna glanced at each other, then back at Kit.

"No wonder you don't remember being hit," Reed commented. "You were drugged."

"Drugged!" Kit raised his brows. "No, surely . . ."

"You just said you had only a couple of whiskies. That is what Dr. Felton said, too. So you weren't so inebriated you couldn't stay awake."

"No."

"Yet you said that you were unusually sleepy. So sleepy you could barely keep your eyes open. Perhaps you don't remember the blow because you simply lost consciousness and fell from your horse."

"Of course!" Anna agreed. "The killer wouldn't have had to worry about Kit's recognizing him — or about his fighting back. He would simply have waited until Kit passed out, then moved in. Either Kit hit his head when he fell, or the killer hit him just to make sure he wouldn't wake up."

Kit stared at them in astonishment. "You're serious. You really think the killer is after me?"

"I told you. I saw someone bending over you!" Anna exclaimed. "If Cooper and I had not come up, I don't know what would have happened to you. Don't you believe me?"

"Yes, yes, of course I do. It's just — I can't quite take it in. I kept thinking that somehow you must have been mistaken. This is — it's just so bizarre."

"I know it must seem so," Reed told him. "But you have to believe it. You have to take precautions — not only for your own sake, but for Anna's, as well."

"Anna! My God, do you think he will try to hurt her, too?" Kit looked at his sister, clearly horrified. "Why would anyone be doing this?"

"We don't know, but we cannot afford to be lax or complacent," Reed said firmly. "I told Anna that I want the two of you to come to Winterset."

"Oh, no. We could not do that," Kit told him.

"She said the same thing — and pointed out that Holcomb Manor is smaller and more easily defensible. So I think you should set up a nightwatch. Have two or three of your best servants take it in turns."

Kit nodded, and Anna agreed. "We will. It's the sensible thing to do."

"I want to send a couple of my servants over here, as well," Reed went on. "To keep watch on the outside of the house."

"See here, Moreland," Kit said, looking offended. "I am able to take care of my sister myself."

"I am sure you are," Reed countered.

"But it would set my mind at ease to know that you have extra help. And there is no harm in their being here. I would tell them, of course, to answer to you while they were here."

Unexpectedly, it was Anna who said, "Yes, of course. This is scarcely a time to stand on pride, Kit. You have already been attacked once. I say we should guard the house as fully as possible."

"Yes, you're right, of course," Kit agreed. "Thank you." He inclined his head toward Reed.

Reed turned toward Anna. "This makes it seem more likely that the doctor is the killer."

"What!" Kit exclaimed. "Are you saying that you suspect Martin? But that's absurd!"

"I know. I find it very hard to believe," Anna told him. "I am sure that in the end it will turn out that he is not, but we have to consider all the evidence."

Reed explained their reasoning regarding the doctor's knowledge of the first killings, then added, "It seemed unlikely, however, that he could have followed you that closely or gotten there ahead of you the other night. But this puts a whole new light on the matter."

"He is a doctor, so he would have something readily at hand to put in your drink to make you sleepy," Anna reasoned. "Then, knowing that you would lose consciousness on the ride home, he would not need to hurry. He needed only to follow you a few minutes later and find you lying in the road."

"No," Kit said firmly. "I cannot believe that it is Dr. Felton."

"I think it is safe to assume that if Sir Christopher was indeed given something to render him unconscious, it was most likely done at the card game," Reed said. "We can all agree on that, can't we?"

Anna nodded, and Kit, after a moment's thought, said, "Yes. Although I cannot imagine that it was any of the others, either. Mr. Norton was there, along with the squire and his son. And last night Mr. Barbush joined us."

"Who?" Reed asked.

"He's an older gentleman," Anna told him. "A confirmed bachelor. He has a small competence, and he retired here, oh, six or seven years ago. I believe he was at Lady Kyria's party."

"Maroon waistcoat," Kit described succinctly.

"Ah, yes, I remember. What do we know about him?" Reed frowned. "When you say 'older,' do you mean he would have been alive at the time of the first murders?"

Anna shrugged. "Alive, probably, but I would think no more than a child."

"I don't know much about his life," Kit mused. "He used to live in London, I believe, for he often talks about the City. 'When I was living in the City . . .'" Kit assumed a rather pompous voice. "I think he once said his cousin was a baron. I rarely see him except when he comes to Felton's card games." He paused, frowning. "You know, it doesn't have to have been one of the people playing cards. It could have been one of the servants. Or another person entirely could have slipped in sometime and put something in the whiskey. We meet there every week for our games. Everyone knows about it. And there are always all sorts of patients in and out of Felton's house."

"I suppose we cannot rule out an outsider," Reed agreed. "Certainly a servant could have slipped something into your drink or food. Who was serving you?"

"A maid brought in the food," Kit said. "I don't remember what she looked like. I believe the doctor poured the drinks himself." He paused and looked at Anna and Reed. "That doesn't mean he put anything in them. And," he added, "we don't even know that anything was put into my drink or food at his house. It could have happened earlier. Perhaps the potion took a long time to work. Or perhaps I just got sleepy, so I didn't notice when someone sneaked up behind me and knocked me on the head."

"You are right. We don't know. Doubtless there are others who know about sleeping drafts besides the doctor." Reed glanced toward Anna, and she knew that his thoughts had turned toward Nick Perkins, who certainly knew a great deal about all sorts of remedies. But she could conceive even less of his committing these crimes than she could Dr. Felton.

"It must be someone else," she said, half to herself.

"I think it's worth checking into the others," Reed agreed. "I'll have my man in London look into this Mr. Barbush. If he did indeed live there, my man will be able to learn of his past. I think I'll have a talk with the constable, too, to see what information he may have been able to find out about the murders."

They talked for a few more minutes before Reed took his leave. Anna and Kit ate their dinner in a subdued silence, having little to say about anything other than their recent conversation and having no desire to talk about that in front of the servants.

Kit made arrangements with the butler for two of the footmen to take watch that night. Kit himself volunteered to take the first one. Anna went up to her room early. She tried mending a few things, then reading, but she could not concentrate on anything, for her thoughts kept straying to the murders, going over and over the same paths. Finally she gave up the effort and got ready for bed.

Before she got into bed, she peered out through the drapes. There was no sign of the ominous visitor she had spotted the other night. Looking closer to the house, she saw a man standing just beyond the side door, smoking a pipe as he looked around him. He was one of Reed's servants, she supposed.

They were as safe as they could make themselves, she reminded herself, but it did little to calm her jittery nerves. When she lay down, it took a long time to fall asleep, and her dreams were troubled. She awoke twice, once with her heart pounding and a vague memory of being chased by a looming, faceless form, and the other time with her loins warm and heavy and Reed's name upon her lips.

She rolled over with a groan, wishing the

empty ache between her legs would cease. Was this the way the rest of her life would be — always wanting, never having? It had been better before Reed came back, she told herself. She had been resigned to her life — content, really — the heartbreak and yearning years in the past. Now every day brought anew the knowledge of just how much she had given up, a fresh reminder of how much she wanted him.

Yet she could not wish that Reed would leave. No matter how much she ached when she was with him, still she wanted him there.

She rode over to Winterset the following morning after breakfast, with one of the grooms riding with her. She chafed at the restriction, but she was not foolish enough to ride out without escort. As she had told Kit, it was only sensible to take precautions.

The butler led her to the drawing room, and a moment later Reed entered. They had planned to visit Nick Perkins that morning, but Anna had had another idea.

"I have been thinking about what we were talking about yesterday — about trying to use my 'gift' or 'curse,' whatever you call it, to discover more about the murders. I want to try it this morning."

"Now? Here?"

Anna nodded. "I thought I could try sitting down somewhere and opening up my mind to it, encouraging such thoughts. I — I would feel better if you were with me. I'm sorry, but it's a little frightening."

"Of course it is. I am not at all sure you should even try it," Reed said, his brow knitting in concern.

"I think I have to. We must try everything we can."

"All right. Well, shall we try it here?"

They looked around the elegant room, decorated in heavy mahogany furniture, the blue velvet cushions faded from time. It scarcely seemed the place to try something so odd, but, then, Anna did not suppose anywhere would seem really suitable for such an experiment.

She sat down in a chair, and Reed took a seat on the couch that lay at right angles to her. Anna settled back into the chair, holding her hands loosely in her lap, and closed her eyes. She felt extremely foolish.

She tried to clear her mind of all thoughts. It was difficult to do, knowing that Reed was sitting only a foot away from her. She thought of Estelle, instead, remembering the day when she had seen her sneaking in the back door at the Manor. She remembered the guilty look on Estelle's face, the fear that Mrs. Michaels would discover her, and the saucy, grateful smile she had tossed at Anna when she did not give her away.

Nothing came to Anna's mind. No feeling struck her. She tried instead to remember the way she had felt in the woods the day she met the twins, but while she could recall the feelings she had had, she could not feel them flooding her again. She sighed and opened her eyes. Reed was watching her. She shook her head.

"Nothing. I'll try again."

She closed her eyes and thought this time of the body that she and the twins had stumbled upon. Again she could remember the sick horror, the fear and pain that had stabbed her like a knife, but again it was like pulling out a memory, not experiencing it once more.

Anna opened her eyes. "I'm not feeling anything. I tried thinking of Estelle, of the Johnson lad, but I don't feel anything. I'm sorry."

"No, don't apologize. It may not be anything you can make happen. Or it may take a lot of practice." He stood up, extending his hand to her. "Come. Why don't we take a stroll? Perhaps some other place will present itself as a better spot to use."

"All right."

Reed offered Anna his arm, and she slipped her hand through it. As always, it sent a little tingle through her to touch him.

They strolled out into the foyer and down the central hall. A long hall stretched down to the left, across the back of the house. It was a gallery, lined with windows on one side looking out into the Winterset gardens. On the opposite wall hung paintings, and at various spots there was a bench upon which to sit, or a long, narrow table.

It was a lordly sweep of hall. Anna could faintly remember running down it when she was a child. It had seemed a marvelous place in which to run full tilt, her shoes clattering on the marble floors. She had not been in it much in recent years. The area had been little used by her uncle and had remained largely closed off. It was along here, she remembered, that the caretaker, Grimsley, had spoken of seeing the ghost of the old lord walking.

Reed glanced at her. "Are you cold?"

Anna smiled. "No, just a shiver from thinking about ghosts."

"Ghosts?" He lifted a brow, then chuckled. "Ah, yes, I remember now. This is Grimsley's ghostly walkway, isn't it? I must say, they have not disturbed me."

Anna's steps slowed, and she looked

across at the inside wall. There were doors set at intervals into the interior wall, all of them closed. But one particular door somehow drew her. She wasn't sure why, but she could not resist stepping across the hall and trying the knob. It opened inward, and Anna stopped in the doorway. A jolt of fear slammed through her almost like a physical force.

She froze, startled, her pulse beginning to race. She looked into the room, which was largely devoid of furniture.

"Anna." Reed's voice was sharp with concern as he followed her to the door of the room. "What is it? What's the matter?"

She glanced at him, unable to express the feelings that were dancing through her, drawing her into the room. She moved inside, not really wanting to, but feeling compelled. Slowly she walked to the middle of the room, looking around her.

Fear and pain were ricocheting around her, not as strong as the feelings she had had in the woods or when she had had her vision about Kit, but the same sort of panicked emotions.

Reed, watching her, saw her face go pale. She swayed a little, and he stepped forward quickly, his hand wrapping around her arm. "Anna! What is it? Do you feel ill?"

"Something happened here," she murmured. She turned toward him slowly, her eyes huge in her white face. "Murder."

Chapter Sixteen

"What?" Reed stared at her in astonishment. "What are you saying?"

"It didn't happen outside. It happened here," Anna said.

"The murder?" Reed asked. "You're saying Estelle was murdered here, in this room? How could that be?"

"No. Not Estelle. It is something much older than that."

Reed continued to gape at her, speechless. Anna turned away and walked around the room. "It isn't as strong, but I can feel it." She stopped, her eyes blank and vague, looking at something that Reed could not see.

"There was furniture here, and a rug — a blue-and-gold Persian rug. And it's — it's covered with blood," she told him. She raised her hands to her temples. Her breath came more quickly in her throat; her heart began to pound. "The Winterset maid — Susan Emmett. This is where she was killed! Not Weller's Point." Anna whirled and looked at him, her eyes focused now, and blazing with emotion. "I am certain of it!"

"My God." Reed stared at her in consternation, then took Anna's arm and led her from the room.

She was trembling, her face paper white, and he thought she might faint. He slipped an arm around her waist and guided her over to a green velvet bench with rolled arms. He pulled her down onto the padded bench with him and took both her hands in his. They were cold as ice, and he chafed them gently.

Anna shuddered and closed her eyes. "Oh, Reed! That poor girl. There was so much blood."

He wrapped his arms around her, pulling her tightly against his side. "It's all right. Don't think about it." He pressed his lips to the top of her head.

"I can't keep from thinking about it," Anna murmured. She realized that they should not be sitting this way, where any servant might come upon them in such a far too intimate pose. Worse, it felt much too good to be in his arms, and soon, she knew, the soothing comfort of his embrace would turn into something dangerously exciting. It was foolhardy to put herself in the way of temptation.

With a small inward sigh at the loss, Anna

sat up, pulling away from his arm. "I think we should go see the maid again."

"Mrs. Parmer?"

"Yes. I thought she was holding something back yesterday, and now I am certain of it."

"All right. I'll have our horses brought round."

They started walking back down the hall to another room with a bell pull, so that Reed could summon a servant.

"I noticed something about the housekeeper's house and Mrs. Parmer's, too — they were very nice, weren't they? Not large, but well built and pleasant. And each of the women had a servant. Do you think it is common for a retired housemaid to live that well?"

"The housekeeper did have a stipend from your uncle. And Mrs. Parmer married. Perhaps her husband was able to afford it."

"Perhaps."

Reed looked at her. "But I agree. It is odd. Do you think someone . . . bribed them?"

Anna gave him a level look. "Something happened here. I am certain of it. And Mrs. Parmer did not tell us everything she knew."

"What makes you think she will now?" Reed inquired.

"We shall just have to make her," Anna replied.

Mrs. Parmer looked somewhat disconcerted to see Anna and Reed on her doorstep again. "My lord. Miss Holcomb." She looked from one of them to the other. "What can I do for you?"

"You can start by telling us the truth," Anna told her crisply.

Mrs. Parmer blinked, surprised, and took a step back. They seized the opportunity to step inside the house, even though she had not invited them.

"I — I'm sorry. I'm afraid I don't know what you're talking about," the old woman said warily.

"Mrs. Parmer, I fear that you were less than open with us yesterday," Reed said. "I am hoping that you will change your mind and tell us the truth now."

"I don't know what you're talking about," she repeated.

"I know what happened in the room off the gallery," Anna said flatly, watching the other woman's face.

Mrs. Parmer's eyes widened, and one hand fluttered up to her throat. "How could you —"

"Susan Emmett was killed there, wasn't she?" Anna asked.

The old woman's mouth worked a little,

but she did not say anything; instead her gaze darted from Anna to Reed, then back.

"Mrs. Parmer . . ." Reed took her hand gently, gazing down into the woman's face. "Don't you think it's time for Susan's death to be explained? You worked with her. You knew her. Do you think it is right that she should have been sent to her death, yet it was never avenged, never atoned for?"

The woman looked uncertain. "Dead is dead. What difference does it make?"

"I should think it would make some difference with your conscience," Reed suggested gently. " 'Tis a harsh thing to have on your soul. . . ."

"I had nothing to do with killing her!" Mrs. Parmer gasped, jerking her hand from his grasp. She hesitated, then said, "All right. I guess it doesn't matter anymore." She glanced at Anna. "And seeing as how you're his granddaughter . . ."

She turned, nodding her head for them to follow her, and led them back into the parlor where they had sat the day before. Anna's heart sank at the old woman's words. It was what she had been fearing from the moment she had stood in the room off the gallery.

"Then . . . it was my grandfather who did it? Lord de Winter?" Anna asked stiffly when they were seated in the parlor, the door closed.

Reed, without saying anything, reached over and curled his hand around hers.

"Aye," Mrs. Parmer responded. "The old lord." Her mouth tightened. "He was always a hard one, that one. Never treated Lady de Winter right, I always said. Cold, he was. And odd. But, then —" She shrugged. "He was gentry, wasn't he, and they're often odd."

"What happened in that room, Mrs. Parmer?" Reed asked.

"I don't know exactly," she replied. "I wasn't there when it happened. It was only afterward — the housekeeper woke me up in the middle of the night, and she dragged me downstairs to that room." Even now, the woman blanched a little at the memory. "There was blood everywhere. It was horrible. Mrs. Hartwell told me to clean it up and keep my mouth shut, so I did. I washed up all the blood, and she and I rolled up the rug — it had blood all over it, you couldn't ever get that clean — and had it put in the attic. Mrs. Hartwell told me that I would be taken care of, as long as I didn't talk, so I didn't. They gave me money, a nest egg, so after a few years I could leave there and marry, and we were able to build this house."

She lifted her chin a little defiantly.

"You're thinking I'm wicked, aren't you, miss, not to tell and to take the money for it? But I wanted out of that life — forever taking orders and cleaning up after folks, my hands red and raw all winter — and when they offered me that money, I saw it was my chance to get away. So I took it. Besides, who'd have believed me, even if I *had* told? The lord and lady would have sworn it wasn't true, and Mrs. Hartwell, too, and I'd 've been turned off without a reference."

"You were in a difficult situation," Reed told her sympathetically.

Anna let out a soft groan and brought her hands to her head. "Oh, God, he was mad, wasn't he?"

Mrs. Parmer nodded. "I'm sorry, miss. But he wasn't right in the head. And he got worse."

"But no one told you that it was Lord de Winter who killed Susan?" Reed asked. "Did they?"

"Who else could it have been?" Mrs. Parmer retorted. "One of the servants, they wouldn't have done all that to cover it up, now would they? And Master Charles was only a lad. Who else would have been in that room with her? Then, after Will Dawson was killed, too, her ladyship locked Lord Roger up. In the nursery, see, where the windows had bars on them. They added a good stout door with a lock on it, and only Mrs. Hartwell had the key. He had several rooms there to walk around in, and his valet did for him, you see."

"So was his madness common knowledge?" Anna asked.

"Oh, no, miss, the other servants weren't told. Nobody saw him except when he would go walking in the gallery with his valet or her ladyship. They put out the story that he was ill, weak. His valet always took his meals up to him. The servants knew he was odd, and there were whispers, of course. But her ladyship was a sweet woman — kind, she was, and nobody wanted to hurt her. And the pay was good. Nobody wanted to get dismissed. So no one talked much outside the house. The doctor knew, of course. He used to come and check on him, bandage him up when he hurt himself, give him something to make him quiet. You know."

Anna thought of the missing pages in the doctor's journal. Had they referred to his visits to the mad Lord de Winter?

"The solicitor knew, too, I guess — the old one before Mr. Norton, I mean. Oh, and Perkins. He used to come by, regular-like. He'd help the valet sometimes, when the old lord was too wild. There was another servant, too, one they hired to help the valet. He was a big, strong fellow, but he never talked much with any of the rest of the servants."

"What was Lord de Winter like?" Anna asked her.

The old woman shrugged. "He never talked much to me. Whenever I went in to clean his room, the valet would take him out to walk in the garden or somewhere. Sometimes they'd go down to the summerhouse — he liked the summerhouse. But he looked at you, and his eyes . . ." She gave an exaggerated shudder. "They weren't like normal eyes. I can't explain it, but there was this look in them I never saw in anyone else, and I hope never to see again. Just being in his rooms was bad enough, what with all the masks and writings and such."

"Excuse me?" Reed interrupted her. "Masks? Writings? I don't know what you're talking about."

"Oh. No, I guess, they would all 've been taken down. He liked to collect masks, Lord de Winter did. Strange looking things from all over the world. They looked like animals, some of them. And others were like something I've never seen — demons, maybe. Wicked-looking things, they were. He'd always collected them, see, and he was that fond of them. So they hung them all around in the nursery, so he could have them around. Whenever I was cleaning the rooms, it always felt like someone was watching me, 'cause of all those masks."

"You mentioned writings," Anna prodded when the woman fell silent.

Mrs. Parmer nodded. "Sometimes, when the spells took him, he would write on the walls. They painted them over now and then, but he'd always go back to writing on them." She shook her head. "Couldn't make heads nor tails of it, I couldn't. Some of it didn't even look like English."

Anna thought of the symbols her uncle drew, and her stomach constricted. Was her uncle like his father? Was his madness, too, the kind that drove a man to kill?

"What was Lord de Winter like before he descended into madness?" Anna asked. "You said he was hard."

"Oh, my, yes. Everything had to be just so, and woe betide anyone who put things out of place or wasn't quick enough. And servants weren't the only ones. Her ladyship could never please him, except for giving him a son. I heard him take her to task something terrible. He even hit her sometimes. But she and Nurse were good about keeping Master Charles out of his way. A child could never be neat enough for that one."

Her uncle, too, wanted things done just a certain way — utensils in the correct order, the stones lined up according to his plan — and he did not like anything changed. But he had never been one to erupt into violence, or even shouting, if things were not done exactly to his plan. He simply worried and stewed about it. Charles' personality was mild, and surely, Anna thought, that made all the difference between him and his father.

They left not long after that. Anna was reeling from the information that they had received.

"My own grandfather!" she exclaimed as they rode back toward Winterset. "No wonder Nick was reluctant to tell me about the murders. He must have known the truth, and he could not bear to tell me that my grandfather was a murderer."

"It explains a great deal," Reed agreed. "It is little wonder that the murders went unsolved. There was obviously a conspiracy of silence to protect Lord de Winter."

"The doctor must have known," Anna said. "Or at least suspected that Lord de Winter was the culprit. He knew he was insane. He knew that they locked him up after the murders. And after that the murders stopped."

"Yes, I would think he must have wondered about it. Perhaps those pages torn out of the doctor's journal were about Lord de Winter."

Anna nodded. "That is exactly what I was thinking."

"I would like to look at that nursery myself," Reed commented. "Obviously I should have trusted more in what Grimsley said. Lord de Winter did live in the nursery."

"That poor woman," Anna said, shaking her head. "Lady de Winter, I mean. Think of being married to a monster like that. Knowing what he was, what he had done — yet she must have felt she had to shield him from the law because of her children. She would not have wanted them branded as mad, too. The scandal would have tarnished their name beyond repair. I can understand why she covered up for him. But to continue to live with him in the house, to see him . . . Why, Mrs. Parmer even said sometimes Lady de Winter walked with him in the gallery. She was with him in the summerhouse when they had the fire."

Reed looked at Anna. "That is where they both died, isn't it?"

Anna nodded, her expression changing. "Are you thinking — that he killed her, too?"

Reed shrugged. "One has to wonder what

they were doing there alone, if he had been locked up for the past several years in the nursery. What started the fire? Given his history, I would be suspicious."

"Yes, no doubt you are right." Anna could not help but think with horror of what ran in her family, lurking in her own flesh and blood.

When they reached Winterset, they went straight up the stairs to the nursery. The door to the nursery was indeed a sturdy door with a lock. Fortunately it was not locked, so they did not have to search for the key. Reed opened the door, and they stepped inside.

The rooms were dark, the curtains drawn, and Reed strode over to push aside the curtain and let in some light. Anna looked at the bars crisscrossing the window, and she could not suppress a shiver. Reed looked at her in some concern.

"Are you all right?"

Anna nodded. "Yes. It is just . . . a little unsettling." She rubbed her arms, feeling cold despite the fact that it was summer. She wasn't sure why she felt unnerved here — whether she actually sensed something abnormal, or whether her emotions were simply colored by what Mrs. Parmer had told them about the place.

They walked through the rooms — three

small bedrooms and a larger schoolroom. The rooms were clean, the shelves empty. There was no sign that anyone had ever lived here, including children. What furniture there was, was all adult-size. A large humpbacked trunk stood against one wall in the schoolroom, and Reed crossed over to open it.

"Well," he said, looking down into the trunk. "Here are the lord's masks."

Anna went quickly to his side and peered into the trunk. The inside was filled with masks, some metal, others wooden, and still others made of clay or cloth or — Anna reached down and touched one — of animal hide. Reed began to pull them out and line them up on the floor. Some were amazingly realistic renditions of animals — there were a few that even had protruding snouts. Others were more like stylized drawings of animals, and others seemed to be mythical beasts or more human-looking beings that were what Anna supposed Mrs. Parmer had termed "demons." Teeth were painted on some; others had actual animals' teeth glued to them.

Even laid out here on the floor, the masks looked eerie and bizarre. She could well imagine how frightening they would appear hanging all over the walls, teeth bared.

"Lord de Winter seemed to favor wolves," Reed commented.

Anna nodded, glancing over the masks. There was, indeed, a preponderance resembling wolves.

Reed lifted out the last mask and laid it down, saying, "There are books on the bottom of the trunk."

"His journals?" Anna looked in at the rows of identical brown books.

"I presume." He reached in, took one out and began to glance through it.

Anna did the same. The pages were filled with words in a small, cramped hand. She glanced through them. Though at first glance they appeared to be sentences, with periods and commas, the strings of words made little or no sense.

"Gibberish," Reed said, flipping through the pages.

"I can make out a few things. This looks like *king*, maybe. Oh, and here, I think this says *Wolf People*." She could make out little else. Some of the words were written, as Mrs. Parmer had noted, in something that was definitely not English — nor any other language Anna had ever seen.

She laid the book aside and picked up another one. It was much the same. As she went down through the stack, she noticed, however, that there were more and more words that made sense and even sentences that were understandable, although wildly irrational.

"Reed, look — here it says, 'We are the descendants of the Beast.' And here, 'not cursed, but blessed.' "

Reed moved closer, reading over her shoulder, " 'At night I roam with my . . .' What is that?"

Anna peered at where he pointed. " *'Brethren?'* "

Reed nodded. " 'At night I roam with my brethren. None can see us. None know the power we hold. We walk between the worlds, and all is dark.' "

"His mind was clearer at this time," Anna mused. "Perhaps they are earlier books, or maybe he went through more lucid periods. Didn't Mrs. Parmer say that he had 'spells,' or something like that?"

Anna flipped through more pages. "Here — wolves again. 'We are the Children of the Wolf. The power is in us. None can reach us, none can stop us.' Who is this 'we'?" she asked.

"God knows. The wolves? People that only he saw?"

"Oh, look. 'When I was fifteen, the King of the Wolves spoke to me.' But this makes no sense — 'Come down from the mountain and bury beneath my skin.' " She turned the page. "Here is some more about the King of the Wolves talking to him."

Reed picked up another journal and paged through it. "This one is gibberish again." He searched through the others remaining in the trunk, glancing through them and setting them aside until he found one that was more intelligible.

"All right," he said, his eyes scanning down the page. "Here he says something about being superior, part wolf, part man. Apparently he thought he had the sense of smell of a wolf and their acute hearing. 'I walk upright, but I have the heart of my brothers. At night I walk in the woods and converse with them. But none hear, for we speak without words.' "

Anna shuddered. "Ugh. This is all horrid. I cannot bear it."

She set the journal back in the trunk and glanced around the room. "It is so cold in here." She rubbed her arms again. "I want to leave this place."

"Of course." Reed took off his jacket and draped it around her shoulders. They had been kneeling on the floor beside the trunk, and he stood up, reaching down to offer his hand to her.

Her hand was ice cold. Reed looked down

into her face. It was pale, her eyes huge and haunted. He put his arm around her shoulders, sweeping her out of the room and down the stairs to his study.

"Here. Sit down." He led her to the sofa that sat at one end of the room, then turned and walked across the room to the liquor cabinet, where he poured whisky from the decanter into two cut crystal glasses. He returned to Anna and handed her one. "Drink this."

Anna looked doubtfully down at the strong-smelling liquid, then back at Reed.

"Trust me. It'll put some color back into your cheeks," he told her, taking a sip of his own drink.

Anna took a sip, and the whisky roared back through her throat and down into her stomach like liquid fire. She coughed, her eyes beginning to water. "How do you stand that?"

"You get used to it." Reed smiled. "Take another drink. You'll feel better."

Obediently, Anna had another swallow before she set her glass on the table beside her. "I don't know if I will ever feel better."

"Did you feel something from the room?" Reed asked. "The way you did in the room off the gallery?"

"Not at first — or, at least, only a little. It wasn't the same as the feelings I've had before. It just made me . . . uneasy, I guess, is the word for it. But the longer we stayed there, as we looked through his journals, I felt more . . . a kind of dark anger and . . . something that was like pleasure, but sick and repulsive. It was so cold, down-to-the-bone cold. I thought I might start shivering and never stop."

"Cold. Like he was," Reed commented.

"Oh, Reed, I cannot bear to think that that man was my grandfather!" Anna exclaimed. "He was evil through and through." She turned to look at Reed, her blue eyes shining with tears. "I feel so ashamed, so sick, that I am related to him. His mania, his illness, runs through us. It is bred in me."

"No, no!" Reed quickly set his drink aside and reached out to Anna, pulling her into his arms. "You are not mad. Whatever was wrong with Lord Roger de Winter, it is not in you. There is no evil in you — of that, I am sure."

"But these things I see . . ." Anna cried out softly. "My feelings, my visions, whatever you want to call them. Don't you see? *He* saw things, heard things. My uncle sees things, too. The Angel Gabriel speaks to him."

"That doesn't make you mad," Reed retorted. "The things that your uncle sees, that the old Lord de Winter saw — those were figments of their imagination. The things you have sensed, or 'seen,' were things that had actually happened or were about to happen. They were very real things. Besides, you did not believe that they were playing out in front of you. You knew they were visions, that they had happened at some other time or in some other place."

"Yes . . ."

"But your uncle believes that the angel is standing right there talking to him."

"Yes, that's true."

"So what you see is different. You are not like your uncle, and certainly you are not like your grandfather."

"I wish I could truly believe that," Anna sighed.

"Believe it. Listen, I have a large number of relatives whom I would rather not possess. We all do. My grandmother was the terror of the family. And my great-aunt, Lady Rochester, has a tongue that would blister paint. Great-Uncle Ballard lives in fear of her still. And you think they aren't peculiar? My grandmother swore that she talked to her dead husband — and he answered. Lady Rochester has a vast array of wigs, all of them quite atrocious, which she switches as if they were hats, believing, apparently, that none of us notice that her hair is red one day and black the next. And my cousin Albert is an utter nodcock."

"But none of them have murdered people."

"Not that we know of, though, frankly, I would not put it past my grandmother. My point is that we cannot choose our relatives. We are simply stuck with them. But their actions, their lives, do not determine ours. I am not like my grandmother. You are not like your grandfather. I know you regret what he did. I do, too. But you are no more responsible for his actions than I am. You must not blame yourself. It took place almost fifty years ago. You cannot change what happened. You cannot put it right. And the man who did it has nothing to do with you. Whatever he was, you are a wonderful, kind, beautiful human being. That is what is important, not your grandfather."

"Oh, Reed . . ." Anna let out a breathy little sigh. "It is so easy to believe that when I hear you say it. When I am with you, nothing seems to be so bad."

"There is nothing bad. Not in you." He kissed the top of her head. Her hair was like silk beneath his lips; her perfume teased at his nostrils. He raised a hand to her cheek, gently running his finger along it. "You are so beautiful."

Anna's heart seemed to skip a beat. The whisky she had drunk had turned her warm inside, making the cold recede. At the touch of Reed's finger upon her cheek, the heat spread out through her body. She turned her face up toward his, and she was caught in his gaze.

"Anna . . ." His voice was barely more than a whisper, and the sound of it sent a tremor through her.

For a long moment, they did not move. Indeed, they scarcely seemed to breathe, as though the slightest movement might break the moment.

Then, knowing that she should not, Anna stretched up toward him. She wanted to feel the touch of his lips upon hers. She wanted to have his hands on her body. Everything inside her yearned for him.

His lips brushed hers, caressing first her top lip, then the bottom. His hands came up, cupping her face and sliding back, his fingers tangling in her hair. His skin was faintly rough against the soft flesh of her face as his thumbs stroked over her cheek-bones.

Anna's eyes fluttered closed, and her skin flared with heat. Her breasts felt swollen and heavy, the nipples prickling as desire flooded her loins. She remembered his fingers upon her breasts, caressing and arousing her, his hands sliding up her legs, seeking the hot, moist center of her. She ached there, her whole body alive and tingling with need, trembling with desire.

He kissed her, his lips soft and supple on hers, enticing and seducing her. Anna quivered, lost in his taste, his scent. His hands slipped down her neck and over her chest, coming to rest on her breasts. A soft moan escaped her as he caressed her, and she wanted to be free of her clothes, to feel his skin upon her naked flesh.

Her hands went to his chest, sliding up across his shirt. She could feel the musculature of his chest beneath the material, firm and strong. She wanted to slip her hands beneath his shirt and caress his bare skin, to know the texture of him. She thought of tasting him with her mouth, of sending the tip of her tongue lazily gliding over his skin.

Reed's kiss deepened, and his hands dug in at her waist. He turned, bearing her back against the sofa. In another moment, Anna knew, she would be lost, unable to stop the hurtling force of their passion.

"No!" she gasped out, twisting away. "No. We cannot."

Her hands came up to her face. She could not bear to look at him, knowing that even a glance might break her resolve. Anna jumped to her feet. She heard him rise behind her, and she whirled, one hand out.

"Please . . . no." She looked at him, wanting with all her heart to throw herself back into his arms.

Color flamed along Reed's cheekbones, and his chest rose and fell in uneven rhythm. He had never looked so handsome to her, so desirable, as he did in that moment, and Anna clenched her hands at her sides, fighting her own treacherous instincts.

For a long moment they stood like that, caught in the tangle of their desire, and then, with an almost physical wrenching, Anna whirled and ran from the room.

Chapter Seventeen

Someone tried to break into Holcomb Manor that night.

In the middle of the night, Anna was pulled from her sleep by the sound of raised voices. She got up and wrapped her dressing gown around her, then hurried downstairs to the music room, where several of the servants were already gathered. Kit hurried in almost on her heels.

"What the devil is going on here?"

"Someone broke the window, sir," one of the footmen answered, turning to Kit and Anna. "I was keeping watch, sir, like you told me, and all of sudden I heard this sound like glass breaking. So I called for John, here, and we started looking around. When we got to the music room, we found the pane broken and the window up. Someone had reached in and unfastened the lock, looks like. But I guess we scared them off."

"Close the window and board up that pane," Kit ordered. "We'll have the glazier in tomorrow. Hargrove, set someone on that. Then get the rest of the men. We are going to search outside the house."

While the butler snapped orders to the servants, Kit strode out of the room and down the hall toward the kitchen. Anna hurried after him.

He turned. "Where are you going?"

"With you," Anna replied. "Where else?"

"You should stay in here."

"I shall be with you," Anna countered.

Kit started to protest, then raised his hands and let them fall. "All right. I can't waste time arguing."

They continued into the kitchen area, where Kit picked up the lantern by the back door and lit it. Hargrove followed them, handing out lanterns to the servants in clusters of two or three, and the entire group trooped out the back door, spreading out to cover the immediate grounds.

Kit and Anna walked through the garden, glancing in either direction, heading toward the trees at the back. They had not reached them when a cry went up from near the house.

Turning, they hurried back through the garden to where Hargrove and a footman were bending over something on the ground. When they grew nearer, they saw that it was one of the outside guards whom

Reed had sent over. He was stretched out, unconscious.

"He's been knocked out," Hargrove told them. "I can feel the bump on the back of his head."

They carried the man inside and laid him out on the servants' table, where Anna could tend to his wound. The others returned to their search of the gardens, but few had any hope of finding the intruder.

Anna bandaged up the man's head, and, when he came to, she gave him some of the powder Dr. Felton had left for Kit's headaches. Everyone returned before long with the expected news that they had found no signs of any person on the grounds.

Anna looked at Kit worriedly. Obviously, whoever had tried to hurt Kit was not giving up on his plan. She had to find out who was doing the killings — and soon.

Anna and Reed went the next morning to visit Nick Perkins. The old man greeted them warmly, though he looked surprised at their visit.

"Come in, come in. Let me brew some tea for us."

"I don't know that we will be staying that long," Anna said somewhat stiffly.

She wasn't quite sure how to act around

Nick now. Looking at him, she felt the same friendship and affection that she always had. Yet she could not help but think about the fact that he had aided Lady de Winter to cover up the murders her husband had committed. She understood that he had not told her the truth about the murders because he was trying to protect her from the knowledge that her own grandfather was a killer and a madman, but, still, there was a pinprick of hurt, knowing that he had lied to her.

"Is something the matter, Miss Anna?" he asked, his forehead knotting in concern.

"We learned some things yesterday," Reed said. "And we need to talk to you about them."

The old man looked at them a trifle warily, but he led them into the main room of his cottage, gesturing them toward the chairs. He sat in a chair across from them.

"All right, then," he said. "What is it you're wanting to know?"

"We found out yesterday that it was you who discovered Susan Emmett's body," Anna said flatly.

Perkin's eyebrows rose. "Aye, that I did."

"Yet when I asked you about that murder you said nothing about it."

He shrugged. "I don't know how that could have helped you, miss."

"But surely you can see that it would have been of interest to us that you helped cover up those killings," Anna shot back, unwanted tears springing into her eyes.

Perkins stared at her in dismay. "Miss Anna . . . how . . . who told you that?"

"I see you cannot deny it," Anna said, her voice laced with hurt. "Nick, how could you do that?"

The old man sighed, seeming almost to shrink before their eyes. He cast a look at Anna and said, "You're right. It was a wicked thing to do. You cannot blame me more than I blame myself. If it weren't for me and what I did, old Will Dawson wouldn't have died."

He paused, rubbing his hands over his face, then went on. "My family's been loyal to the de Winters for generations. We've worked for them, farmed their land, even fought for them back in the old days. My first instinct, I guess, was loyalty, even though I never liked Roger de Winter. He was a hard, cruel man." Nick's face tightened as he spoke. "When I came upon him standing over Susan's body — he had carried her out to Weller's Point after he killed her in the house — my first thought was to get him away from there, to get him back to the house."

Nick stood up and began to pace. "He took my helping him as his due, of course. That is the arrogant sort he was. Everyone else existed to serve Lord de Winter. But Lady Philippa — his wife — was a wonderful woman. She didn't deserve the shame, and neither did their son. It would have stained the de Winter name forever. When I told her what I had found, she begged me to help her. So I did. What was done, was done, I thought. His going to the gallows wouldn't have brought the girl back. I told the constable that I had found Susan and led them to the body, but I said nothing about his lordship. And, of course, no one ever questioned him or Lady de Winter. There was no indication that her death had come at Winterset. Lady de Winter saw to it that the room was cleaned up."

He sighed again and turned toward Anna. "We thought we could control him. His valet stayed with him, and at night they locked him in his bedchamber. He assured us that he understood, that he would abide by the rules. He said he had not meant to kill the girl, and I guess we were eager to believe him. Of course, we saw our mistake after he got away from his valet one night and killed poor Will."

"But still you did not turn him in," Reed commented.

"No. We had already concealed the first murder. I could scarcely go forward then and have Lady de Winter accused of being an accessory. She locked him up after that, put him in the nursery and got a burly guard to watch him, as well as his valet." Nick turned haunted eyes toward Reed. "I've never forgotten or forgiven myself. If I had been a better man, a stronger man, I would have taken him straight to jail when I found him. But I wasn't . . . and I could not hurt Lady Philippa like that."

"Why did he do that?" Anna burst out. "We found those masks, his journals, but we could make very little sense of them."

"He was mad," Perkins said bluntly. "He grew worse and worse until he died. He had some crazy idea that the legends about the Beast of Craydon Tor were true. He said it was the de Winter curse, but it had turned out to be a blessing. He thought that periodically through the years one of the de Winters, like him, would be one of the 'Children of the Wolf.' He said that sort of thing. These 'Wolf People' were superior to everyone else, he thought. They had gifts, he said — they had heightened senses of smell and hearing, as if they really were wolves.

They were attuned to the woods, to nature, and they had the courage of a wolf. Because he was one of the 'Wolf People,' he was not subject to the laws that governed lesser folk. He believed that he hunted and then killed, like a wolf, and that it was his right, part of his superiority."

Perkins paused, then went on. "He used to put on those masks and wear them about his rooms. He had strange clawlike nails that he would slip on his fingers. I think he must have worn them when he killed his quarry. Perhaps the first time, when he killed Susan in the house, it might have been a sudden impulse. But I think when he killed Will Dawson, he put them on and went hunting."

Anna shivered. It was a horrible image and one that she knew she would not be able to get out of her head for a long time.

Nick turned to her and said earnestly, "I'm sorry, Miss Anna, but I could not tell you all that. I know what I did was wrong, but I can't regret it, not when you and your brother and your mother would have had to live with that stigma. You may hate me, but —"

"Oh, Nick." Anna sent him an anguished look. "I cannot hate you."

She knew that she was grateful he had

done what he did, that she and Kit had not grown up with the black cloud of their grandfather's evil deeds hanging over them. God knows, she wished that she did not know about them even now. At the same time, she hated what he had done, and she was not sure that she could ever feel the same way about him again.

They left not long afterward, but when Reed turned his horse toward the road, Anna reached out and put her hand on his arm, stopping him.

"I want to go the other way," she told him.

Reed's eyebrows soared upward. "By the footbridge? Are you sure?"

"Yes. I have been thinking about it. Even though we have found out who killed those people almost fifty years ago, I'm not at all sure that we are any closer to finding out who the killer is right now. Everyone who lives around here has heard of those killings. You and I have proved that with a little research, a person could find out the essential elements of those killings and repeat them. Remember how Grimsley told us of seeing lights in the nursery and walking along the gallery? He assumed that they were ghosts, because that is the way his mind works, but clearly it could have been someone who sneaked into the house while it was empty. They could have found Lord Roger's journals. Perhaps there are other journals, ones that talk about the killings, ones that we did not see, and this person read them and became intrigued."

Reed nodded. "Yes, it's obviously a possibility."

"But we still have absolutely no idea who that person is," Anna pointed out. "So I thought that I ought to try again what we talked about — but this time go to the scene of the crime and see if I can sense more about the murder. Perhaps, if I tried, I could see more of what happened, get a clue about who the killer is."

Reed frowned. "I don't like the idea of your exposing yourself to such pain. I saw how you reacted in the room off the gallery, and that was an old murder. Where the killings have been so recent, it will be worse. I don't want you to suffer that sort of pain."

"I have to," Anna insisted.

Finally, with a sigh, Reed agreed, and they turned toward the footbridge.

On horseback, it did not take them long to reach the stream. Anna could feel her stomach tightening as they drew near the location. They dismounted and tied their horses to a tree, then walked over to the spot where Anna and the twins had stumbled upon Frank Johnson's body.

As she approached it, the tense, uneasy feeling inside her chest began to grow, the pain twisting and turning inside her. She stood over the place where he had lain, looking down, remembering his body lying there. She wanted to look away, to close her mind to the memories, but she forced herself to think about it, seeing again the gruesome wounds, the blood pooling on the ground. . . .

Shock jolted through her, along with a burst of pain in her head, and Anna gasped. It was not as strong as it had been the first time, but she could feel again the sensations that had assaulted her when she had been in this place before. She could see the darkness, feel herself stumbling forward, falling with a thud.

Unconsciously, Anna reached out her hand. She did not realize she had done so until she felt Reed take it, his fingers curling around her palm. She squeezed his hand tightly, grateful for its reassuring strength.

With a sigh, she opened her eyes.

"Are you all right?" He was looking down at her, his brow creased with concern.

She nodded. "It isn't as intense as when I

felt it the other day. I'm not sure how much is the feeling and how much is remembering what it felt like then."

"What could you tell about the murder?" he asked.

"Not that much. It was quick. I think the killer must have jumped out from behind something and hit the boy in the head, because I felt surprise at almost the same time as I felt the flash of pain. Then he stumbled forward, I think, and fell to the ground and lost consciousness. I could never see the killer. I think he was behind Frank. Poor boy."

She looked up at Reed. "I'm afraid it isn't much help."

"You have established a pattern. Wasn't your brother knocked in the head, as well?"

Anna nodded. "Yes. He must hit them with something, and then, when they are incapacitated, he goes after them with a knife or whatever it is he uses to cut them."

"Shall we go on to the farm where your maid was found?" Reed asked. "Do you feel well enough?"

"Yes. I'm fine. Really, it wasn't nearly as bad as before."

So they rode on, crossing the stream and turning east, rather than continuing on the path to Winterset. They went through a pleasant meadow and up a rise, and there they dismounted.

"Dr. Felton said her body was above the meadow and not far from the clump of oak saplings." Anna gestured toward a small stand of slender young trees.

They crisscrossed the area on foot, but Anna remained strangely unaffected. Finally she stopped with a sigh. "I don't understand. Perhaps I have the place wrong. Or maybe it has been too long."

"But you felt the murder in Winterset, even though it had been many years," Reed countered. He looked thoughtful. "When you first felt that something had happened to Estelle, you were elsewhere, were you not?"

Anna nodded. "Yes, in the woods near my house." She looked at him. "Do you think that is where she was killed? That we should try there instead?"

"I don't know. But Lord de Winter took Susan Emmett's body from where he killed her to another spot. Perhaps our killer is that slavishly devoted to following the original murders."

"It's worth a try."

They mounted their horses again and trotted back the way they had come, taking the narrow path that led toward Holcomb

Manor. When they reached the edge of the woods, they dismounted and walked into the trees, leading their horses.

"This is the place where the twins found their dog," Anna said, pointing. "I still wonder if his wounds might have been caused by the same person. They were similar. Or maybe it was his pain I felt that day. The spot is not far from here."

She wound through the trees, trying to remember the precise location where she had felt that slamming fist of fear. She drew in her breath sharply as little prickles of awareness suddenly danced over her skin.

"Do you feel something?" Reed asked.

Anna nodded. "Yes, a little. It's near here."

She walked on, and now the fear was sweeping through her like a tide of cold. Her steps grew quicker.

"She was scared," Anna said, her eyes blank, looking at the area in front of her without really seeing it, focusing on something in her mind. "The fear came before the pain. She — she's running." Anna's voice grew a little breathy. "It's behind — behind her, and it's catching up."

She hurried through the trees, her voice going higher with fear, her breath coming in little pants. "She screams. She wants him — the man she was going to meet. I can't — can't get his name. And then — and then —"

Anna came to a dead stop, holding her hands out a little from her sides. "Here. The pain comes here. It's different — not on the head. Something slams into her from behind, and I can't — *she* can't breathe. She's fallen, and then it's on her. She's paralyzed with fear. And then there's pain, tearing pain, and a flash of something — a face or something that terrifies her. I can't really see it well. I just feel what she's feeling."

She let out a breath and glanced around her, feeling as if she were returning suddenly to her own place and time. Her hand was in Reed's, and she was clutching it to her; she realized it with some embarrassment and released him.

"I'm sorry."

He shook his head, dismissing the need for any apology. "Was that everything you could see?"

"Yes. I didn't see his face. I never can. But it was different with her. She ran from him, and he didn't hit her on the head first."

"It was the first. Perhaps it was unplanned. Or maybe he learned from the first

one that he needed to render them unconscious quickly."

"Or because they were men, he presumed
he needed more advantage."

Reed nodded. "No one but us — and the
killer — knows that this is where the murder
actually took place. So the constable has not
searched the area."

Anna nodded. "You're right. We should
look around, see if we can see anything. One
of her earbobs, perhaps. Penny said she was
wearing a set that the man she was meeting
had given her."

"Were they still on her body?"

"I'm not sure. I mentioned them to
Estelle's family, but they had no idea what I
was talking about. So I would think that
they were missing from the body — or perhaps, in their grief, they didn't even notice."

"All right. Let's begin to look. Starting
here, since this is where you think she went
down."

They bent over, searching the ground
carefully, walking away from each other and
returning in narrow zigzags. After a few
minutes, Reed let out a cry of discovery.
Anna was instantly at his side.

"What? Did you find anything?"

"Look at that." Reed pointed at the

ground at his feet. Just this side of a small shrub, lying against a small, fallen branch, lay a glitter of gold.

"What is it?" Anna leaned closer, and Reed bent to pick it up.

"A cuff link," he said, holding it out to her in his palm. "Do you recognize it?"

It was a gold cuff link, with a small onyx set in the center. Anna shook her head indecisively.

"I don't know. I — it seems as though I have seen it somewhere, but . . . it's not really familiar."

Anna sighed. She had had such hopes of finding out something pertinent, but when they *had* found something, it hadn't turned out to be of much use.

Reed saw her expression. "Don't be downcast. Now we know where the murder really took place, and we know that he lost a cuff link."

"But it's scarcely something we can take to the constable," Anna pointed out. "What would we say? We found this lying in the woods, nowhere near where either body was found? Or that I somehow knew the murder really took place here?"

"No. But we know more than we knew before." He smiled down at her. "We have a link to the killer."

"I know. It's just — I am worried about Kit. After last night . . . I don't think he will stop until he has hurt Kit. We *must* find out who it is. And soon."

"We will," Reed assured her, taking her hand and squeezing it. "Now . . . let me escort you home, and then you shall invite me to stay for dinner, and we'll spend the evening, you and Kit and I, racking our brains for answers to our puzzle."

Anna had to smile, as he had planned. "All right."

They did, in fact, follow Reed's proposed schedule for the evening, riding to Holcomb Manor and joining Kit for supper, then sitting down afterward in the sitting room and discussing their progress concerning the murders. Their revelations regarding Lord Roger de Winter left Kit stunned and almost speechless.

"Our grandfather?" he asked in amazement. "Are you jesting?"

"It's hardly something I find funny," Anna told her brother. "Yes, it's true. Both the maid we went to see and Nick Perkins admitted it. They helped Lady Philippa conceal it from everyone."

"I cannot imagine."

"What worries me most," Anna said, "is

that our uncle lived in that house until ten years ago. He was alive when it happened, about ten or so — old enough, perhaps, to have had some idea of what was going on. It might have . . . influenced his madness."

"Yes, but Uncle Charles is not like that," Kit argued. "The way you described Lord Roger . . ."

"I know. But none of us knows what really goes on in Uncle Charles' mind. It's quite likely he saw those masks, even read the journals. Couldn't he have developed a similar obsession?"

"It does sound like the type of delusion that Uncle Charles has. But I have never heard anything about those particular beliefs in all his ramblings. You know that what he believes is all about the Queen and how he is the heir to the throne and all that." He cast an embarrassed glance at Reed. "I am sorry to involve you in all this."

"No need to be," Reed responded casually. "I've told Anna all about my myriad peculiar relatives."

Anna cast him a warm look. It pleased her to see Reed and Kit talking together so easily. They could be friends, she thought, letting her mind drift for a moment in a pleasant dream. If only things had been different . . .

The evening wound to a close. Reed rode home, and Anna went up to bed, leaving Kit to take the first watch of the evening, as he had told his servants he would.

It was raining. The ground was wet and slick, and thick drops clustered on the leaves of the trees, rolling off them. She was walking through the woods. Everything around her was silent and gray, with the faint light one found beneath the trees on a rainy day.

Ahead of her, she saw a man lying on the ground, unmoving, his face turned up to the sky. Raindrops pattered on his face, rolling down his cheeks, and he did not stir. She moved closer, fear clutching at her throat.

She stood over the man and looked down at him. His face was pale and still as death, raindrops clustering on his eyelashes, soaking his hair.

"No!" Her scream ripped through the woods.

"No!" Anna sat bolt upright, her eyes flying open.

The dream had been so real that for a moment she was unsure where she was. Her heart was pounding in her chest as though it might explode, and she was cold with horror. *Reed was dead!*

She threw back her coverlet and jumped out of bed. She lit a candle with shaking fingers, then hastened to her wardrobe. *She had to go to him. She had to see! Maybe it wasn't too late.*

With icy fingers, she pulled out a simple dress that buttoned down the front, easy to put on by herself. She whipped off her nightgown and dressed, shoving her feet into slippers.

She hurried out the door and ran down the stairs, her unbound hair floating in a tangle down her back. Once outside, she ran across the yard. It was her first instinct to run all the way to Winterset, but her mind was working well enough to conquer that thought. It would be much faster to ride.

It was almost dawn. She could see the lightening of the sky in the east, though the sun had not yet appeared over the horizon. The birds were beginning to move and twitter in their trees, but the stables were still dark, the grooms not yet tending to their business.

She ran in and hurried along the stalls to where her horse was kept. She grabbed a bridle from a hook on the wall, and at that moment a groom came clattering down the stairs from the sleeping quarters above.

"Miss!" he exclaimed, hurrying toward her. His hair was still mussed from sleep, and his shirt hung outside his trousers. "What's the matter?"

"Saddle my horse," Anna said, shoving the bridle at him.

"Now, miss?" He gaped at her.

"Yes! Now! Hurry!"

He blinked at her in amazement, but he moved to do as she bid, going into the stall and putting the bridle on her mare. Anna waited impatiently, pacing up and down the center aisle of the stables, as he bridled and saddled her horse.

"But ye need a groom to go with ye," the groom said as he led the mare to Anna. "Yer not going out without a groom, are ye? Master Kit said —"

"I am leaving now," Anna said firmly. "Give me a hand up. You can follow if you wish, but I'm not waiting."

The man was too used to obedience to refuse to do as she said, and he tossed her up into the saddle, then stood, scratching his head, as he watched her ride out of the stables and into the yard beyond.

Anna took the faster route through the fields to Winterset, grateful that it was growing lighter by the moment. She gave her horse its head, her only thought to reach Reed. She thundered along the narrow dirt path and across a meadow, sailing over a low stone wall, and then headed on to the path to Winterset.

The sight of Reed's cold, lifeless face plagued her thoughts. She had been so stupid, she berated herself. She had been so caught up in her fear for her brother that she had not even thought about Reed. He was as likely to be in danger as anyone — more, even, since he was actively involved in searching for the killer.

The sun was just peeping over the horizon as her horse pounded up to Winterset. The house stood still and quiet, though there was some sign of activity out in the stables. A startled groom stuck his head out the stable door and started forward when he saw Anna jump down from her horse. She left the reins dangling for him and ran through the formidable gates and up to the front door.

She crashed the knocker against the door repeatedly until a footman pulled the door open.

"Reed! Where is Reed?" she cried, pushing past the astonished servant into the foyer.

"Uh, uh, in his bedchamber, I imagine, miss," the footman began, but realized he was speaking to Anna's back as she rushed past him and up the stairs.

"Miss!" he exclaimed in a scandalized voice and started after her.

"Reed!" Anna called as she darted up the stairs and into the hall. She looked around, not knowing which room was his, and called his name again as she started down the hall, opening one door after another.

The footman jittered along behind her nervously, pleading with her to stop, to let him announce her to the master. Down the hall, a door was flung open and Reed stepped into the hall.

"Anna!" He had obviously pulled on his clothes hastily, for he wore only trousers and a shirt, hanging open down the front, and his hair was still tousled from sleep. "What is it? What's the matter?"

He started forward. Anna ran toward him. "Reed!"

She flung herself into his arms. "Reed! Oh, thank God! I was so worried about you."

Reed held her close, motioning at the gaping footman to leave, which the man did, albeit with some reluctance.

"Worried about me?" Reed asked, surprised. He stepped back into his room, pulling Anna with him, and closed the door. "Now, why would you be worried about me?"

"I saw you!" she cried, stepping back and looking searchingly into his face, as though she could not quite believe that he was alive and well, even though the evidence was standing right in front of her.

"Saw me?" he repeated. "What do you mean?"

"In a dream. I dreamed about you lying out in the woods in the rain, dead. You were so pale, so still. Oh, Reed, I was so scared!" She threw herself against him, her arms going around his waist and holding on tightly. "I thought you were dead. I don't know what I would do if you were dead."

Anna looked up into his face. Her eyes were huge and dark blue in her face, sparkling with tears, and the color was high on her cheekbones, staining them red. Her hair hung in a long tangle down her back, careless and windblown.

Reed's breath caught in his throat. He had never seen her look so desirable.

"Oh, Reed . . ." Anna breathed, and she brought her hands up to cup his face.

She felt the roughness of his unshaved skin beneath her hands, and she was suddenly aware of his shirt hanging open, revealing a strip of bare skin down the front of his chest and stomach. Her heart began to hammer, and the nerves all over her skin sizzled to life. She felt the heat flood his face beneath her hands, and her own insides turned hot and molten.

Anna trembled, rose up on her toes, then pulled his head down to meet her mouth.

Chapter Eighteen

Reed's mouth clamped down on hers greedily. All the passion that had been held back stormed through them, sweeping aside the concepts of propriety and duty. There was no thought, no feeling, other than the desire that raged in them.

He lifted her into him, pressing her body against his. She could feel the fierce hunger in him, the heat that exploded in his body, surrounding her. He kissed her wildly as his hands roamed up and down her back, digging into her buttocks and moving her against the rigid length of his desire.

Her own hunger was like a ravening beast inside her, clawing to be free of the restraints she had put on it for so long. She wrapped her arms around Reed's neck, clinging to him as her lips gave back to him, kiss for kiss.

Lost in a haze of desire, they made their way toward the bed, turning, sliding backward, never pulling apart long enough to walk the few feet. He fumbled at her buttons, and she slid her hands beneath his shirt, roaming with pleasure across his bare skin. The feel of his flesh beneath her fingers, the smoothness of skin and the faint roughness of hair, stoked the flames of her passion still higher.

Anna felt as if she could scarcely breathe, could not last another moment without touching him, kissing him, all over. She wanted him with a kind of desperation she had never experienced, a hunger that would not be denied. She wanted to know him, to have him inside her, to belong to him in the most elemental way.

"Love me," she murmured, lightly dragging her nails down his bare back beneath his shirt.

Reed jerked at her touch and let out a groan. "I do, I do." He kissed her deeply and whispered, "I will."

He jerked at the last few buttons, popping off two of them, and shoved her dress down off her arms. In her haste, Anna had donned none of her petticoats, only her chemise and pantalets. Reed stopped, gazing down at her lithe body, clad only in these two simple cotton garments. Her breasts swelled above the top of her chemise, pale and round and succulent. A strand of her hair fell in front of her shoulders, curling and tangling down over her breast, and the sight of it sent hunger crashing through him.

Reed ached to take her immediately, to consume her all at once, and at the same time he wanted to take his time, to taste each and every delight of her flesh. He wanted to smother her with long, leisurely kisses, to roam over every inch of her smooth skin, to caress and arouse her to a quivering, begging hunger. And he wanted, too, to sink deep within her right now, to drive to his exploding satisfaction.

He reached down and took the strand of hair between his fingers, sliding down it, his knuckles brushing over the silken skin of her breast, and his skin trembled at the touch. He laid the tress back over her shoulder and bent to press his lips upon the soft, yielding top of her breast. He smelled the scent of her skin, the faint trace of perfume. His lips made their way across the tops of her breasts, kissing and teasing, his tongue circling designs over the quivering flesh.

Untying the bow between her breasts, he slipped loose the ribbon that laced up the chemise, and it sagged apart. He slipped his hands between the two sides and pushed back the fabric, exposing the full white orbs. Reed cupped her breasts, delighting in the contrast of her pearly skin with his tanned hands.

Her nipples tightened boldly under his gaze, and he grazed his thumbs across them, sending shivers through Anna and hardening the buds even more.

"You are so beautiful," he murmured, and bent to kiss her breasts again.

He wrapped his arms under her hips, lifting her up so that he could feast more freely upon her breasts. His tongue traced around a nipple, teasing it into an even tauter state, lashing and circling and finally pulling the hard button of flesh into his mouth, suckling it.

Anna trembled beneath his ministrations, sparks of sensation shooting through her with every tug of his mouth. Her abdomen blossomed with heat, desire pooling between her legs. She groaned, her hands roaming restlessly over his shoulders and neck, and tangling in his hair.

She had never known anything like the feelings that flooded her now. An insistent ache grew between her legs, yearning for a completion that only Reed could give her. He had lifted her off her feet, and now she wrapped her legs around him, pressing herself wantonly against him.

A half groan, half laugh escaped Reed,

and he murmured shakily, "You will un-man me."

He eased her feet back onto the floor and threw off the scrap of her chemise, still clinging to her arms, then unfastened the bow of her pantalets and ran his hands beneath them, pushing them over the curve of her buttocks and down her legs, until they fell in a pool at her feet.

Anna tugged at his shirt, pushing it back and off his shoulders. Then her hands went to his trousers, inexpertly seeking the buttons that fastened them.

"You should do this," she said shakily. "I am all thumbs."

"I enjoy more the way you do it," he told her, smiling.

In response, she tossed him a saucy grin and slid her hand boldly into his trousers, and he groaned, biting back an oath. She started to withdraw, but he clamped his hand over hers.

"No, stay."

Surprised at her own audacity, Anna did as he said, her hand searching out the hard male length of his desire and curling around him. Her other hand slid beneath the waistband of his trousers, and she pushed them down, gliding over his buttocks as his hand had moved on hers. He sucked in his breath, and the sound aroused her. She could feel the quiver of his flesh beneath her hands, and that aroused her even more.

Reed grasped her shoulders and kissed her, his mouth claiming hers, as she continued to caress him. His lips ground into hers, his tongue probing. He wrapped his arms around her, his skin searing hers, and they tumbled back onto the bed.

He kissed her again and again as his hand went between her legs, finding the tender flesh there, slick with the moisture of her desire. He caressed her, his fingers moving delicately, expertly, exploring and exciting her. Anna dug her fingertips into the soft flesh of his buttocks as the passion built in her to almost unbearable heights. She moaned his name, lost in her hunger, aching for him.

He parted her legs and slid between them, sinking into her slowly, gently opening her and filling her. Anna gasped, but it was wonder, not fear, that spread through her as he eased into her, and despite the brief, sharp slice of pain, her desire only increased, swelling and growing in her with each slow thrust.

Reed moved within her, and Anna wrapped her arms and legs around him, trembling with urgency. Something was building in her, strange and sweet and at the same time almost unbearable in its intensity. She clutched at his back, almost sobbing in her need for release. And now he was moving more quickly, thrusting into her hard and fast, and she was rushing, rushing. . . .

Then the pleasure broke within her, startling her and flooding her with the most intense sensation she had ever known, sweeter and brighter and more explosive than anything she could have imagined. He cried out, jerking as his own shattering release reached him, and he collapsed against her.

They lay there for a long moment, spent and replete. He rolled from on top of her, wrapping his arms around her and taking her with him, so that she lay across his chest.

Dazed, Anna lay limply, listening to the hard, triphammer beat of his heart as it gradually slowed. She could not speak, could not even really think, only lie basking in the pleasure that permeated her body.

Then, much to her surprise, his hand began to move over her again, smoothing down her back and hips and thighs, stroking and caressing her, his fingertips lightly teasing over her skin. Amazed, she felt his maleness move against her.

"Again?" she asked, rolling onto her side and staring at him.

He grinned at her. "I have been waiting for this a long time."

Reed pushed her gently onto her back and rose onto his elbow. "This time, I mean to take my time with you."

And he did. He lay looking at her, his fingers drifting over her skin. He aroused her slowly, teasing and caressing with his fingers and mouth, stoking the fires of her passion bit by bit, until her whole body was once again alive and thrumming. Only then, when she was moaning, her hands reaching for him, urging him on, did he slide once more inside her. Slowly, he stroked in and out, building the desire in them both to the melting point, teasingly keeping them just out of reach of that supreme release, until their bodies were stretched taut, aching and almost at the breaking point.

Then he plunged deeply, hurtling them both over the edge into blissful oblivion.

Anna's eyes drifted open, and she lay for a moment, aware of the soft, sated contentment that permeated her body. She felt warm and languid, and she was aware of her body in a way she never had been before. She closed her eyes, letting herself enjoy this last moment of unadulterated happiness.

Then, with a sigh, she sat up. Beside her,

Reed opened his eyes at the movement and smiled at her. His face was unlined and content, his eyes filled with happiness.

Bleakly, Anna knew that she was about to ruin that happiness.

"I must go," she said softly. She could not resist leaning over and kissing him.

Reed wrapped an arm around her shoulders, holding her for a longer, deeper kiss than she had planned. When he released her, she sat up, her eyes bright and her breathing a bit unsteady.

"Don't go," he murmured. "Stay. We are doubtless already a complete scandal to the staff. We may as well luxuriate in our wickedness. There is no avenue for us now save marriage, anyway, and that will cure all transgressions."

"No, please, don't joke about it," Anna said, sliding off the bed and picking up her clothes.

She felt suddenly embarrassed at her nakedness, and she turned away, hastily pulling on her undergarments and dress.

"I'm not joking," Reed said, his voice turning a trifle wary. He sat up, feeling at a disadvantage, and got up to don his own trousers. "I may have said it lightly, but I meant it just the same. I want to marry you."

When Anna did not respond, he walked around to face her. She started to turn away, but he put his hands on her shoulders, stopping her. "Anna. Look at me. Say something. I am asking you to marry me."

"I cannot," she said wretchedly. "You know it is impossible."

"No, I don't know that," he responded tightly. "There is nothing impossible about it. We have only to do it. And I intend for us to do it very soon."

"No!" Anna jerked away from his grasp. "Reed, please, don't make it any more difficult."

"I shall make it damned difficult," he rasped. "You act as if I am hurting you. I am asking to marry you! I want to love you and care for you for the rest of our lives."

"I want it, too!" Anna cried, facing him. Tears shone in her eyes. "But you know that we cannot."

"We can! I don't give a damn about your family and whatever madness may lie in them. I love you, and I want you, mad family and all. I don't plan to spend the rest of my life the way I have the past three years, missing you, *aching* for you, all because of your stubborn pride."

"It is not stubbornness, nor my pride. I am doing what is right, and you know it. You just want to pretend that the problem doesn't exist, but it does."

"You don't understand. I know very well that it is there. I just don't care. I refuse to let the fact that your uncle is insane ruin both our lives."

"You cannot allow that into your family. Reed, think! Yours is one of the highest, oldest families in the land. You cannot let their blood be mingled with de Winter blood. You cannot subject future generations to that."

"Then we won't have children. Anna, listen to me." He went to her, taking her hands between hers. "There are ways to avoid having children."

"You cannot be certain," Anna said.

"Dammit, if it takes never being able to experience again what we just did, then I will do that," Reed told her roughly. "I want you as my wife."

"We could not keep that from happening again, and you know it," Anna retorted. "And, besides, you should have children. You will make a wonderful father. I know it. I have seen you with Con and Alex. You deserve to have children."

"I would rather have you," he replied bluntly.

"It isn't even just the children," Anna told

him. "The madness comes upon us late in life. Although my uncle showed only slight signs when he was in his twenties, the madness grew worse and worse as he got older. It could still happen to me. I could go mad, and then you would be saddled with an insane wife. I can't do that to you. I couldn't bear for you to see me like that."

"And I cannot bear to live without you," Reed snapped. "I want to be with you for the rest of my life. And if you should go mad, then I will live with you mad."

"That would only be a half life!" Anna argued.

"I would rather have a half life with you than years and years with some other woman. Bloody hell, Anna! I love you! And I am willing to take whatever comes." His eyes flared with anger. "I think it is just that you are afraid. You don't love me enough to marry me."

"That's not true!" she flashed back. "I love you more than anything. More than life itself. I love you to the very depths of my soul." Tears clogged her throat, and she had to force out her last words, "And that is why I will not marry you."

Anna turned and ran from the room.

"Anna, dammit!" Reed let out an oath and whirled, picking up the nearest object, a small lamp, and sending it crashing against the opposite wall. He stood for a moment, then turned and ran after her.

She was already running down the stairs, and Reed started after her, heedless of the startled gazes of his servants, many of whom seemed to have found some task that needed doing around the staircase. "Anna! Wait!"

Anna did not pause, but ran out the front door. By the time Reed reached the door, she was already mounted on her mare. She glanced back at him, and he saw her tear-streaked face. Then she dug her heels into her horse and was gone, leaving him staring after her.

By the time Anna got back to Holcomb Manor, the righteous anger that had sustained her at first had all drained away, leaving her feeling only an empty ache.

She knew that she had to stop seeing Reed. The situation was impossible. She had been living in a dream world, believing that somehow she could be with him and enjoy his company and not give in to her passions, but obviously that was not the case. Nor could she marry him. Despite what he had said, it would be wrong and cruel of her to tie him to a wife who might grow mad, a wife who could not give him children. He deserved so much more. Some other woman could give him that.

Anna tried to ignore the jealousy that gnawed at her when she thought of him marrying another, more proper, wife. She had to be reasonable, she told herself, and just because Reed was not adhering to reason, that was no excuse for her to abandon it. Indeed, she had to be reasonable for both of them.

When she reached her house, she ran up to her room and threw herself onto the bed to indulge in a good cry. Then she sat up and washed her face and rang for Penny to draw her a bath.

After a long soak in the tub, she got dressed and let Penny do up her hair, then went downstairs and started listlessly on her tasks. She found it difficult to concentrate, and the household problems she dealt with seemed inordinately petty.

She half expected Reed to come calling. He was not the sort of man to give up on something he wanted. She did not know how she could continue to refuse him when everything inside her yearned for exactly what he was offering. How could she be strong enough to deny them both the happiness they wanted?

She was in the midst of such gloomy thoughts late that afternoon, staring out the window at the garden, when she saw a figure moving through the trees toward the house. The day had turned as gray and dreary as her thoughts, and there was a fine mist in the air, obscuring the scene. Anna leaned closer to the window, peering out, her stomach tightening.

The man stopped at the edge of the garden, looking uncertainly toward the house. Anna's eyes widened. It was Arthur Bradbury, her uncle's manservant.

She walked quickly out of the room and down the hall to her brother's study. "Kit. Arthur is here."

"What?" He looked up from his work, his brow drawing together in confusion.

"Arthur Bradbury."

"But what is he doing here?"

"I don't know. But it must be important for him to leave . . ."

"Yes, of course. You're right."

Kit stood up. He had been working in his shirtsleeves, but now he picked up the light gray jacket from the arm of the chair across from his desk and shrugged into it as he followed Anna out of the room. "Where is he?"

"I saw him out among the trees at the

edge of the garden. I think he must be waiting, hoping one of us will come out."

Anna picked up her everyday bonnet from the coatrack by the back door and tied it on as they went outside and through the garden toward the trees beyond. As they drew closer, she could see Arthur's large form beneath the trees. He was pacing anxiously, a frown on his face. His expression lightened when he saw Anna and Kit approaching him, and he swept off his cap as he stepped forward to greet them.

"Sir! Miss! I'm that glad to see you. I was just trying to think of a way to get your attention 'thout anyone seein' me."

"What is it?" Kit asked. "Is anything wrong with our uncle?"

Arthur shifted a little. "Fact is, sir, well, he's missing, like."

"Missing?" Anna asked, her voice rising in dismay.

"When I got up this morning, he weren't anywhere to be found. It's not like him to stray outside his ring of stones in the day, miss. I was a mite worried, and the longer I waited, the more worried I got. So after a while, I went out lookin' for him. And I haven't found him anywhere." He looked from one of them to the other, as though hoping they would have an answer.

"Oh, Lord," Kit sighed. "Has this ever happened before?"

Arthur shook his head. "No, sir. Not this long. He don't like to be outside the ring when it's light. I'm worried something might have happened to him. I can keep looking, but with just one person . . ." He shrugged.

"We will help you," Anna said.

"I'll get Rankin." Kit named their gamekeeper, who carried supplies up to Arthur and their uncle. Only he, of all the servants, knew about their uncle's presence in the woods. "I think you should return to your house, Arthur, in case Uncle Charles should go back there. He would be alarmed to find you gone."

"Yes, sir, you're right about that."

Kit turned to his sister. "You should stay here."

"Stay here?" Anna echoed, astonished. "I will not. You will need all the help you can get searching the woods."

"It is not safe, not with everything that has been happening. And you can't take one of the servants with you, since none of them know about Uncle Charles," Kit reasoned. He hesitated, then added, "If you must go, come along with me. That will be safer."

"That takes away the whole point of

having an extra person to search," Anna pointed out. "I will search one section alone, just as you and Rankin do."

Frankly, she was not much inclined to strike out into the woods on her own, given the recent murders. But she could not simply stand by and do nothing while her uncle was missing.

"I shall be fine," she assured her brother. "You need not worry about me. I know the woods as well or better than you, and there are few enough of us to search, as it is. Nothing will happen to me. It's daylight, and the killer has not struck during the day. Besides, it isn't me he has tried to harm, it is you. If anyone should stay home, it should be you."

Kit snorted at the absurdity of that suggestion.

"Really, Kit, don't make a fuss. Nothing is likely to happen, and if I do stumble upon someone suspicious, I shall scream, and you and Rankin can come to my rescue."

"If we are close enough to hear you," Kit pointed out. He sighed. "I am sure I should not allow you."

"Allow me?" Anna's eyes flashed dangerously.

"But I know you would pay no attention to me if I did forbid it," he finished, long accustomed to dealing with his older sister. "So we may as well not fight about it."

"I agree."

Arthur, relieved to have passed on his burden, returned to the hut by Craydon Tor to await their uncle, and Anna and Kit went back into the house briefly, Kit to locate Rankin and enlist his help, and Anna to put on a sturdier pair of walking boots.

Soon they were making their way through the garden and across the fields behind the house into the woods beyond. The mist had thickened in the past few minutes, and Anna was glad for the bonnet that kept the moisture out of her face.

When they reached the edge of the woods, the three of them fanned out, heading off at different angles. Before long, Anna could no longer hear the sounds of either her brother or Rankin as they moved through the trees. It was, she admitted, a trifle eerie to be walking in the thick woods all alone. Even the slight noise of a squirrel scampering across a branch was enough to make her jump, and when a bird exploded out of the brush in front of her at her approach, she could not suppress a little shriek.

She clapped her hand over her mouth, hoping that her utterance had not been loud enough for either her brother or Rankin to hear. Scolding herself for being such a nervous ninny, she pressed on.

The mist was growing heavier now. In fact, she realized as drops hit the brim of her bonnet, the mist had evolved into rain. As she trudged on, the rain grew harder, and she wished that she had thought to throw on a light cloak over her dress. At least, she thought, her boots would hold up to the rain and mud.

Anna shivered and wrapped her arms around her body, hugging herself for warmth. She slipped on the wet leaves and grabbed at a sapling for balance. It was then that fear slammed into her.

She gasped, her knees giving way, and if it had not been for her grasp on the small tree trunk, she would have fallen to the ground. She leaned against the tree, wrapping her arm around it to hold her up, dreading what she knew was coming.

She feared it was her uncle — some horrible vision was going to unroll before her eyes concerning her uncle. But when it came, it was far worse.

First was the insidious fear, pervasive, and so intense it made her ill. Then she saw Reed's face, just as she had seen it in her dream the other night, pale, eyes closed, looking as if he were dead.

A moan escaped her, and Anna sank down to her knees, unable to stand. Not Reed, she prayed, please, not Reed.

But there was no mistaking his face or the blood trickling from his temple. His face was wet, the rain running down it, and she knew with a certainty that this was no fore-warning as last night's dream must have been. It was no false vision, as she had let herself believe. It was now. It was real.

And Reed was in terrible danger.

Chapter Nineteen

Terror surged in her, and her first instinct was to close her mind to the vision, to pull away from it. It was what she always did. The intensity frightened her, and she would pull her mind back.

But she knew that she could not do that now. She had to see more. She had to know where Reed was and what was happening to him. It was the only way to save him.

So she remained on her knees, hanging on to the slender trunk of the tree with both hands, and forced her mind to stay on what she saw inside it, opening herself up to the horror and pain.

Reed was lying on his back on the ground, and there were trees around him. A man was kneeling over him, his back to her, a black cloak wrapped around him so that he was little more than a dark shape. He was leaning forward.

"No!" Anna cried, and staggered to her feet. She ran forward blindly, consumed by fear, and it wasn't until she slipped in the mud and fell down that she stopped and pulled her thoughts together.

The vision was gone now, though the sick, quaking fear lingered in her body. She made herself remember it, made herself think, not of Reed and the danger that threatened him, but of the area around him. *She knew that place!* She was certain of it.

She closed her eyes and made herself stay still, remembering the placement of a large rock just beyond Reed's shoulder and the spreading branches of an oak a little farther away.

Anna jumped to her feet, suddenly certain of where Reed was. It was in these very woods as they ran toward Winterset land, away from Craydon Tor. She was, she knew, not very far away from it.

She ran, dodging around trees and bushes, lifting her skirts to keep them from snagging, slipping now and then on the wet ground. The rain grew hard, drenching her, and a tree branch caught her bonnet, tearing it from her head. She paid no attention, just ran, her breath rasping in her throat, fear growing in her with every moment.

And then, at last, she saw them ahead — a man lying stretched out on the ground, a dark shape bending over him.

"No!" Anna screamed, throwing herself at the kneeling figure.

At her cry, he whipped around, rising and throwing out his arm. He caught Anna in the chest, knocking her backward onto the ground. She looked up at him and gasped, a paralyzing fear gripping her. The face of the figure looming over her was not human.

It took a moment for her to realize that the man, draped in a cloak, wore a mask similar to the ones they had found in the old Lord de Winter's chambers. It was made of hide, white-and-gray-mixed fur, fitted to the face and ending across the cheeks and nose. The hood of the cloak was pulled forward, revealing nothing of his head but the masked face. Human eyes looked out at her from behind the holes cut into the hide, and the combination of human and animal in the face was somehow worse than either alone would have been.

"You!" he exclaimed, and glanced around wildly. "You should not be here."

Someone she knew, she thought. Someone who knew her. She could not connect this monster in front of her with anyone familiar. She did not know what to do or say, how to stop him from killing Reed.

Slowly she rose to her feet, taking in the situation before her. There was a short club lying on the ground beside him, and there was a knife in his hand. However, the knife had no blood on it, which she hoped meant that Reed was not dead, just knocked unconscious. If she could distract the man, perhaps Reed would wake up and subdue him. Therefore, she should keep him talking and watching her, taking his attention away from Reed. It was not much of a plan, she knew, but it was the only thing she could think of at the moment.

"Leave him alone," she ordered, trying to put as much firm authority in her voice as she could.

He shook his head. "No. No. He has to die."

"Why?" she asked. "He's done no harm to you."

"He wants you!" the anonymous figure shot back. "Don't you see? That is why he keeps hanging about. He wants to marry you. He is trying to disturb everything, and I cannot allow it!"

"I am not going to marry Reed."

"Of course you are not. You are meant for me."

Anna gaped. *What on earth was he talking about?*

"We know that, the two of us," the bizarre figure went on. "But *he* is interfering." He flung a hand toward Reed, turning to look down at his body.

Anna moved forward, afraid that he was about to harm Reed, but the man swung back around, flinging up his hand, and she halted.

"No! Come no closer."

"All right," Anna said pacifically. "I will stay right here."

She thought about what the man had said. It was clear that he was insane. But there must be some way she could use his madness to her advantage.

"I don't understand," she began, "what you mean about me. About my being meant for you."

"We are destined for each other!" He flung his arms wide in a dramatic gesture, and Anna saw that beneath his cloak he wore a plain shirt and trousers, and tucked into the waistband of his trousers was the gardening instrument that Dr. Felton had mentioned, its four sharp tines bent forward like claws.

A shudder ran through her. He had used this on his other victims; he intended to use it on Reed. She swallowed hard against the nausea rising in her.

"We are both the Children of the Wolf," he went on. "I am not the person you think you know. The people who call themselves my parents are not really my parents. I was adopted. I know that now. I realized it several years ago. At first, I didn't understand who I was. I was just relieved that those foolish, weak, ordinary people were not really the ones who sired me. But then I learned that I was heir to the Wolf."

"I'm sorry. I don't know what you're talking about."

"You do! Of course you do! Or have they so indoctrinated you that you do not believe? Don't worry. I will teach you." He placed his hand upon his chest, saying earnestly, "My grandfather was Lord Roger de Winter."

"That cannot be," Anna said before it occurred to her that it was not wise to contradict this unhinged man. "I mean . . . Lord Charles has no children," she went on in a conciliatory tone.

"Not him!" The man waved her mention of her uncle away with a gesture. "I don't know who my father was, but my mother was the illegitimate child of a maid at Winterset. My grandfather was Lord de Winter."

"I see." That was, Anna thought, not an entirely preposterous idea. According to what Nick had said, the old lord had been a terrible husband, and he had clearly been a cold, hard person who would not have balked at seducing, or even raping, someone who worked for him. God knows, he had killed a maid; he would not have stopped at a lesser crime.

Who was this man? His voice, she thought, sounded a little familiar, but she could not place it.

"Winterset should be mine," he went on, his eyes lighting fanatically. "Once I knew that, I got into the house. I searched through it, and finally I found my grandfather's treasure trove."

The lights in the house that Grimsley had seen, Anna thought. "You found the masks."

He nodded. "Yes. You have seen them? Have you read his journals?"

"A little," Anna admitted.

"Then you must know!" he said excitedly. "We are descendants of the Wolf. *He* doesn't belong there." He gestured wildly toward Reed. "It is you and I who should be at Winterset. *I* am the heir to Lord de Winter. It is I who should rule there."

"So you are going to kill him?" Anna asked. "That won't get you Winterset." His belief was so impossible, so preposterous, that she scarcely knew where to begin. "It would go to Reed's heirs. And even if it reverted somehow to the de Winters, you would never inherit the estate. You just said that you are illegitimate."

"Ah, but I have figured that out," he said craftily, his eyes taking on a gleam. "I will come into possession of the property after you and I marry."

"Marry!" She gaped at him. "But how will that — my brother Kit is the heir . . ." Anna's voice trailed off as she realized that it was because of Kit's link to Winterset that this man had tried to kill him.

"You think I would marry you after you had killed my brother?" she cried. "After you killed the man I love? I would never marry you!"

"You must!" he snapped back, his eyes flashing. "We are destined for each other. We carry the de Winter blood. We belong together."

"I may have that tainted blood flowing through my veins," Anna flared. "God knows, I wish that I did not. But I am not like you. I am not like Lord de Winter."

"You are." His eyes flamed with anger. "You and I belong together. We are de Winters!"

"I will never marry you," Anna said slowly and distinctly, her voice like iron. "You repulse me. No matter who you kill or what you do, I will never marry you."

He let out an inarticulate roar, his hand coming up and back, as though he was preparing to strike her with the knife. But he stopped himself and stood for a moment, looking at her wildly.

"It is *him!*" he shouted, whirling around and pointing at Reed's recumbent form. "He is why you act like this!"

He thudded down onto his knees beside Reed, raising his hand. With a shriek, Anna threw herself at him, grabbing his knife hand and pulling back with all her strength. Cursing, he rose and turned, trying to fling her aside, but Anna clung to his arm tenaciously, sinking her nails into his wrist. He howled with rage and clumsily cuffed her with his other hand.

His blow made her head ring, but Anna held on, screaming, hoping that Kit or Rankin might hear her and come to her rescue. He yanked one of her arms from his wrist, but by the time he removed the other, she had grabbed his wrist again, and so they struggled. From the corner of her eye, she saw Reed's legs twitch, and hope surged in her. She struggled on with renewed strength.

She could see her attacker's eyes grow

dark with rage, the insane light burning brighter, and he let out a howl of frustration. With a burst of strength, he flung her away from him, and she stumbled backward and fell onto the ground. Before she could get up, he threw himself at her, raising his knife.

"Let her go!" a voice bellowed, and the next instant, a man barreled into her attacker, knocking him off Anna.

The knife went flying off into the grass, and the two men grappled, rolling across the grass. Anna scrambled to her feet, staring at them in amazement. "Uncle Charles!"

The other man landed a hard hit on her uncle's chin, knocking his head back, and then he rolled out from under him, but her uncle lunged at him, hitting her attacker around the knees and toppling him over again. Anna looked around for something to use as a weapon and spied the fallen club lying beside Reed. She ran to pick it up and turned back to the fight.

Her uncle was on the ground on his back, the killer straddling him, his hands around her uncle's throat. Anna ran to them and brought the tree branch down as hard as she could. She intended to hit his head, but at the last moment he dodged, and it cracked across his back instead, breaking in two. He turned toward Anna, snarling, and started to rise.

At that moment Reed lunged into the scene and brought his hand down sharply, rapping the killer on the head with his own club. The man wavered for a moment, then collapsed.

"Reed!" Anna launched herself into his arms, and he caught her, staggering back a little shakily.

"Sorry." He gave a little half laugh. "I'm not quite steady."

"Of course not." Anna stepped back and looked up into his face. "You're bleeding. He must have cracked you on the head."

She dug into her pocket for a handkerchief and pressed it against the wound on Reed's temple. Blood streaked the side of his face and neck.

"I don't know what happened. I was riding along, and suddenly something fell on me. He must have been up in a tree." He turned and looked down at his assailant. "Good God. Who the devil is he?"

"The Queen's spy," Anna's uncle answered. He had gotten to his feet and was standing rubbing his throat.

Reed looked at him. Hastily Anna said, "Reed, this is my uncle. Uncle Charles, this is Reed Moreland. He bought Winterset."

Uncle Charles looked suspiciously at him. Reed reached out to shake his hand, but her uncle backed up, shaking his head. "No. No. Can't do that."

"Uncle Charles doesn't like to shake hands," Anna told Reed. She turned back to her uncle. "Thank you, Uncle, for coming to help me."

Lord de Winter nodded. "Of course. I saw him before. First I thought he was a demon. I wasn't sure what was going on. But Gabriel explained it to me. Said he was an assassin sent by the Queen. He was in disguise. I have been searching for him. Then I heard you scream. I knew he was after you." He turned toward Reed, explaining, "She would be in line, you see, after Kit, if he killed me."

"Yes, of course," Reed answered calmly. "Well, what do you say we see exactly who this chap is?"

He walked over to where the fallen man lay and bent over him. The mask was tied on, and he had to jerk at it strongly to rip it from the man's face. He straightened, and the three of them stared down at the man beneath the mask.

"Miles Bennett," Anna breathed.

"His poor mother," Anna said, shaking her head.

It was the next morning, and she was sitting at Holcomb Manor, pouring tea for Dr. Felton, Reed and her brother Kit. Shortly after Reed had taken off Miles Bennett's mask, Kit and Rankin had arrived, drawn, as Charles de Winter had been, by Anna's screams. They had listened in amazement to Anna and Reed's story, and afterward, while Uncle Charles had returned to his home, Kit and his gamekeeper had helped Reed tie up the squire's son and take him down to the village to jail.

Kit had returned to Holcomb Manor after that, but Reed had accompanied the constable to the squire's house, and he had come to the Manor this morning to tell them what had transpired, arriving right before Dr. Felton.

"Yes," Dr. Felton said now, agreeing with Anna's comment. "I just returned from the squire's house. Mrs. Bennett was prostrate with grief. I had to give her a calming tincture."

"The squire, as well," Reed said. "They apparently had no idea that anything was wrong with Miles, putting his moods and his locking himself away in his room for hours down to his youth and 'poetic' nature."

"The Squire assured me that Miles was not adopted," the doctor went on. "He said that the boy was seized by the notion that he was adopted two or three years ago, but the squire thought he had gotten over the idea. He hadn't mentioned it recently."

"So he could not have been related to Lord Roger de Winter?" Anna asked.

Dr. Felton shook his head. "Apparently it was just another one of his bizarre notions. It would be easy, I suppose, to say that he inherited his madness from the old lord, but it isn't the case. Miles' illness, I think, is merely some sort of perverse fascination with Lord Roger and his misdeeds that mingled somehow with his obsession with you, Miss Holcomb."

"Did you know about Lord Roger de Winter?" Anna asked the doctor curiously. "Did you tear out the pages concerning him in your father's journal?"

Felton shook his head. "No. I had no idea that he had treated Lord de Winter for anything other than the usual colds and such. I suppose my suspicions should have been raised by the fact that there were no accounts of treating anyone at Winterset for any sort of illness, but it just never struck me." He shook his head. "My father would, of course, have protected his patients' privacy, but I cannot believe he knew that Lord de Winter had killed those two people. He would not have helped Lady de Winter to conceal that."

Though Kit, Reed and Anna had agreed that the truth must be told about Lord de Winter's murders, they had not revealed that Nick Perkins had helped Lady de Winter to conceal what had happened. However wrong it had been of him to do so, Anna could not expose her old friend's wrongdoing. Whatever he had done, he had done out of kindness and loyalty to Lady de Winter, and Anna was sure that he had paid for it many times with his burden of guilt.

"Did they find anything at the Bennetts' house?" Anna asked.

Reed nodded. "Indeed they did. Estelle's new earbobs, for one thing. Apparently Miles was her 'gentleman' friend. They had been meeting in the woods secretly for some time, and he gave her the earrings, then took them back after he killed her. I don't know whether he planned all along to kill her that way, or if he did it in a rage and then decided to set it up to look like the original murders. Miles has given the constable almost nothing coherent. He is either silent and brooding, or he raves about the 'Wolf People' and such.

"However," Reed continued. "They found several of the old lord's journals there, as well as another couple of masks. It seems that Miles had also emulated de Winter by writing a journal of his own. I imagine there will be more than enough evidence in that to convict him of killing Estelle Akins and Frank Johnson."

"Thank goodness," the doctor said. "This has been such a terrible thing. It will be good for everything to get back to normal." He looked over at Reed. "Will you continue to live at Winterset, my lord? After all that has happened?"

"At least part of the year," Reed answered, and his gaze slid over to Anna. "It is a lovely house, despite the tragedies that have happened in it. And I would like to fill it with new, better memories."

"Very good." Dr. Felton nodded approvingly. "I am glad that you are remaining."

"We all are, I'm sure," Kit added.

Anna said nothing. She was afraid she could not speak without tears overcoming her. Once the elation of capturing the killer had worn off, she had realized that nothing had really changed between her and Reed. All the reasons why she could not marry him still existed. She didn't know how she could bear to live with him so close by. Nor did she know how she could bear to have him move back to London, either.

"Well, I had better get back to the village,"

481

the doctor said, rising. "I imagine I will have twice as many patients as usual, simply to gossip."

"I'll walk you out," Kit said, standing up as well.

Anna and Reed bid the doctor polite farewells, and he and Kit left the room, pulling the door to behind them. Anna shifted a little uncomfortably in her chair. She had not expected Kit to close the door on them; it was most improper.

She glanced over at Reed and found him watching her intently. Her heart picked up its beat, and she looked back down at her hands in her lap.

"Your brother has a purpose in leaving us alone," Reed told her.

"What?" Anna's eyes flew to his face. "What do you mean?"

"He knows that I am about to ask for your hand in marriage. I already spoke to him about it."

"Reed . . . no. Please."

Reed stood up and crossed the room, going down on one knee beside her and taking her hand. "Once again, with the full approval of your brother, I am asking you to become my wife. It is not often that a woman gets asked three times by the same man," he added, smiling.

"Reed . . ." Anna's voice caught.

"But I have to warn you, if you refuse me, it won't be the last time I ask. I intend to keep at it until I wear you down."

"Reed, you know I cannot. Nothing has changed." Anna looked at him with sorrow. "There is nothing more that I would rather do than marry you."

He brought her hand to his lips and kissed it. "Really?"

"Yes, of course. I love you. But I cannot —"

Reed held a finger up to her lips, stopping her words. "Then the de Winter madness is the only impediment? If it did not exist, you would say yes?"

"Yes! You know I would. But it does exist, and I cannot marry you." Tears glittered in Anna's eyes.

Reed kissed her hand again and released it, rising to his feet. "I want you to talk to someone."

"What?" Anna looked at him, confused. "Who? What are you talking about?"

He simply gave her an enigmatic look and walked to the door. He opened it and looked down the hallway, gesturing with his hand. Anna waited, trying to suppress the spark of hope that was rising within her. She could not let Reed talk her into this, she reminded herself.

To her surprise, when Reed stepped back from the door, Nick Perkins walked through it.

"Nick!" Anna stood up, surprised. "I — come in. Sit down. I am surprised to see you."

"Yes, miss, I'm sure you are." Nick came closer to her, twisting his cap between his large hands. He looked highly uncomfortable. "I'll just stand, if it's all the same to you."

Anna cast a puzzled look toward Reed.

"I was on my way to see you yesterday when Miles attacked me," Reed told Anna, coming over to stand beside Nick. "I had been visiting with Perkins, here, about a matter that had come to my mind. You see, after Mrs. Parmer told us about Lord Roger's insanity, I began to wonder. I went to the cemetery and looked at your mother's tombstone."

"What?" Anna gaped at him. "My moth—"

"I saw when she was born. It was almost a year after the murder of Susan Emmett."

Anna nodded, still looking puzzled. "Yes."

"That was *after* your grandmother locked Lord Roger up in the nursery, after she knew he was mad. I could not help but wonder why Lady Philippa would have been engaging in conjugal acts with her mad husband, a man she knew to be a murderer, a man whose blood she could not have wanted to pass down to another child. It must have worried her terribly, just knowing that her son Charles could inherit his father's illness."

Anna's mouth went dry, and her pulse speeded up. She could do nothing but look at Reed, hope rising within her.

"There were some other things that I had noticed when Perkins was talking to us, a certain way he looked. I was curious as to why he had been willing to help your grandmother cover up her husband's crimes. So I went to talk to him." He turned toward Nick Perkins. "Perkins has something he is eager to tell you."

Perkins did not look as eager as Reed had indicated he was. He twisted his cap and swallowed, then said finally, "His lordship was right. I — I was in love with Lady Philippa. That is why I helped her. I would have done anything for her. She — I — we were together after her husband turned mad. Please don't think bad of her, Miss Anna. She was the best woman in the world, a sweet and wonderful lady. Her marriage was an arranged one. Her parents had heard rumors about Lord Roger. They knew he was older than her, and a cold man, but they wanted the connection something fierce, so they married her to him, anyway. She — she didn't know him well enough to know what he was like, and she was an obedient daughter.

"Well, she found out soon enough. He was a hard, cruel man, and he mistreated her. But she had no choice. She had married him. She stayed with him and tried to protect her son from him as much as she could. But she and I — well, she fell in love with me, just as I did with her. And after she found out what a monster her husband was, she stopped feeling so guilty for not being able to love him or to be the wife he wanted. She — well, the fact of it is, Barbara, your mother, was my daughter, not Lord de Winter's. You and Kit don't have any de Winter blood in you."

Anna stared at him. Emotions and thoughts were flooding through her at such a rate and in such a jumble that she could not speak. His eyes, she thought. Why had she never noticed before? Nick's eyes were the same deep blue as her own.

"We used to meet at the summerhouse. Whenever she could get away," Nick went on, his nervousness gone now, pushed aside by remembered emotion. "I don't know if Lord Roger figured it out, or if he just happened to get loose at that moment. But one night he managed to get free of his guards. He somehow slipped the potion that they gave him to keep him quiet at night into the drink of his larger, stronger guard. Then he overcame his valet, knocked him out. He followed Philippa to the summerhouse. Before I got there, he had attacked her, killed her. I came in, and I saw what he had done. We fought, and in the course of our fight, we turned over the lantern. I —"

He squared his shoulders and looked Anna in the eye. "I killed him, Miss Anna. I killed Lord de Winter. A beam had fallen, and I couldn't get to Philippa. I had to leave them to burn." Tears filled his eyes.

Anna pressed her hand to her lips, tears welling in her eyes. "Oh, Nick . . ."

"I'm sorry, miss. I never wanted you to know any of this. But when his lordship told me how you was worrying over the idea that you might go mad, well, I saw I'd done wrong in never telling you."

"But why didn't you?" Anna asked.

"I didn't know that you had learned about the madness. We'd kept it as secret as we could that Lord Roger was mad. I didn't think you and Kit would find out. And then, well, I never was close to your mother. She grew up away from here, and I didn't know her like I know you. I didn't realize that she

487

had learned about the madness. Until yesterday, when Lord Moreland told me, I thought your uncle had gone to Barbados. I didn't realize it had taken him, too. I never dreamed that you were scared of going mad yourself, or that you and Kit were sworn not to marry because of it.

"You see, thinking that you knew none of that, I thought it was better for you to go on believing that Lord de Winter was your grandfather. I didn't, well, I didn't want you to think badly about your grandmother. She was a wonderful woman. And I didn't think you would like knowing that your grandfather was a common farmer, not a lord. I didn't want you to be ashamed of me."

Anna reached out and took his hand. "I would a thousand times rather that you were my grandfather than Lord de Winter. And I don't think anything bad about you or Lady Philippa. I understand about love and what it can do to people." She flashed a sparkling glance at Reed, who was smiling at her, then turned back to Nick. "And I could never be ashamed of you. I'm proud that you are my grandfather."

Impulsively, she reached out and hugged him. "I'm so happy!"

Nick patted her clumsily on the back. "I'm happy, too, Miss Anna."

Anna stepped back. She was grinning broadly, even though her eyes were shining with tears.

Nick smiled back at her and said, "You know, my mother had the second sight, too."

Anna stared at him. "Visions?"

He nodded. "Like Lord Moreland said you saw. Her family always had that gift." His eyes twinkled as he went on. "There's some as say that her ancestor was the witch who cursed the de Winters."

With that remark, he swung around and left the room. Anna stared after him for a long moment, then turned to Reed.

"Does Kit know about it? Now he is free, as well."

Reed nodded. "Yes. I told him all about it when I asked him for your hand."

"That sly fox!" Anna laughed a little waterily, dabbing at her eyes. "No wonder he has been so merry today. I thought it was just capturing the murderer."

"No doubt it was that, too," Reed said. He came closer to her, reaching out to take her hands. "Miss Holcomb, I will ask you again . . . will you marry me?"

"Yes!" Anna cried, leaping into his arms. "Yes, I will marry you — a thousand times over."

Reed laughed, his arms closing around

her. "I think I can make sure that once is all we will need."

Anna leaned back a little, looking him in the eye and saying seriously, "I love you, Reed."

"And I love you, Anna."

His lips closed on hers.

About the Author

Candance Camp is the bestselling author of over forty contemporary and historical novels.

She grew up in Texas in a newspaper family, which explains her love of writing, but she earned a law degree and practiced law before making the decision to write full-time. She has received several writing awards, including the *Romantic Times* Lifetime Achievement Award for Western Romances.

LP
CAMP

Camp, Candace

Winterset